ABOUT THIS BOOK

This book was edited by Andrea Colvin and designed by Sasha Illingworth. The production was supervised by Bernadette Flinn, and the production editor was Lindsay Walter-Greaney. The text was set in Collect Em Now, and the display type is TastyLight.

Little, Brown Ink
Hachette Book Group
1290 Avenue of the Americas, New York, NY 10104
Visit us at LBYR.com
First Edition: September 2023

Little, Brown Ink is an imprint of Little, Brown and Company. The Little, Brown Ink name and logo are trademarks of Hachette Book Group, Inc.

The publisher is not responsible for websites (or their content) that are not owned by the publisher.

Little, Brown and Company books may be purchased in bulk for business, educational, or promotional use. For information, please contact your local bookseller or the Hachette Book Group Special Markets Department at special.markets@hbgusa.com.

Library of Congress Cataloging-in-Publication Data
Names: Lê, Minh, 1979- author. I Chau, Chan, illustrator.
Title: Enlighten me / Minh Lê; illustrated by Chan Chau.
Description: First edition. I New York : Little, Brown and Company, 2023. I Includes bibliographical references. I Summary: Binh and his family take a trip to a silent meditation retreat, where he learns a lot about himself and how to manage his feelings through Buddhist teachings.
Identifiers: LCCN 2021004739 I ISBN 9780759555471 (hardcover) I ISBN 9780759555488 (trade paperback)
Subjects: LCSH: Graphic novels. I CYAC: Graphic novels. I Spiritual retreats—Fiction. I Buddhism—Fiction. I Meditation—Fiction. I Vietnamese Americans—Fiction.
Classification: LCC PZ7.7.L398 En 2022 I DDC 741.5/973—dc23
LC record available at https://lccn.loc.gov/2021004739

ISBNs: 978-0-7595-5547-1 (hardcover), 978-0-7595-5548-8 (paperback), 978-0-316-39552-6 (ebook), 978-0-316-33267-5 (ebook), 978-0-316-33257-6 (ebook)

Printed in CHINA

1010

Hardcover: 10 9 8 7 6 5 4 3 2 1
Paperback: 10 9 8 7 6 5 4 3 2 1

Enlighten Me

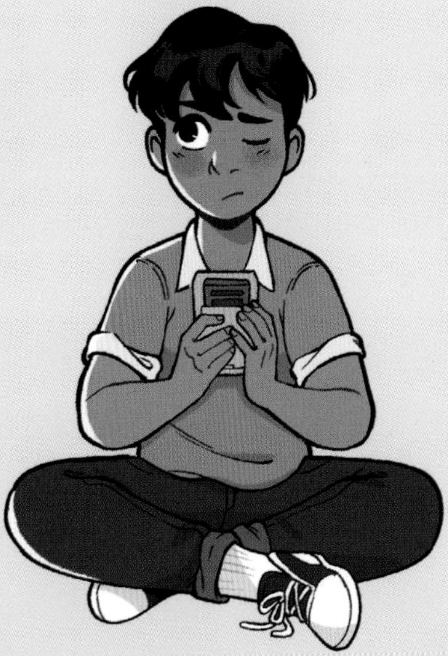

Written by
Minh Lê

Illustrated by
Chan Cha

LB INK
LITTLE, BROWN AND COMPANY
New York Boston

To Cha & Mẹ: for giving me the support and space I needed to find my own path —ML

For mom and dad, Cuong and Phuoc —CC

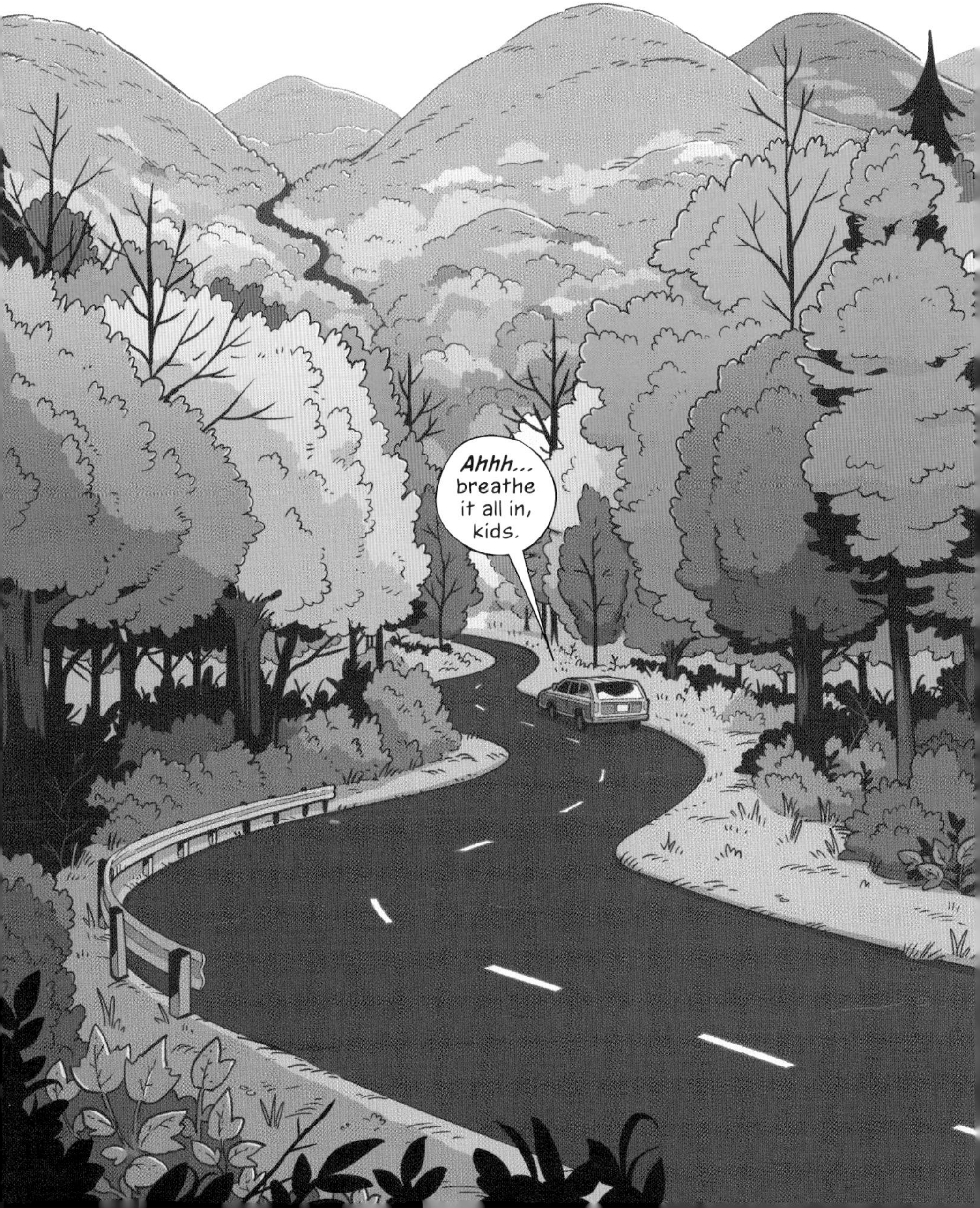
Ahhh... breathe it all in, kids.

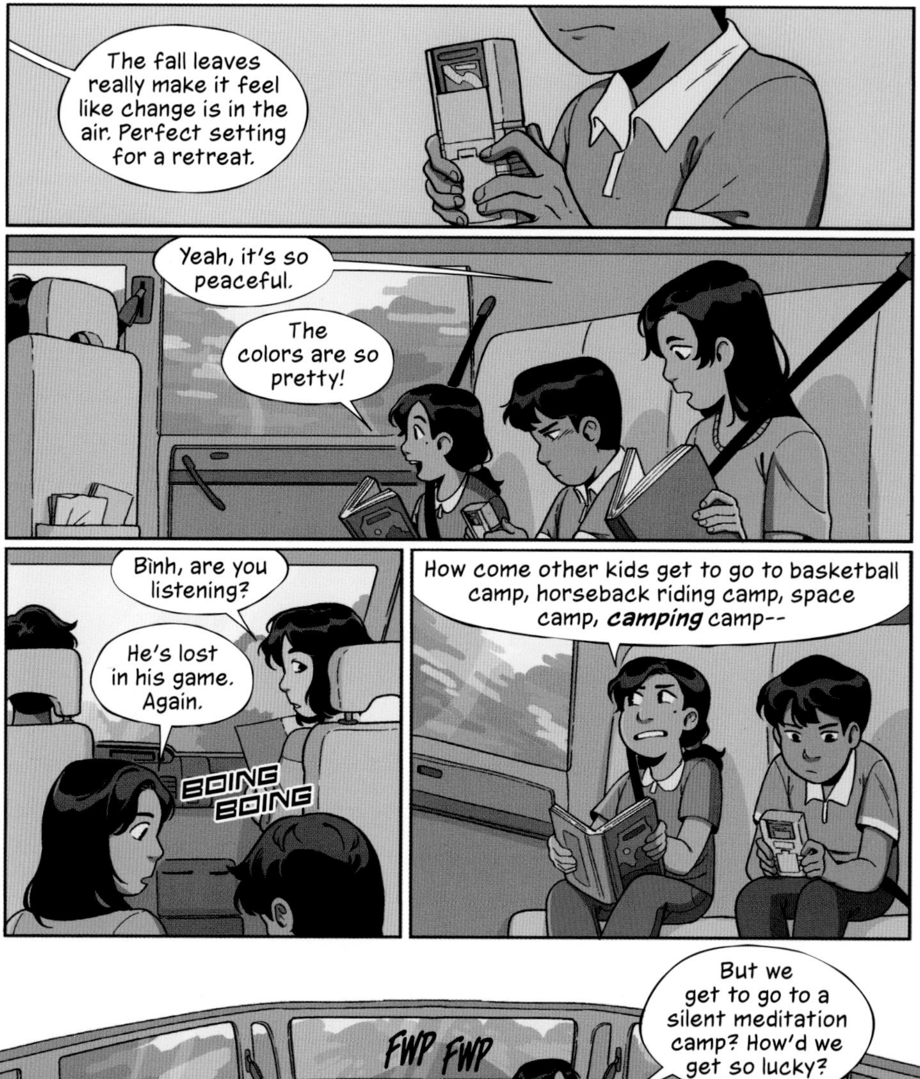

The fall leaves really make it feel like change is in the air. Perfect setting for a retreat.
Yeah, it's so peaceful.
The colors are so pretty!
Bình, are you listening?
He's lost in his game. Again.
BOING BOING
How come other kids get to go to basketball camp, horseback riding camp, space camp, *camping* camp--
But we get to go to a silent meditation camp? How'd we get so lucky?
FWP FWP

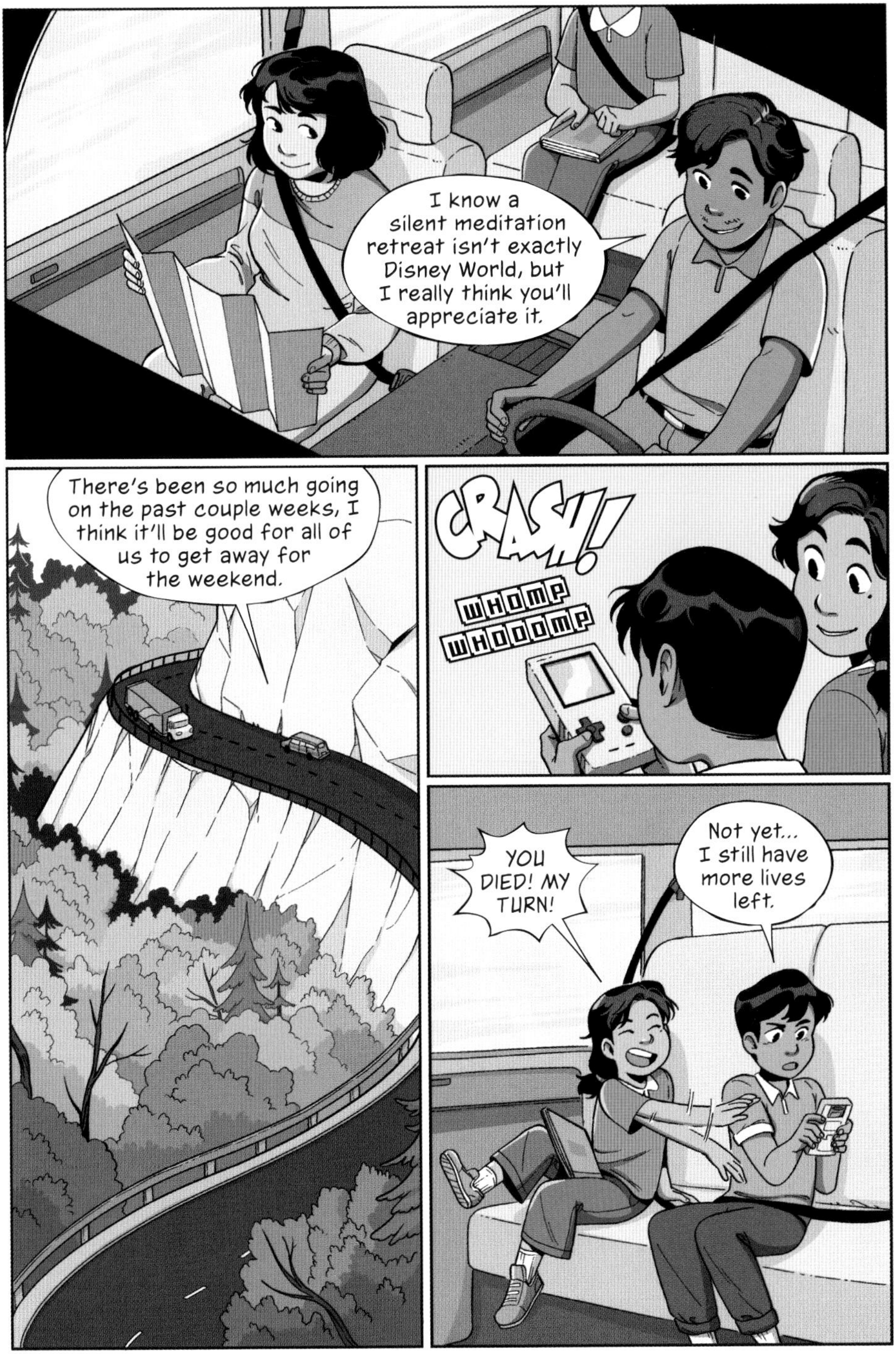
I know a silent meditation retreat isn't exactly Disney World, but I really think you'll appreciate it.
There's been so much going on the past couple weeks, I think it'll be good for all of us to get away for the weekend.
CRASH!
WHOMP
WHOOOMP
YOU DIED! MY TURN!
Not yet... I still have more lives left.

Let Hoa have a turn. I wanted to talk to you anyway.

We heard back from your vice principal, and thankfully the school decided not to suspend you. But he wants you to write an apology to the boy you were fighting with.

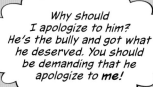

Fine.

Why should I apologize to him? He's the bully and got what he deserved. You should be demanding that he apologize to *me*!

Fighting in school...Why won't you tell us what happened? What made you so upset?

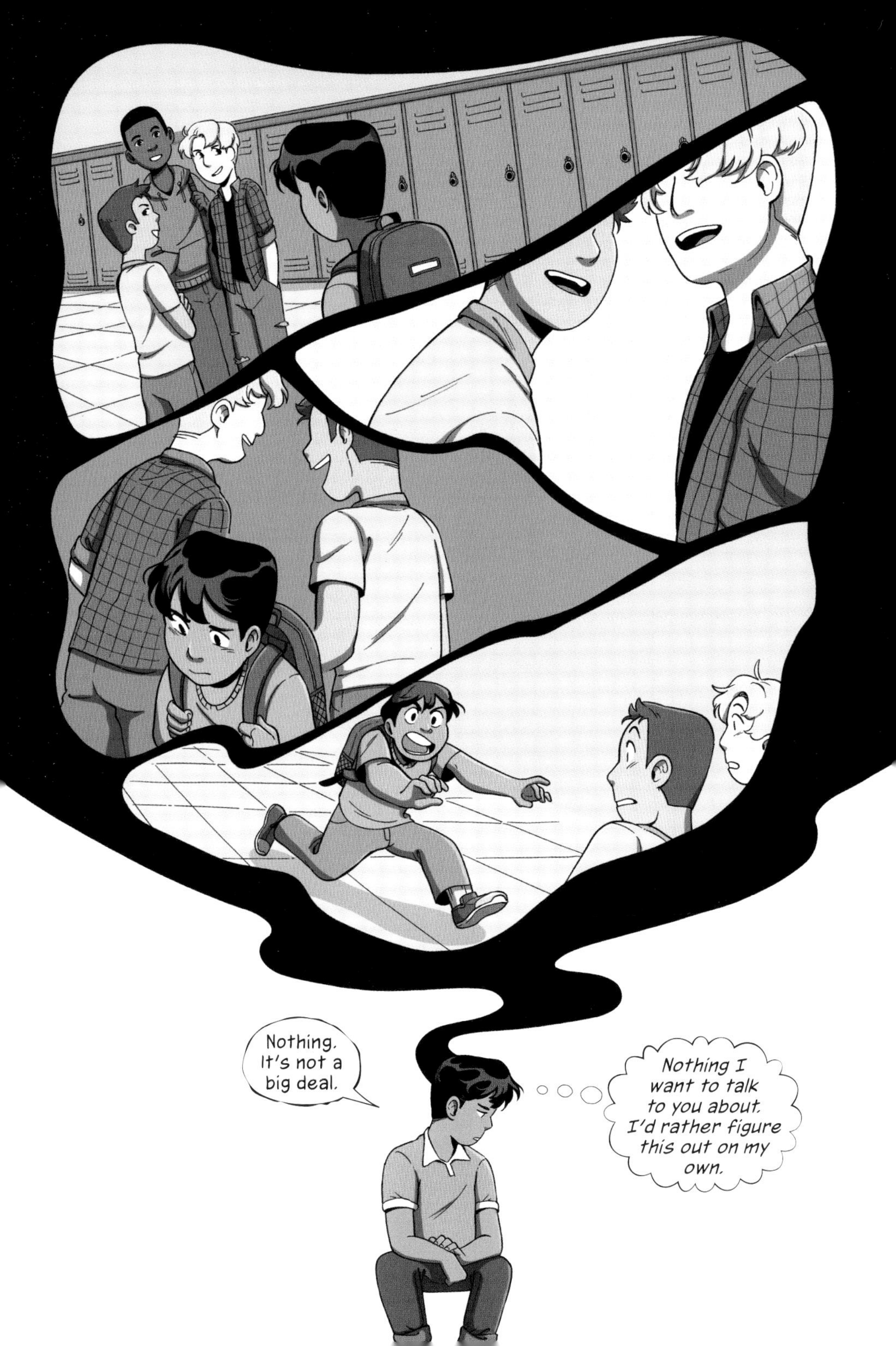
Nothing. It's not a big deal.
Nothing I want to talk to you about. I'd rather figure this out on my own.

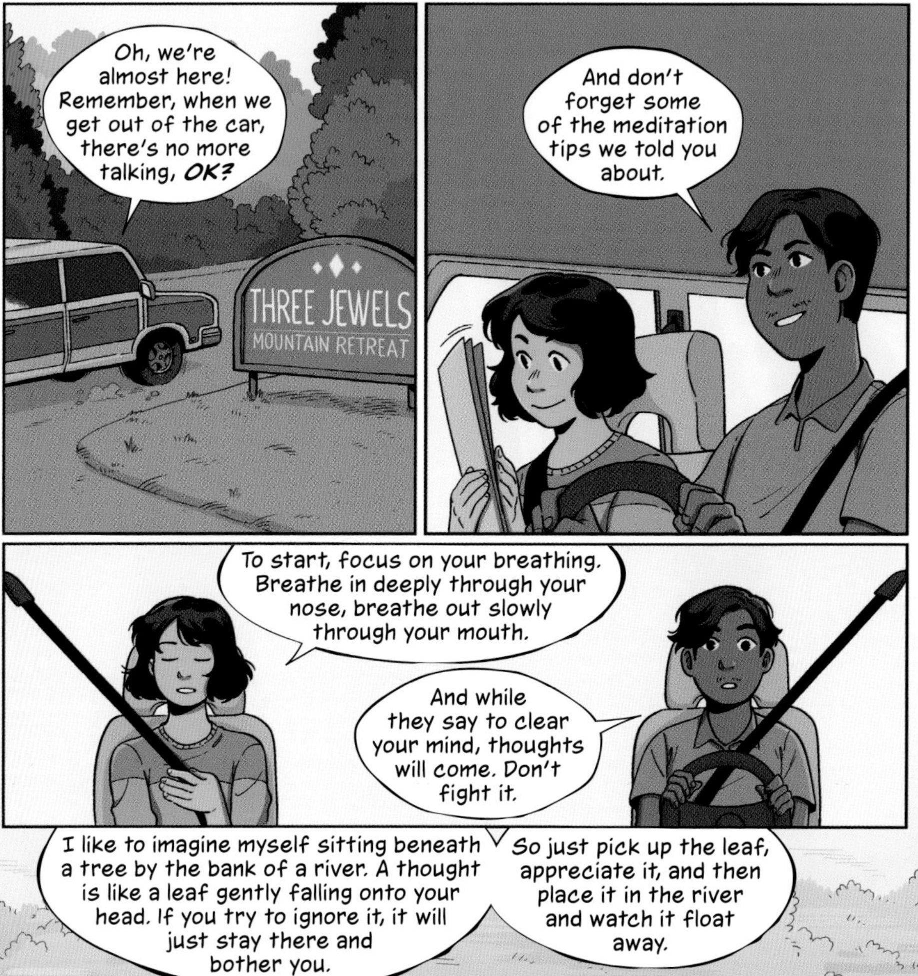
Oh, we're almost here! Remember, when we get out of the car, there's no more talking, OK?
THREE JEWELS
MOUNTAIN RETREAT
And don't forget some of the meditation tips we told you about.
To start, focus on your breathing. Breathe in deeply through your nose, breathe out slowly through your mouth.
And while they say to clear your mind, thoughts will come. Don't fight it.
I like to imagine myself sitting beneath a tree by the bank of a river. A thought is like a leaf gently falling onto your head. If you try to ignore it, it will just stay there and bother you.
So just pick up the leaf, appreciate it, and then place it in the river and watch it float away.

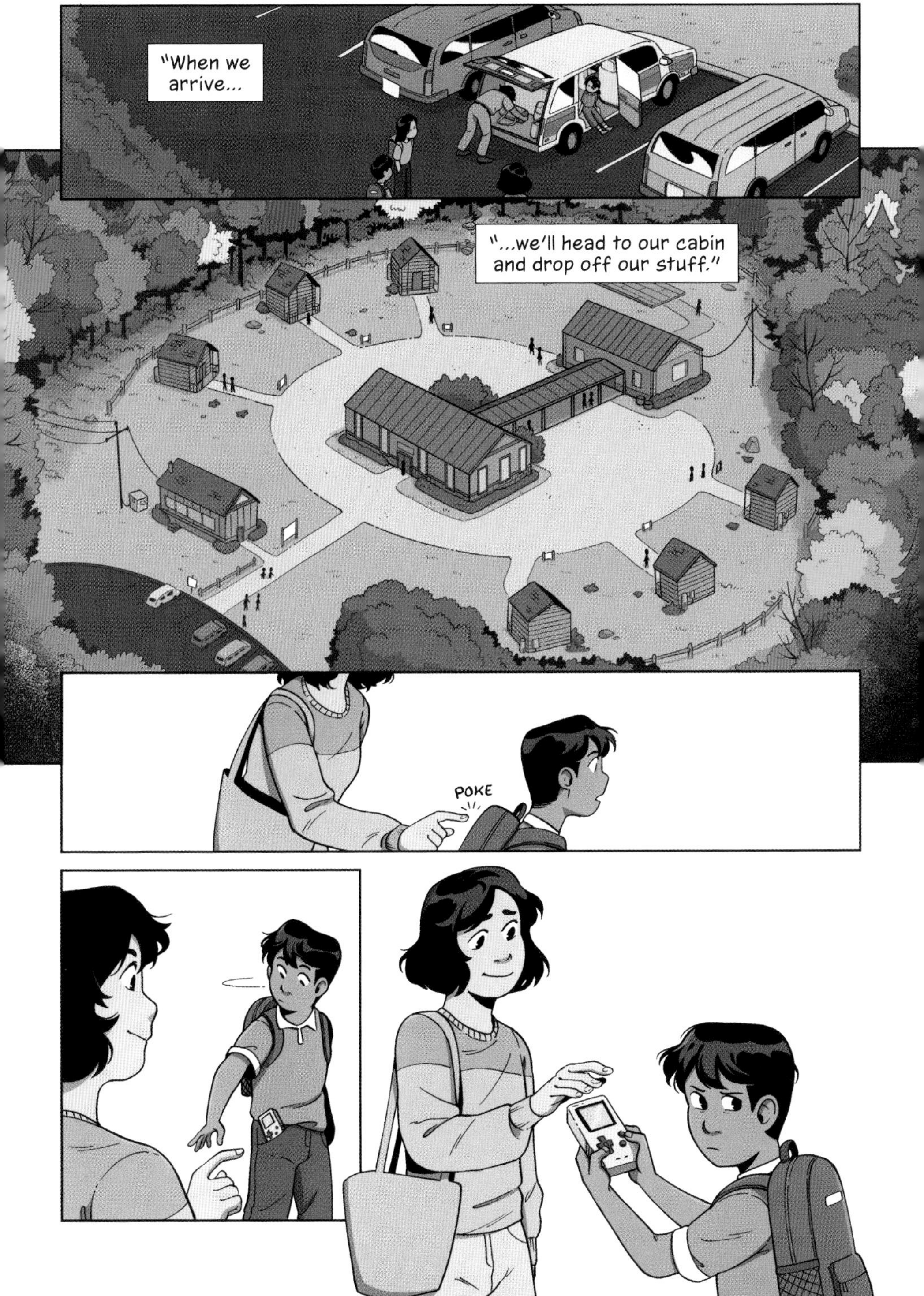
"When we arrive...
"...we'll head to our cabin and drop off our stuff."
POKE

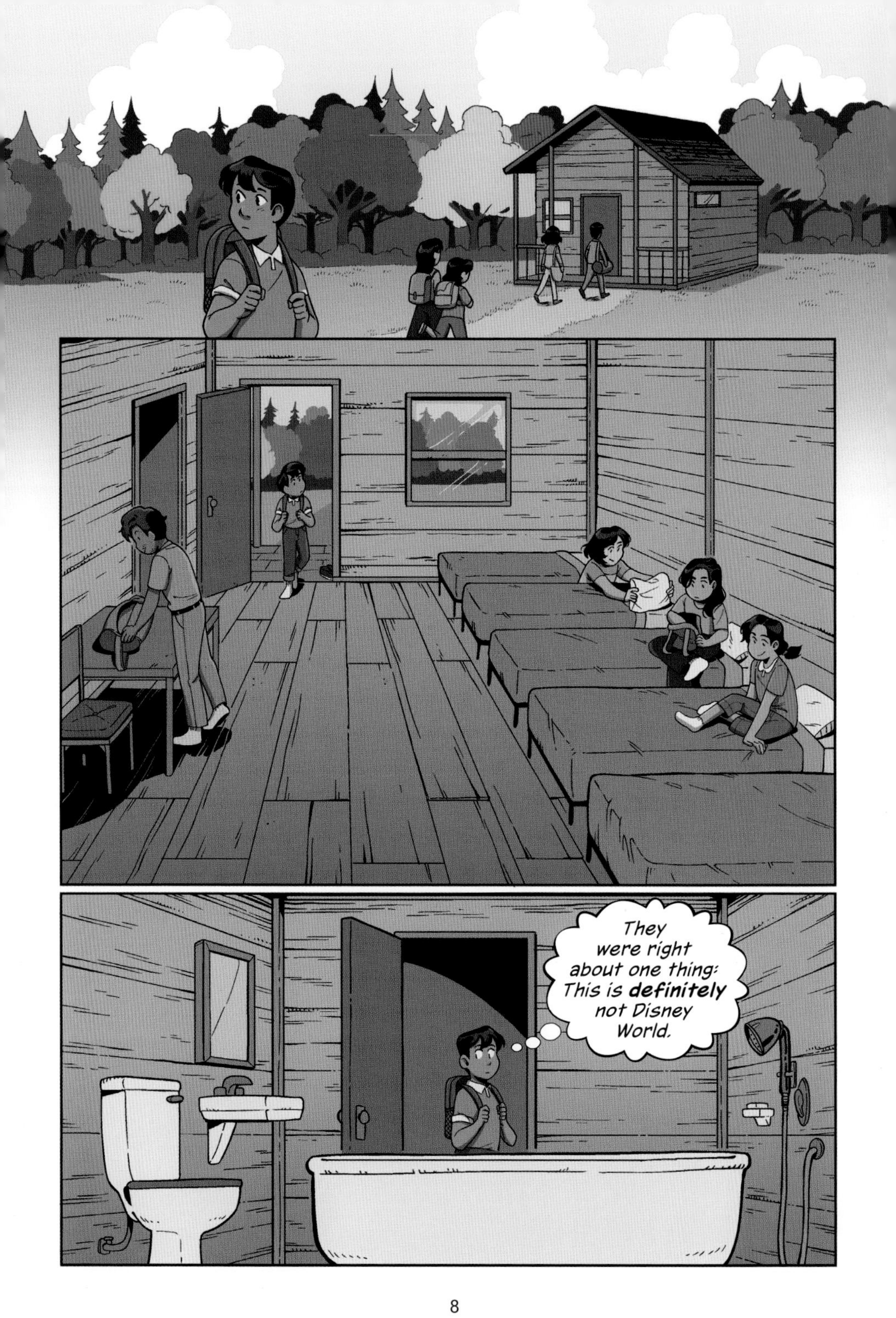
They were right about one thing: This is **definitely** not Disney World.

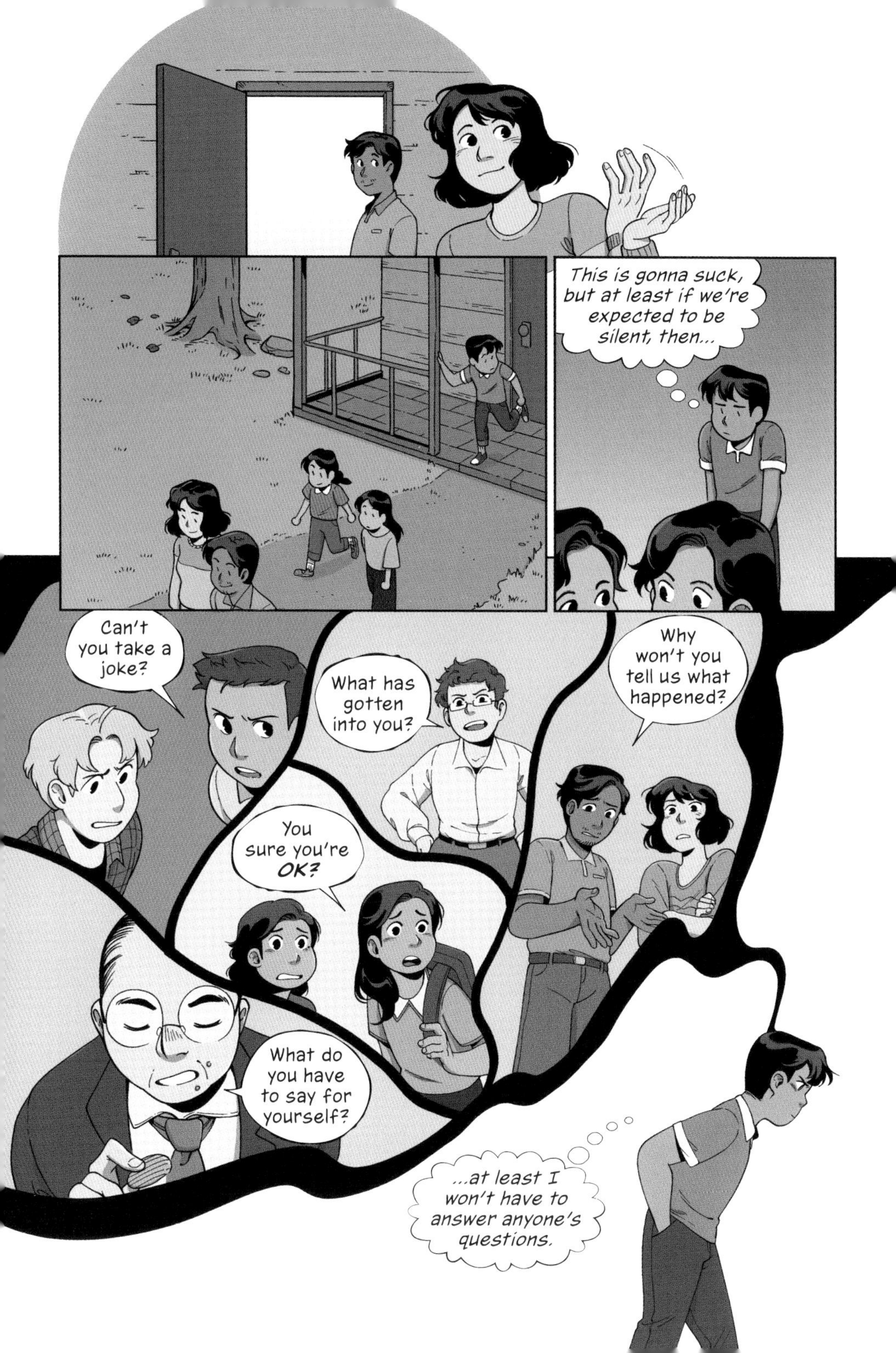
This is gonna suck, but at least if we're expected to be silent, then...
Can't you take a joke?
What has gotten into you?
Why won't you tell us what happened?
You sure you're OK?
What do you have to say for yourself?
...at least I won't have to answer anyone's questions.

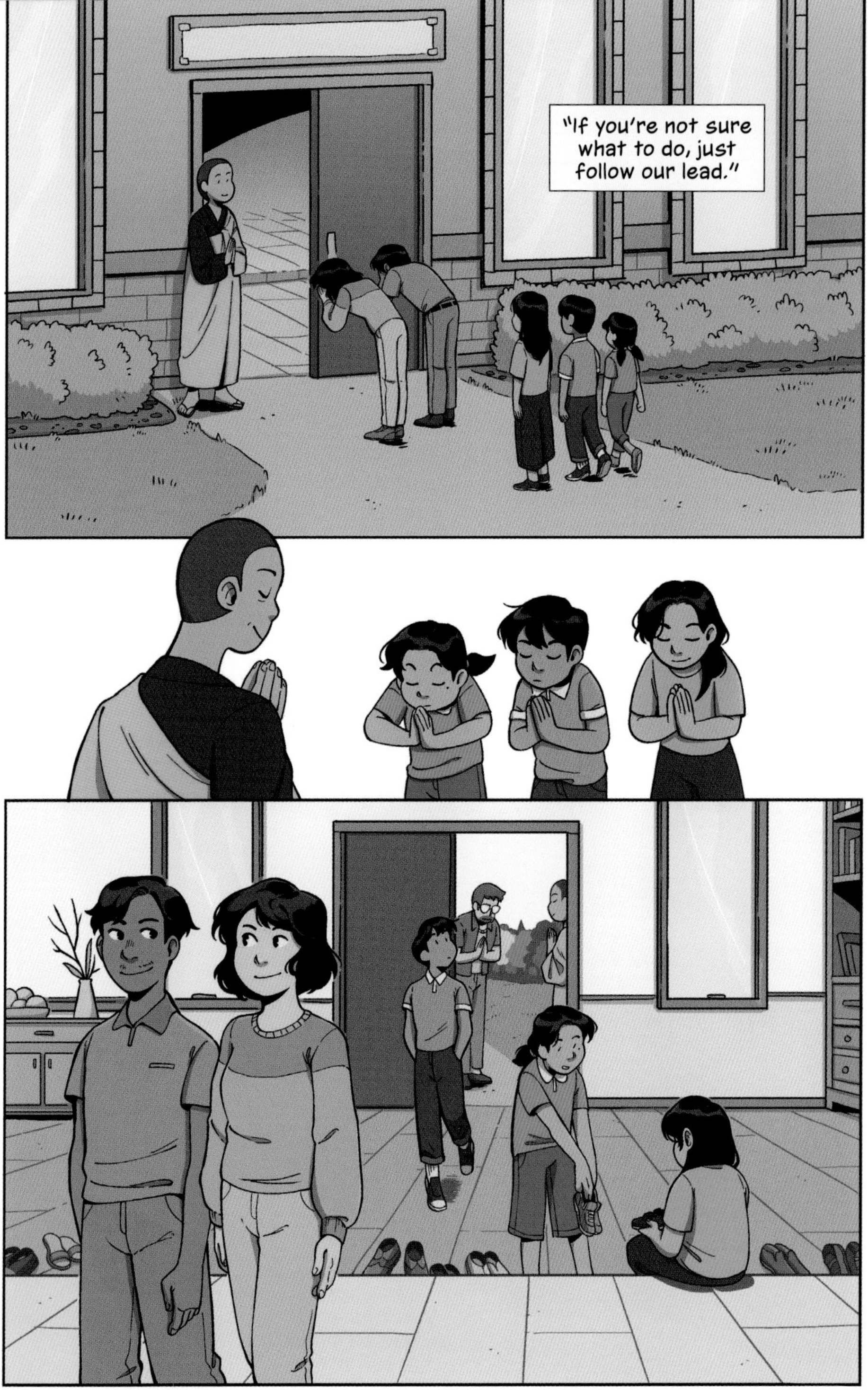
"If you're not sure
what to do, just
follow our lead."

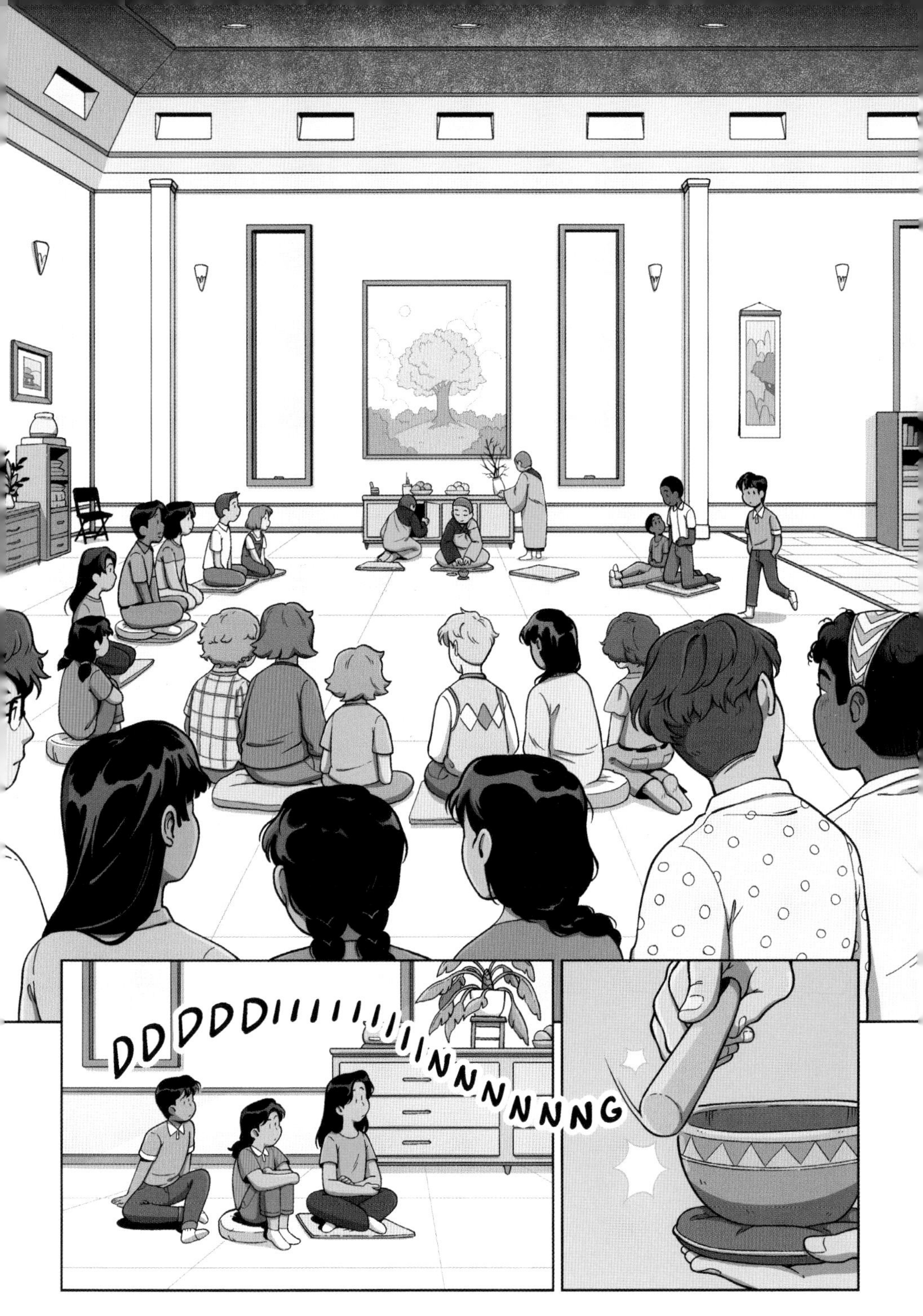
DDDDDIIIIIIIIIIINNNNNNNG

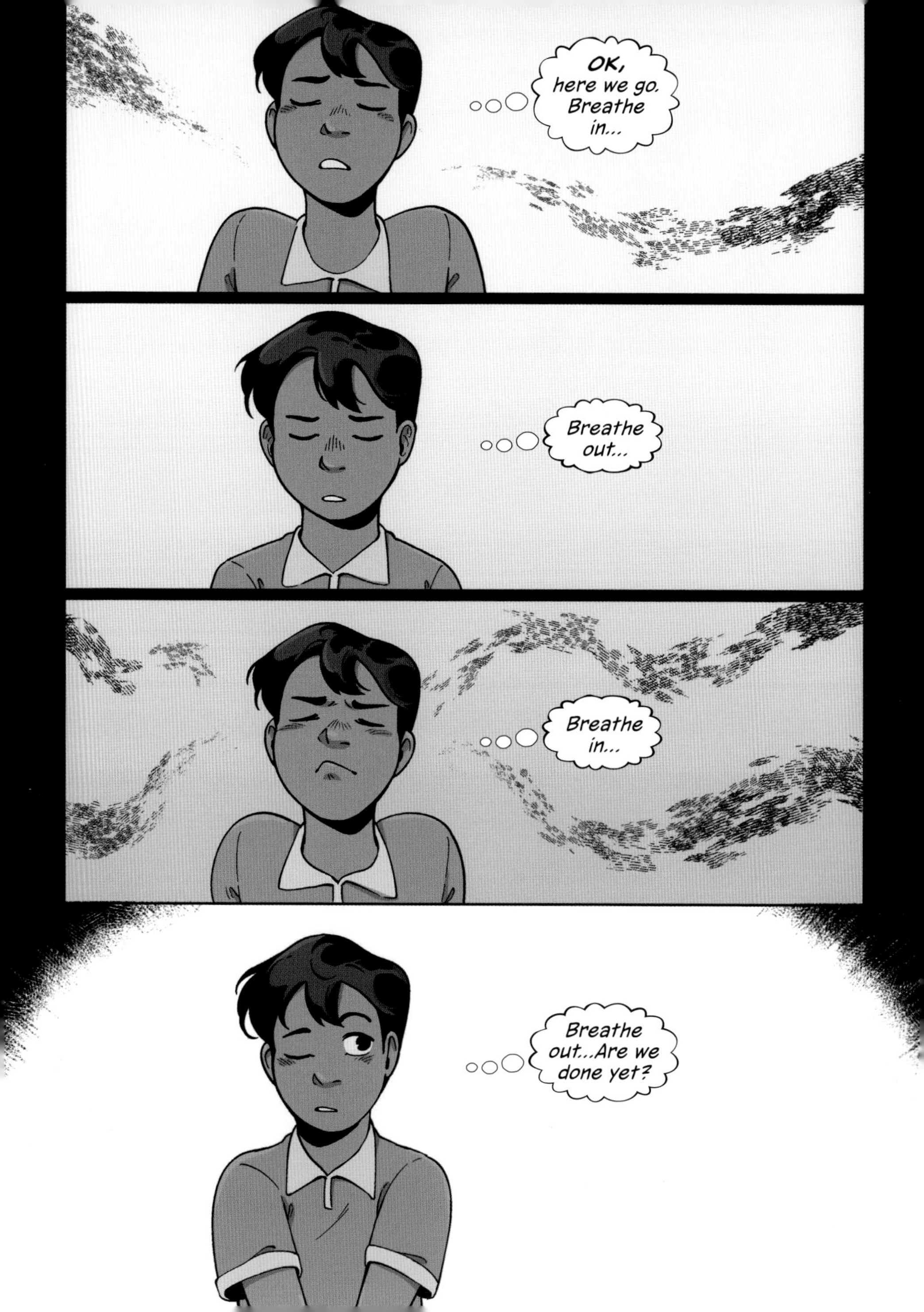
OK, here we go. Breathe in...
Breathe out...
Breathe in...
Breathe out...Are we done yet?

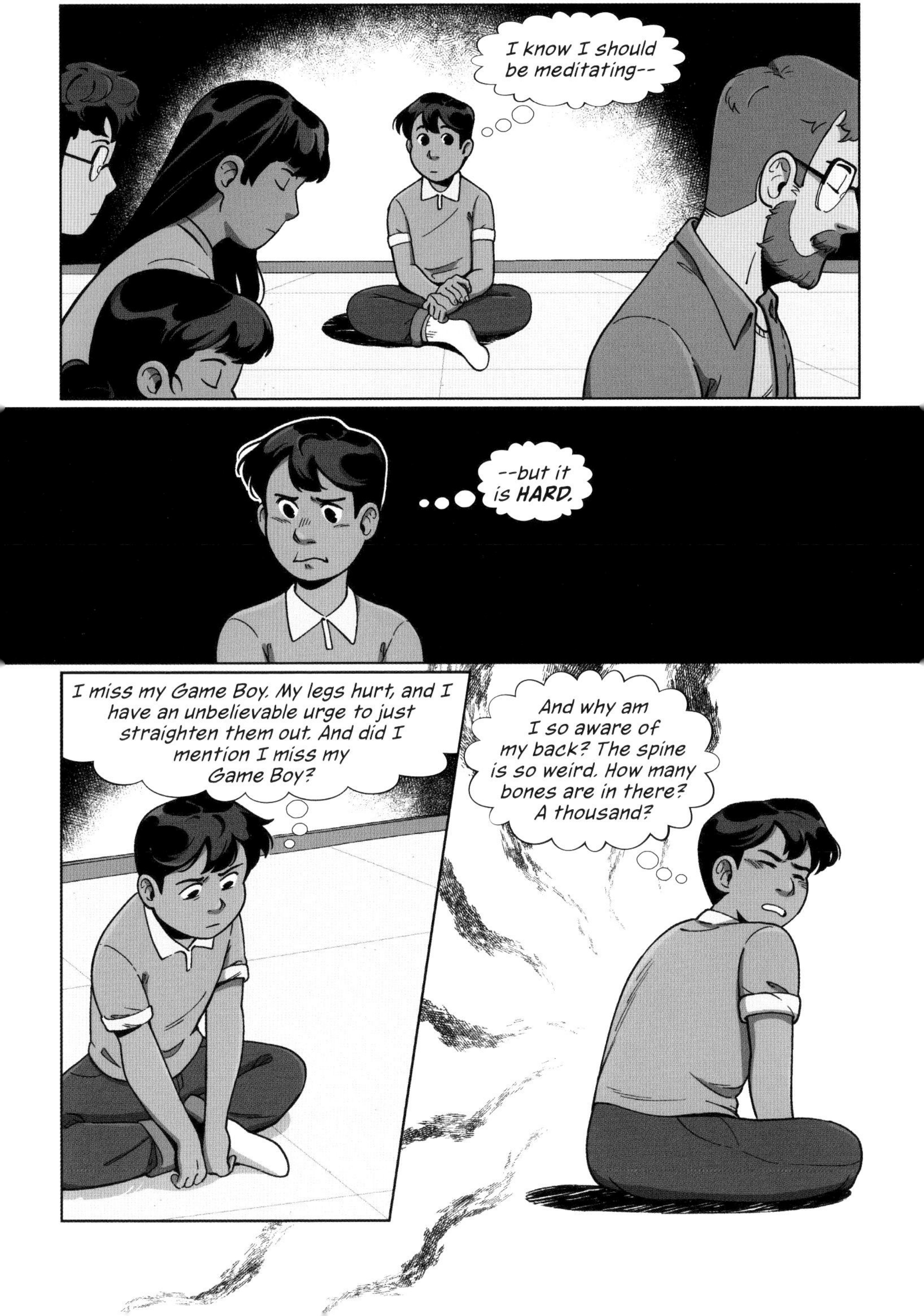
I know I should be meditating--
--but it is HARD.
I miss my Game Boy. My legs hurt, and I have an unbelievable urge to just straighten them out. And did I mention I miss my Game Boy?
And why am I so aware of my back? The spine is so weird. How many bones are in there? A thousand?

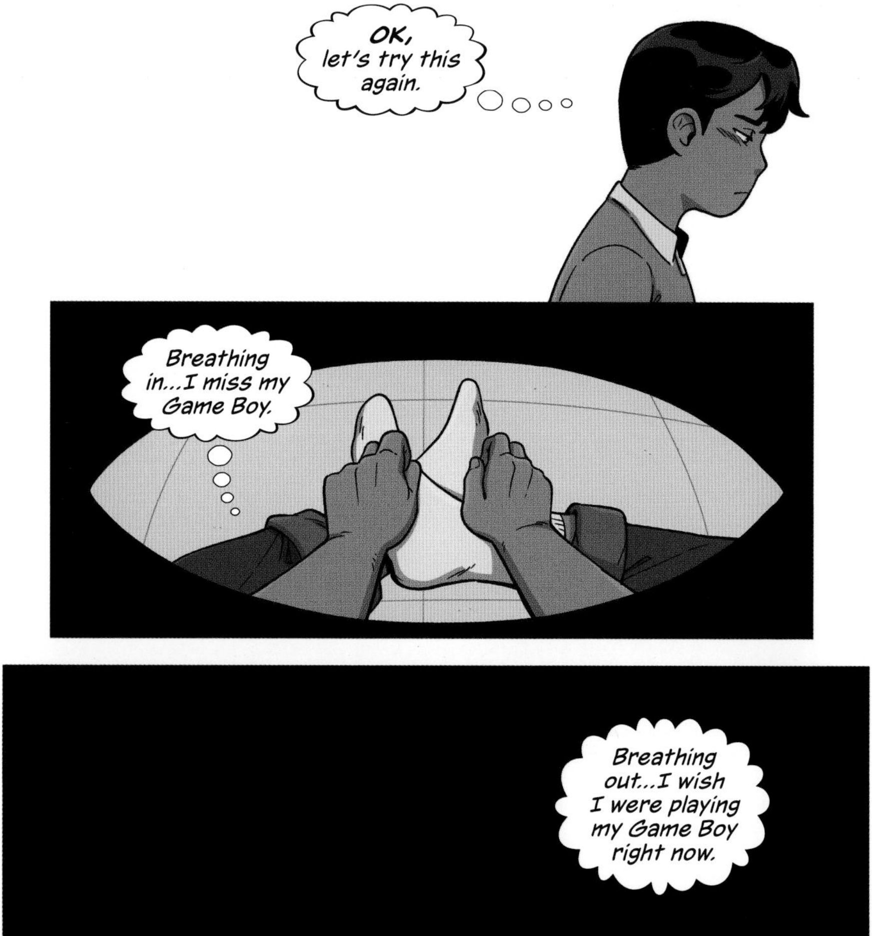
OK,
let's try this again.
Breathing in...I miss my Game Boy.
Breathing out...I wish I were playing my Game Boy right now.

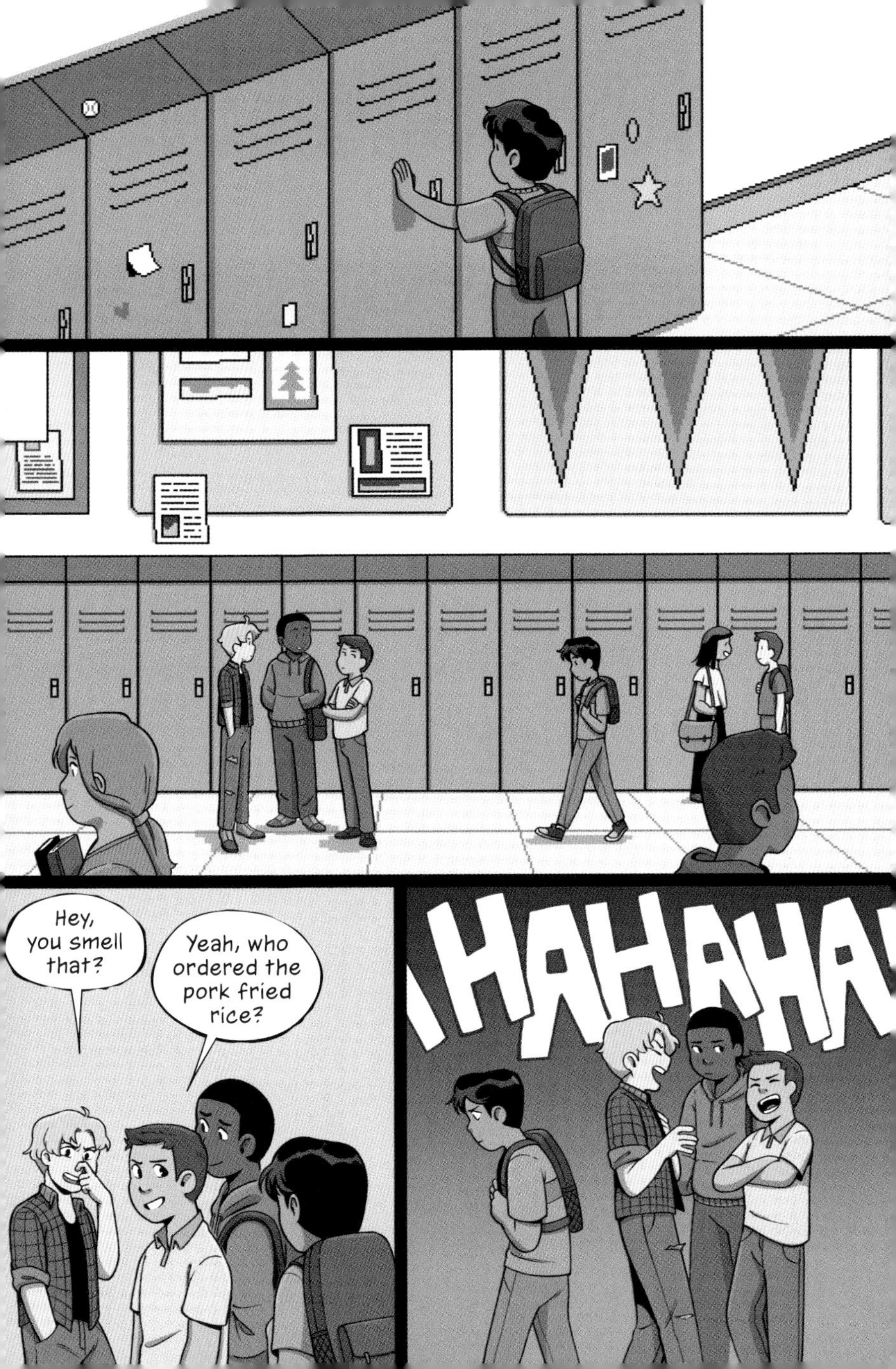
Hey, you smell that?
Yeah, who ordered the pork fried rice?
HAHAHAHA

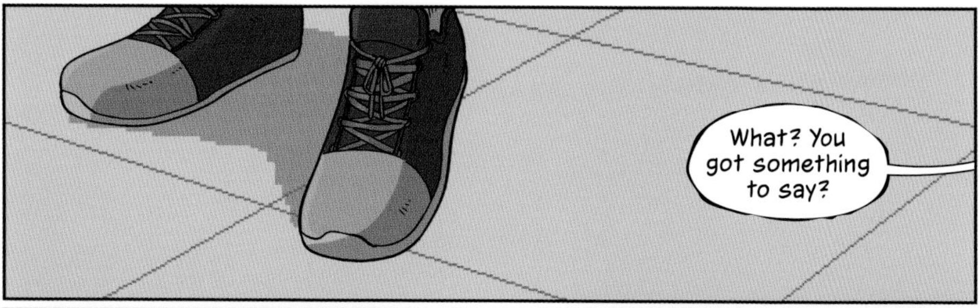
What? You got something to say?

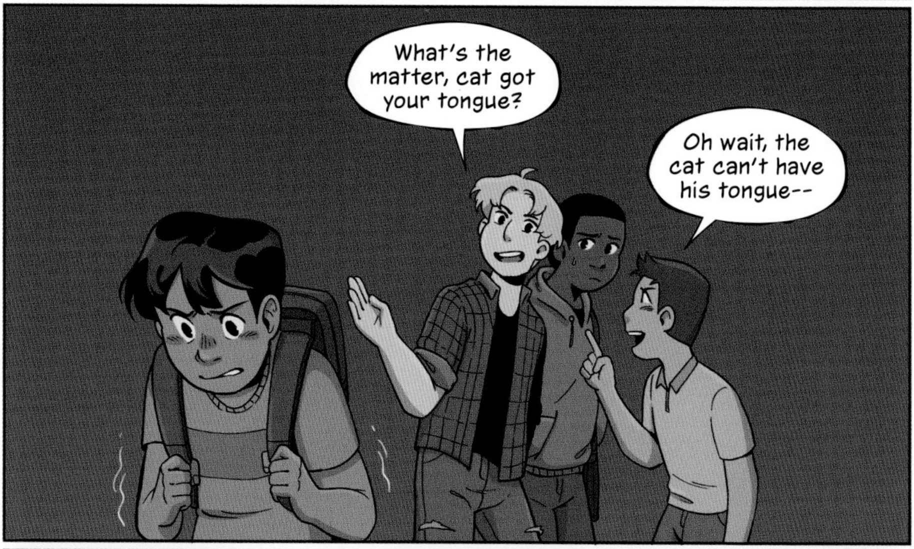
What's the matter, cat got your tongue?
Oh wait, the cat can't have his tongue--

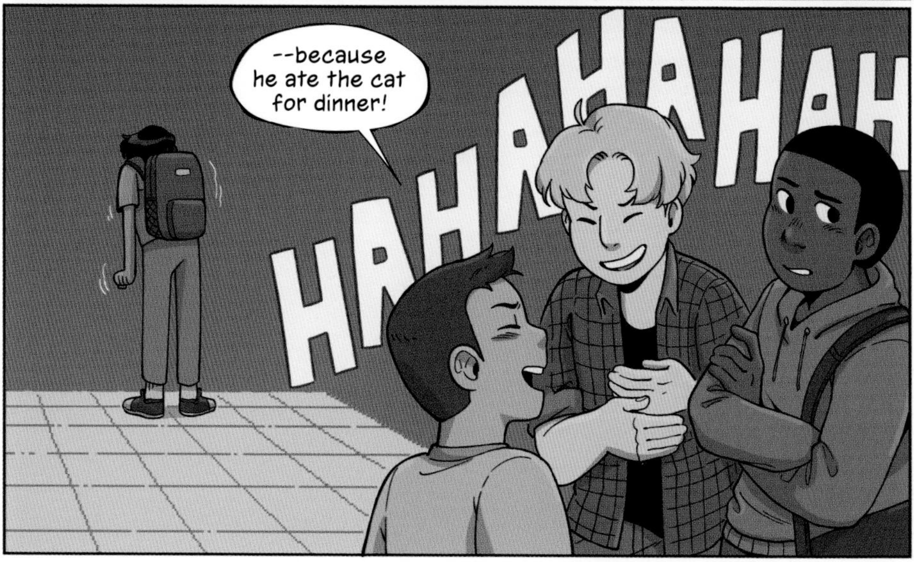
--because he ate the cat for dinner!
HAHAHAHAHAH

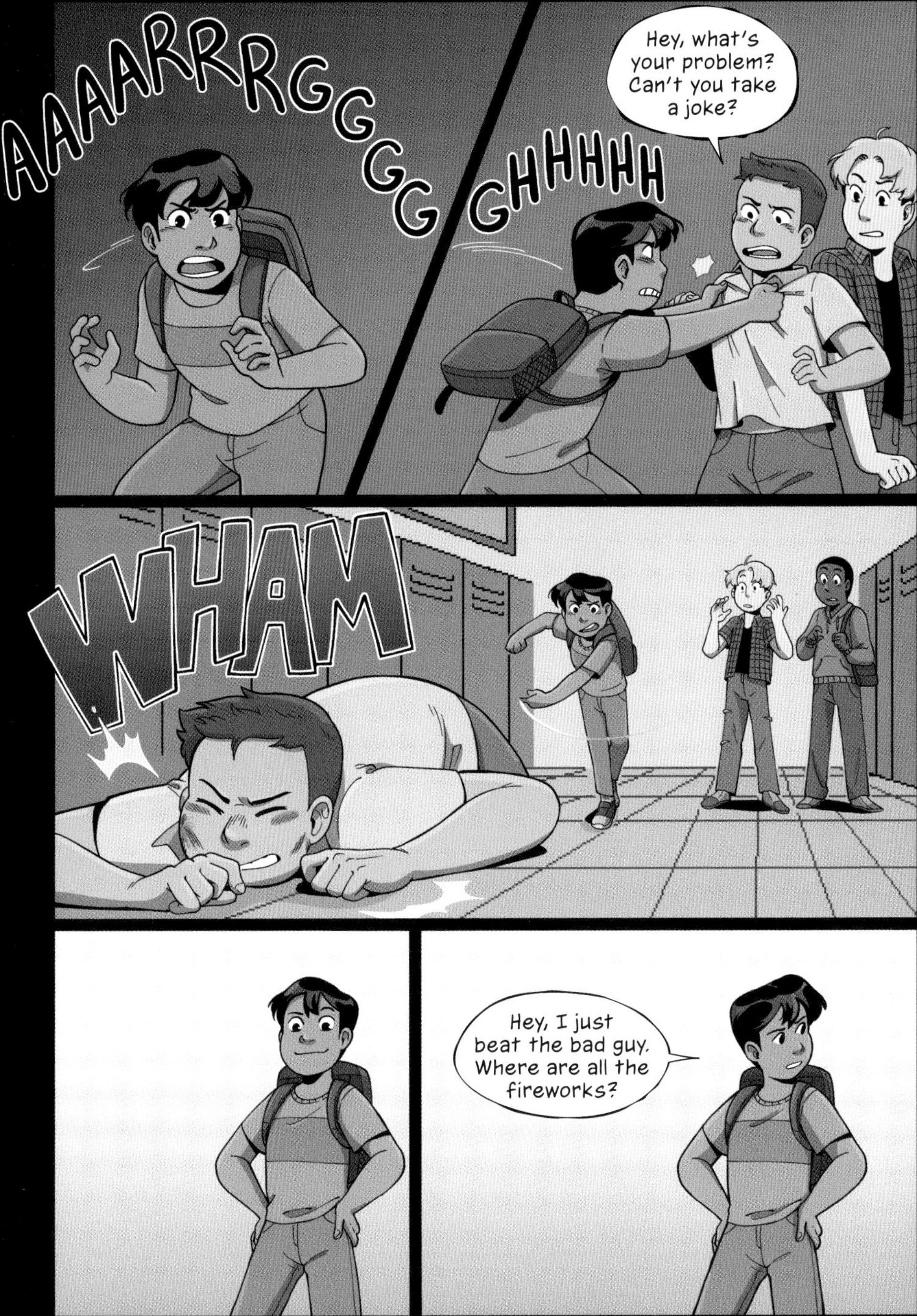
AAAARRRGGGG
GHHHHH
Hey, what's your problem? Can't you take a joke?
WHAM
Hey, I just beat the bad guy. Where are all the fireworks?

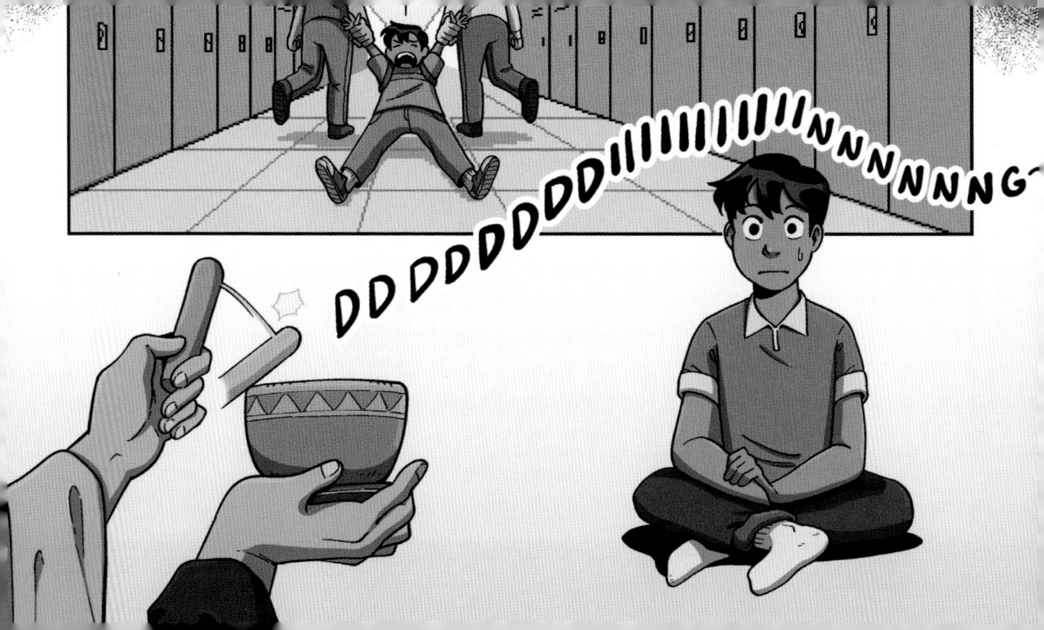
DDDDDDDDDDIIIIIIIIIIINNNNNNNG-

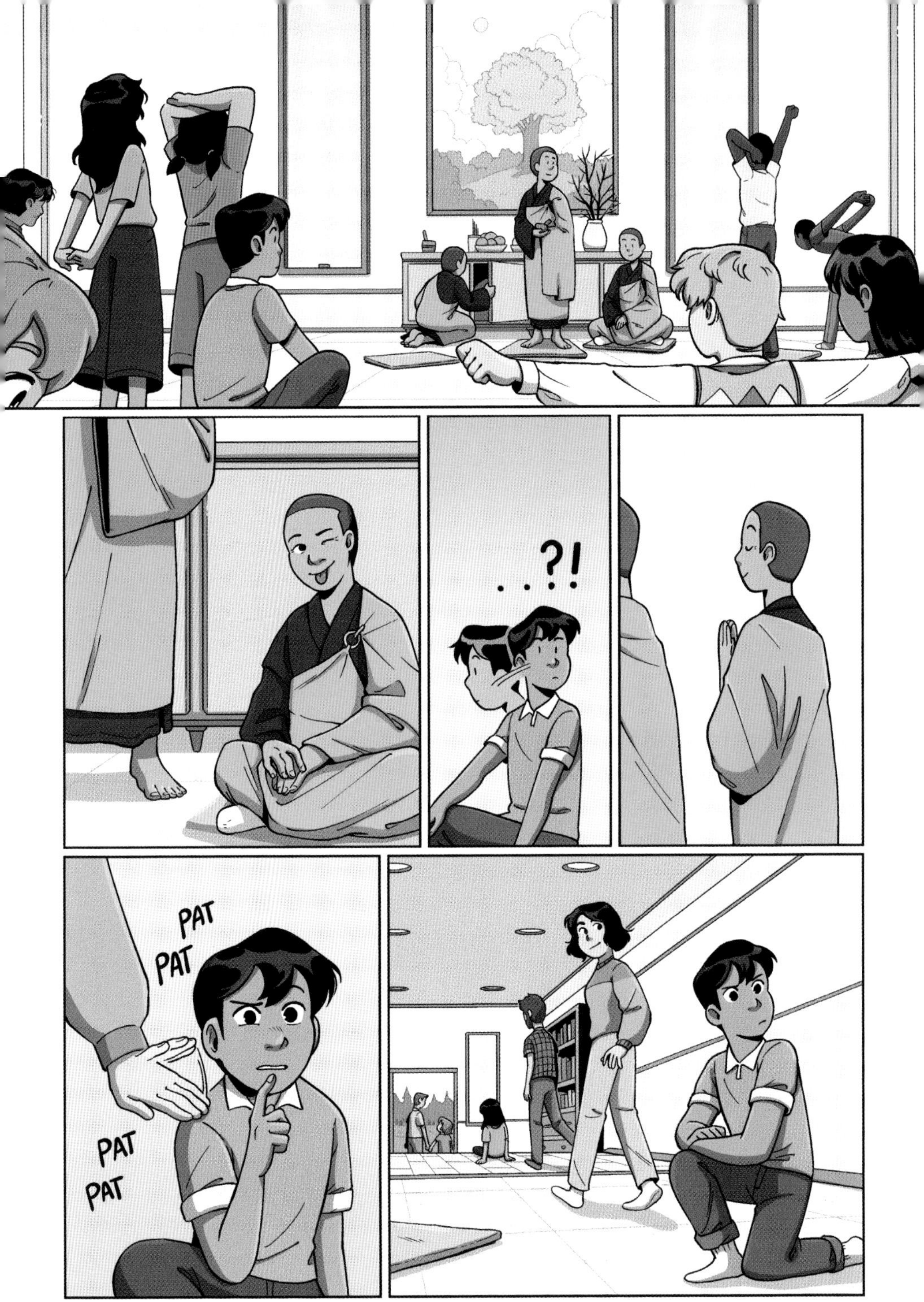

. . ?!
PAT
PAT
PAT
PAT

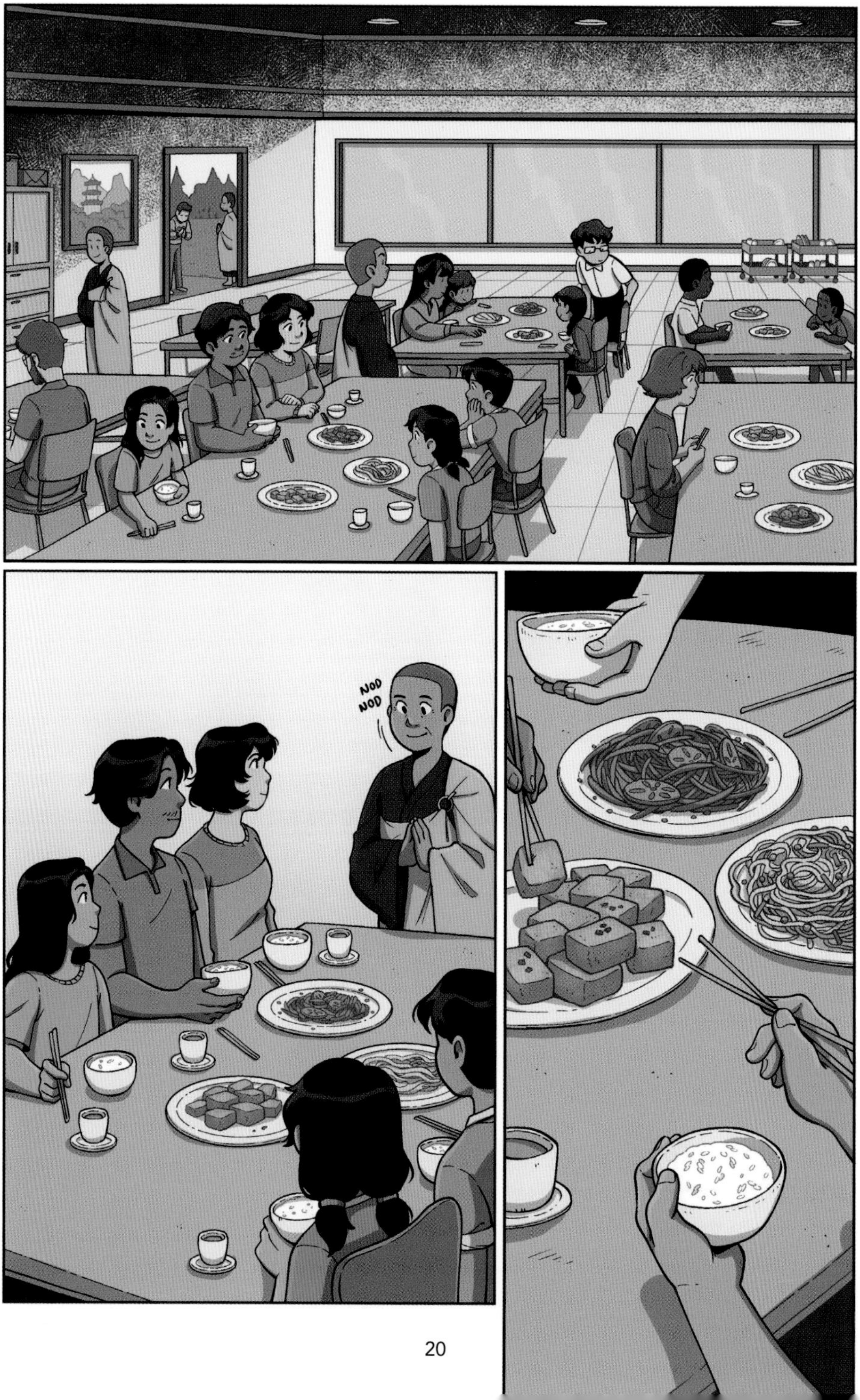
NOD
NOD

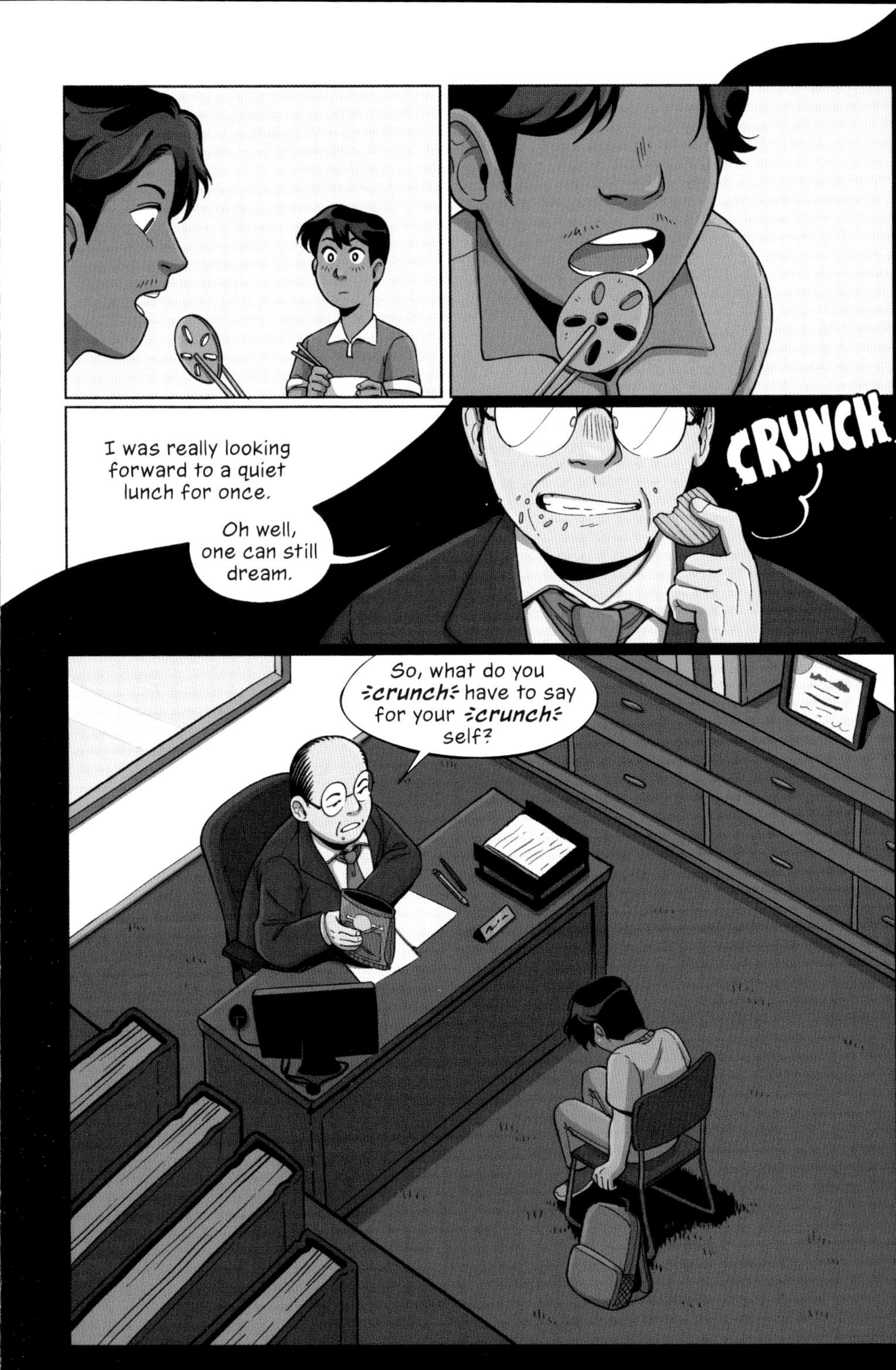

I was really looking forward to a quiet lunch for once.
Oh well, one can still dream.
CRUNCH
So, what do you =crunch= have to say for your =crunch= self?

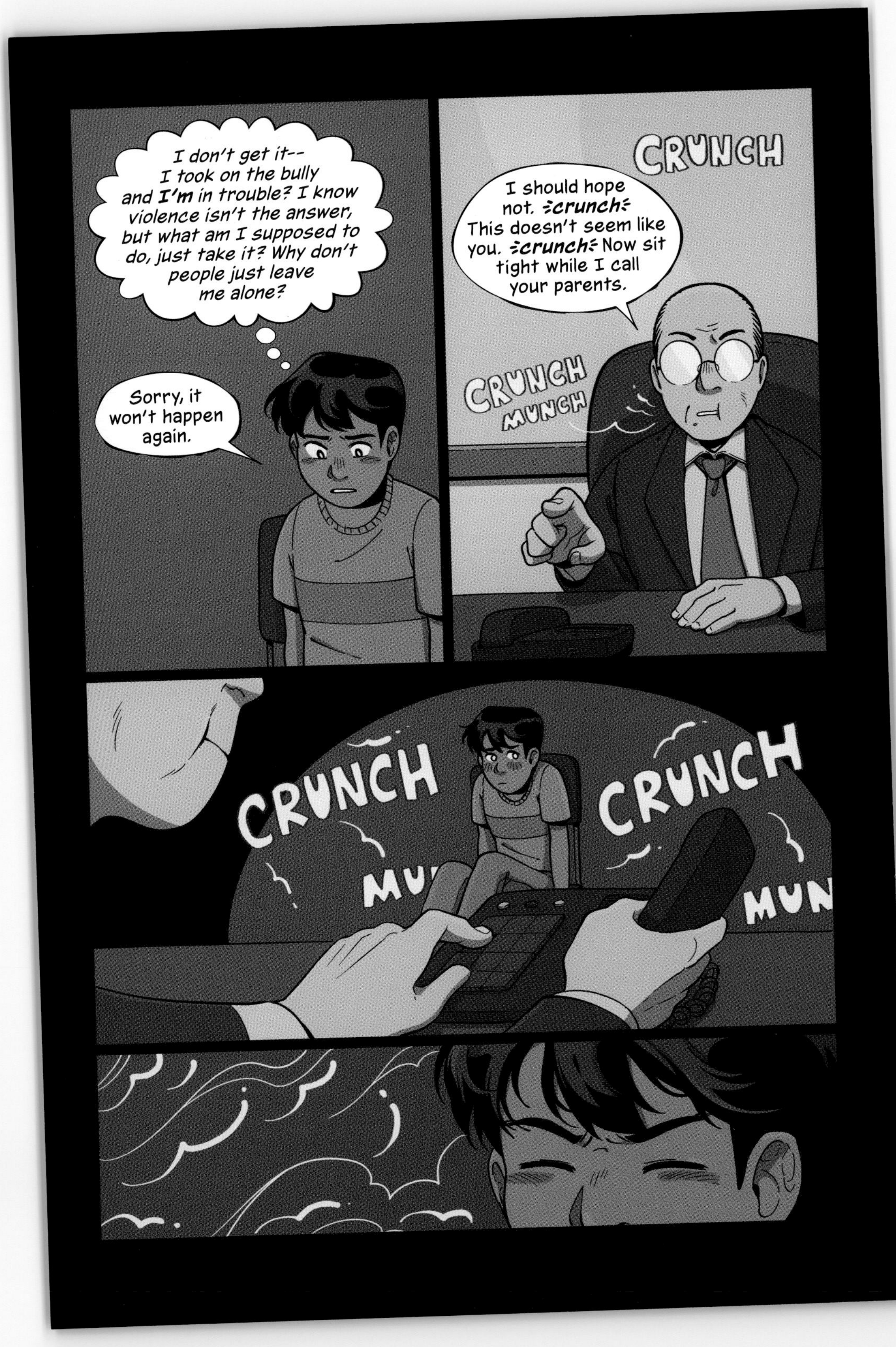

I don't get it-- I took on the bully and ***I'm*** in trouble? I know violence isn't the answer, but what am I supposed to do, just take it? Why don't people just leave me alone?
Sorry, it won't happen again.
CRUNCH
I should hope not. **crunch** This doesn't seem like you. **crunch** Now sit tight while I call your parents.
CRUNCH
MUNCH
CRUNCH
CRUNCH
MUN
MUN

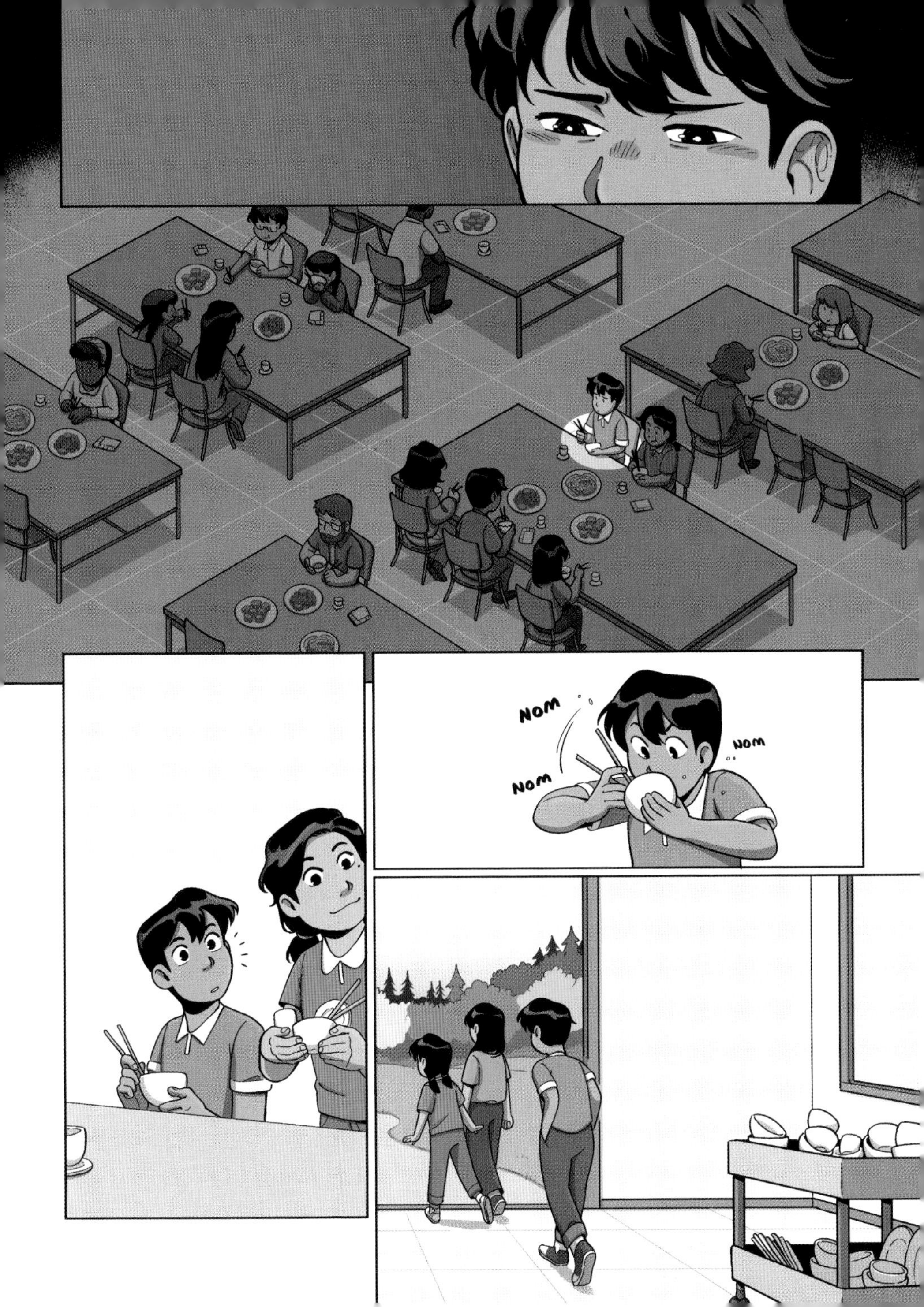
NOM
NOM
NOM

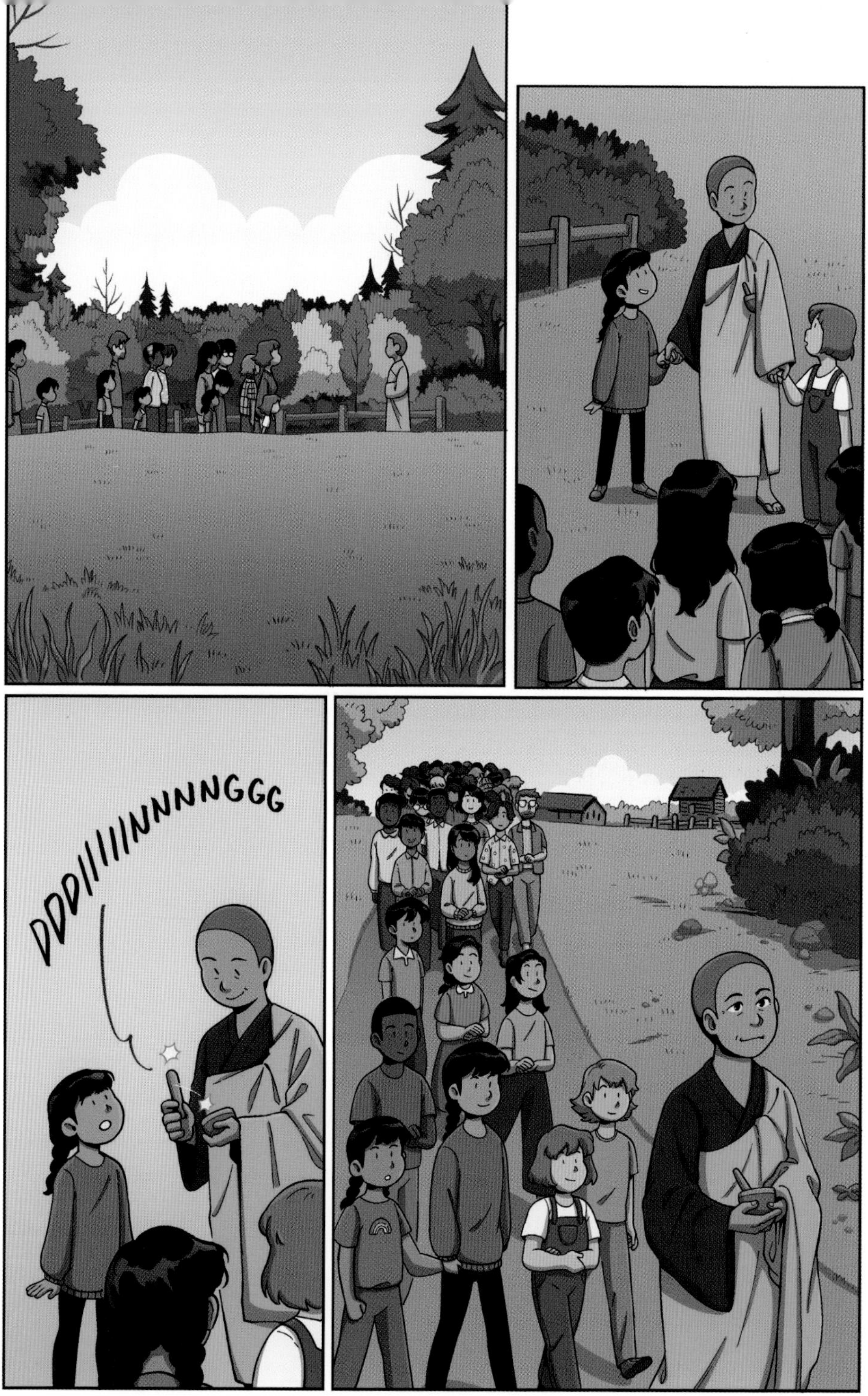
DDDIIIIIINNNNGGG

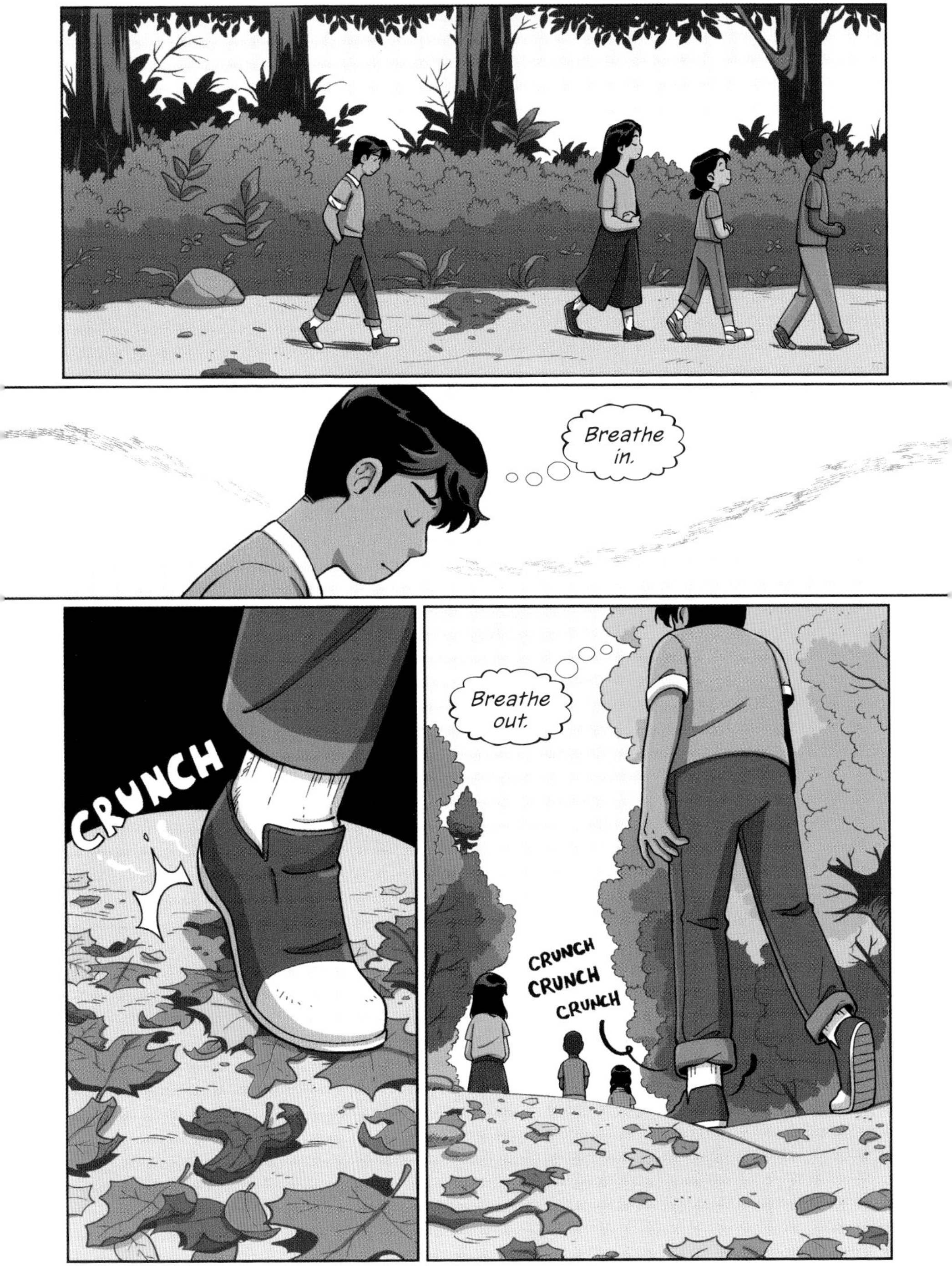
Breathe in.
CRUNCH
Breathe out.
CRUNCH
CRUNCH
CRUNCH

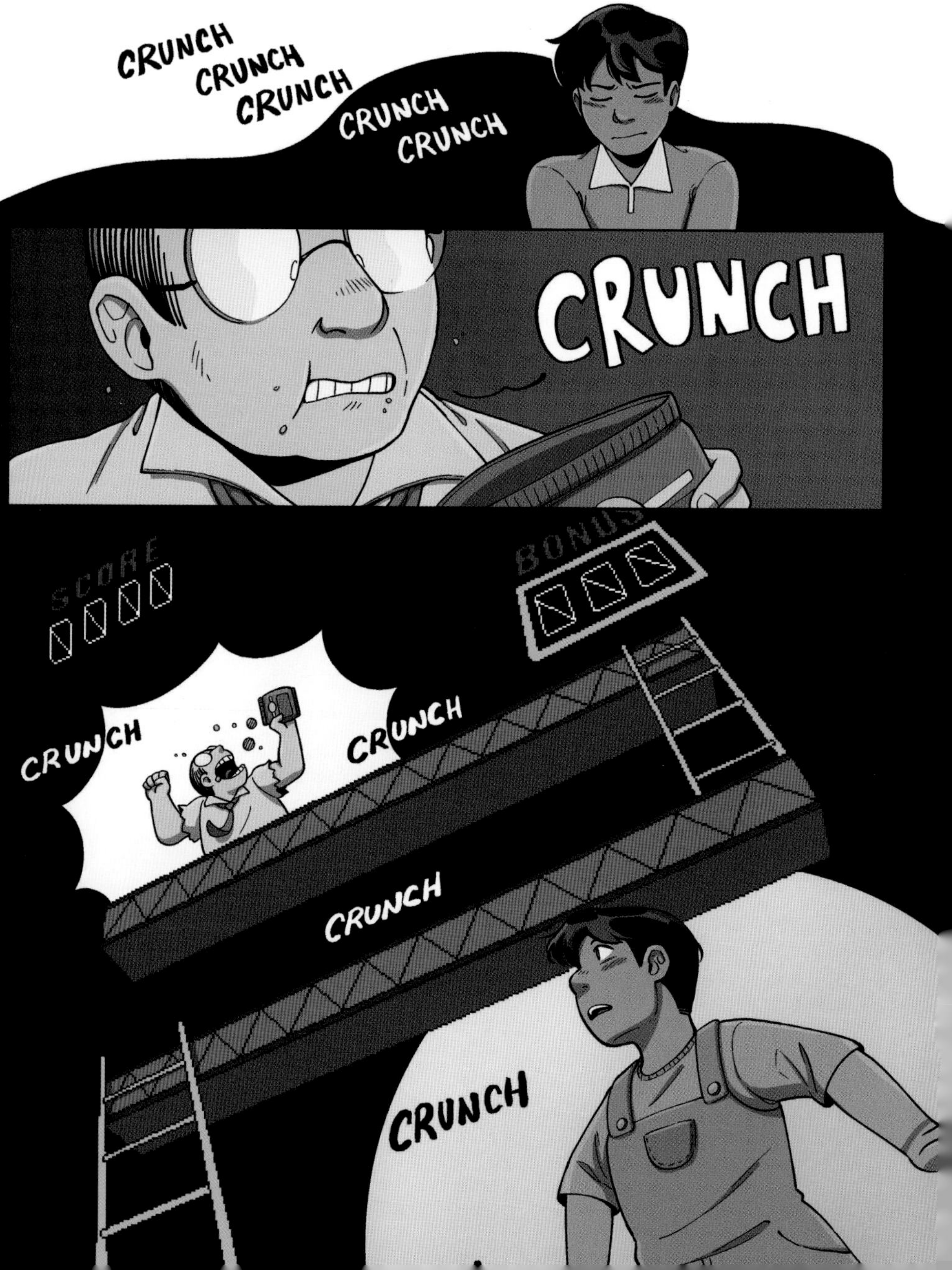
CRUNCH
CRUNCH
CRUNCH
CRUNCH
CRUNCH
CRUNCH
SCORE
BONUS
CRUNCH
CRUNCH
CRUNCH
CRUNCH

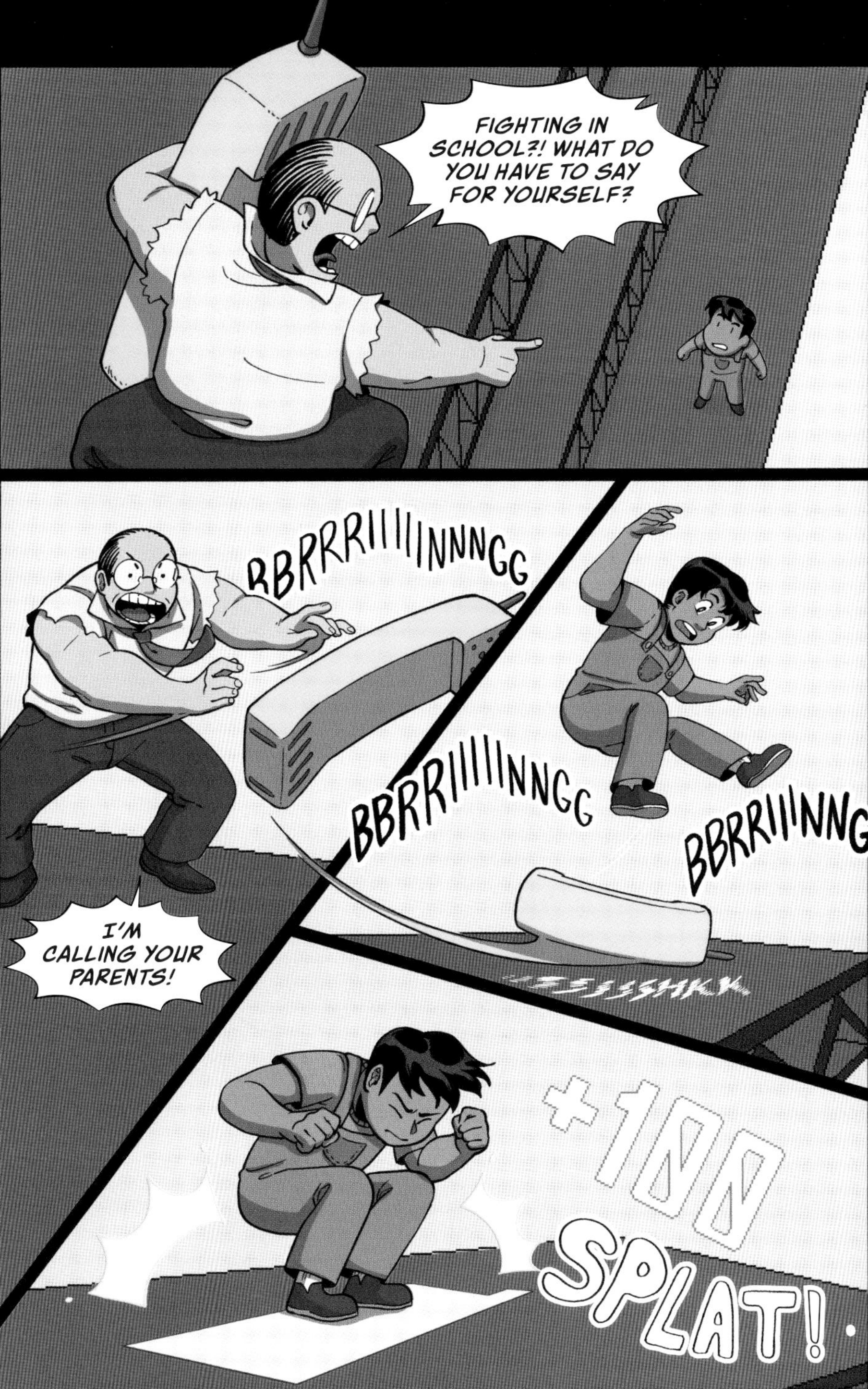
FIGHTING IN SCHOOL?! WHAT DO YOU HAVE TO SAY FOR YOURSELF?
BBRRRIIIINNNGG
I'M CALLING YOUR PARENTS!
BBRRIIIINNGG
BBRRIIINNG
+100
SPLAT!

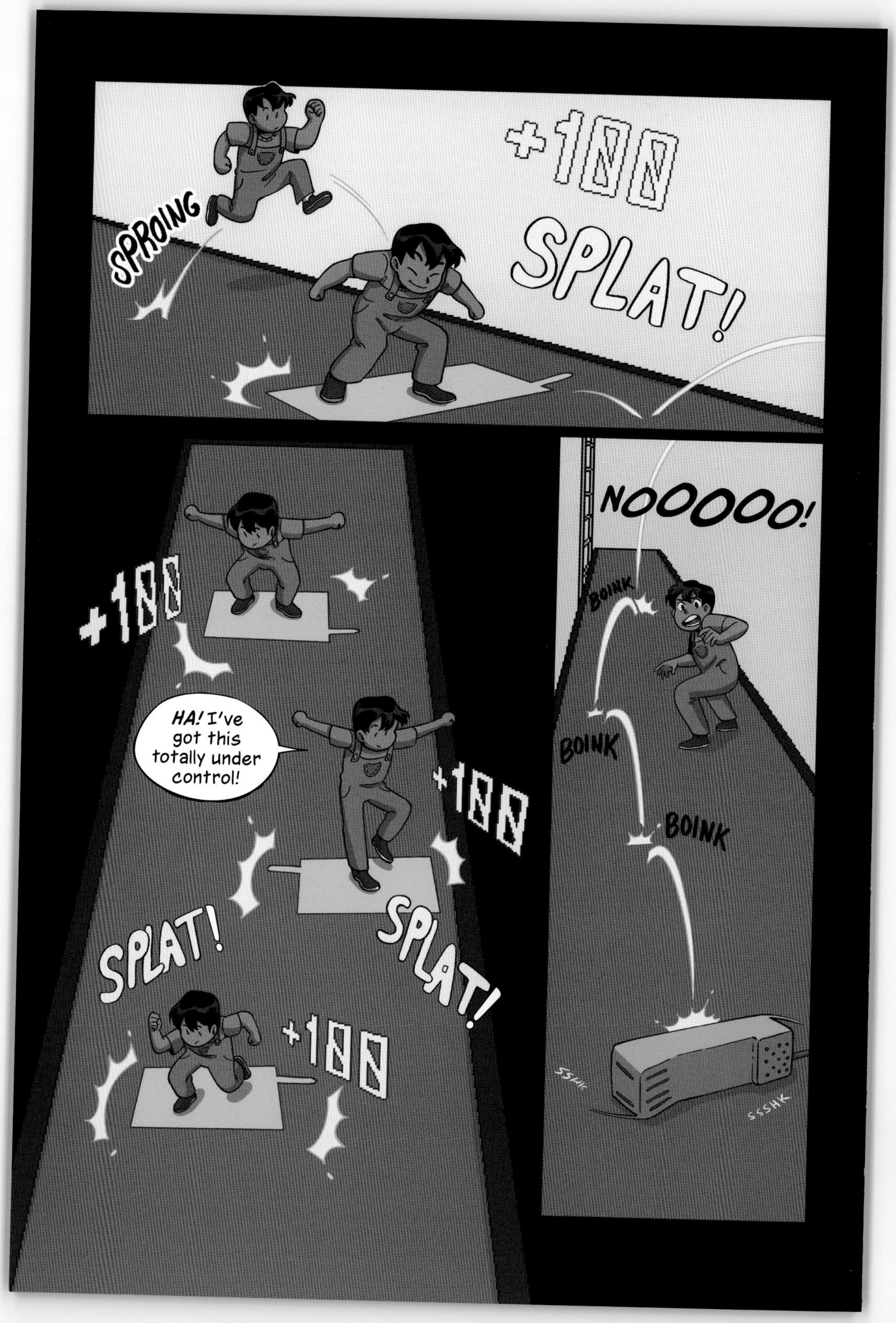
SPROING
+100
SPLAT!
+100
HA! I've got this totally under control!
+100
SPLAT!
SPLAT!
+100
NOOOOO!
BOINK
BOINK
BOINK
SSHK
SSSHK

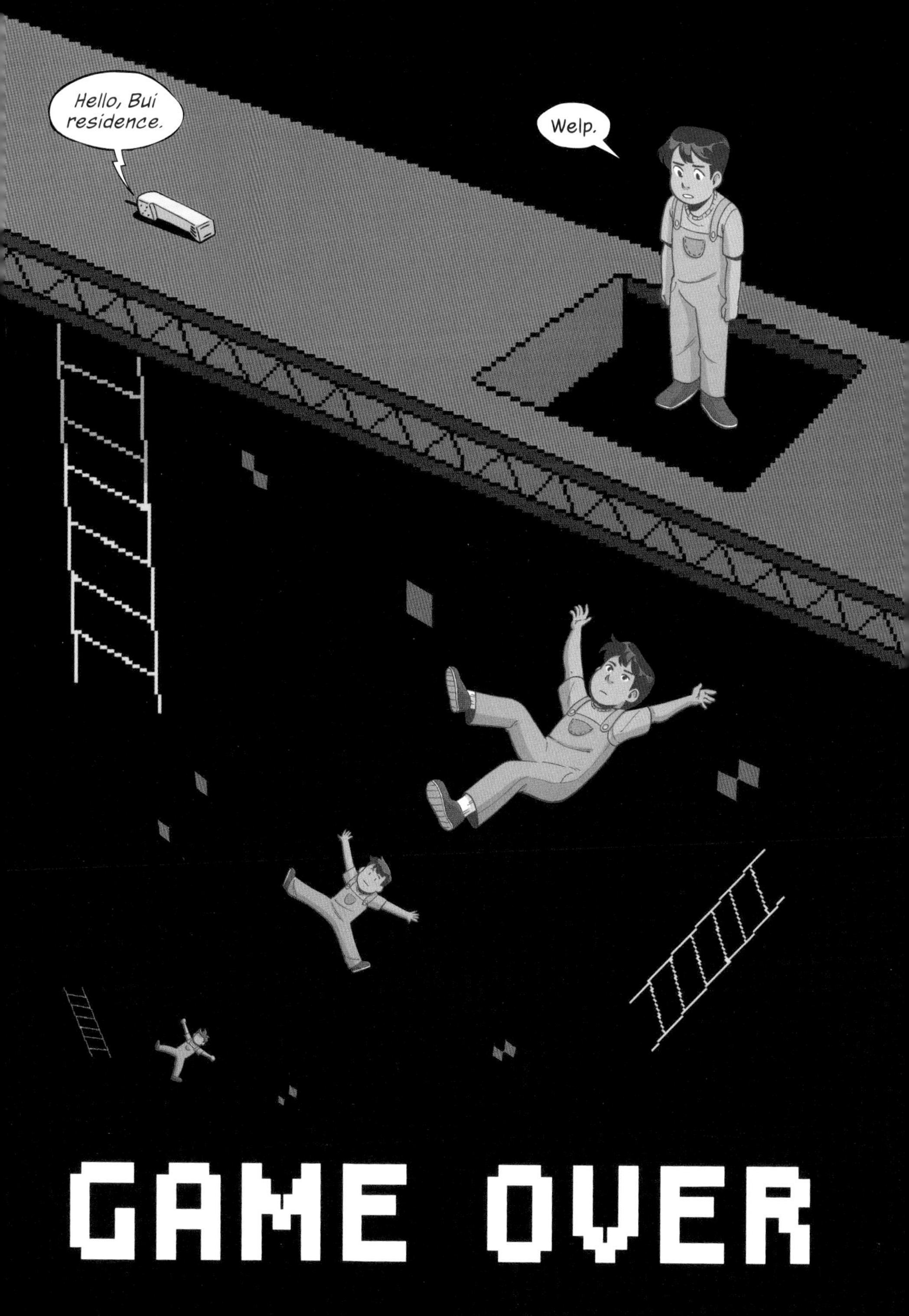
Hello, Bui residence.
Welp.
GAME OVER

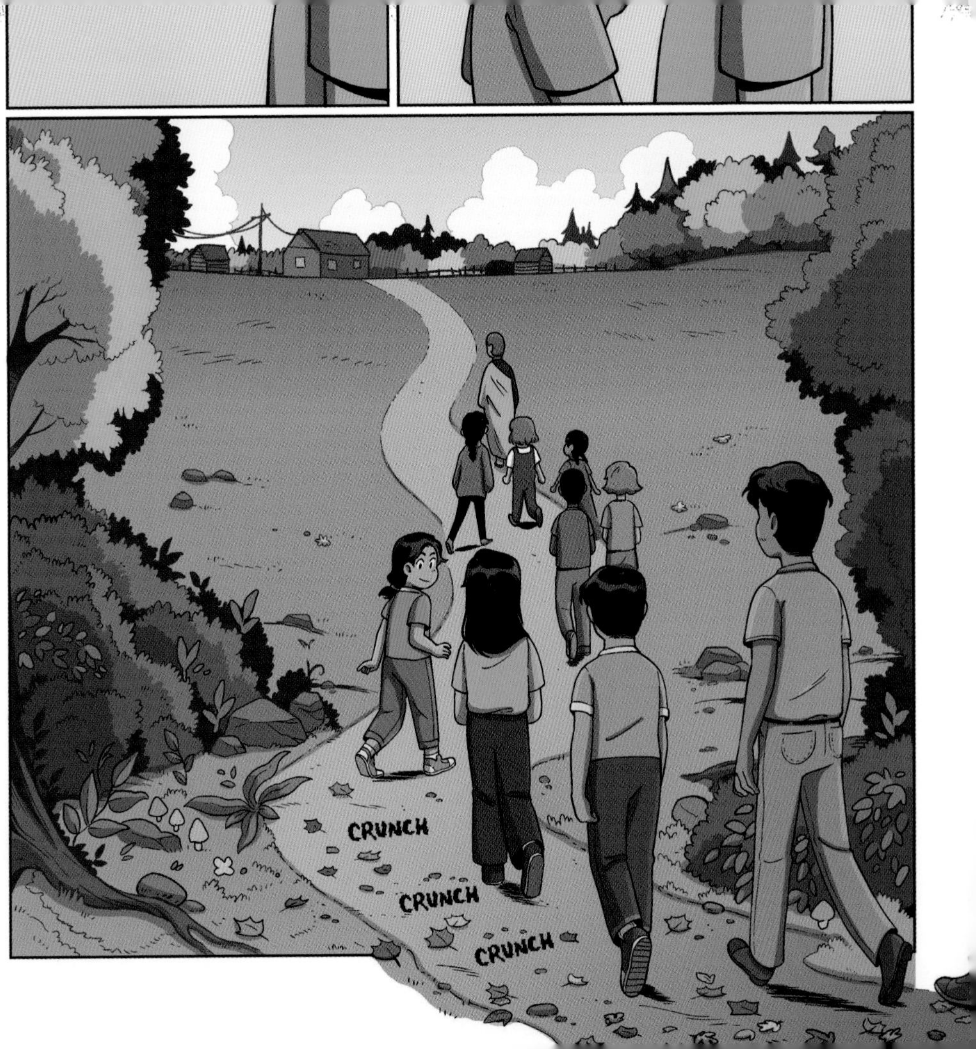
CRUNCH
CRUNCH
CRUNCH

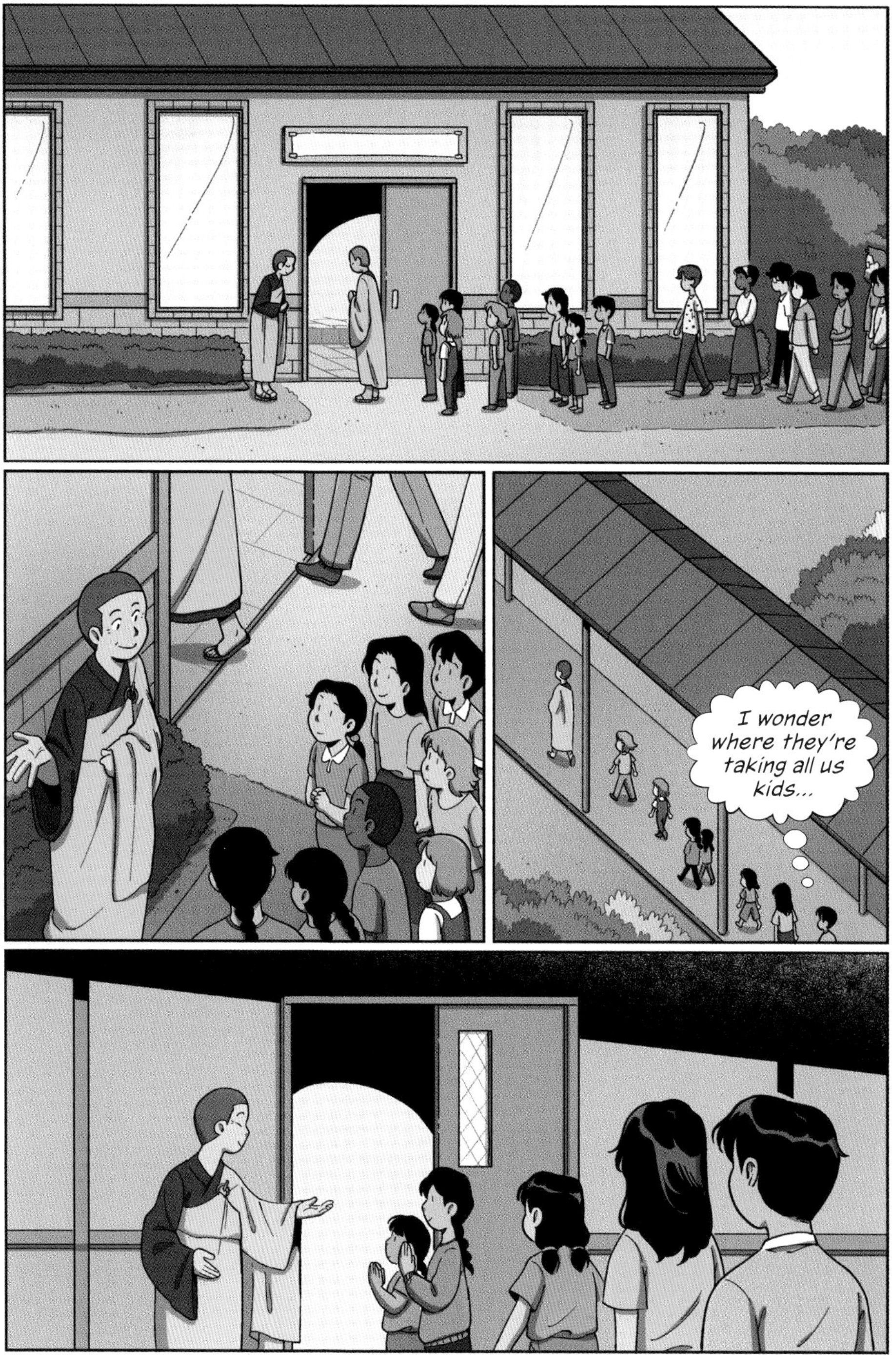
I wonder where they're taking all us kids...

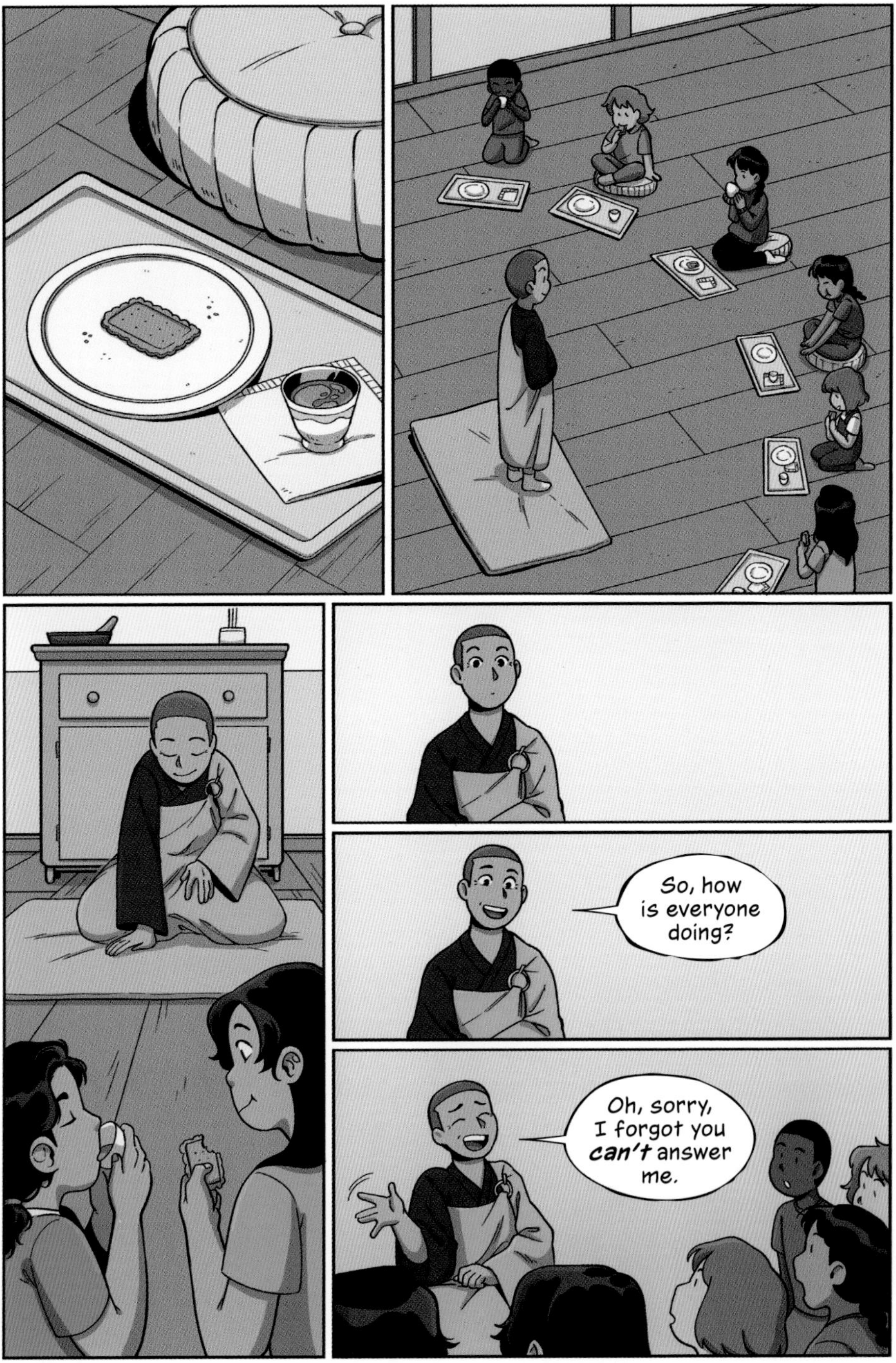
So, how is everyone doing?
Oh, sorry, I forgot you *can't* answer me.

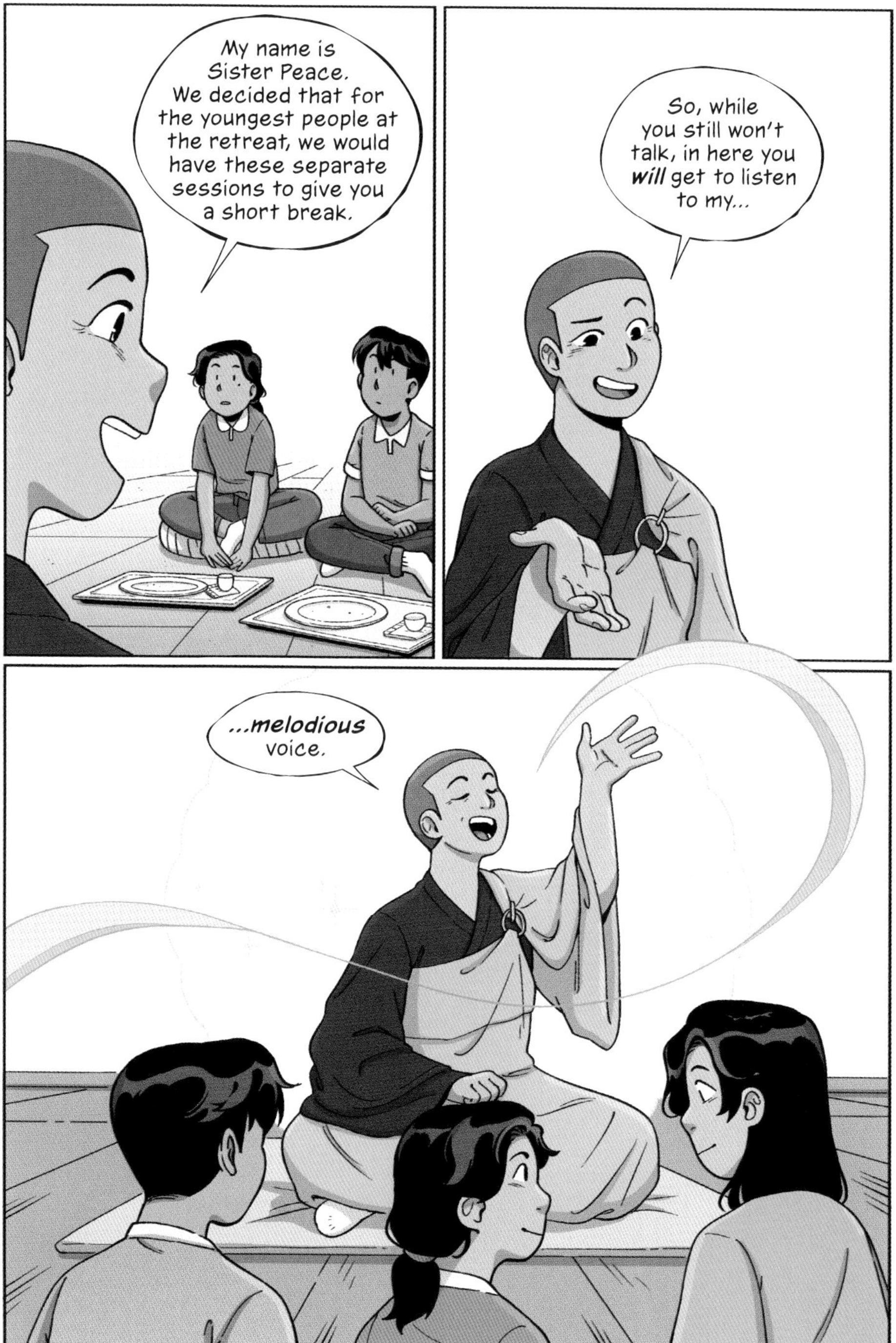
My name is Sister Peace. We decided that for the youngest people at the retreat, we would have these separate sessions to give you a short break.
So, while you still won't talk, in here you *will* get to listen to my...
...melodious voice.

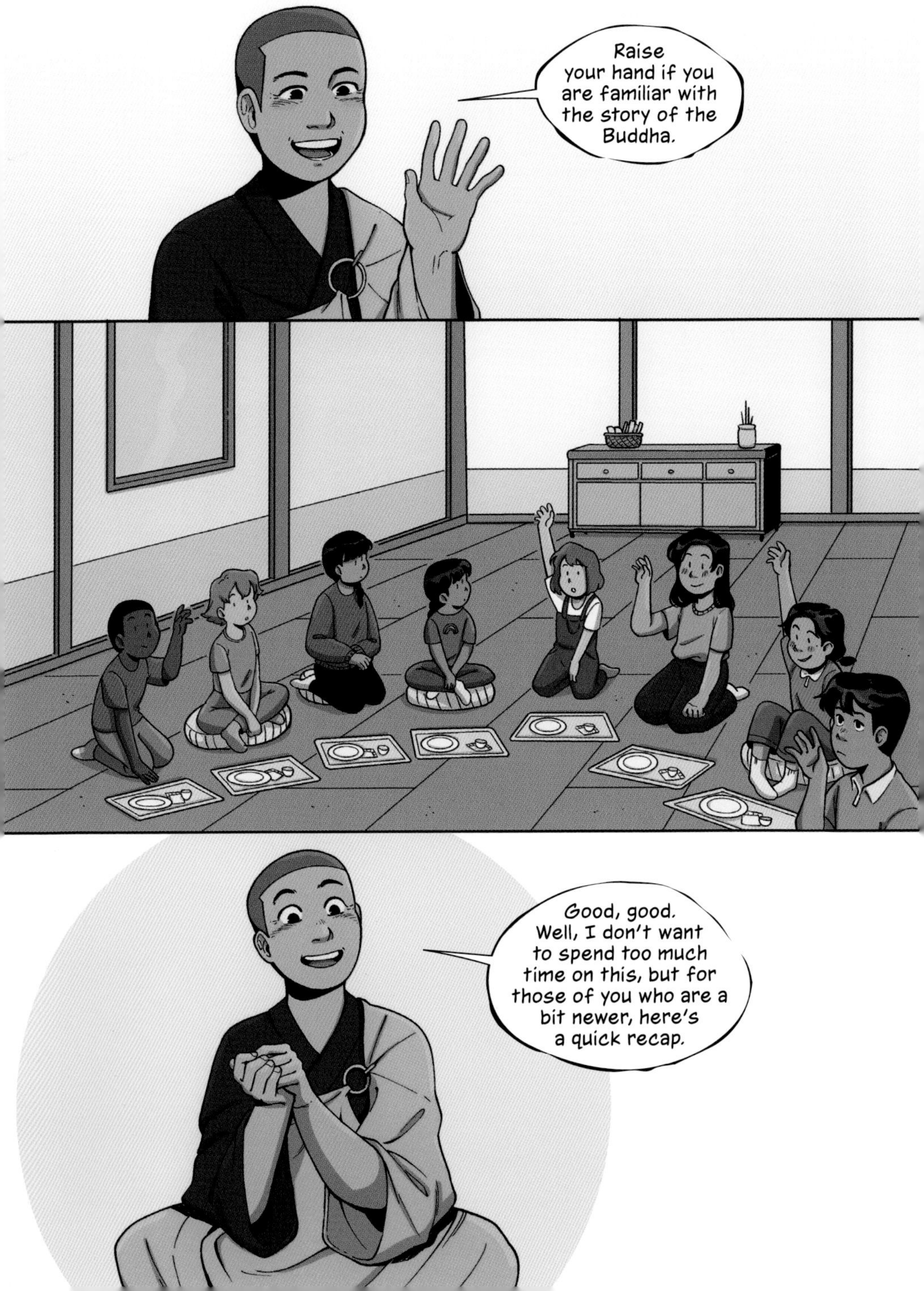
Raise your hand if you are familiar with the story of the Buddha.
Good, good. Well, I don't want to spend too much time on this, but for those of you who are a bit newer, here's a quick recap.

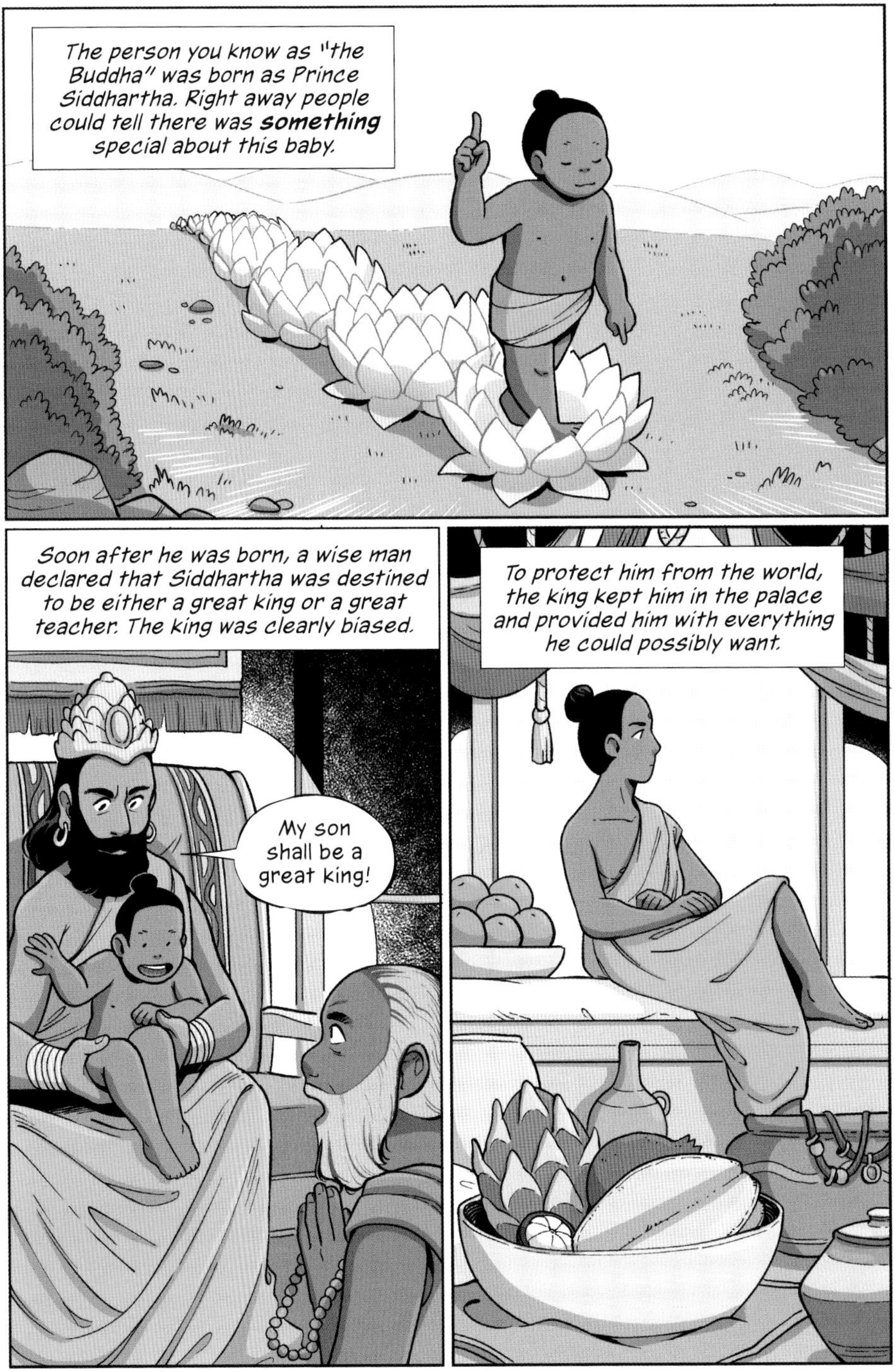

The person you know as "the Buddha" was born as Prince Siddhartha. Right away people could tell there was **something** special about this baby.
Soon after he was born, a wise man declared that Siddhartha was destined to be either a great king or a great teacher. The king was clearly biased.
My son shall be a great king!
To protect him from the world, the king kept him in the palace and provided him with everything he could possibly want.

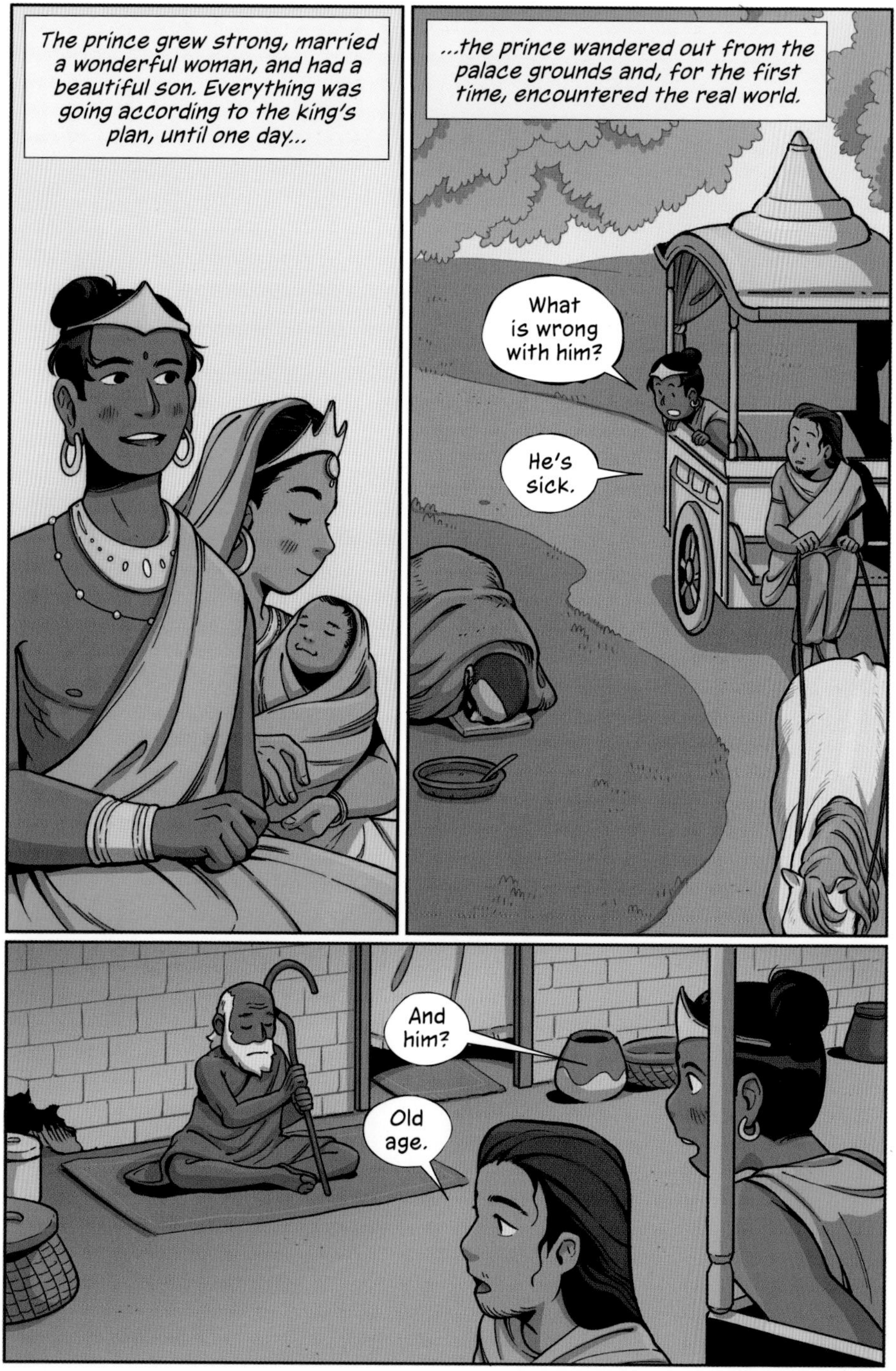
The prince grew strong, married a wonderful woman, and had a beautiful son. Everything was going according to the king's plan, until one day...
...the prince wandered out from the palace grounds and, for the first time, encountered the real world.
What is wrong with him?
He's sick.
And him?
Old age.

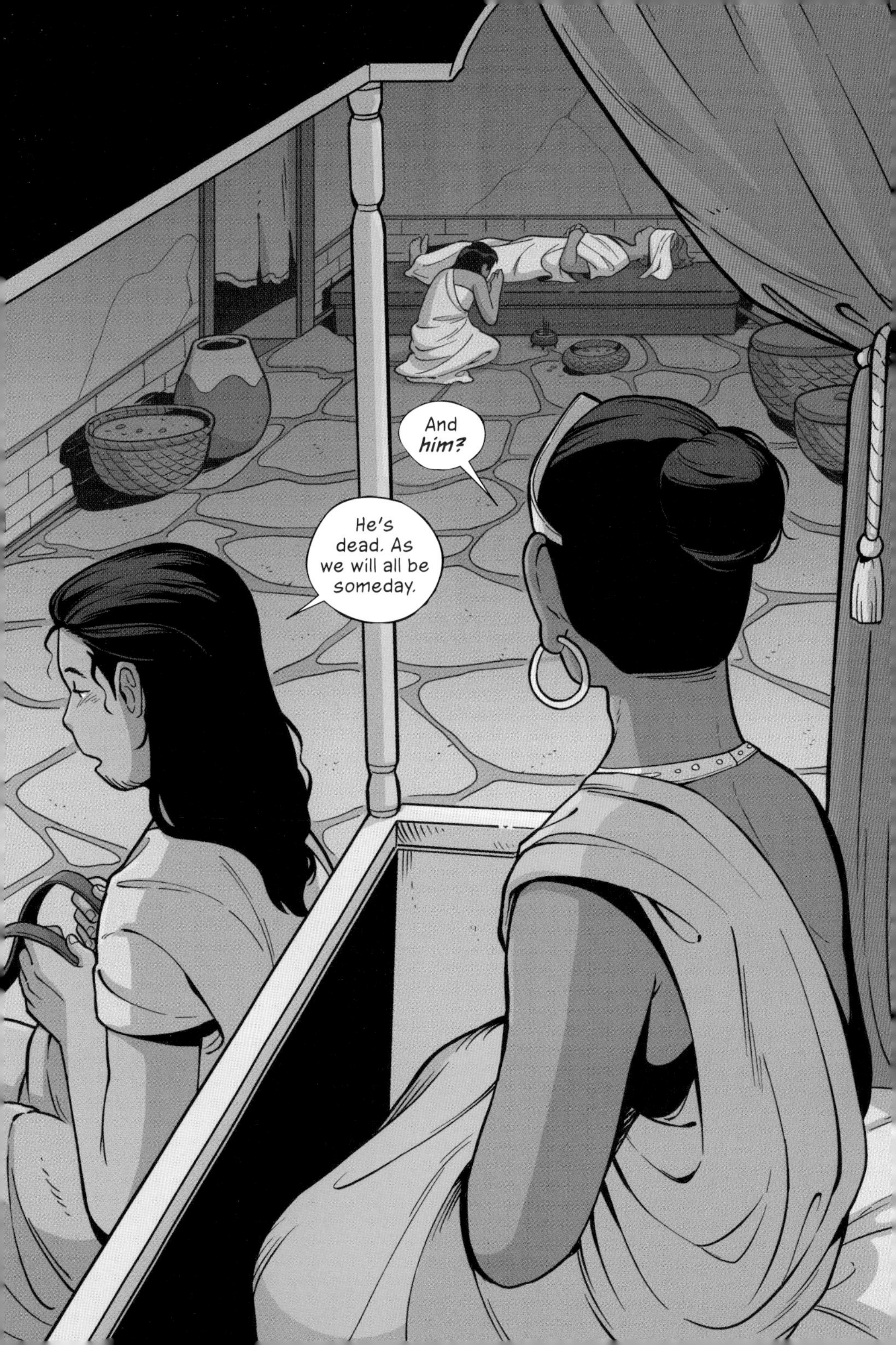
And *him?*
He's dead. As we will all be someday.

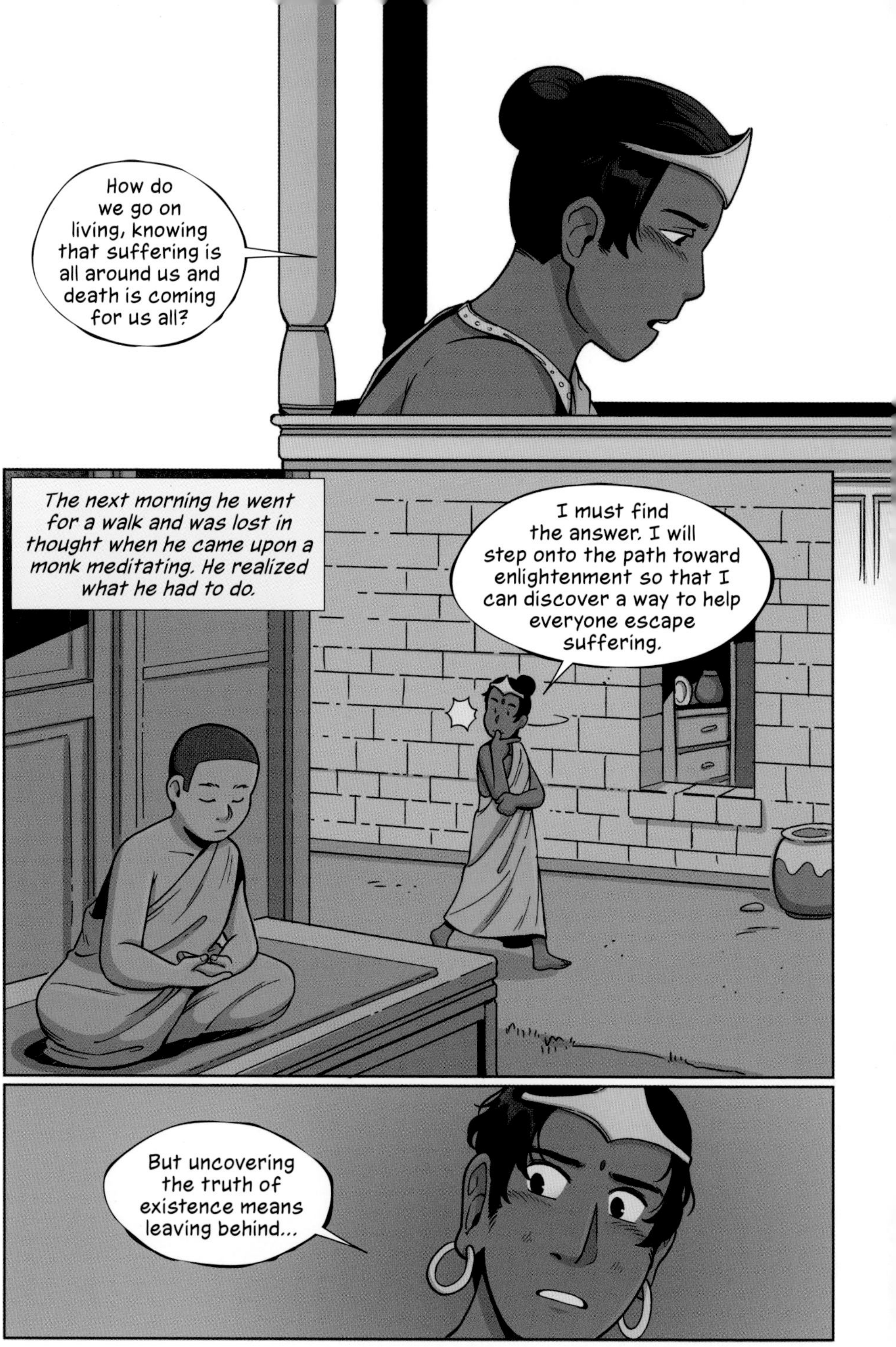
How do we go on living, knowing that suffering is all around us and death is coming for us all?
The next morning he went for a walk and was lost in thought when he came upon a monk meditating. He realized what he had to do.
I must find the answer. I will step onto the path toward enlightenment so that I can discover a way to help everyone escape suffering.
But uncovering the truth of existence means leaving behind...

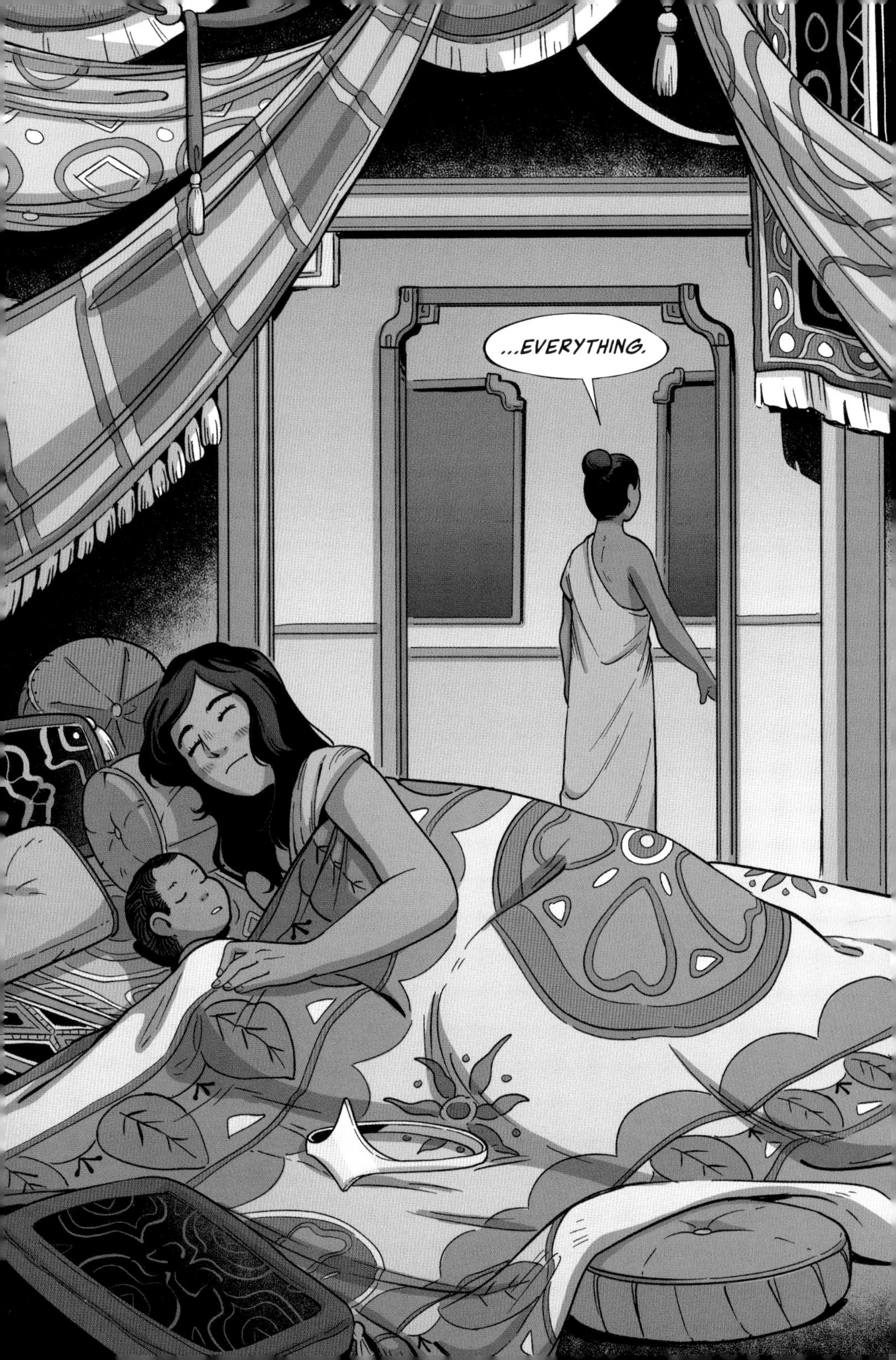
...EVERYTHING.

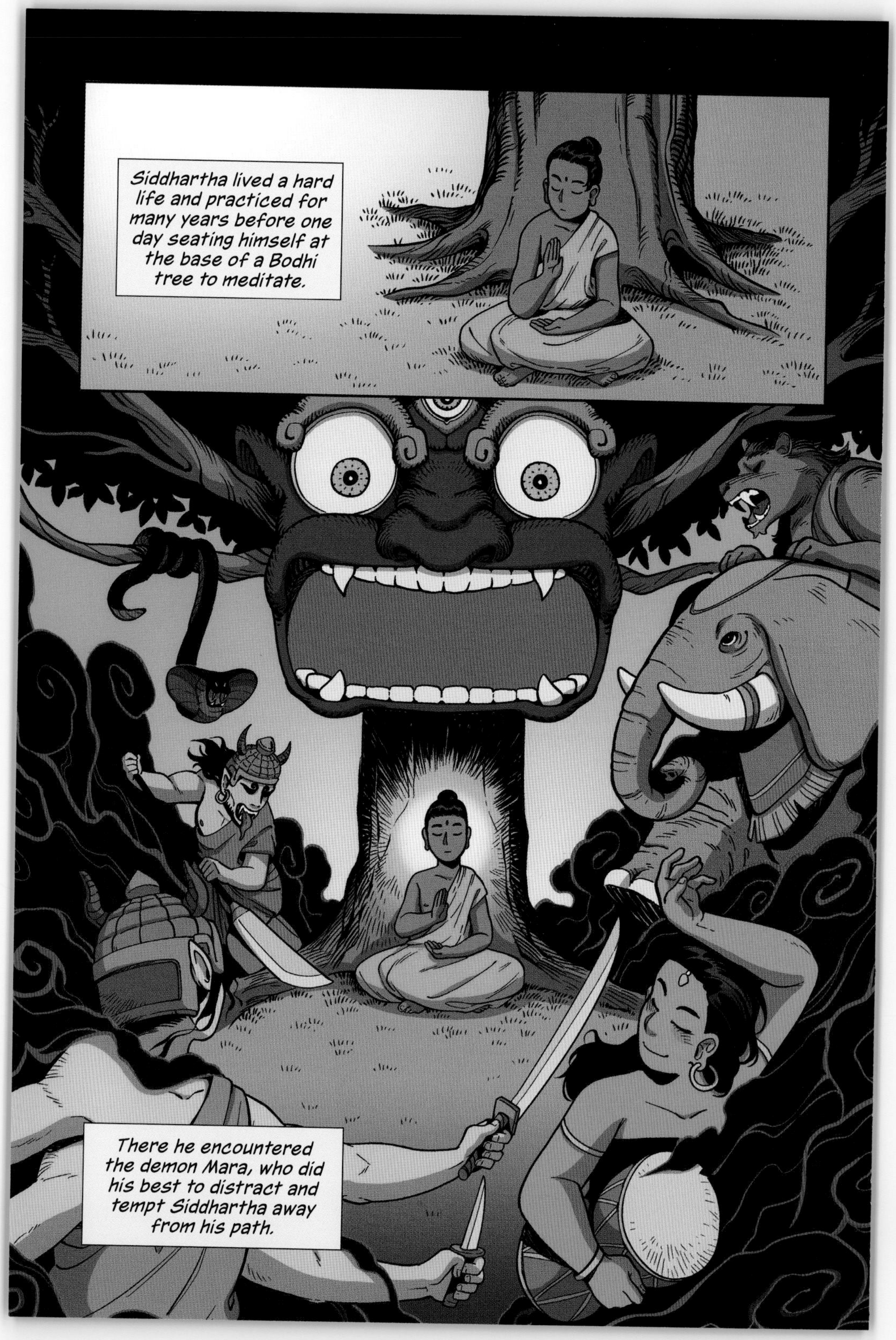
Siddhartha lived a hard life and practiced for many years before one day seating himself at the base of a Bodhi tree to meditate.
There he encountered the demon Mara, who did his best to distract and tempt Siddhartha away from his path.

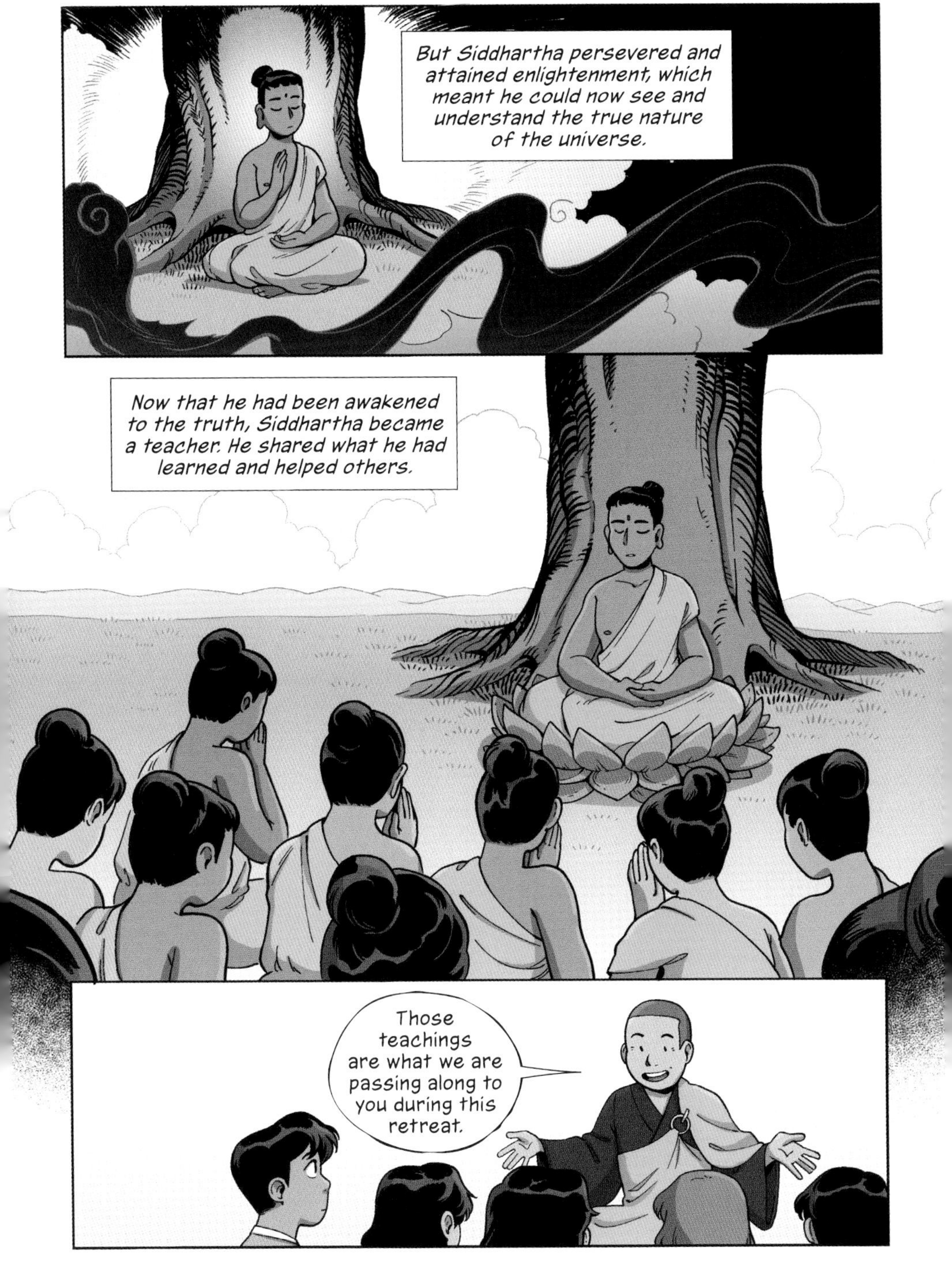
But Siddhartha persevered and attained enlightenment, which meant he could now see and understand the true nature of the universe.
Now that he had been awakened to the truth, Siddhartha became a teacher. He shared what he had learned and helped others.
Those teachings are what we are passing along to you during this retreat.

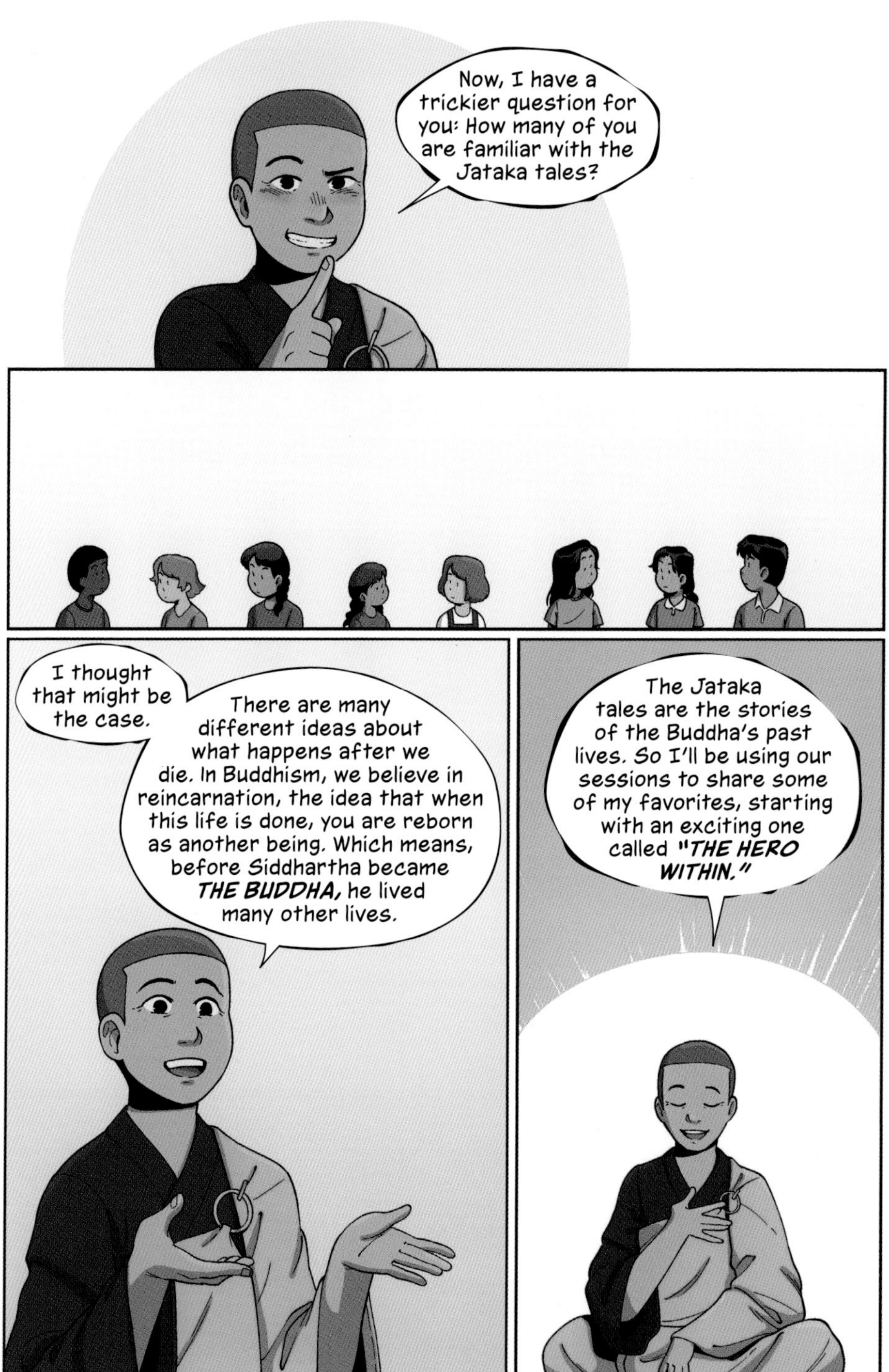
Now, I have a trickier question for you: How many of you are familiar with the Jataka tales?
I thought that might be the case.
There are many different ideas about what happens after we die. In Buddhism, we believe in reincarnation, the idea that when this life is done, you are reborn as another being. Which means, before Siddhartha became ***THE BUDDHA,*** he lived many other lives.
The Jataka tales are the stories of the Buddha's past lives. So I'll be using our sessions to share some of my favorites, starting with an exciting one called ***"THE HERO WITHIN."***

In this previous life, the Buddha was also born as a prince.

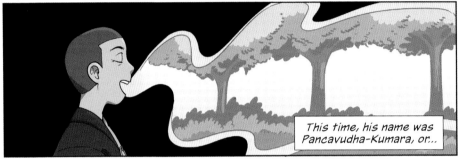

This time, his name was Pancavudha-Kumara, or...

...PRINCE FIVE WEAPONS.

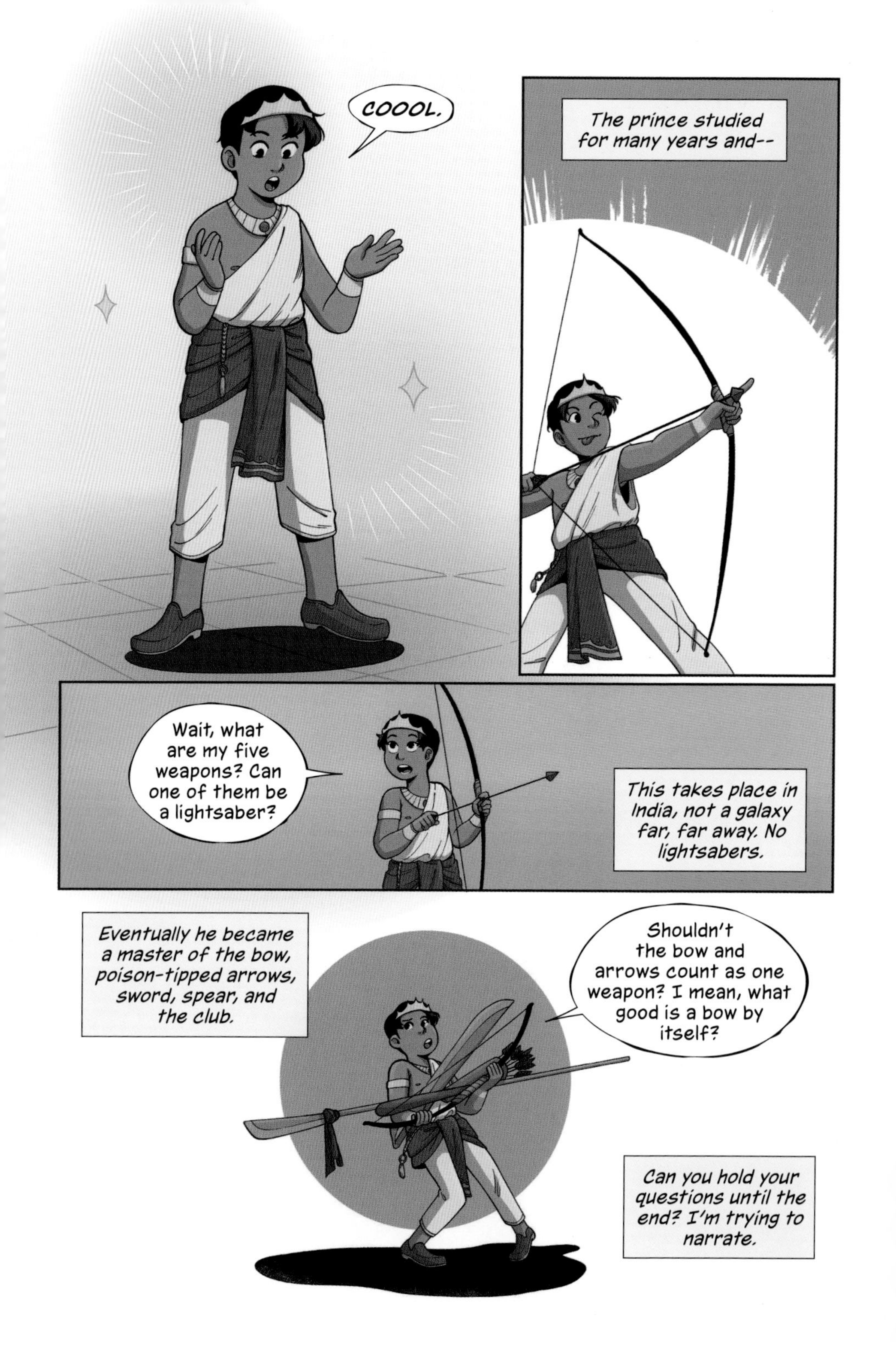
COOOL.
The prince studied for many years and--
Wait, what are my five weapons? Can one of them be a lightsaber?
This takes place in India, not a galaxy far, far away. No lightsabers.
Eventually he became a master of the bow, poison-tipped arrows, sword, spear, and the club.
Shouldn't the bow and arrows count as one weapon? I mean, what good is a bow by itself?
Can you hold your questions until the end? I'm trying to narrate.

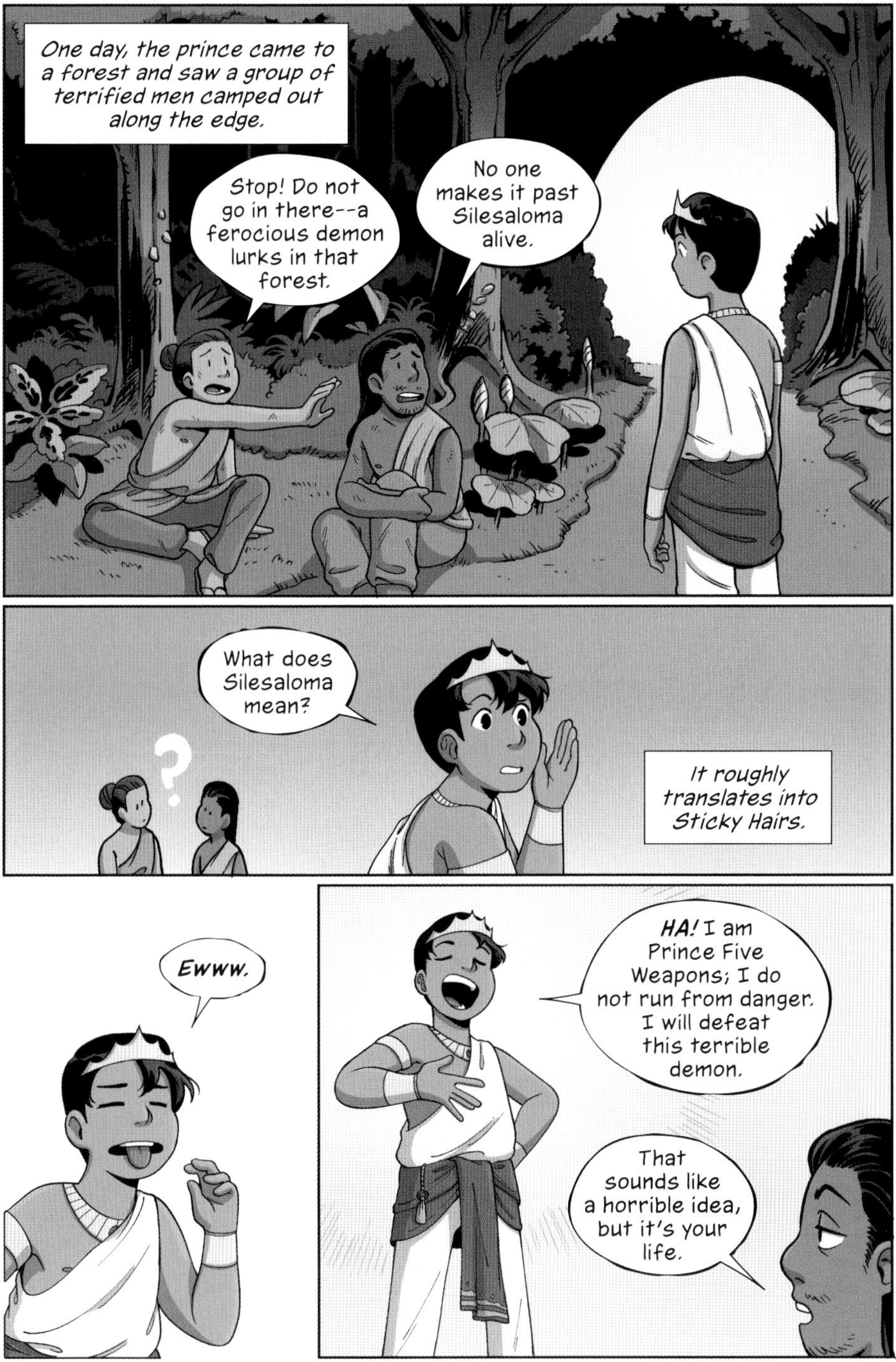
One day, the prince came to a forest and saw a group of terrified men camped out along the edge.
Stop! Do not go in there--a ferocious demon lurks in that forest.
No one makes it past Silesaloma alive.
What does Silesaloma mean?
It roughly translates into Sticky Hairs.
Ewww.
HA! I am Prince Five Weapons; I do not run from danger. I will defeat this terrible demon.
That sounds like a horrible idea, but it's your life.

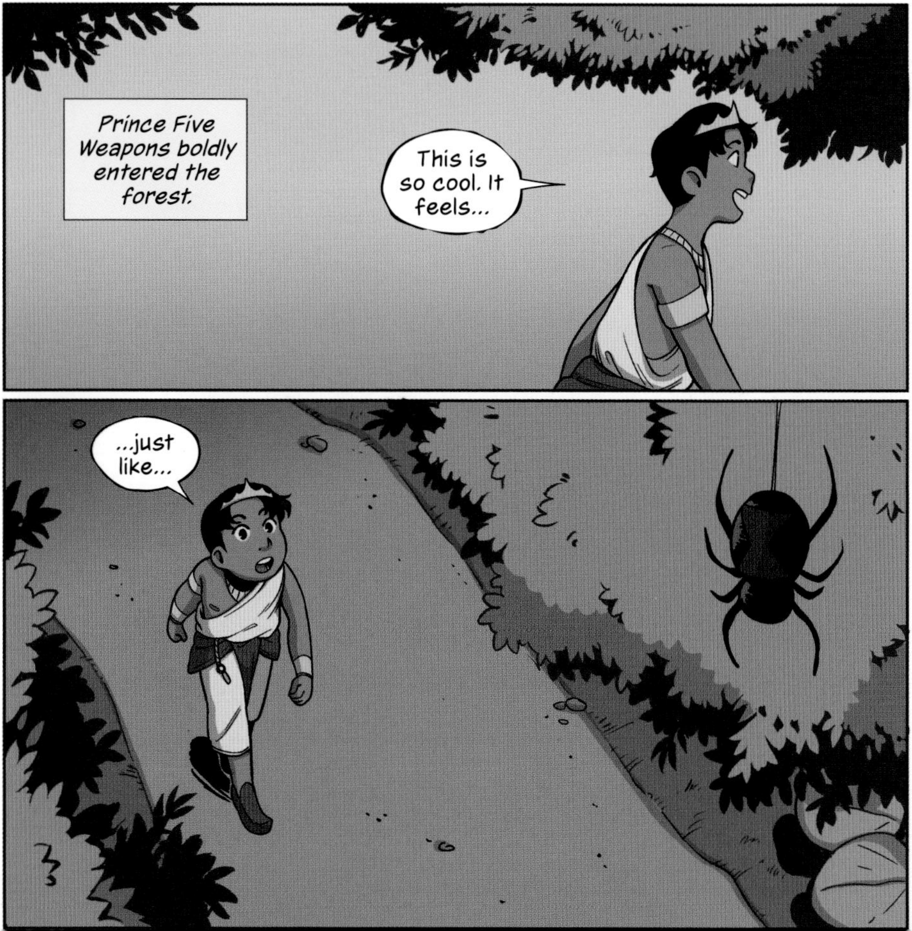

Prince Five Weapons boldly entered the forest.
This is so cool. It feels...
...just like...

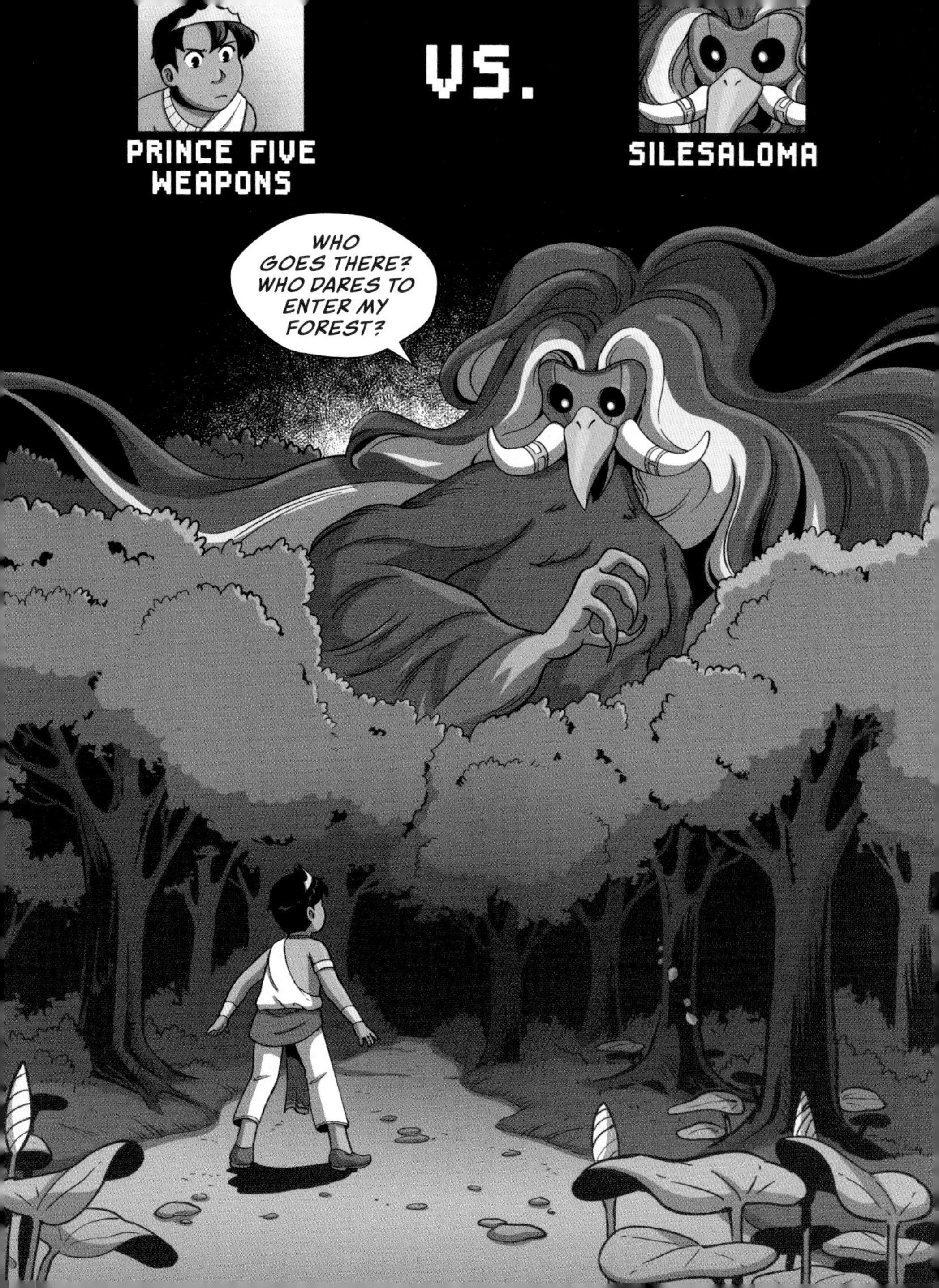
PRINCE FIVE WEAPONS
VS.
SILESALOMA
WHO GOES THERE? WHO DARES TO ENTER MY FOREST?

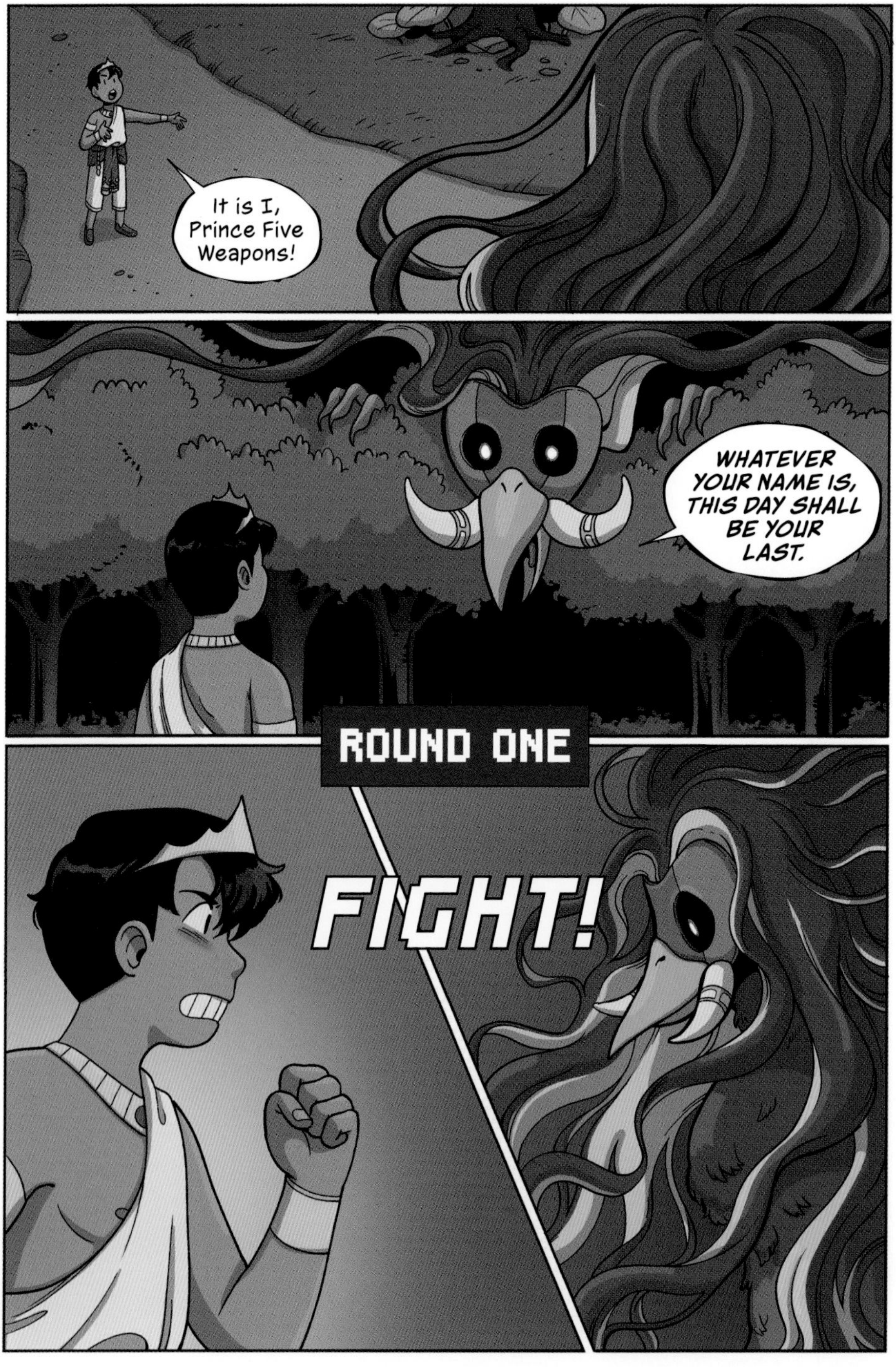
It is I, Prince Five Weapons!
WHATEVER YOUR NAME IS, THIS DAY SHALL BE YOUR LAST.
ROUND ONE
FIGHT!

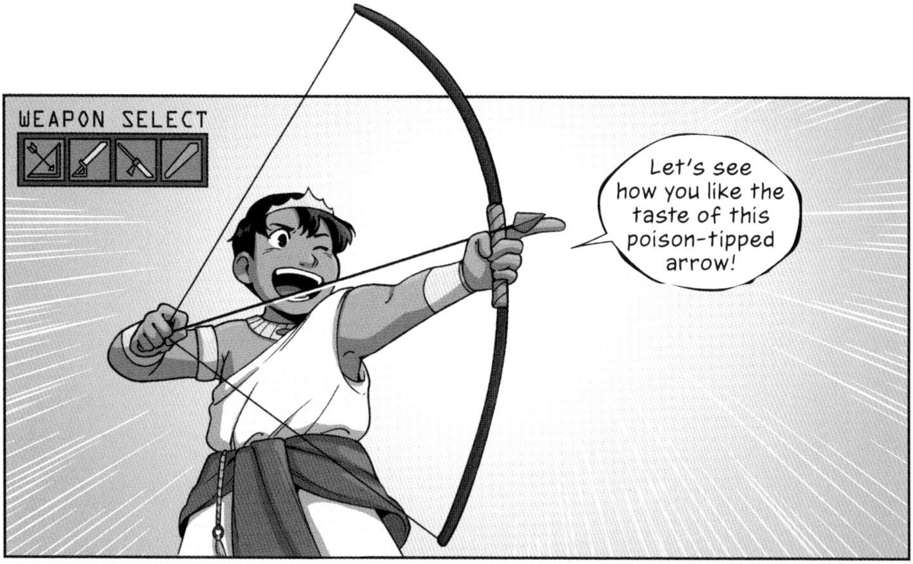
WEAPON SELECT
Let's see how you like the taste of this poison-tipped arrow!
TWIP
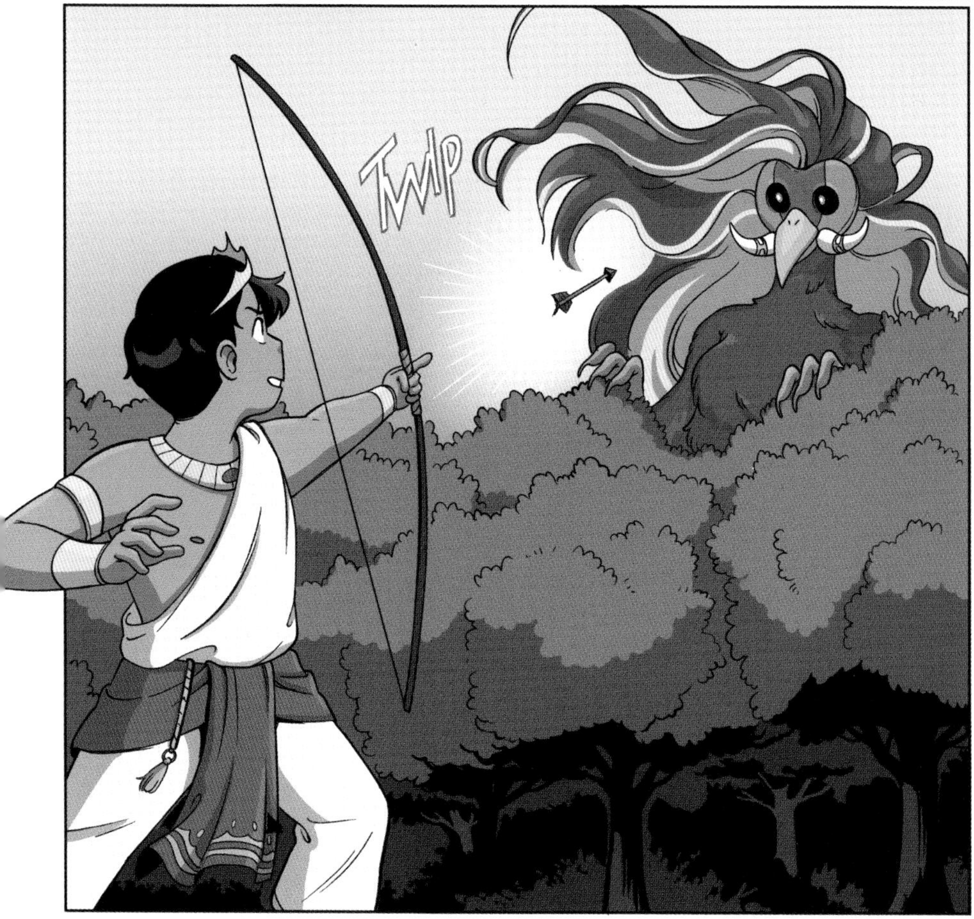

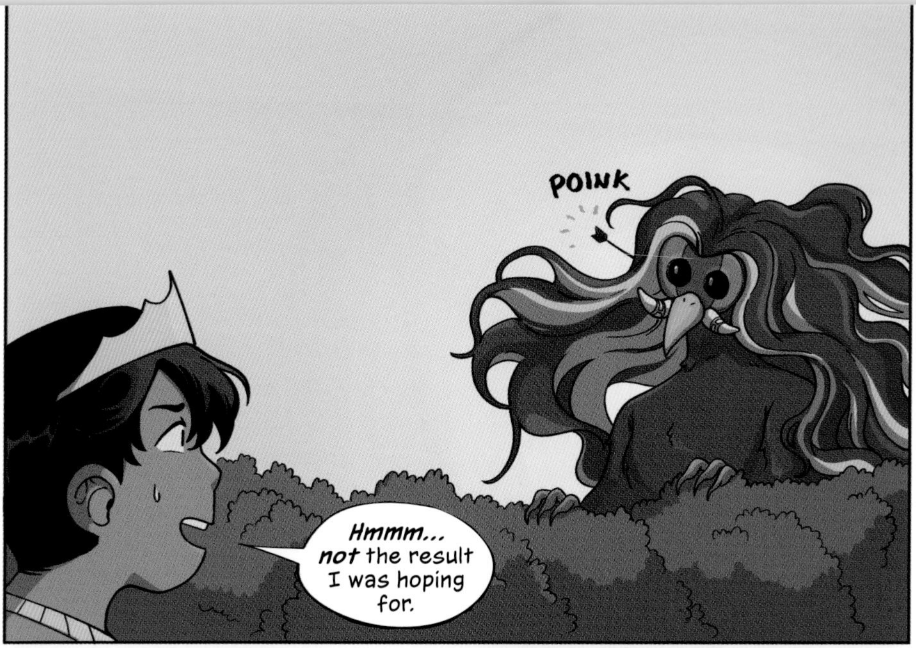
POINK
Hmmm... *not* the result I was hoping for.

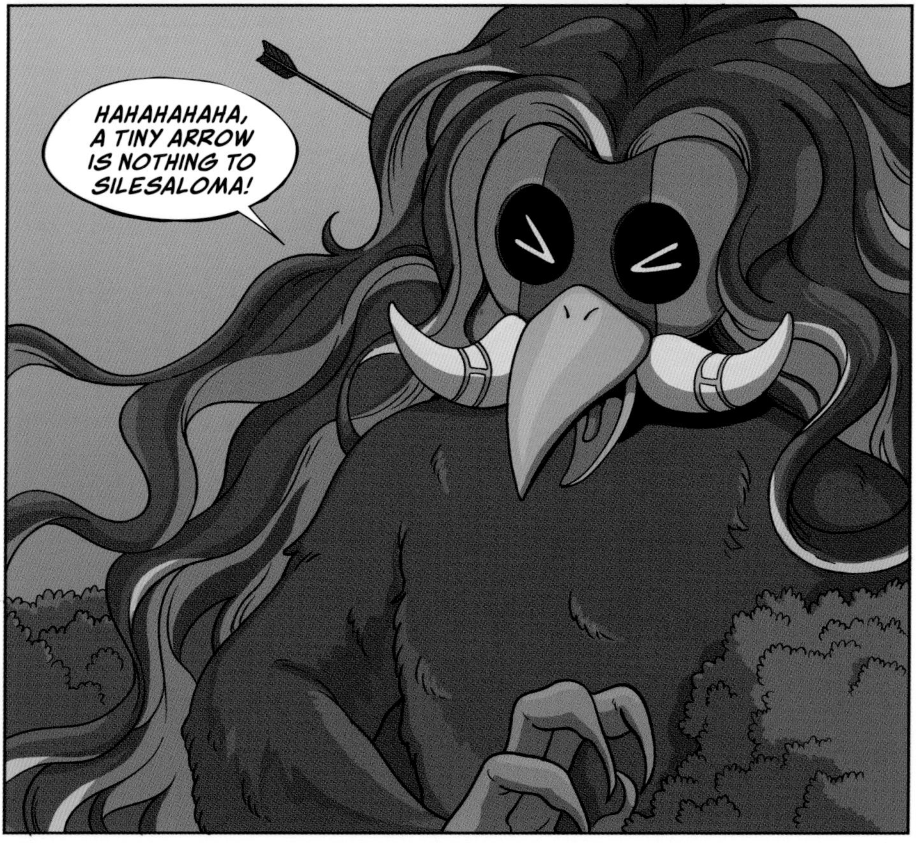
HAHAHAHAHA, A TINY ARROW IS NOTHING TO SILESALOMA!

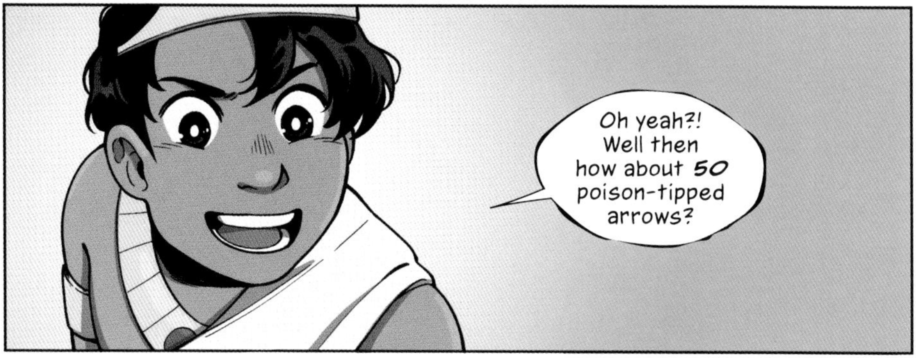
Oh yeah?! Well then how about 50 poison-tipped arrows?

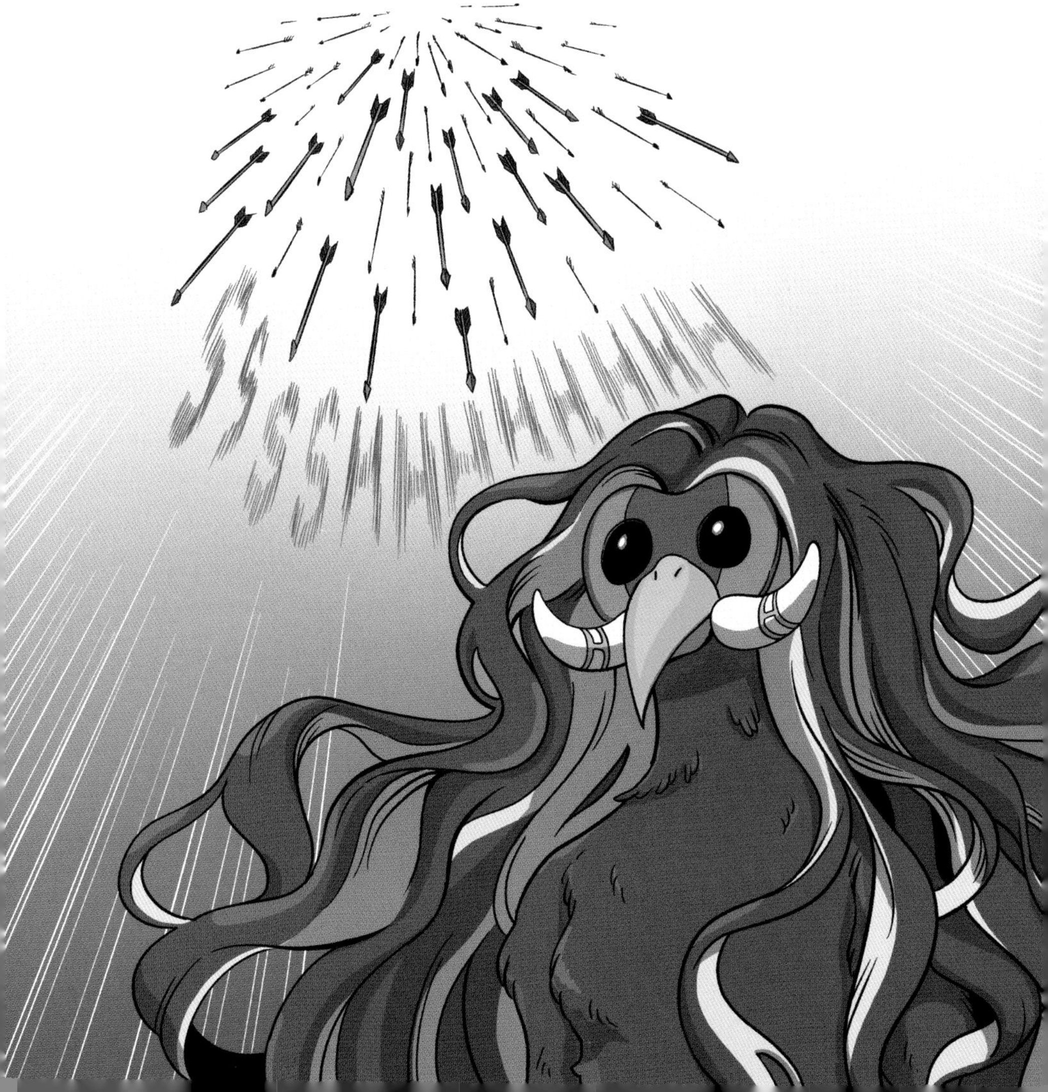

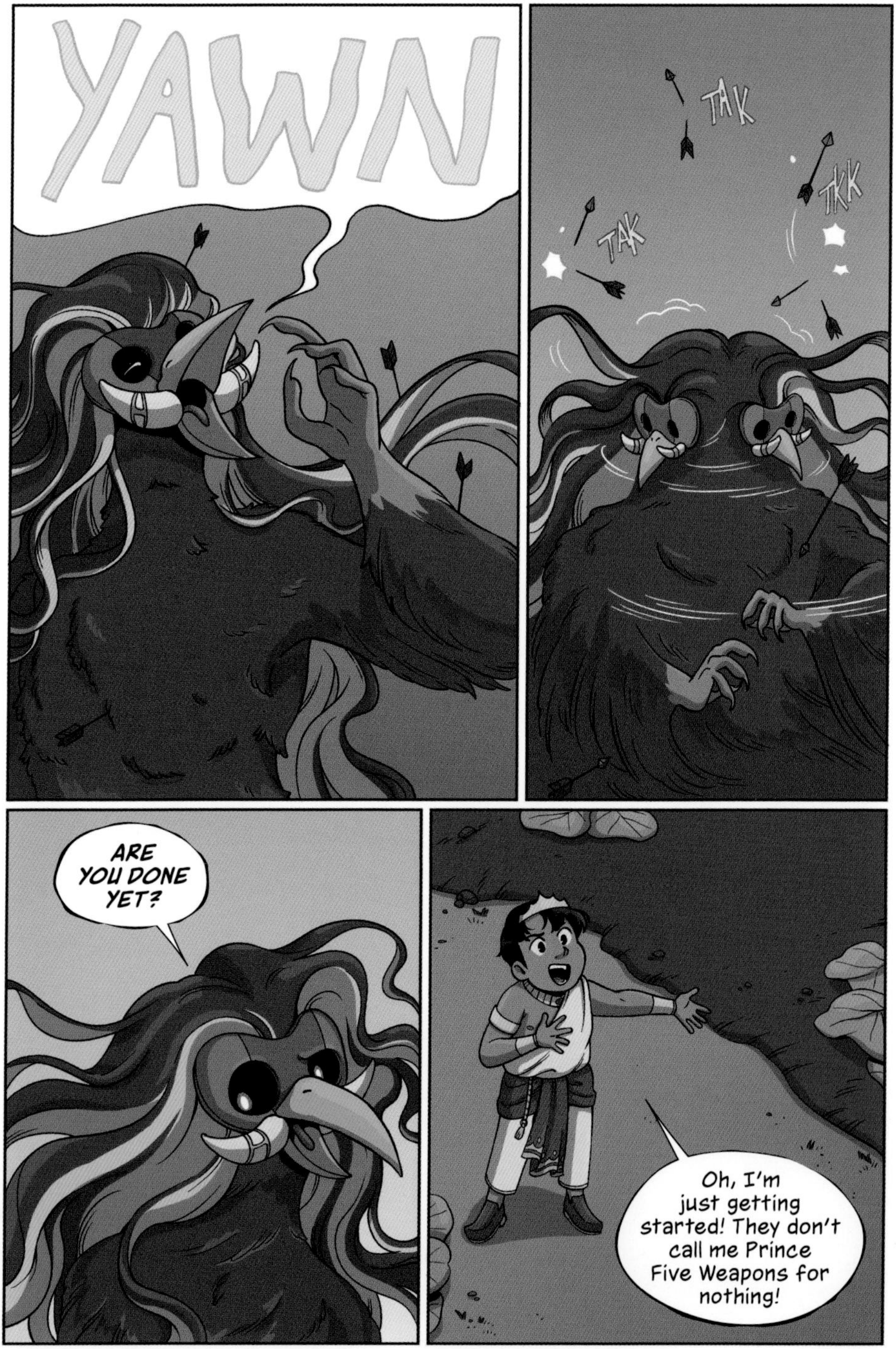
YAWN
TAK
TAK
TKK
ARE YOU DONE YET?
Oh, I'm just getting started! They don't call me Prince Five Weapons for nothing!

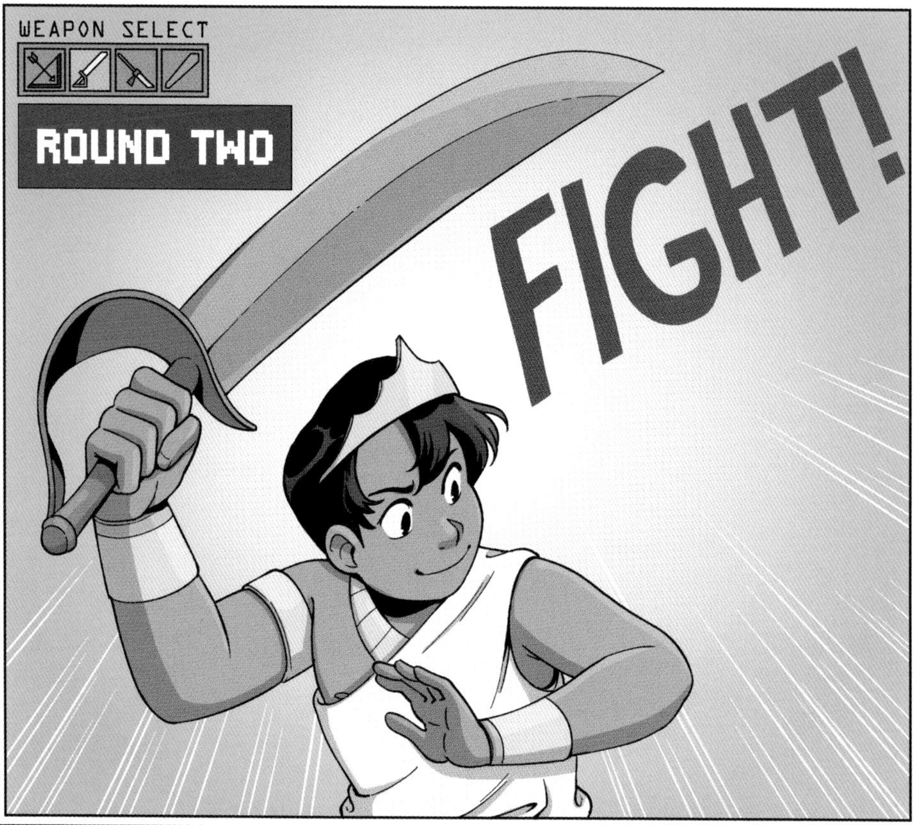
WEAPON SELECT
ROUND TWO
FIGHT!

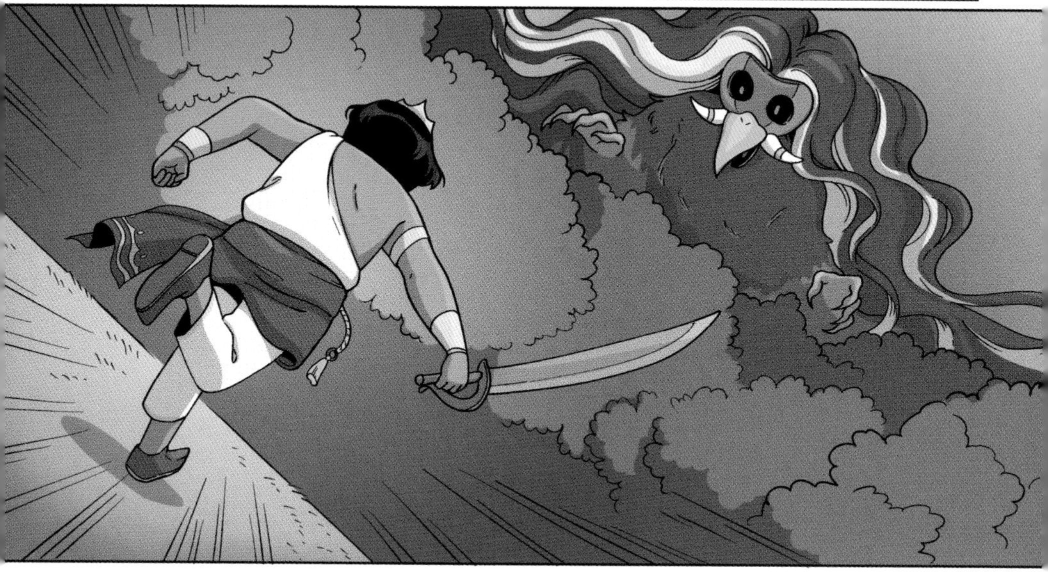

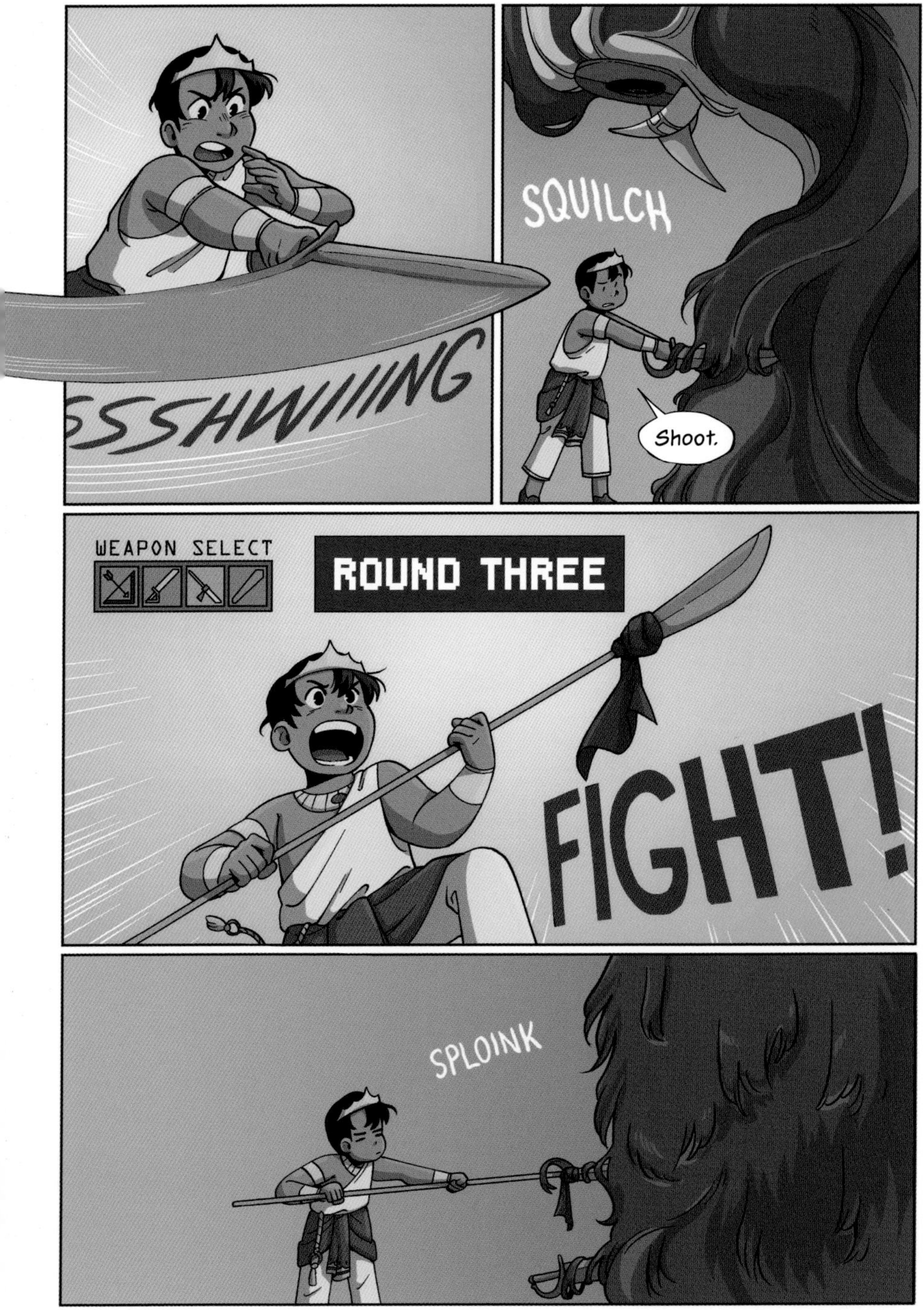
SSSHWIIIING
SQUILCH
Shoot.
WEAPON SELECT
ROUND THREE
FIGHT!
SPLOINK

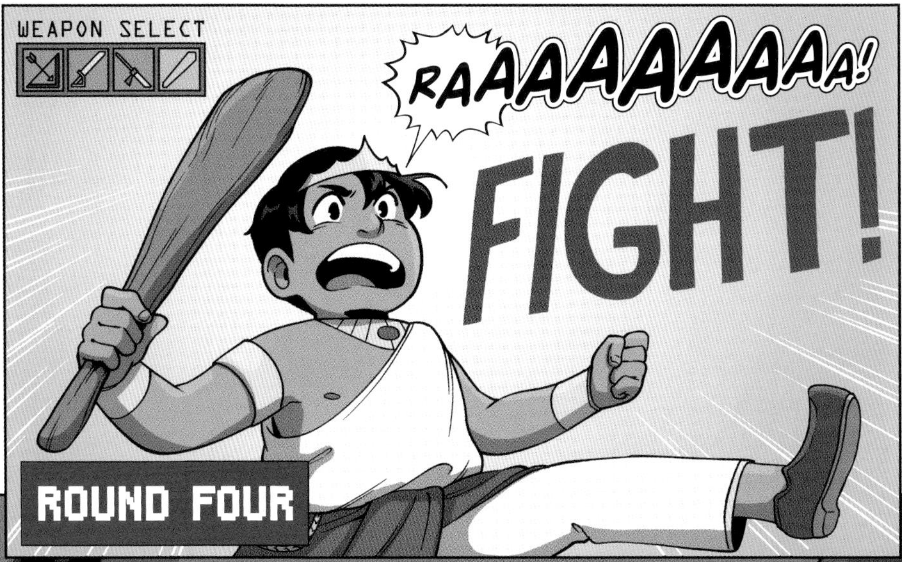
WEAPON SELECT
RAAAAAAAAAa!
FIGHT!
ROUND FOUR

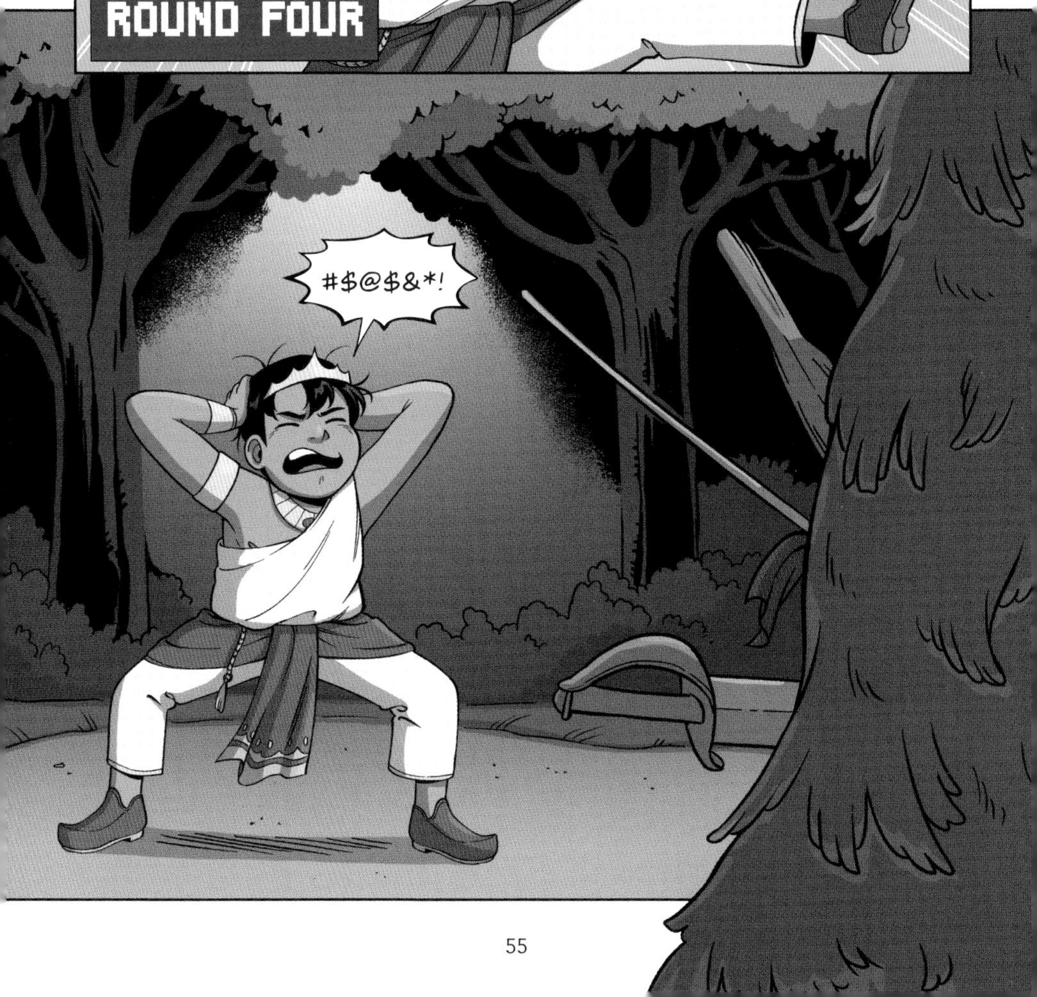
#$@$&*!

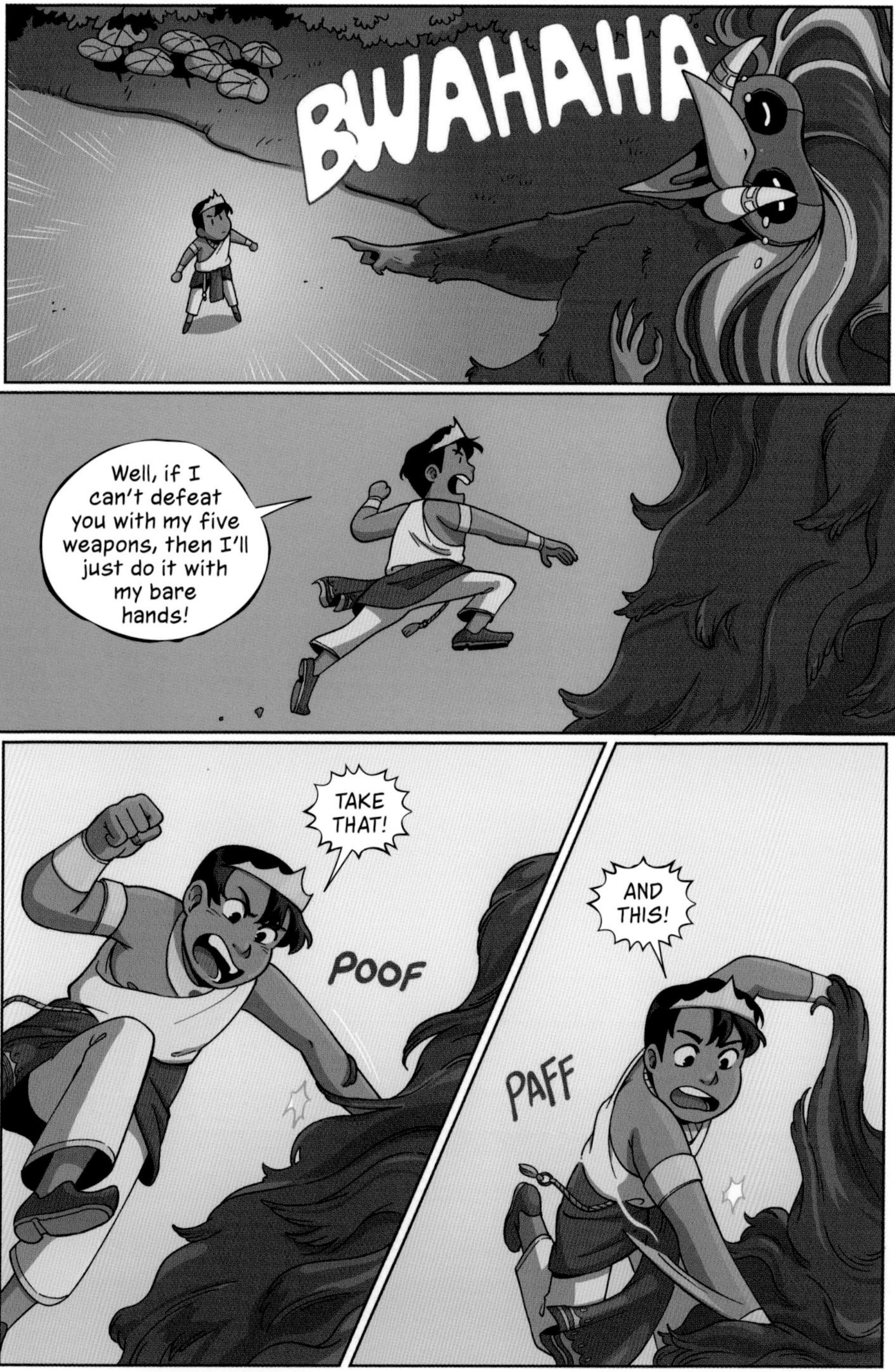
BWAHAHA
Well, if I can't defeat you with my five weapons, then I'll just do it with my bare hands!
TAKE THAT!
POOF
AND THIS!
PAFF

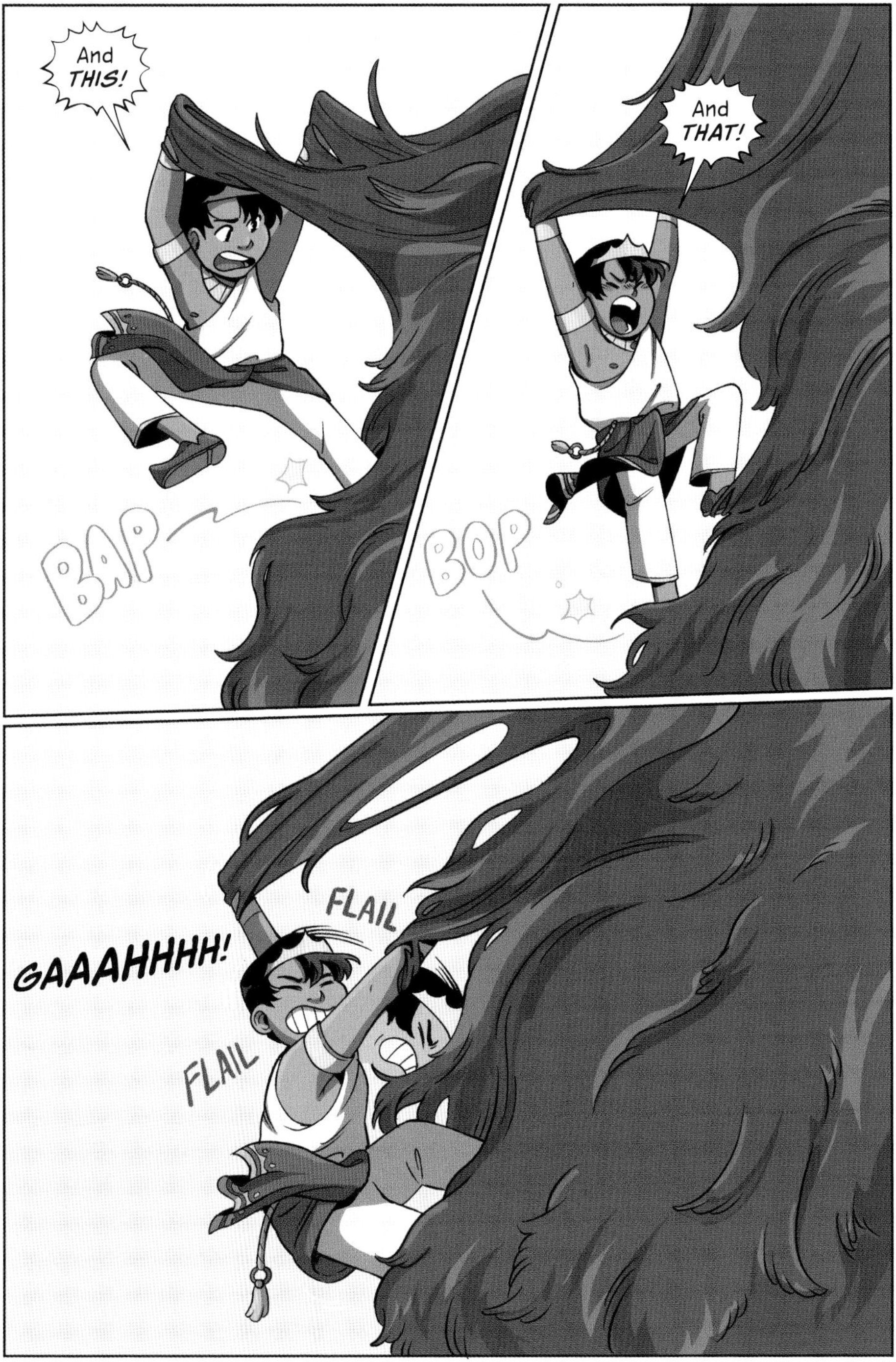
And THIS!
BAP
And THAT!
BOP
FLAIL
GAAAHHHH!
FLAIL

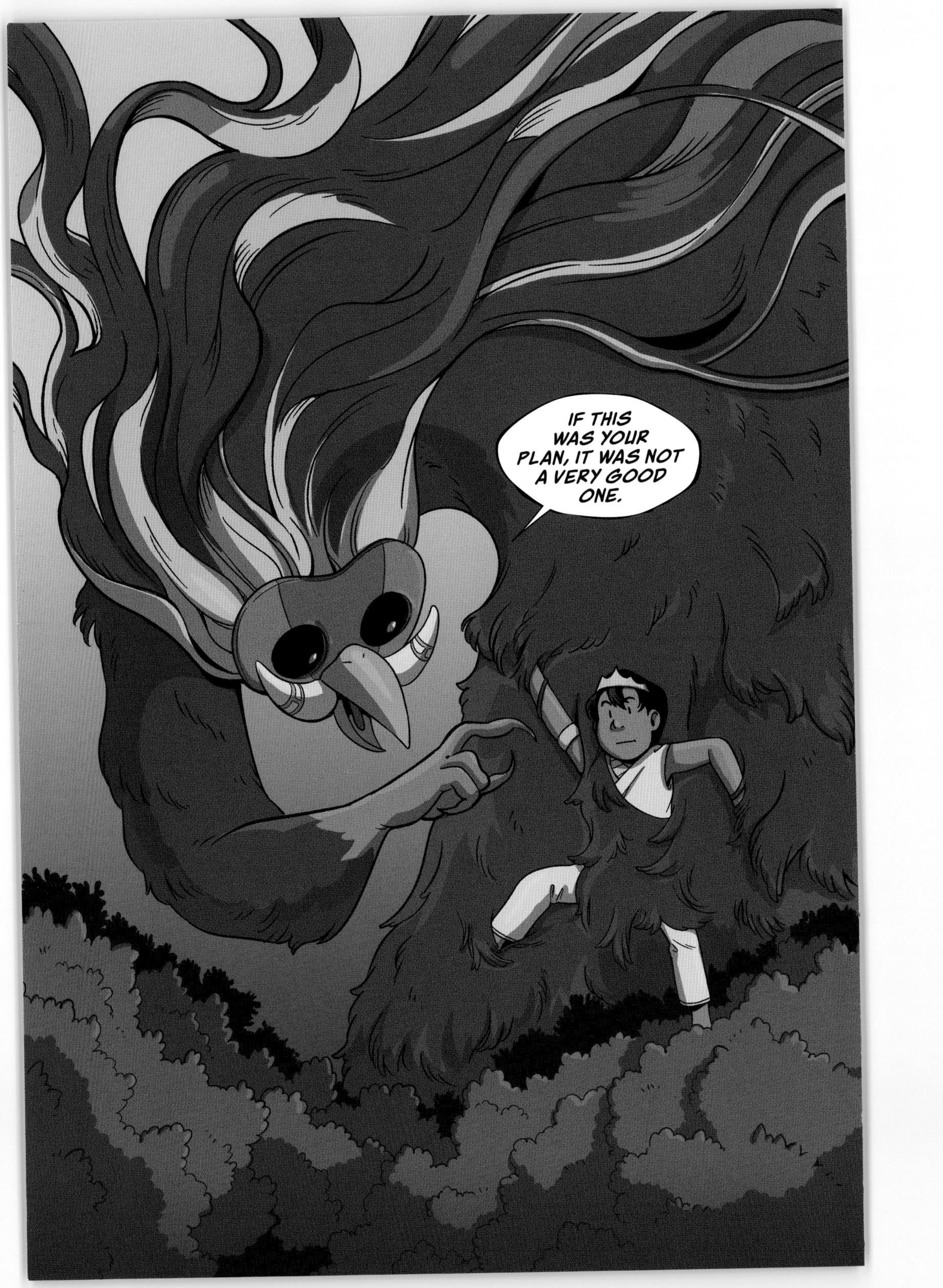
IF THIS WAS YOUR PLAN, IT WAS NOT A VERY GOOD ONE.

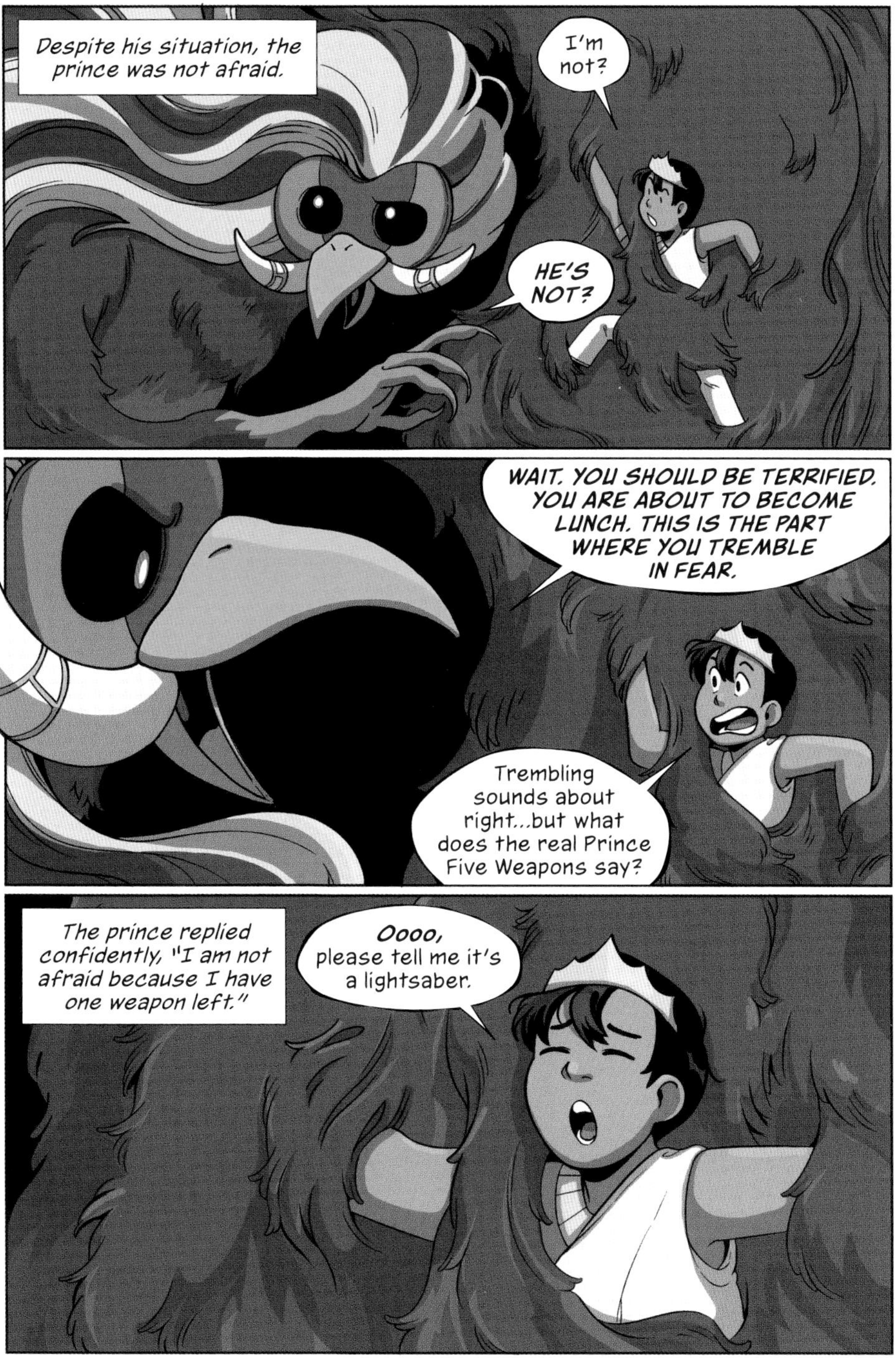
Despite his situation, the prince was not afraid.
I'm not?
HE'S NOT?
WAIT. YOU SHOULD BE TERRIFIED. YOU ARE ABOUT TO BECOME LUNCH. THIS IS THE PART WHERE YOU TREMBLE IN FEAR.
Trembling sounds about right...but what does the real Prince Five Weapons say?
The prince replied confidently, "I am not afraid because I have one weapon left."
Oooo, please tell me it's a lightsaber.

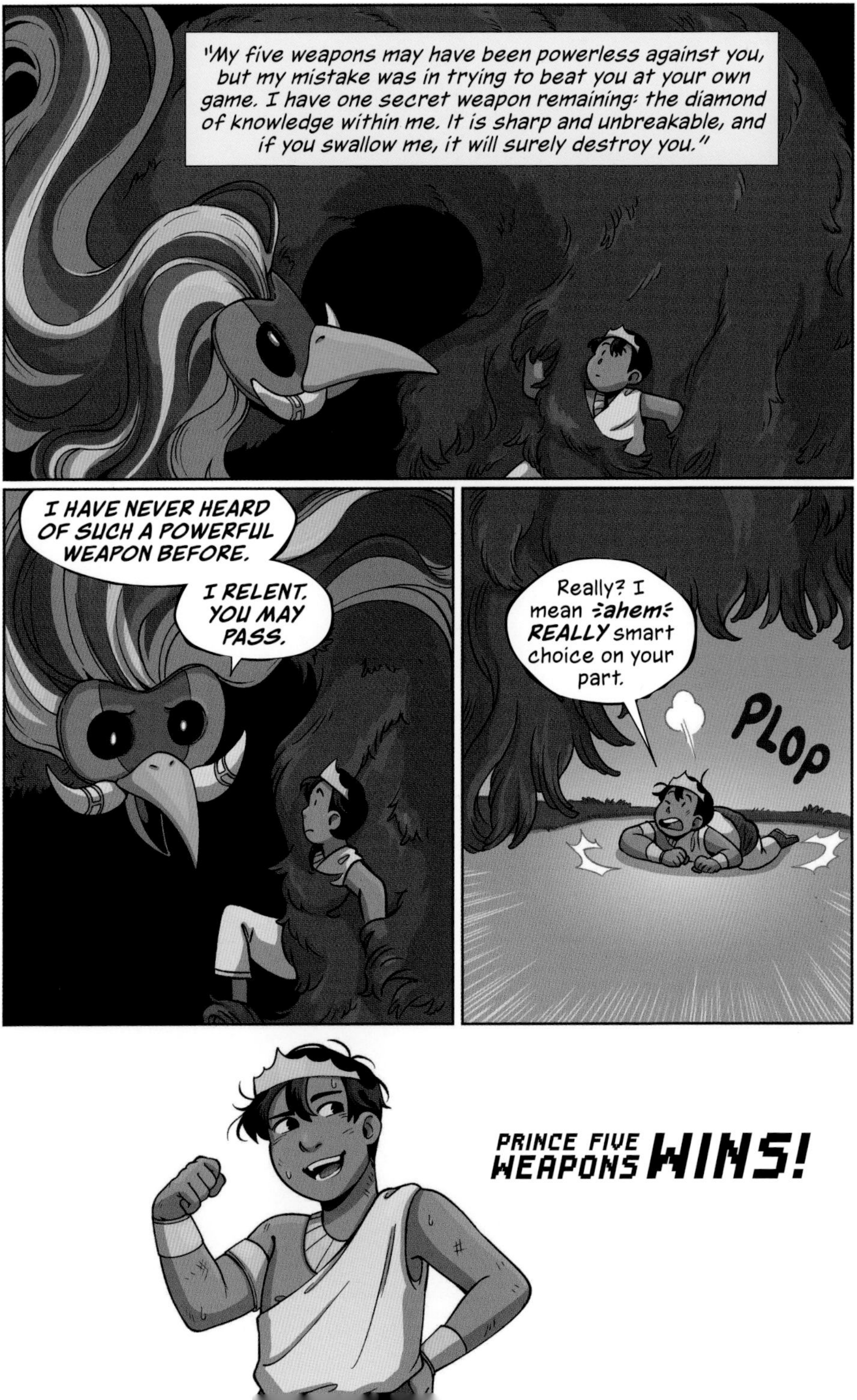
"My five weapons may have been powerless against you, but my mistake was in trying to beat you at your own game. I have one secret weapon remaining: the diamond of knowledge within me. It is sharp and unbreakable, and if you swallow me, it will surely destroy you."
I HAVE NEVER HEARD OF SUCH A POWERFUL WEAPON BEFORE.
I RELENT. YOU MAY PASS.
Really? I mean ahem REALLY smart choice on your part.
PLOP
PRINCE FIVE WEAPONS WINS!

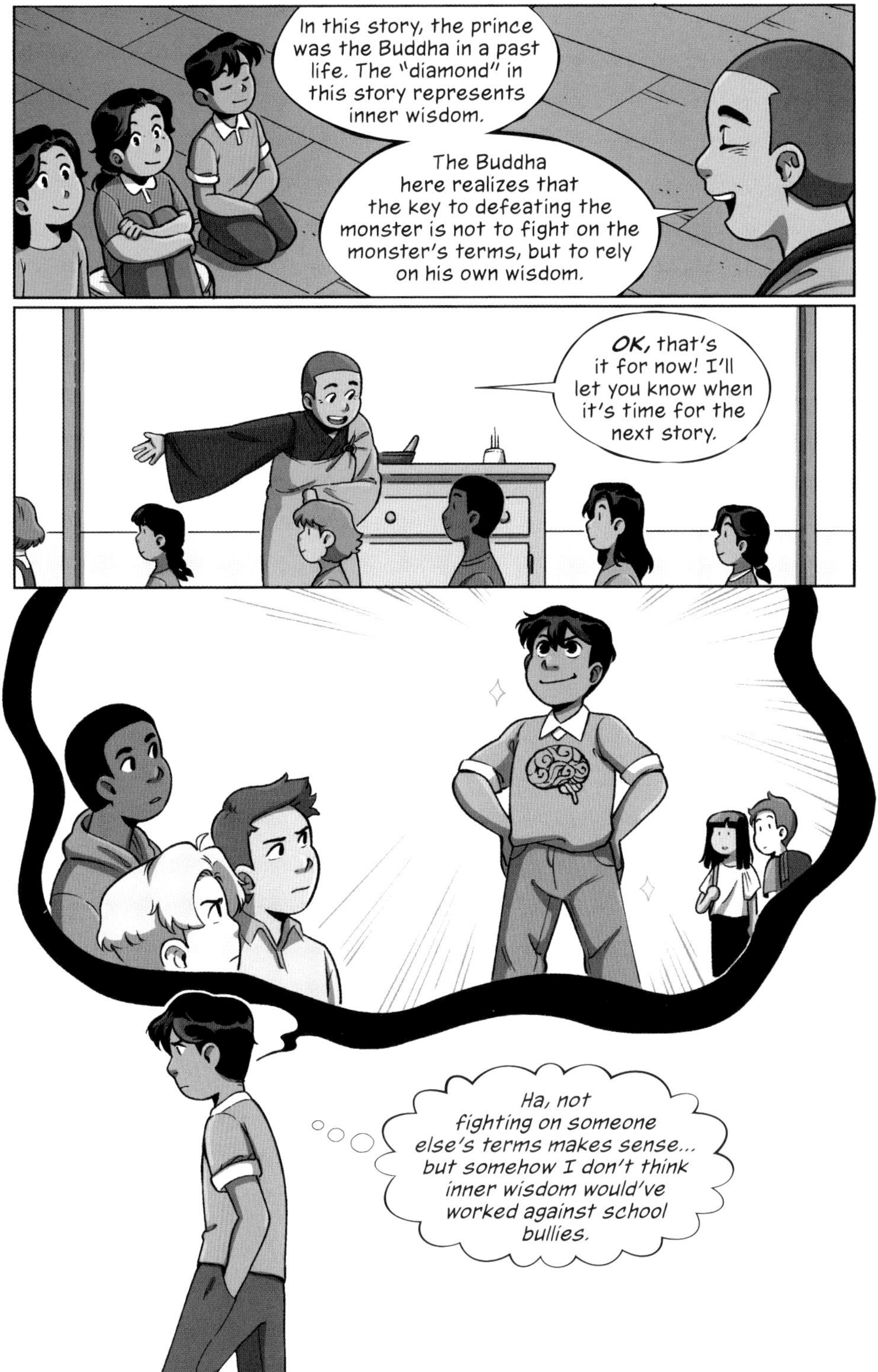
In this story, the prince was the Buddha in a past life. The "diamond" in this story represents inner wisdom.
The Buddha here realizes that the key to defeating the monster is not to fight on the monster's terms, but to rely on his own wisdom.
OK, that's it for now! I'll let you know when it's time for the next story.
Ha, not fighting on someone else's terms makes sense... but somehow I don't think inner wisdom would've worked against school bullies.

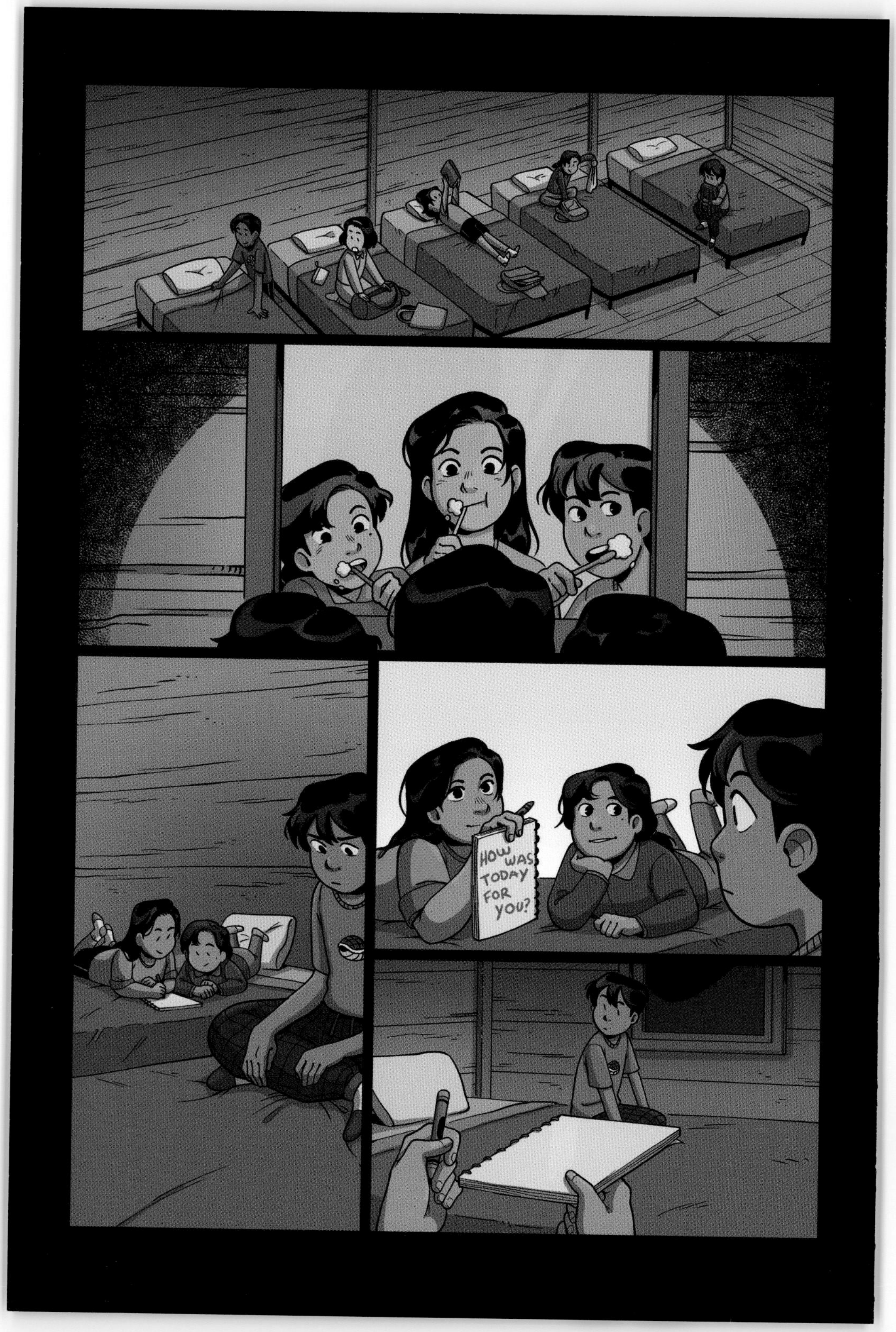
HOW WAS TODAY FOR YOU?

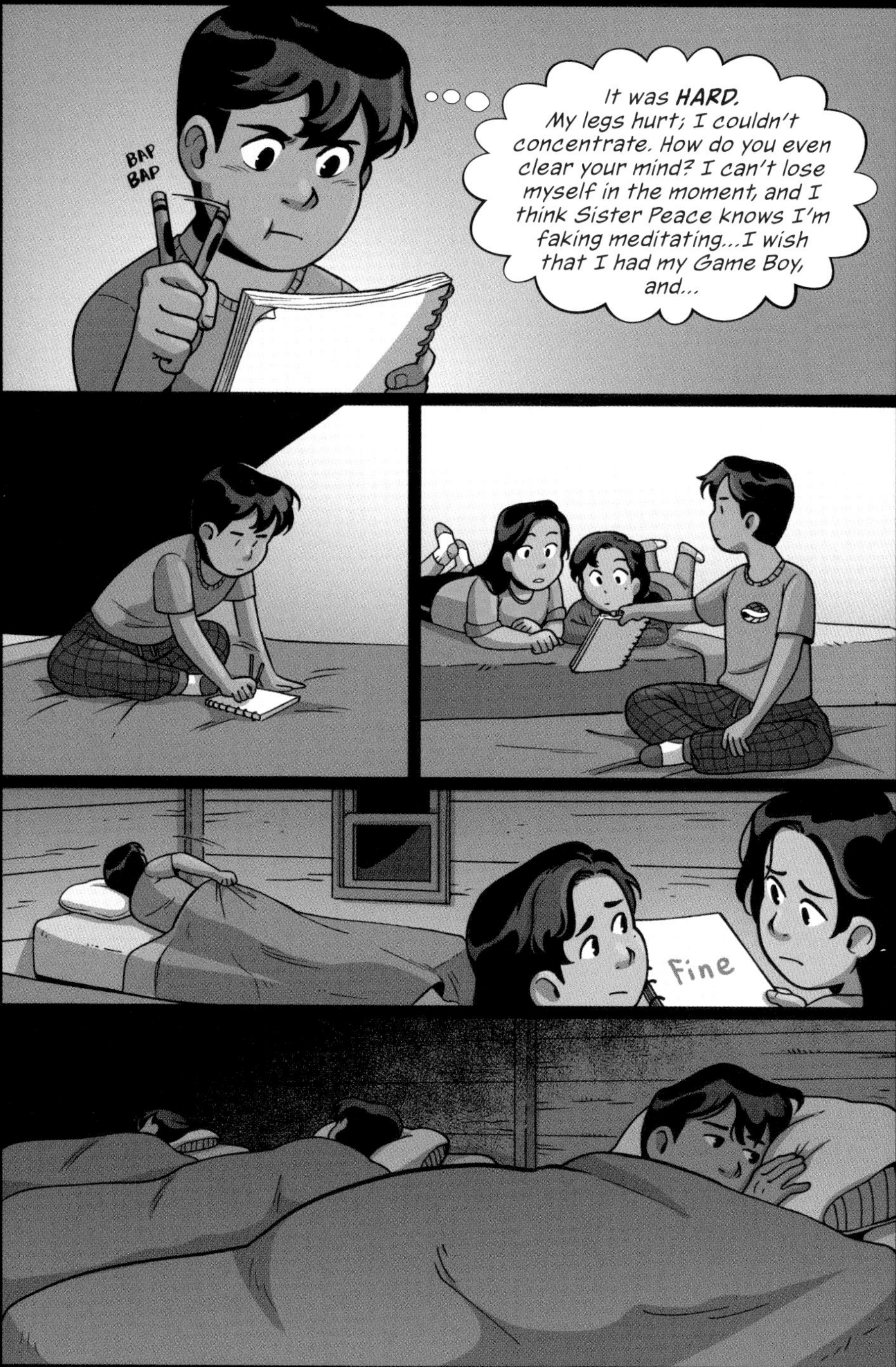
BAP BAP
It was HARD. My legs hurt; I couldn't concentrate. How do you even clear your mind? I can't lose myself in the moment, and I think Sister Peace knows I'm faking meditating...I wish that I had my Game Boy, and...
Fine

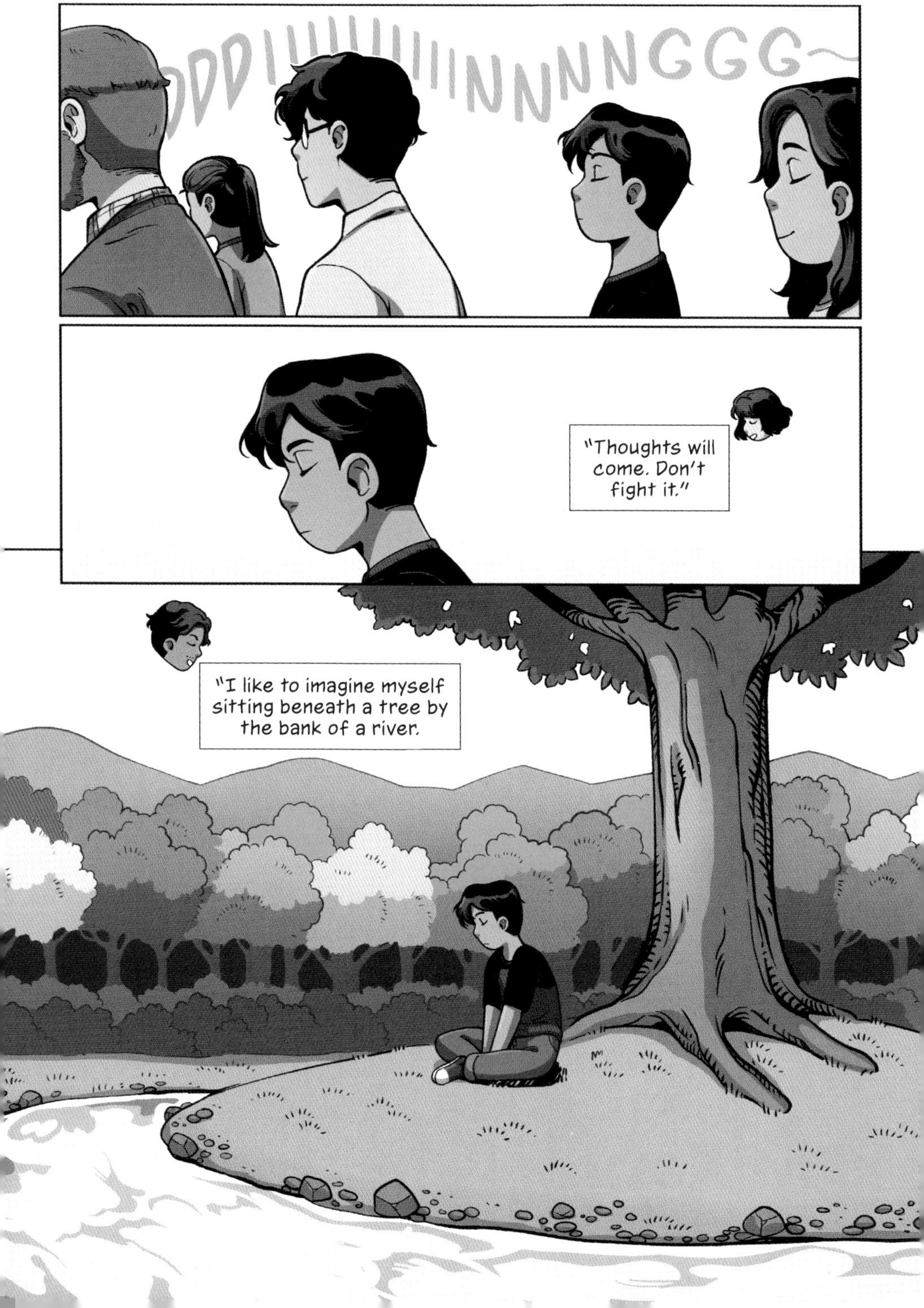
DDDIIIIIIIIIINNNNNGGG
"Thoughts will come. Don't fight it."
"I like to imagine myself sitting beneath a tree by the bank of a river.

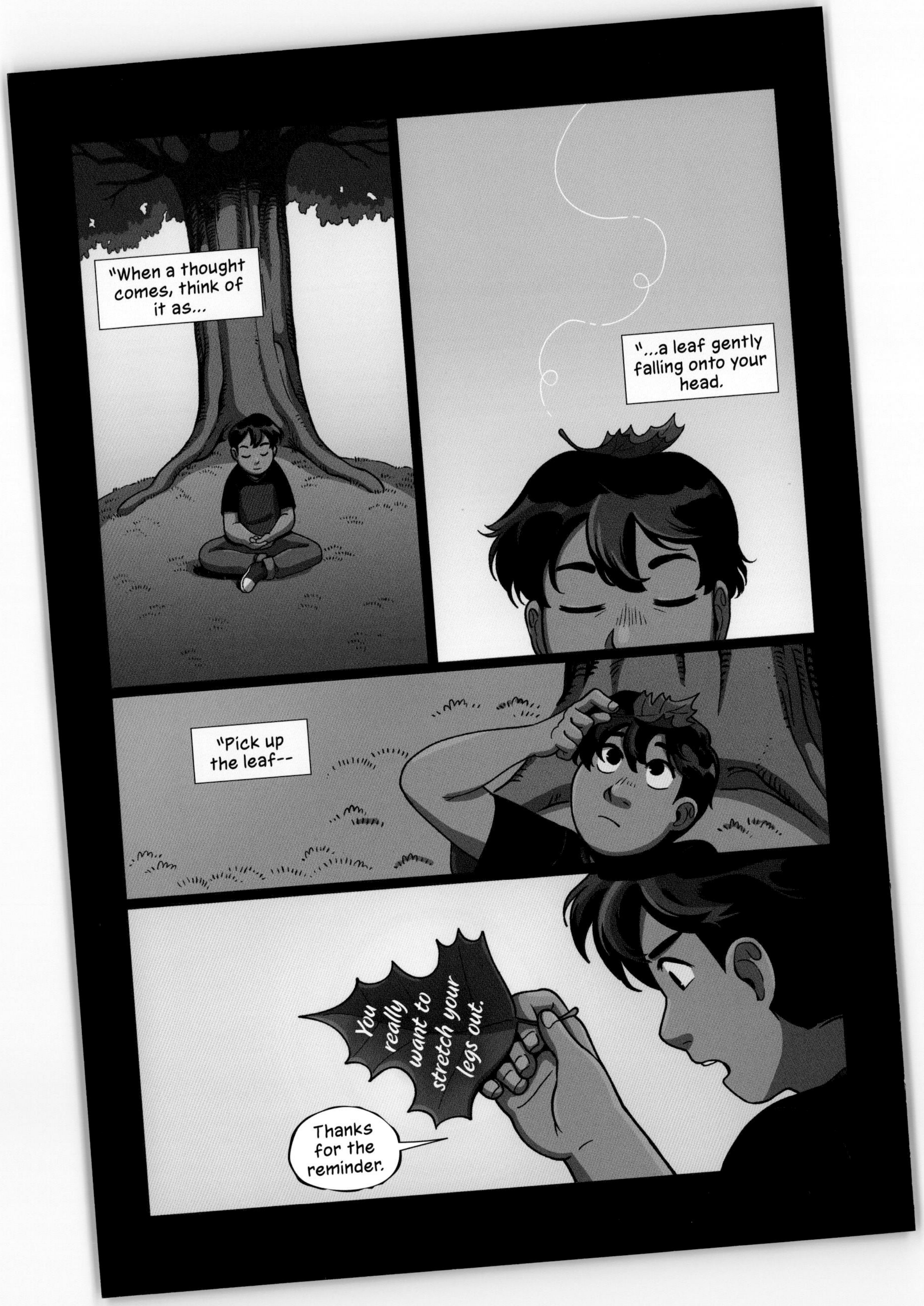
"When a thought comes, think of it as...
"...a leaf gently falling onto your head.
"Pick up the leaf--
You really want to stretch your legs out.
Thanks for the reminder.

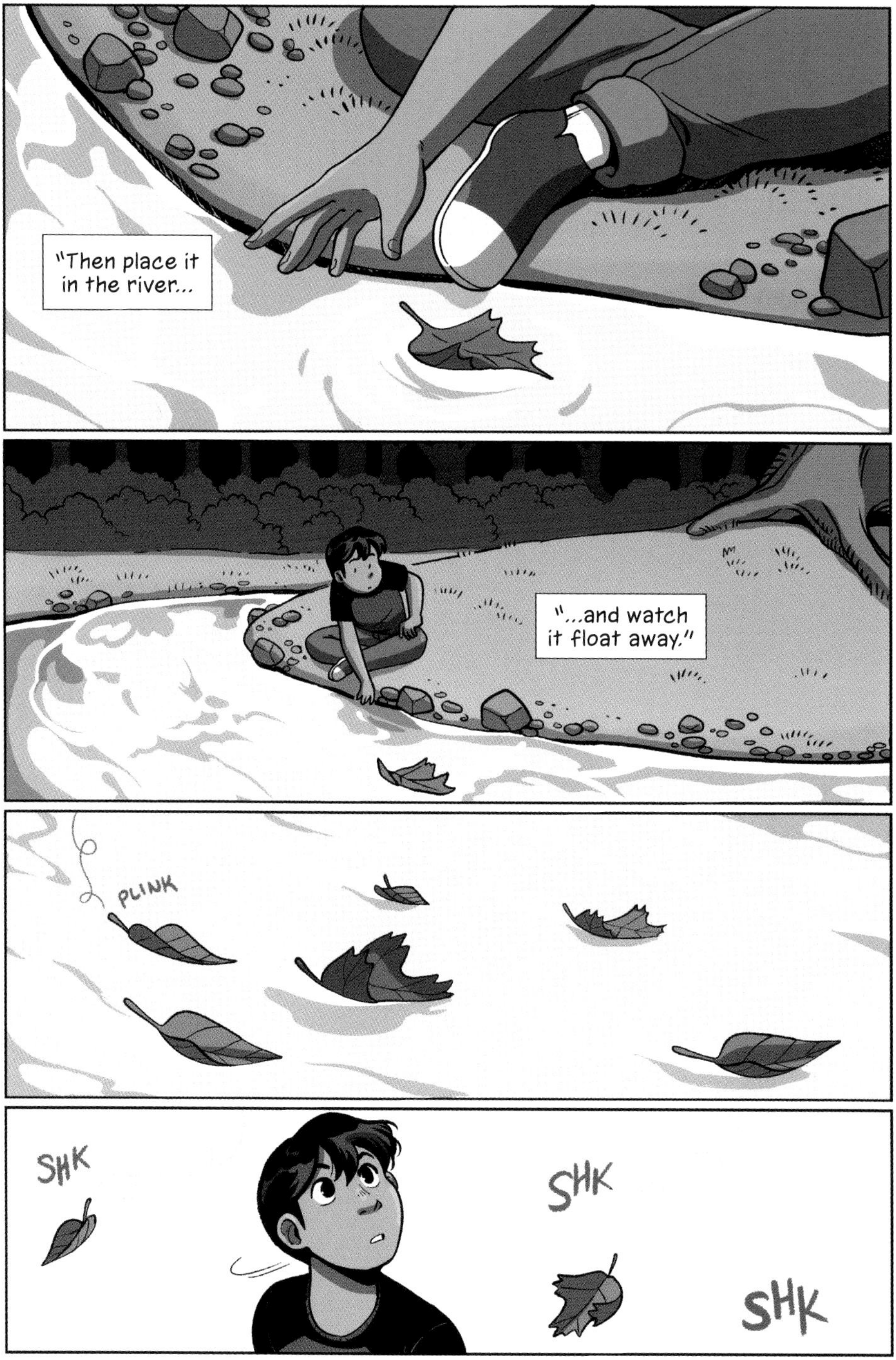
"Then place it in the river...
"...and watch it float away."
PLINK
SHK
SHK
SHK

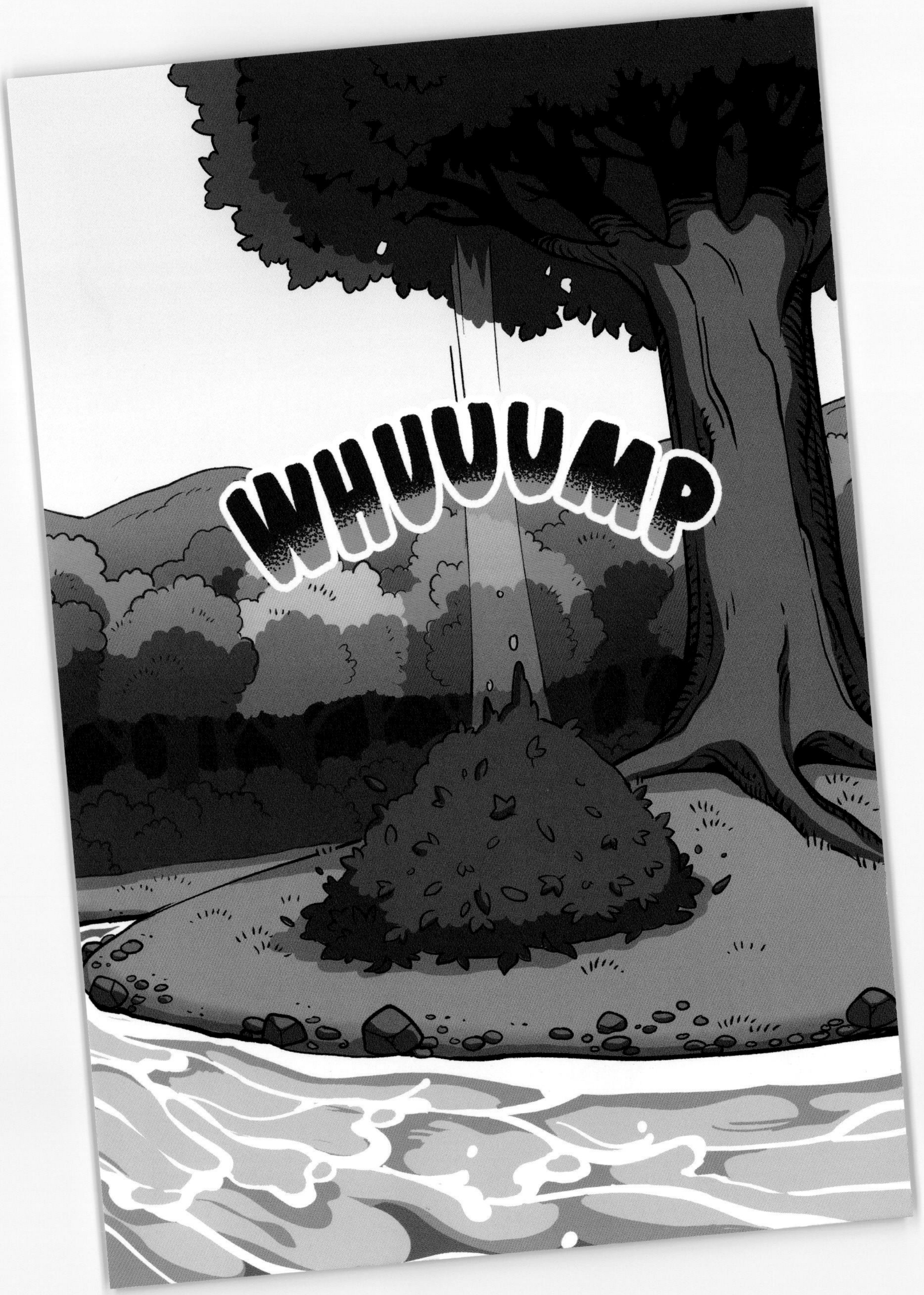
WHUUUMP

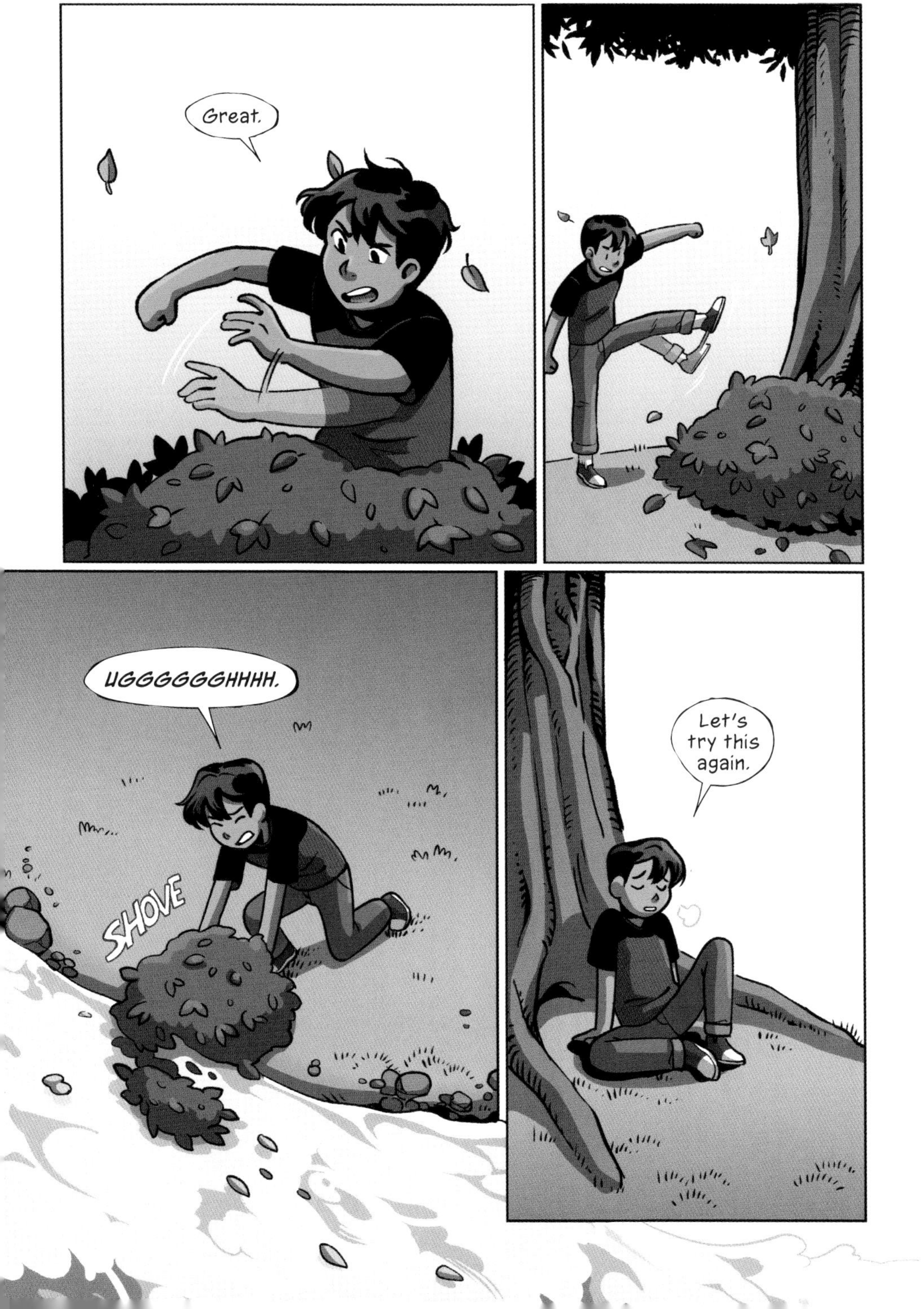
Great.
UGGGGGGHHHH.
SHOVE
Let's try this again.

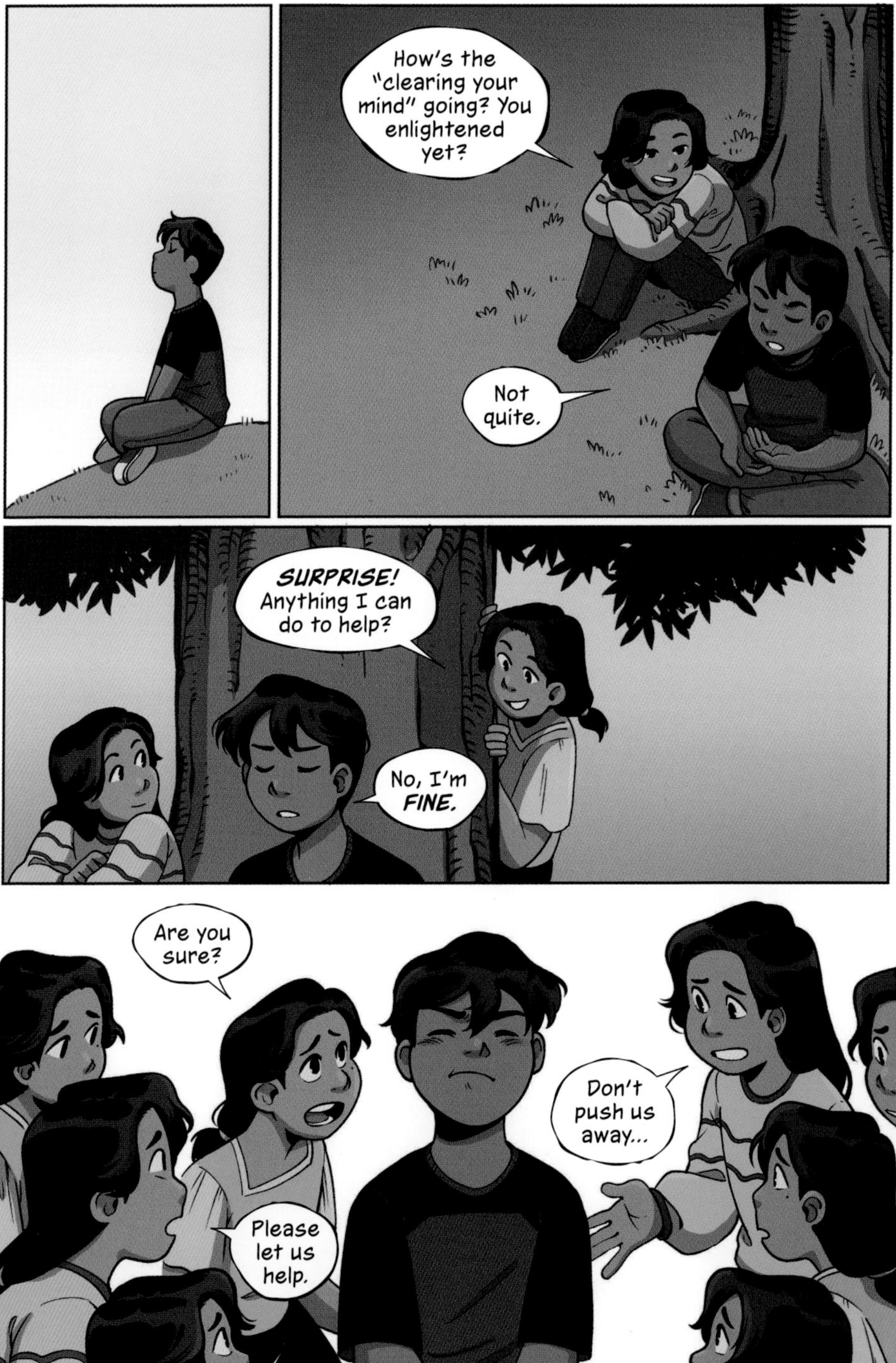
How's the "clearing your mind" going? You enlightened yet?
Not quite.
SURPRISE! Anything I can do to help?
No, I'm FINE.
Are you sure?
Don't push us away...
Please let us help.

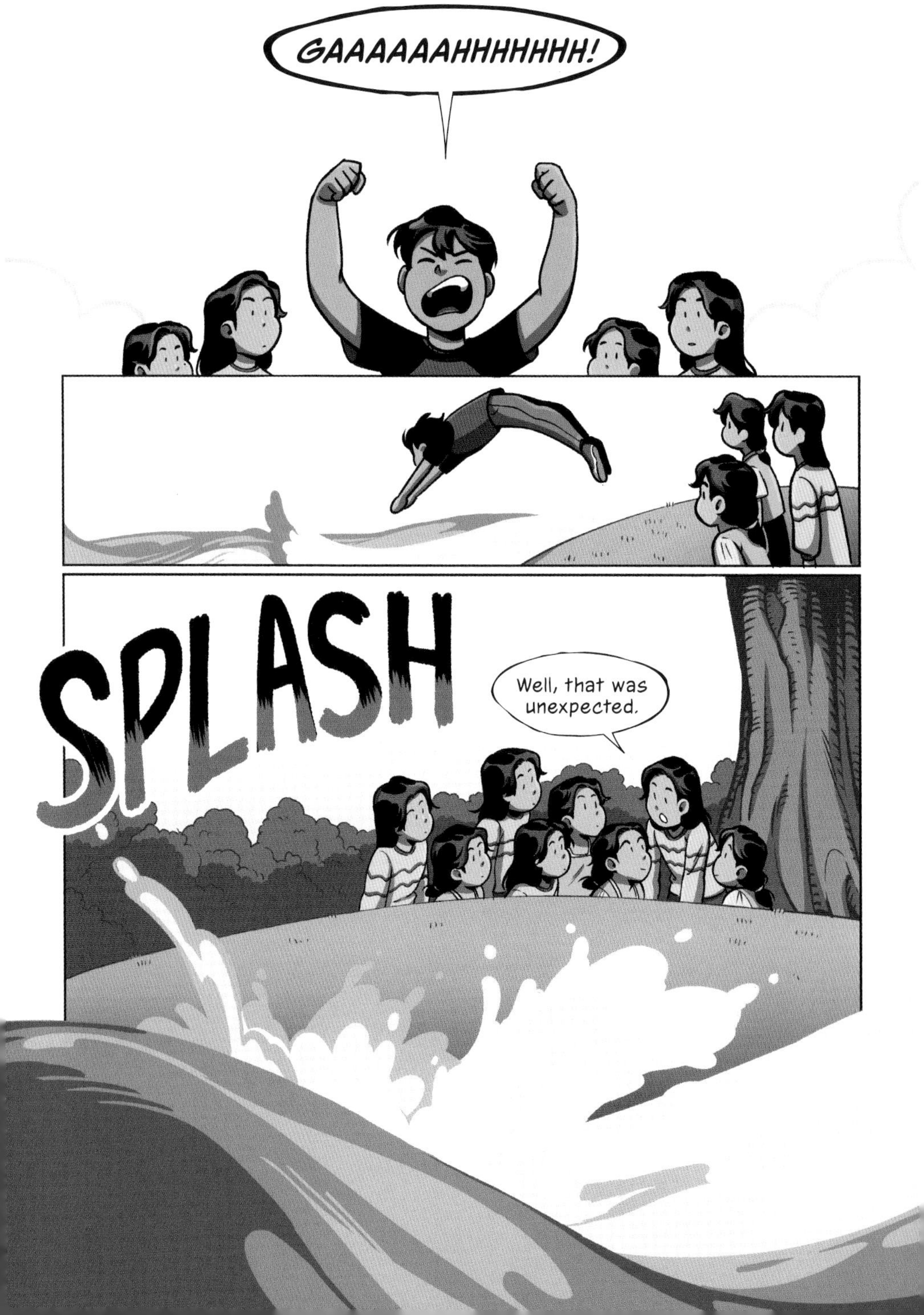
GAAAAAAHHHHHH!
SPLASH
Well, that was unexpected.

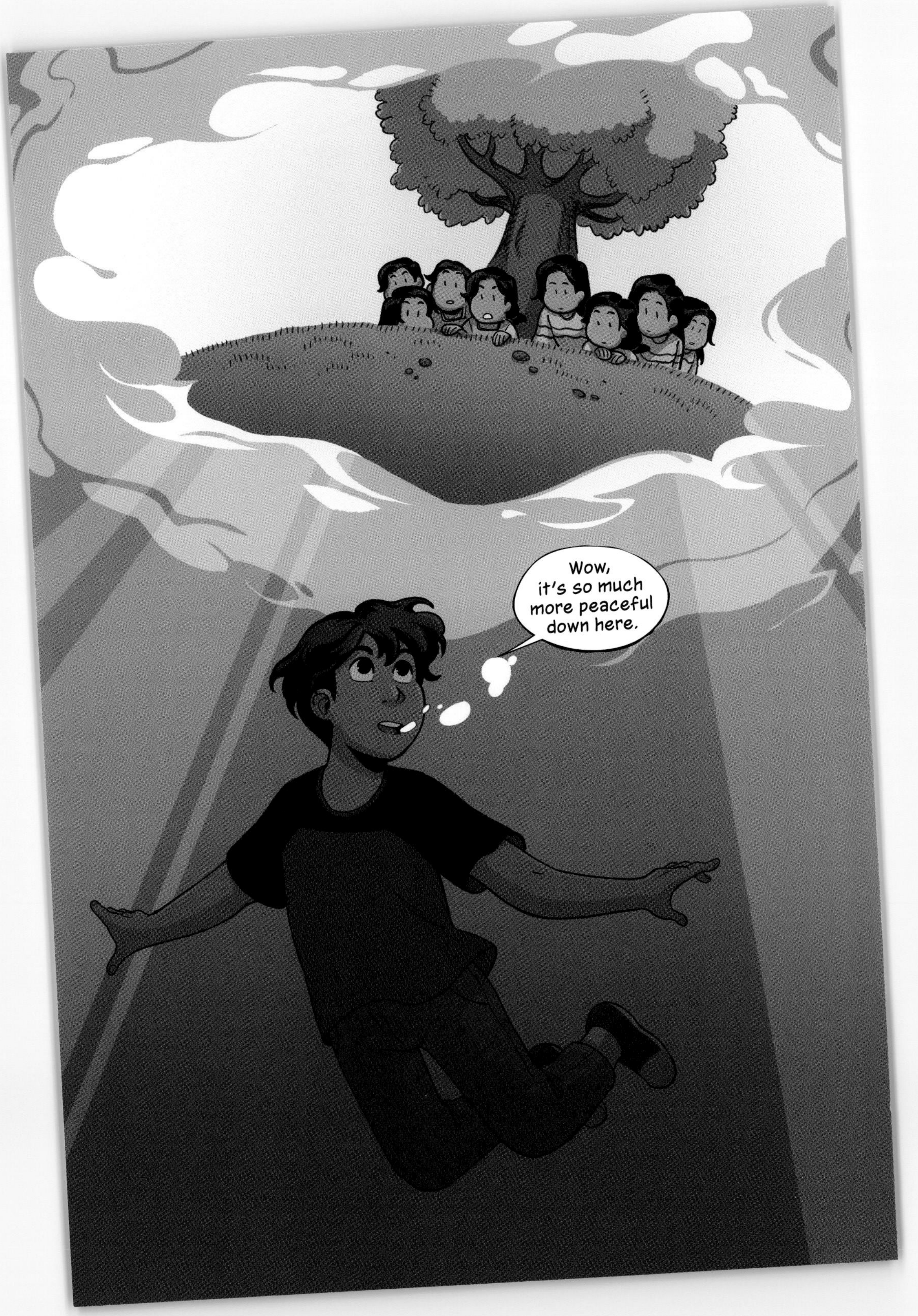
Wow, it's so much more peaceful down here.

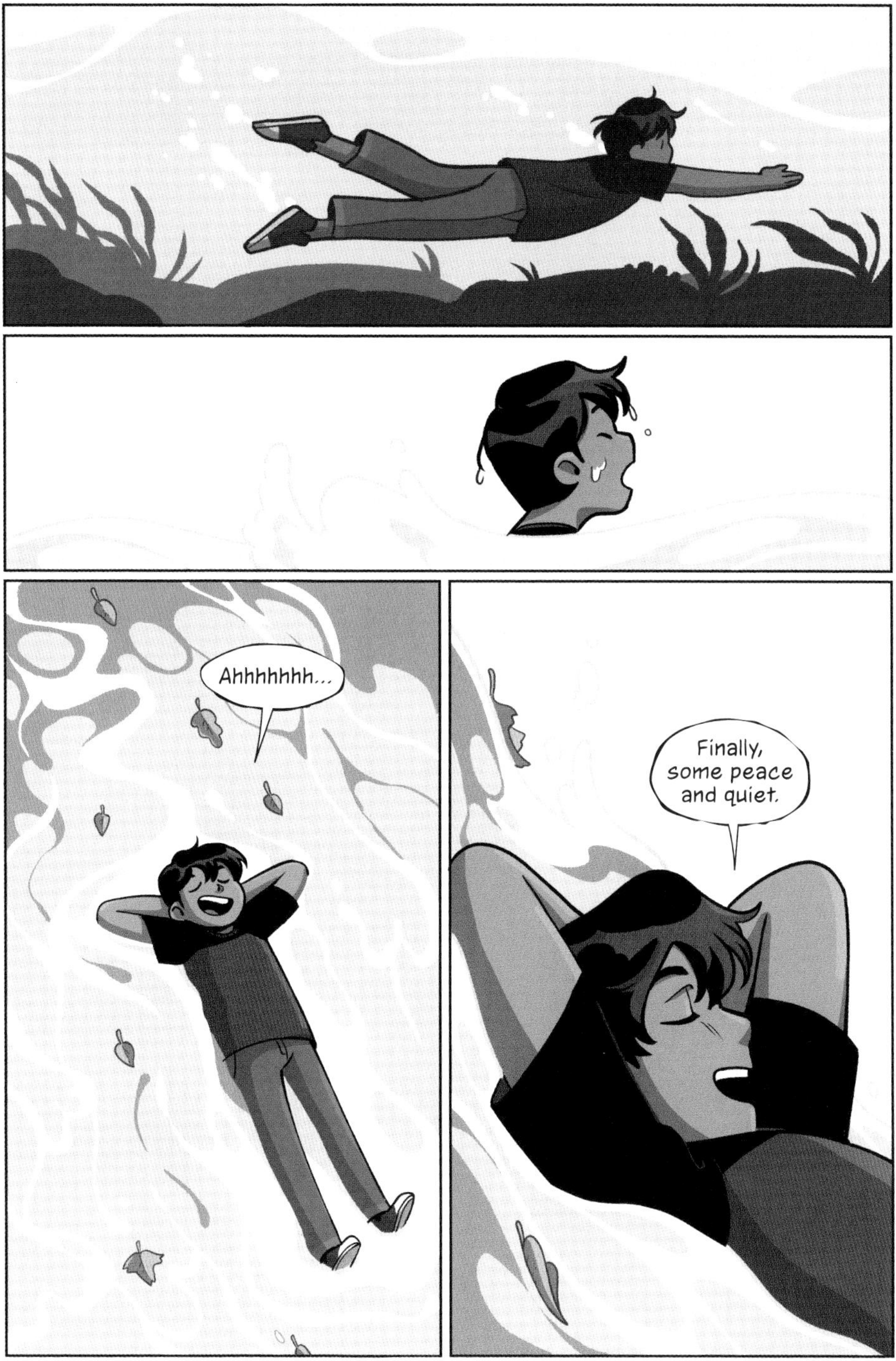
Ahhhhhhh...
Finally, some peace and quiet.

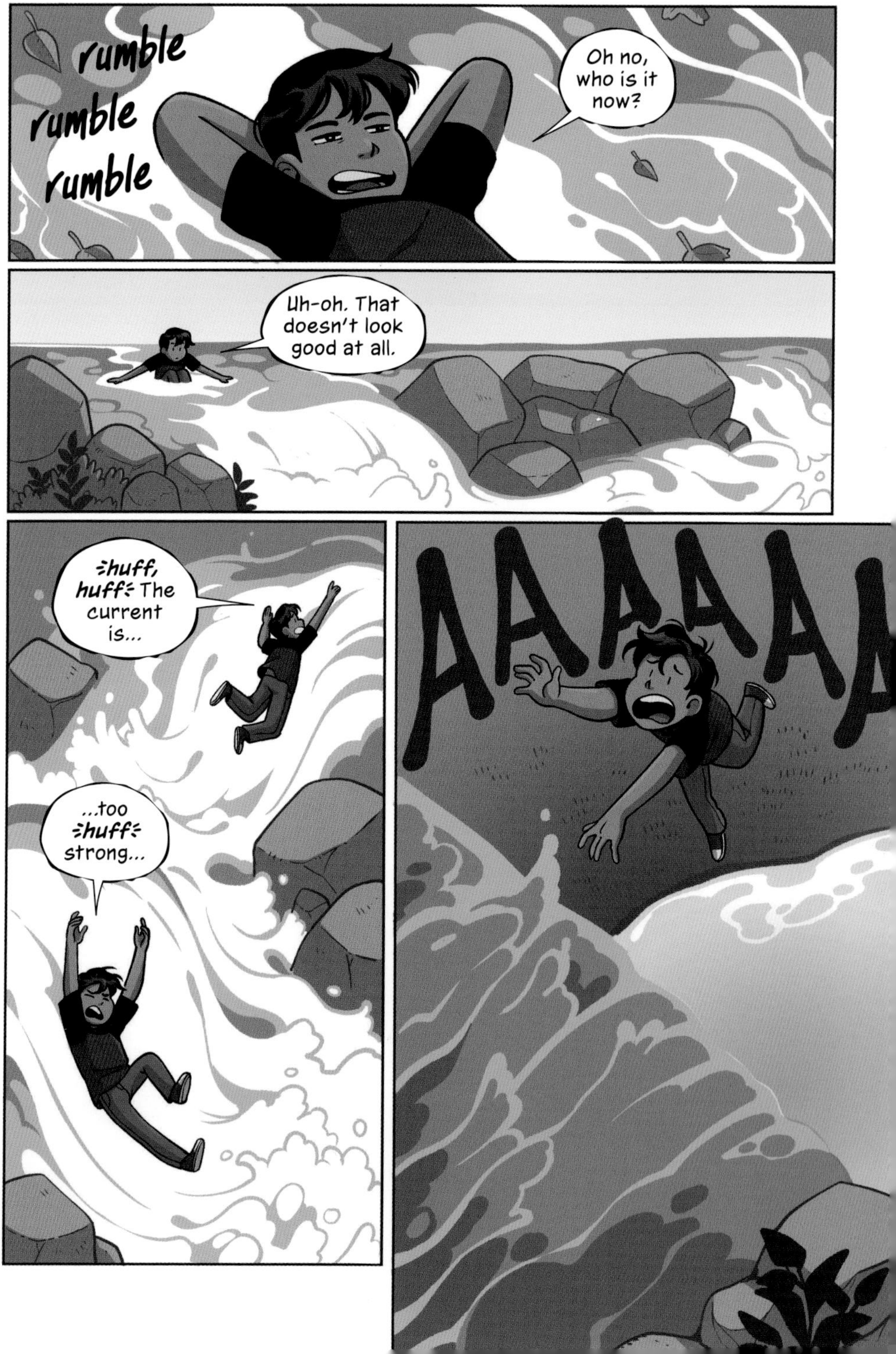
rumble
rumble
rumble
Oh no, who is it now?
Uh-oh. That doesn't look good at all.
huff, huff The current is...
...too huff strong...
AAAAAA

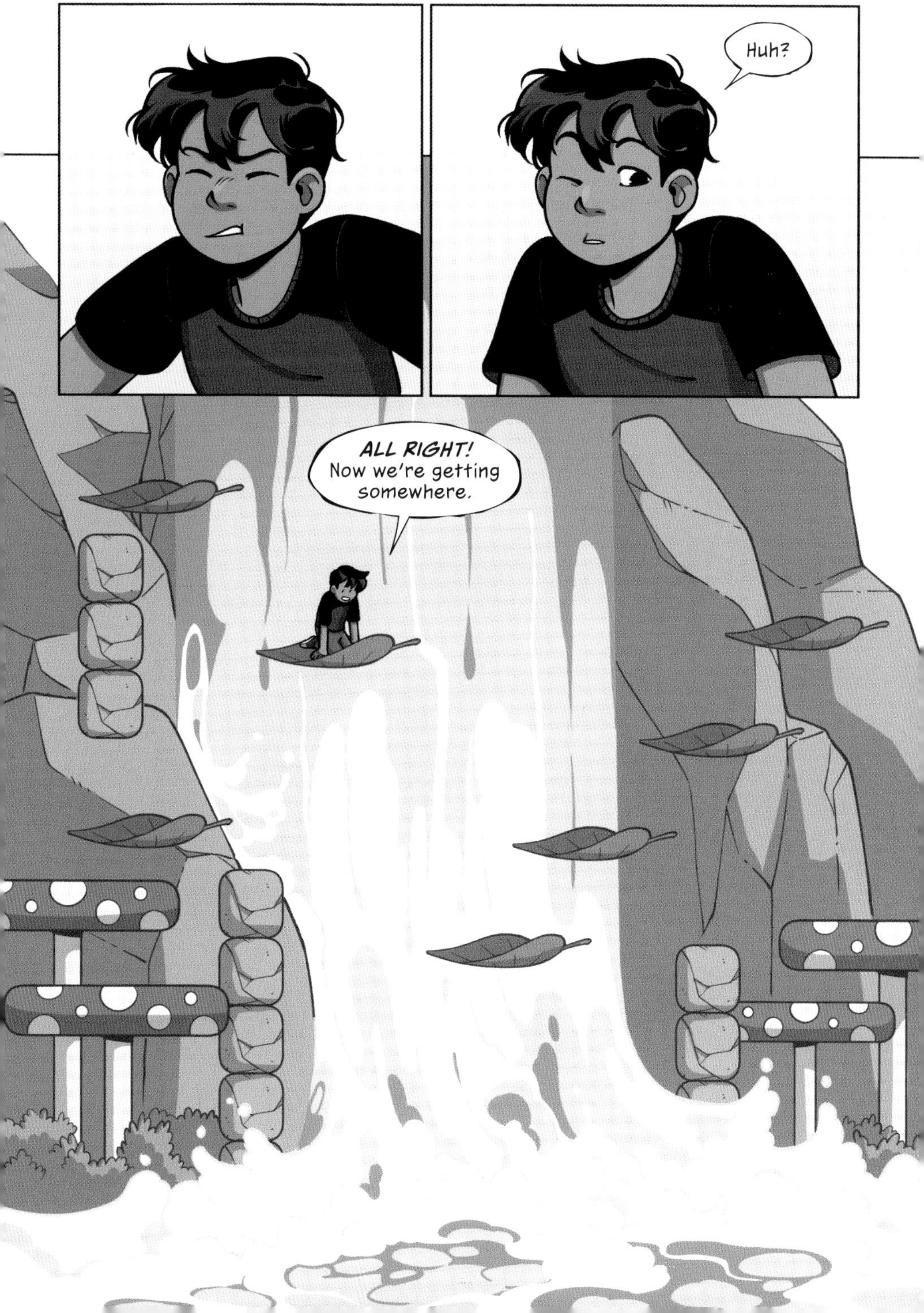
Huh?
ALL RIGHT!
Now we're getting
somewhere.

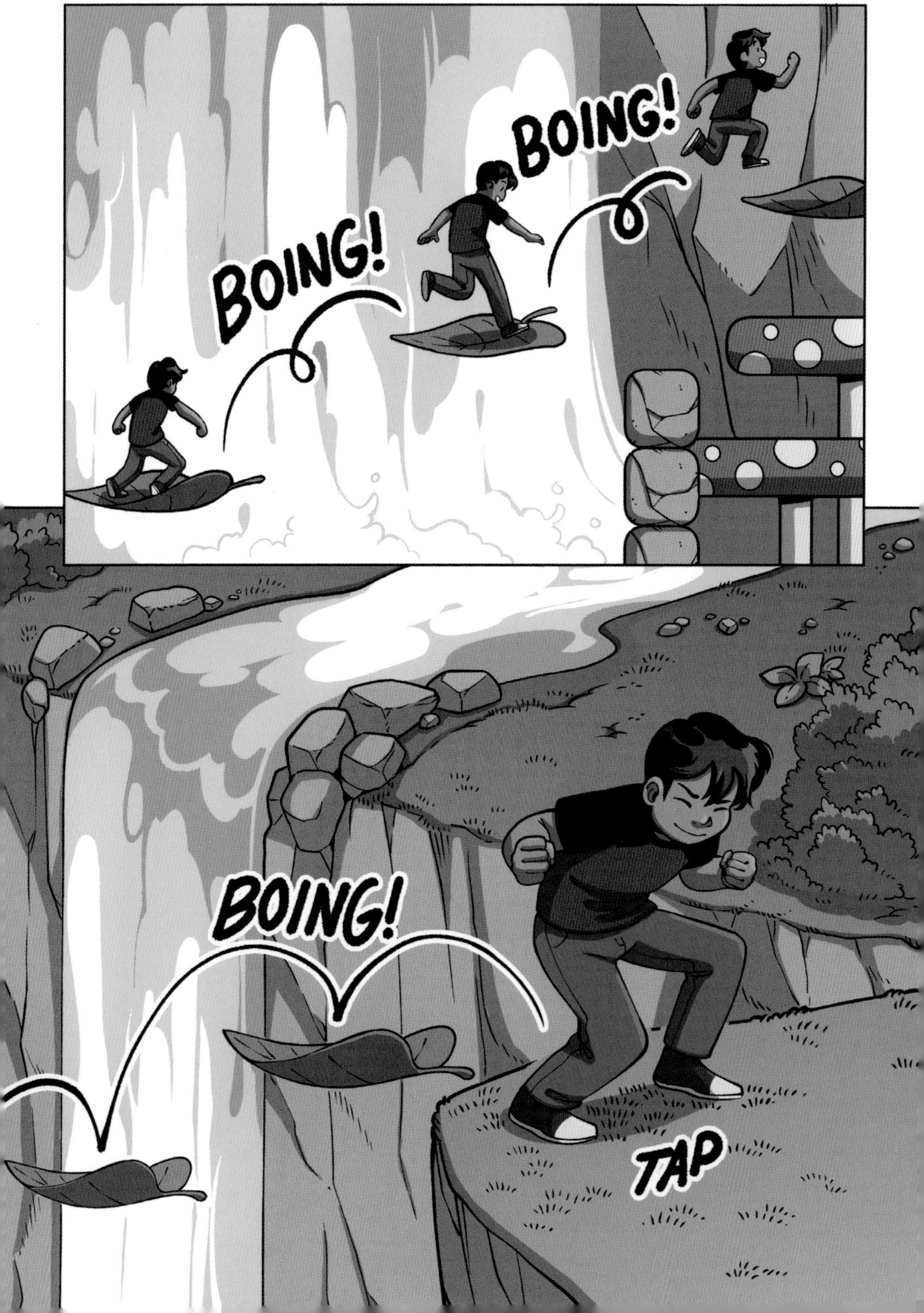
BOING!
BOING!
BOING!
TAP

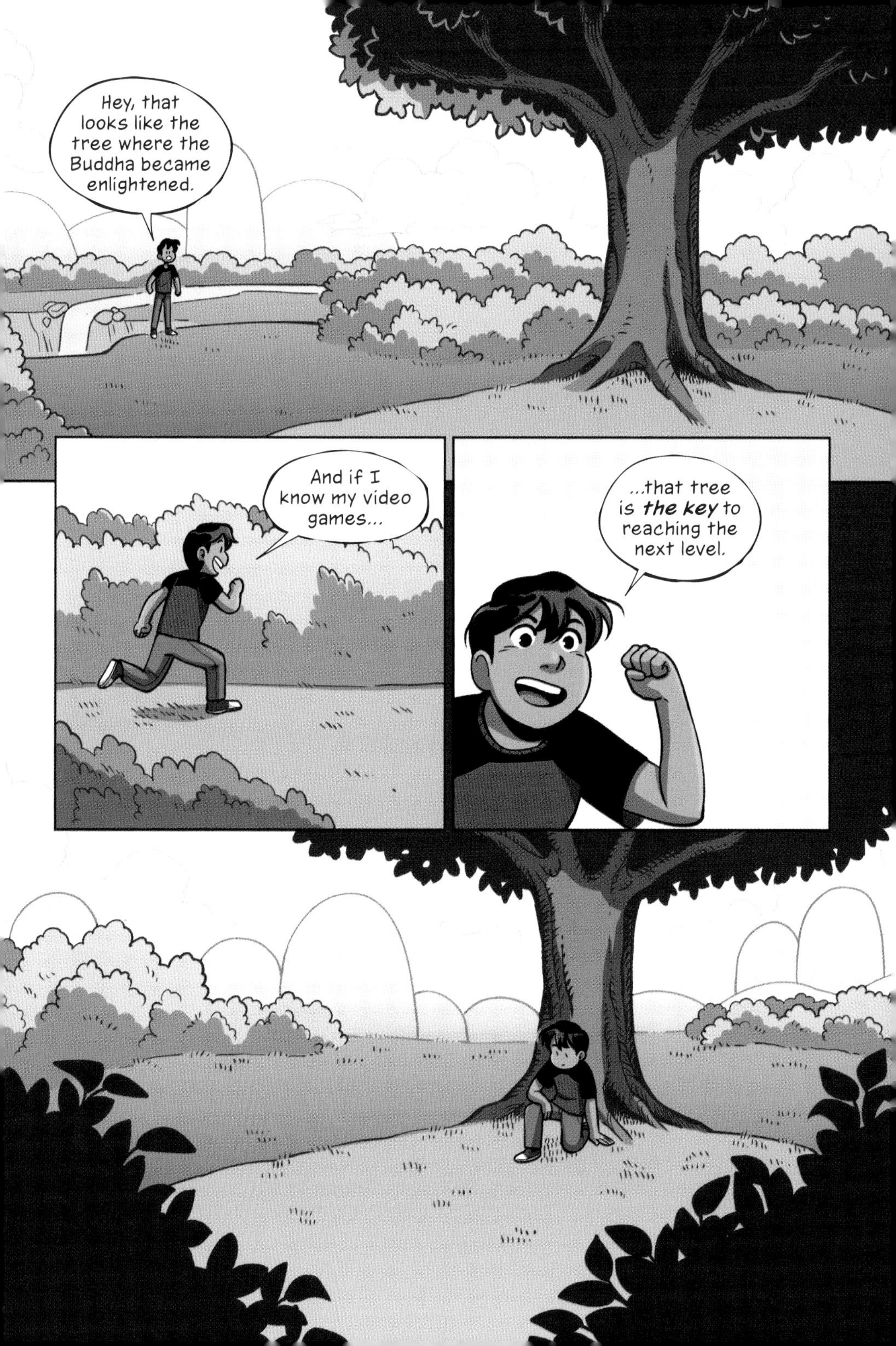
Hey, that looks like the tree where the Buddha became enlightened.
And if I know my video games...
...that tree is *the key* to reaching the next level.

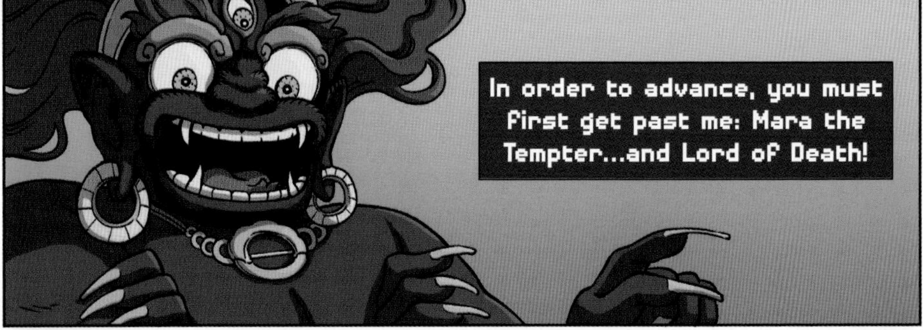
In order to advance, you must first get past me: Mara the Tempter...and Lord of Death!

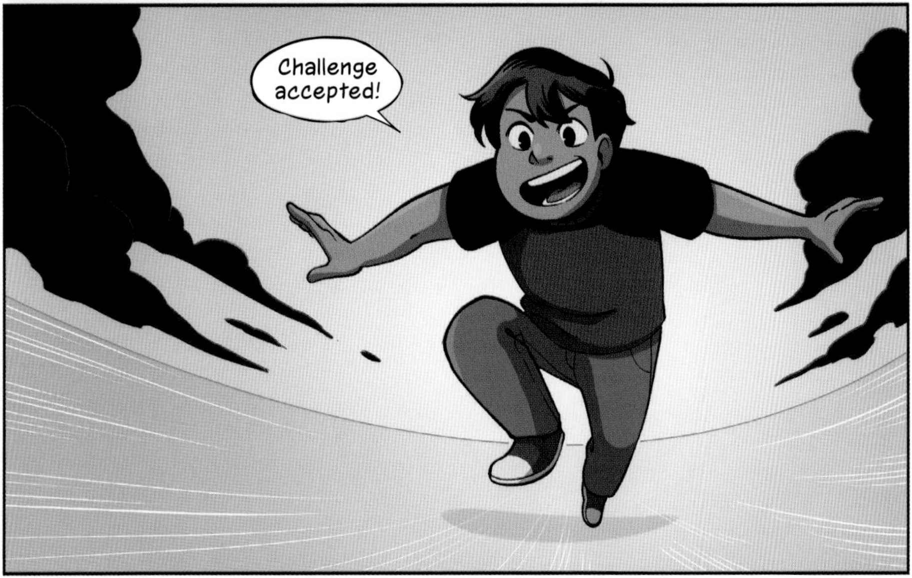
Challenge accepted!

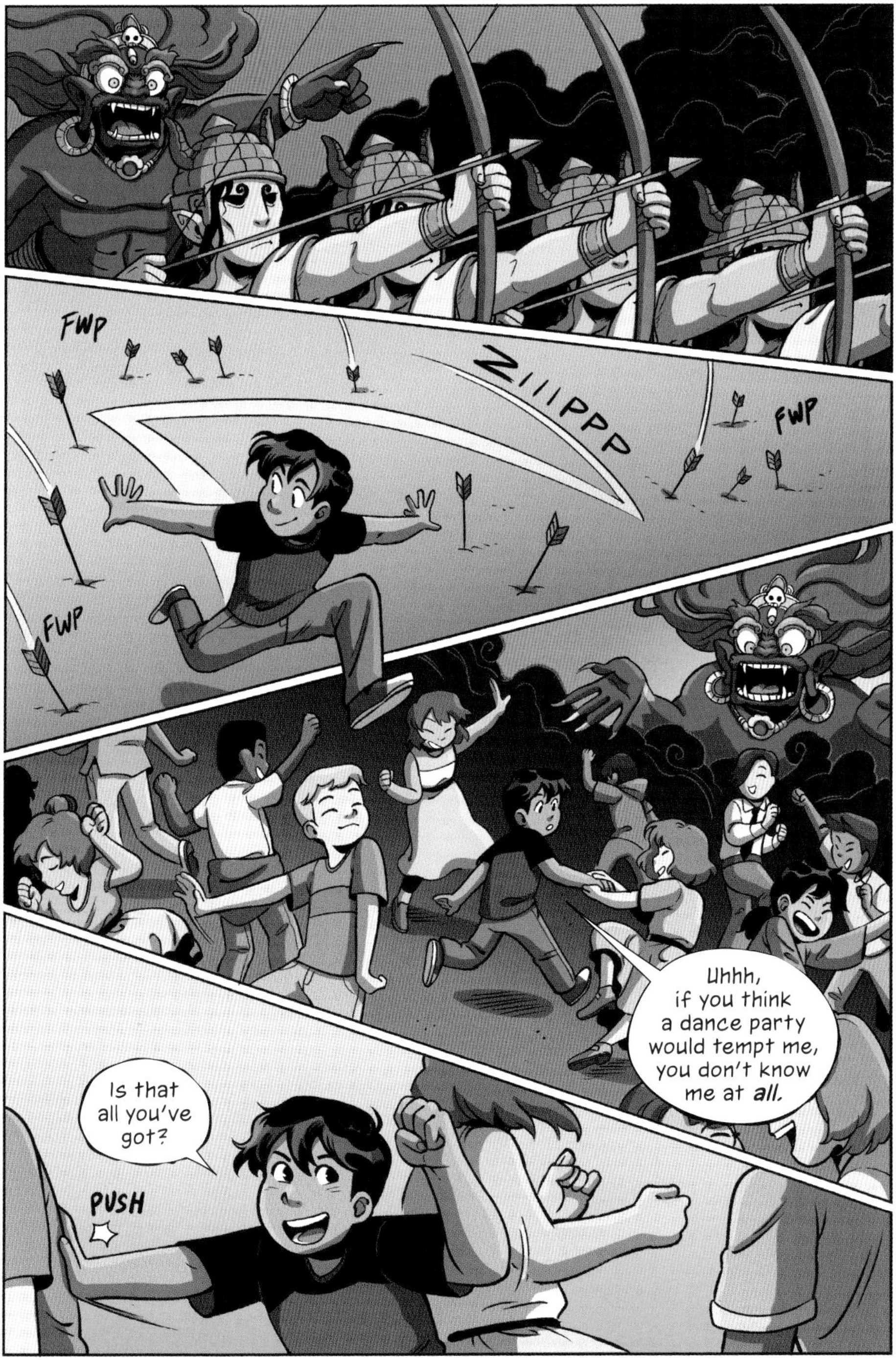
FWP
ZIIIPPP
FWP
FWP
Uhhh, if you think a dance party would tempt me, you don't know me at *all.*
Is that all you've got?
PUSH

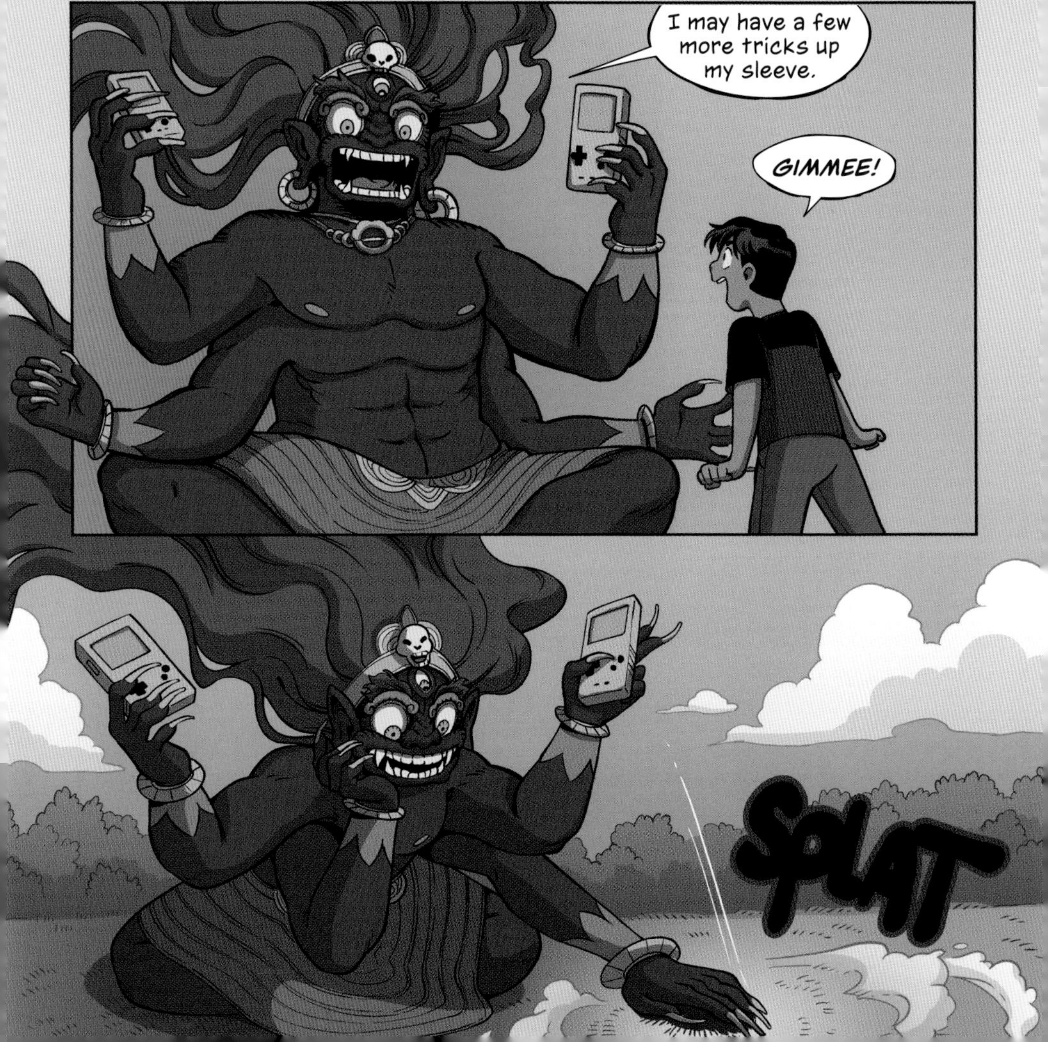
I may have a few more tricks up my sleeve.
GIMMEE!
SPLAT

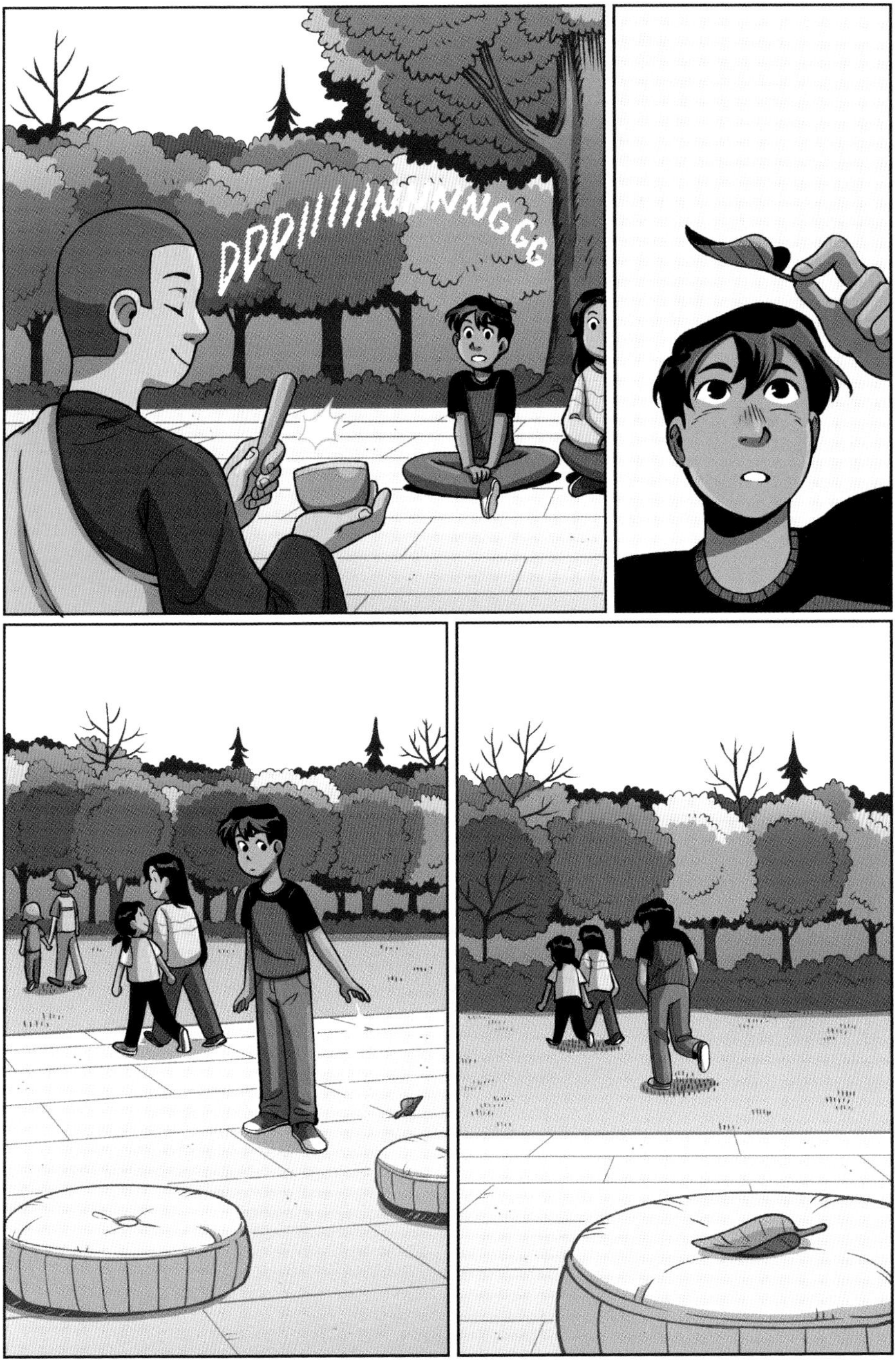
DDDIIIIIINNNNGGG

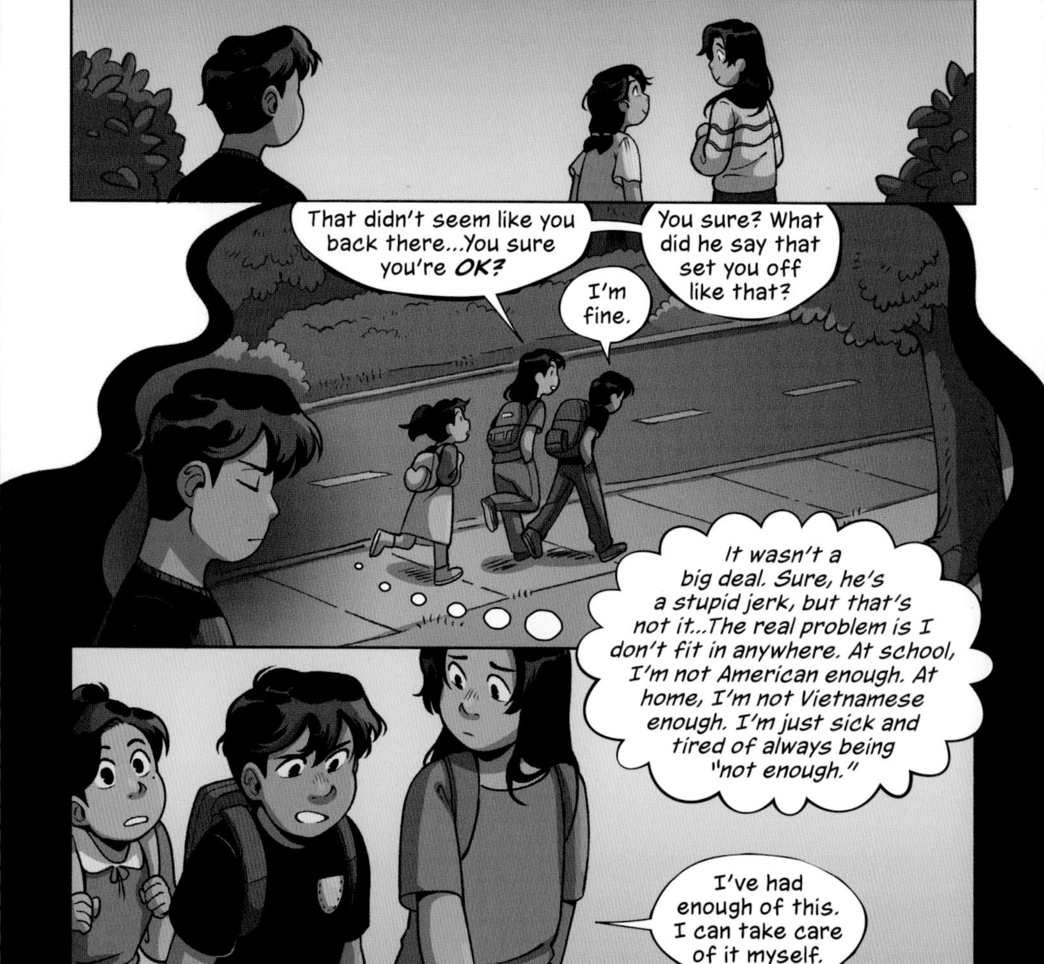
That didn't seem like you back there...You sure you're OK?
I'm fine.
You sure? What did he say that set you off like that?
It wasn't a big deal. Sure, he's a stupid jerk, but that's not it...The real problem is I don't fit in anywhere. At school, I'm not American enough. At home, I'm not Vietnamese enough. I'm just sick and tired of always being "not enough."
I've had enough of this. I can take care of it myself.

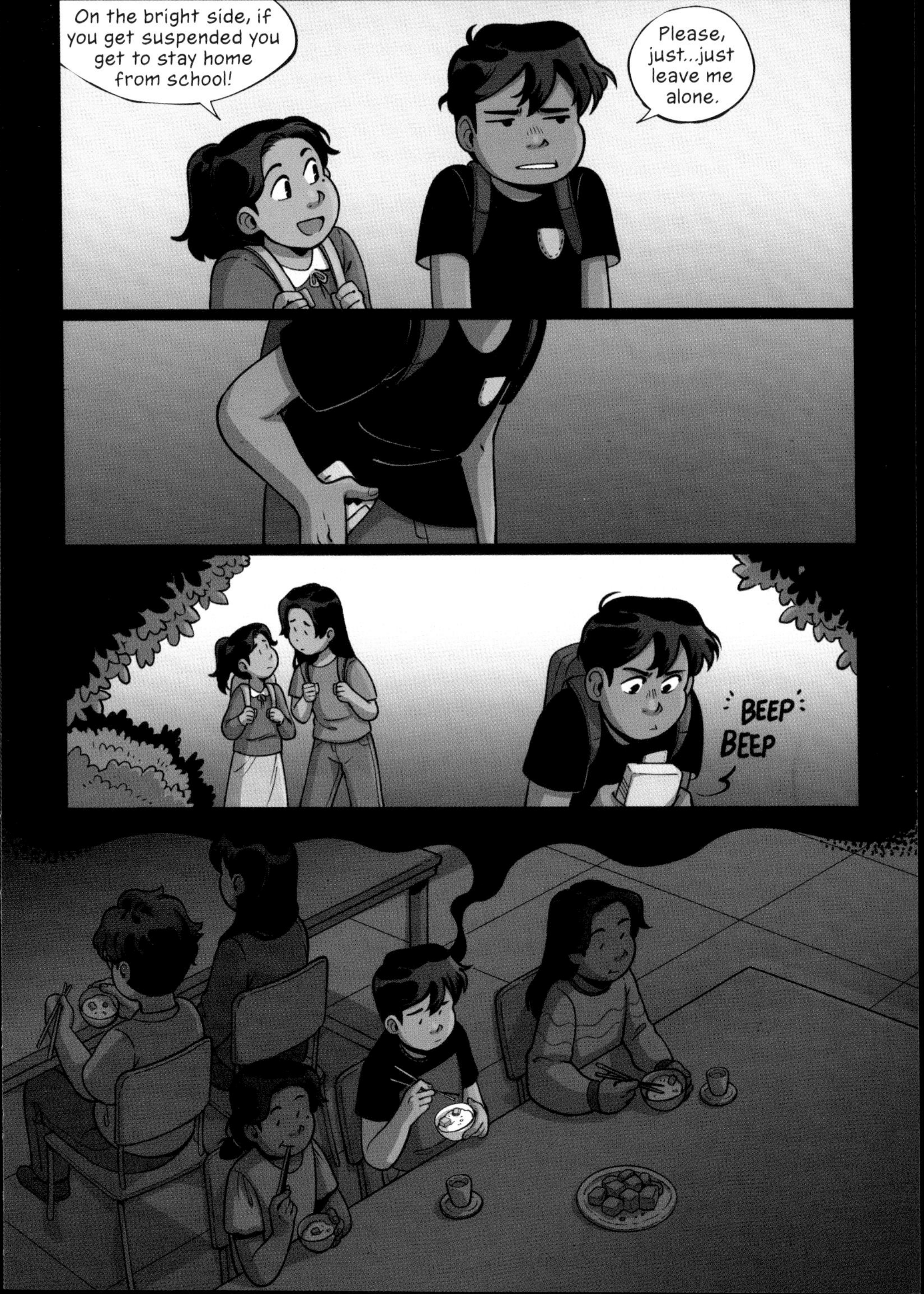
On the bright side, if you get suspended you get to stay home from school!
Please, just...just leave me alone.
BEEP
BEEP

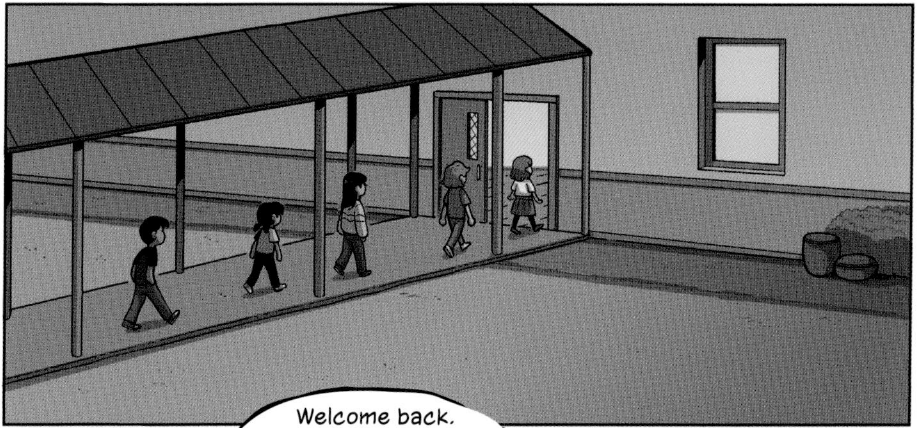

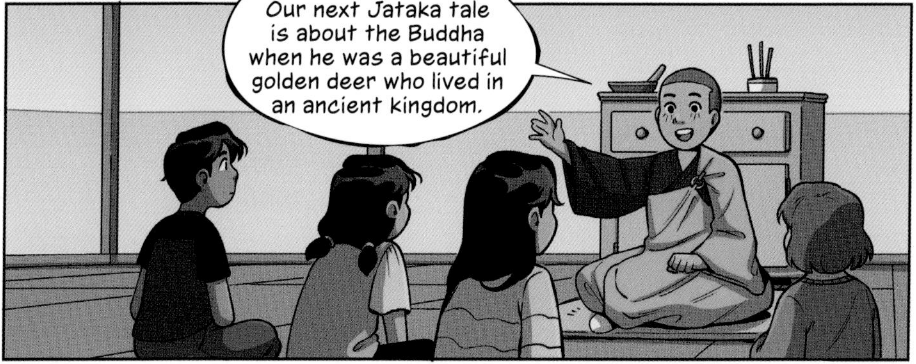
Welcome back. Our next Jataka tale is about the Buddha when he was a beautiful golden deer who lived in an ancient kingdom.

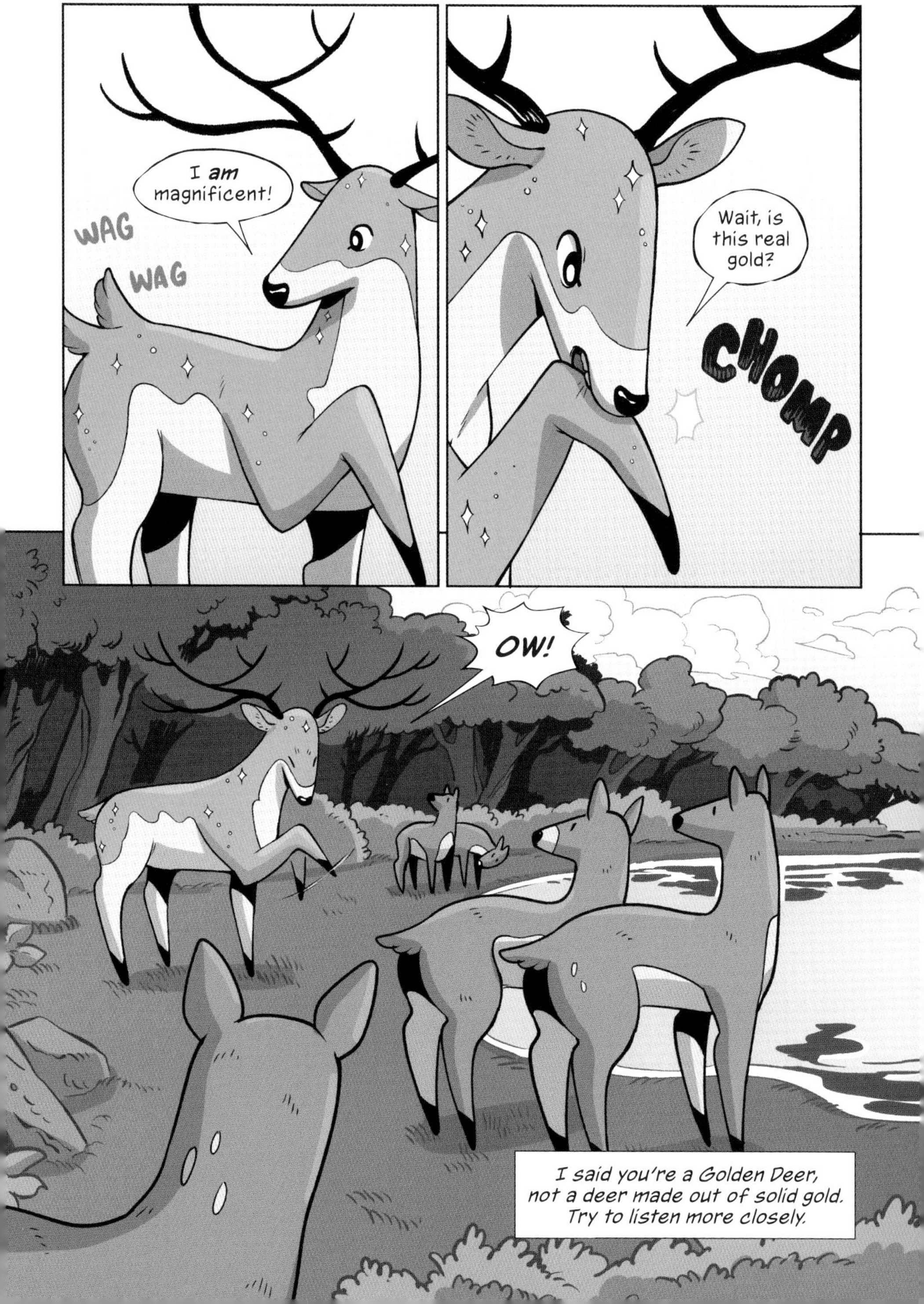
I am magnificent!
WAG
WAG
Wait, is this real gold?
CHOMP
OW!
I said you're a Golden Deer, not a deer made out of solid gold. Try to listen more closely.

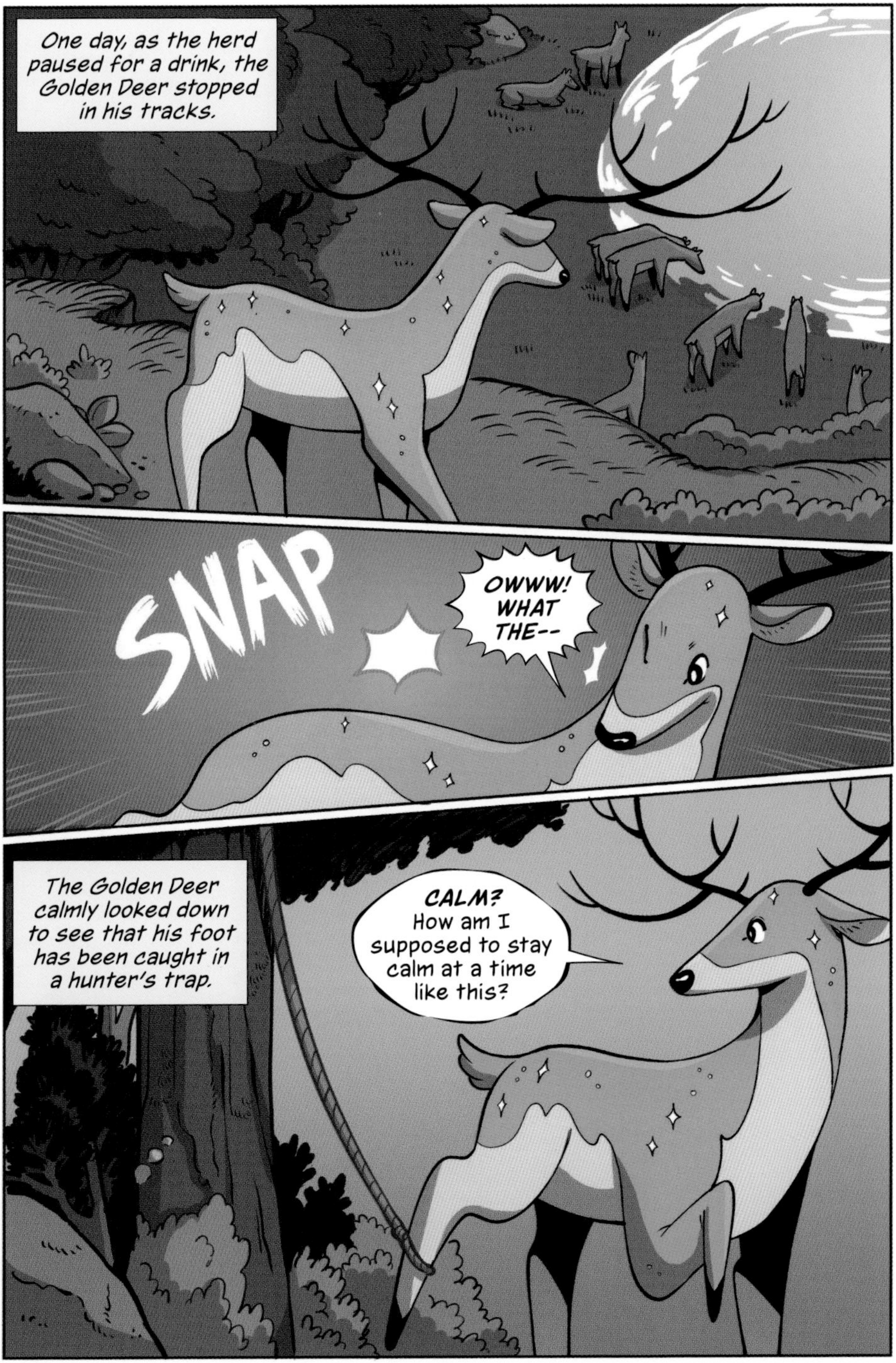
One day, as the herd paused for a drink, the Golden Deer stopped in his tracks.
SNAP
OWWW! WHAT THE--
The Golden Deer calmly looked down to see that his foot has been caught in a hunter's trap.
CALM? How am I supposed to stay calm at a time like this?

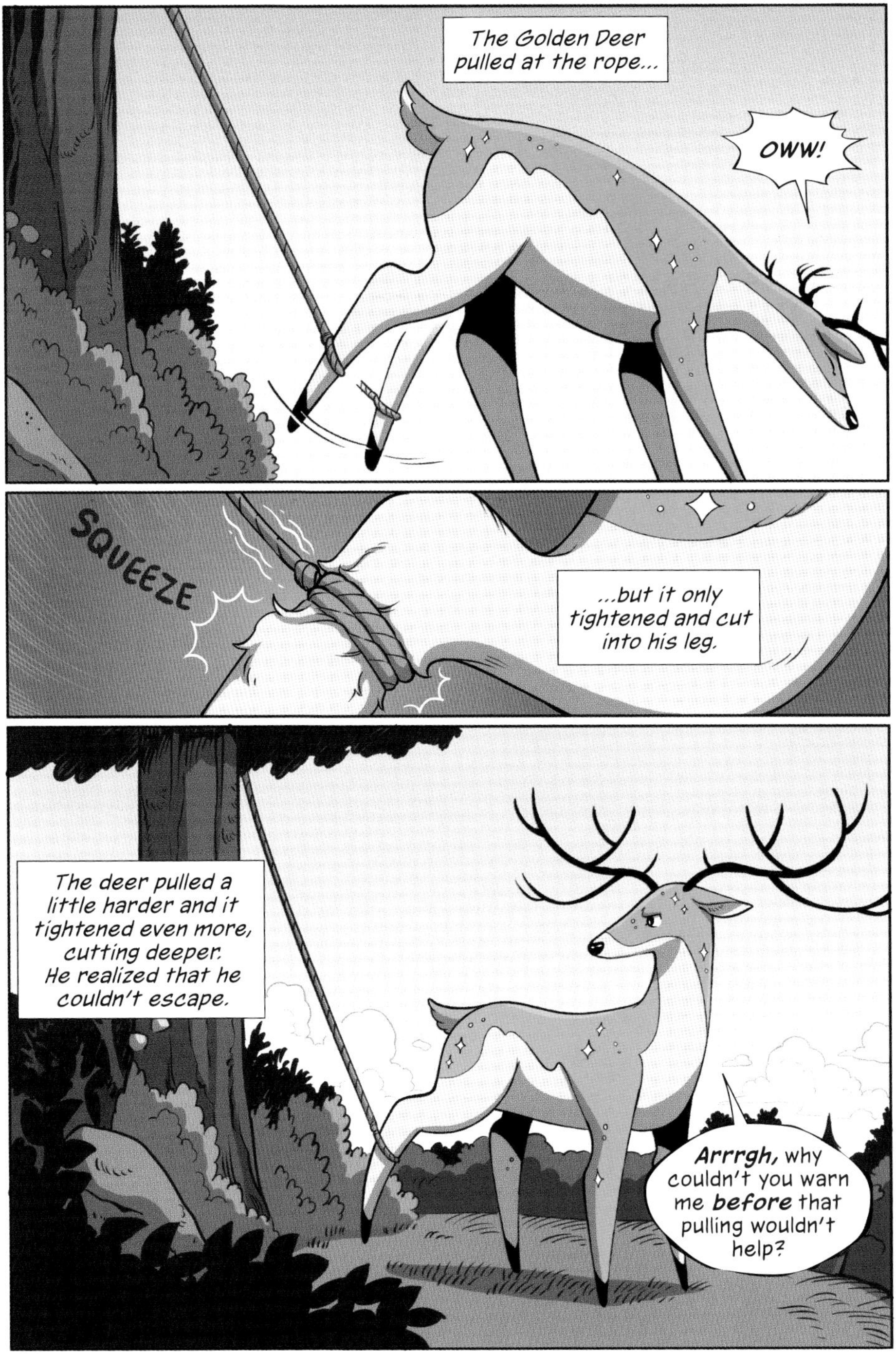
The Golden Deer pulled at the rope...
OWW!
SQUEEZE
...but it only tightened and cut into his leg.
The deer pulled a little harder and it tightened even more, cutting deeper. He realized that he couldn't escape.
Arrrgh, why couldn't you warn me before that pulling wouldn't help?

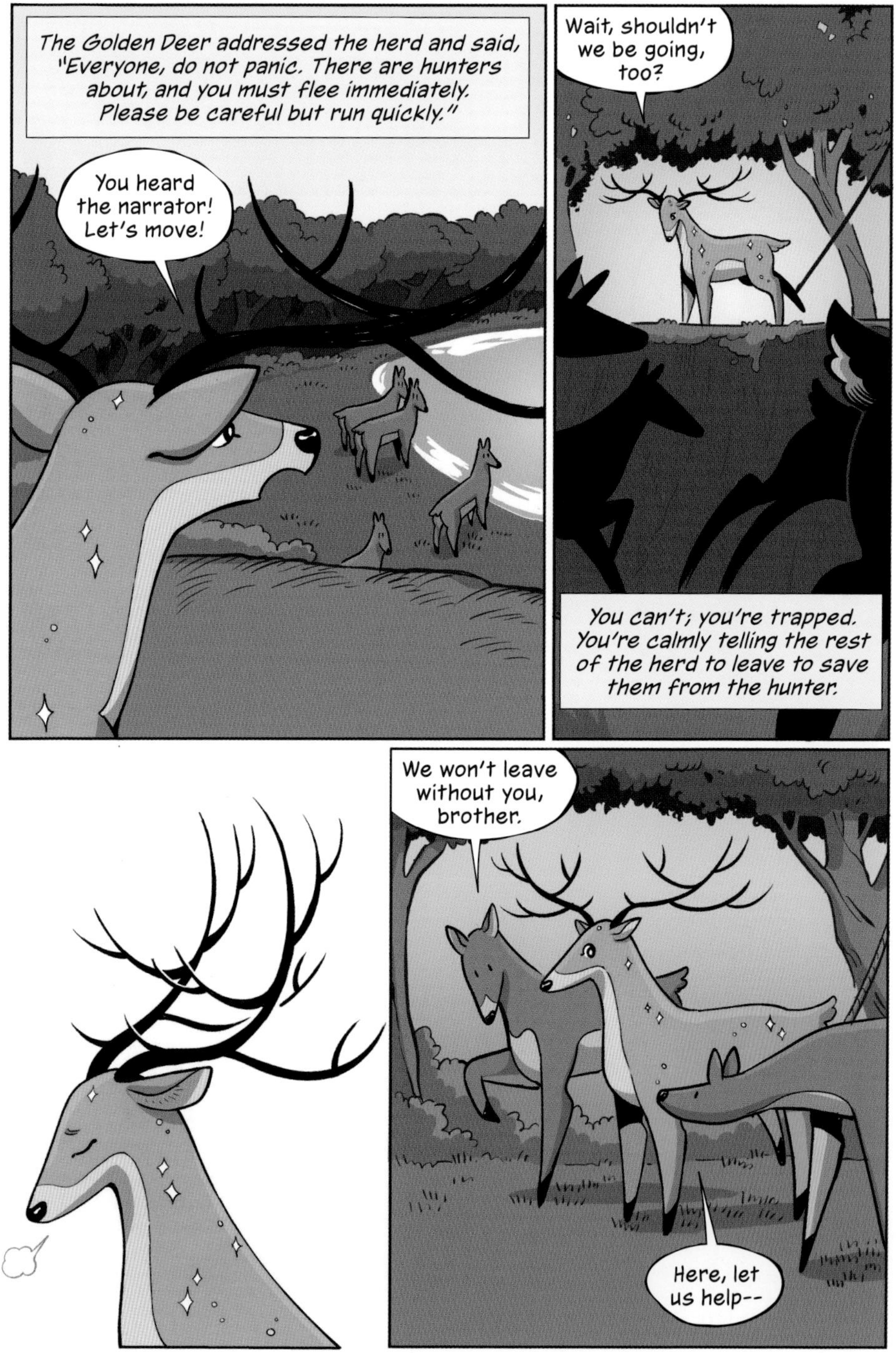
The Golden Deer addressed the herd and said, "Everyone, do not panic. There are hunters about, and you must flee immediately. Please be careful but run quickly."
You heard the narrator! Let's move!
Wait, shouldn't we be going, too?
You can't; you're trapped. You're calmly telling the rest of the herd to leave to save them from the hunter.
We won't leave without you, brother.
Here, let us help--

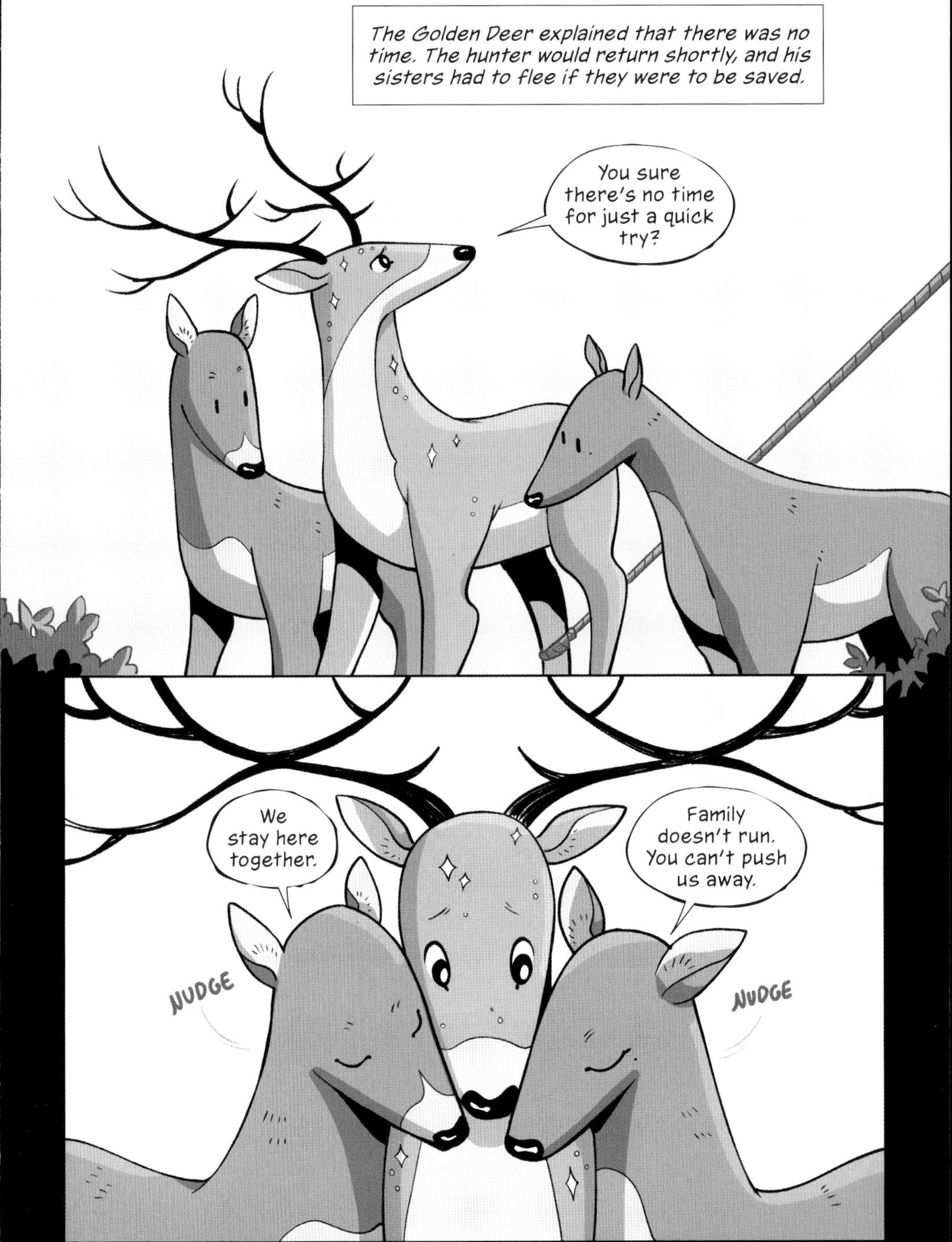
The Golden Deer explained that there was no time. The hunter would return shortly, and his sisters had to flee if they were to be saved.
You sure there's no time for just a quick try?
We stay here together.
Family doesn't run. You can't push us away.
NUDGE
NUDGE

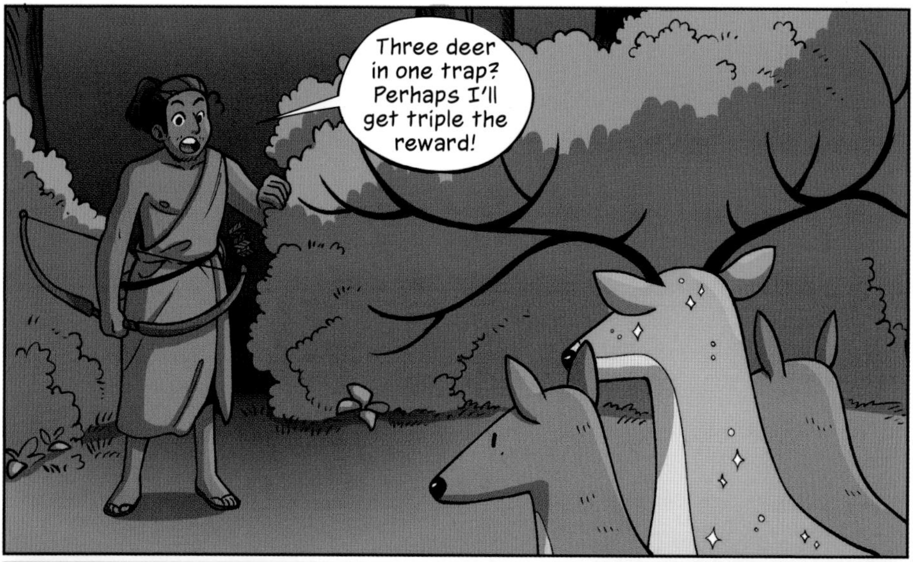
Three deer in one trap? Perhaps I'll get triple the reward!

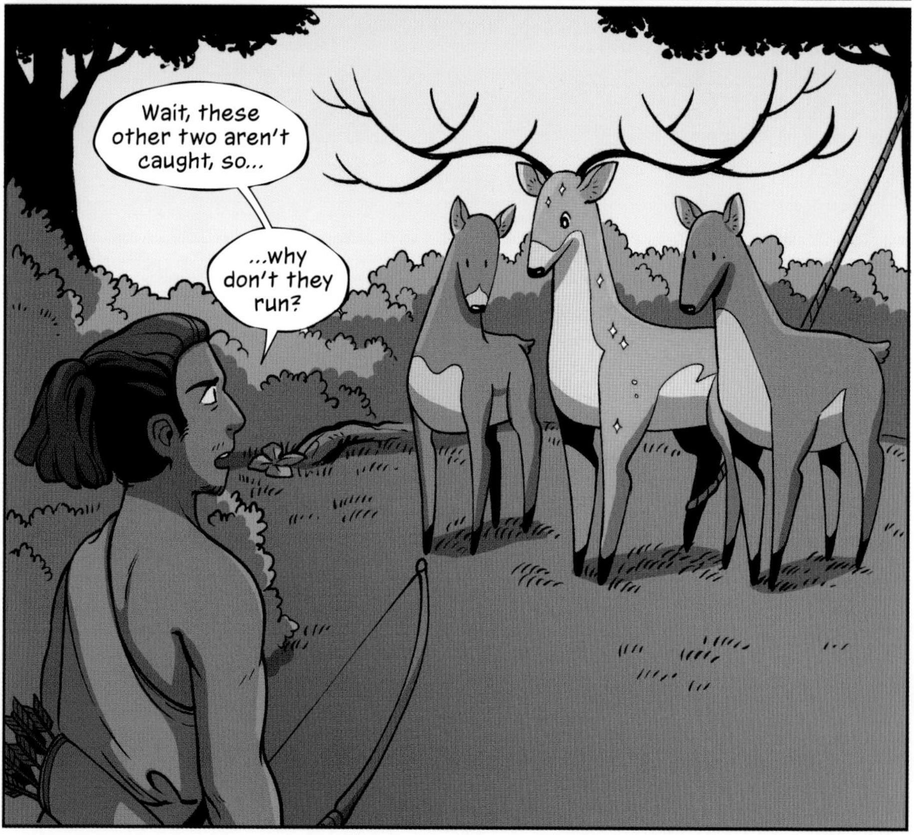
Wait, these other two aren't caught, so...
...why don't they run?

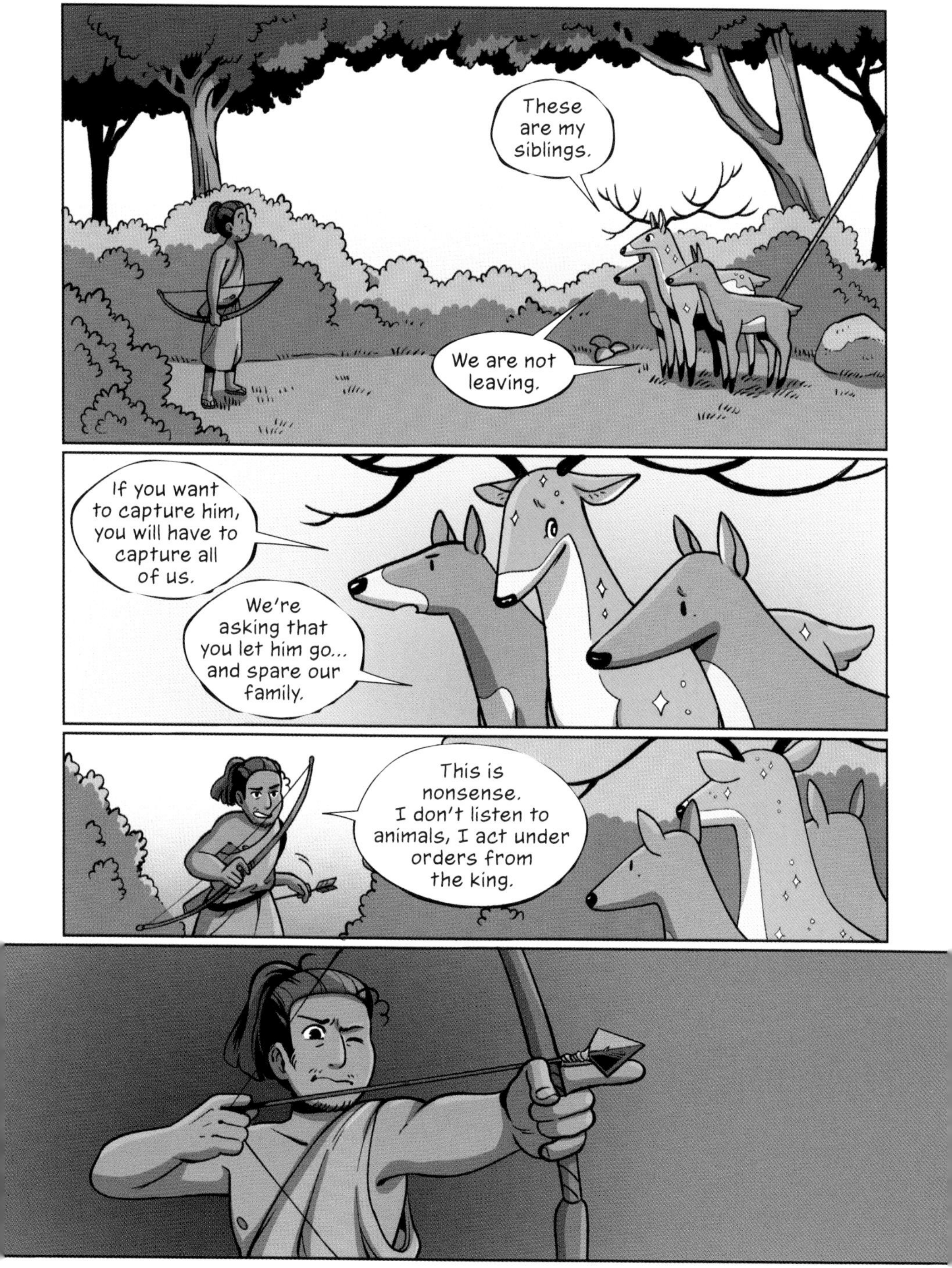
These are my siblings.
We are not leaving.
If you want to capture him, you will have to capture all of us.
We're asking that you let him go... and spare our family.
This is nonsense. I don't listen to animals, I act under orders from the king.

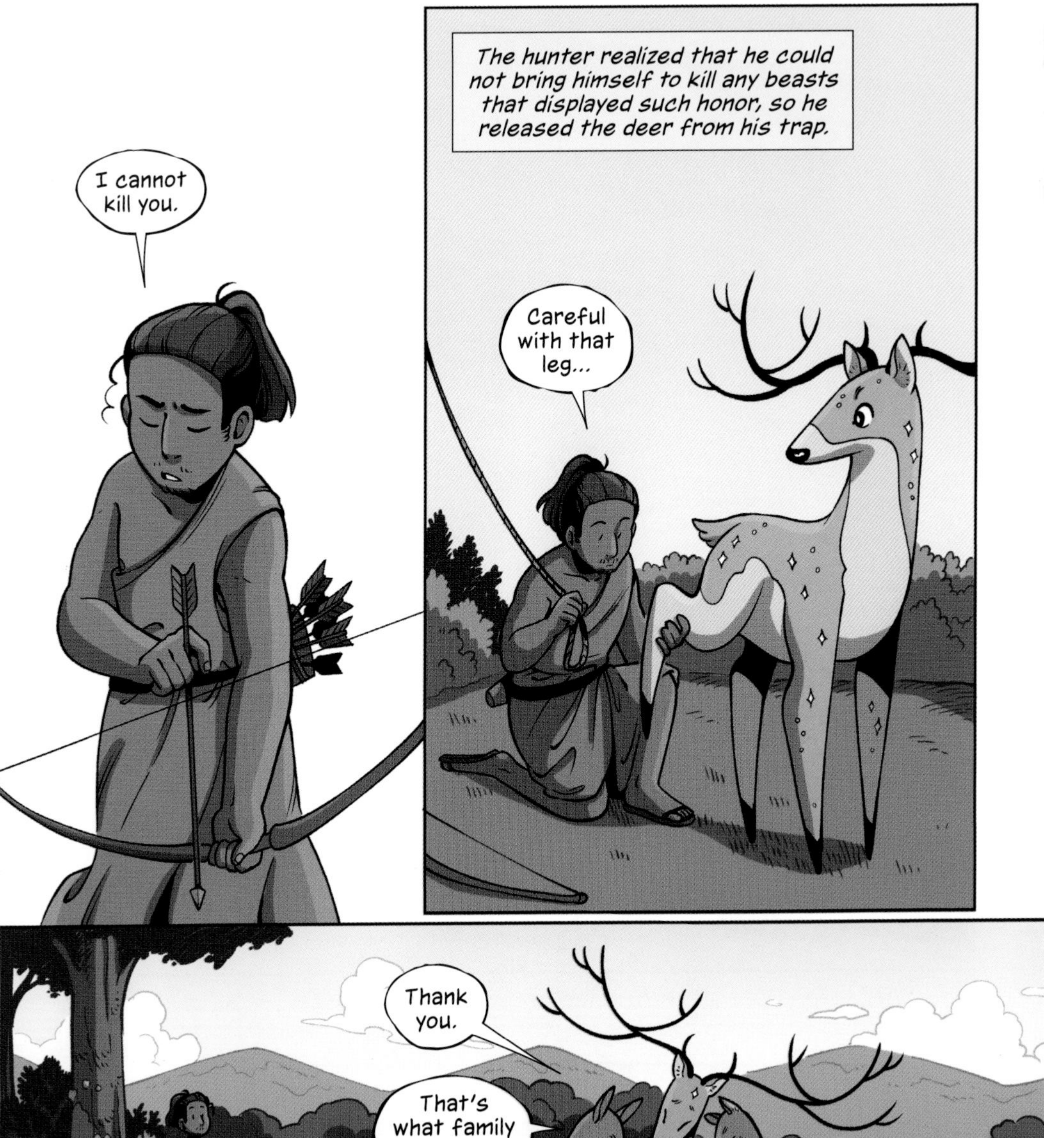
The hunter realized that he could not bring himself to kill any beasts that displayed such honor, so he released the deer from his trap.
I cannot kill you.
Careful with that leg...
Thank you.
That's what family

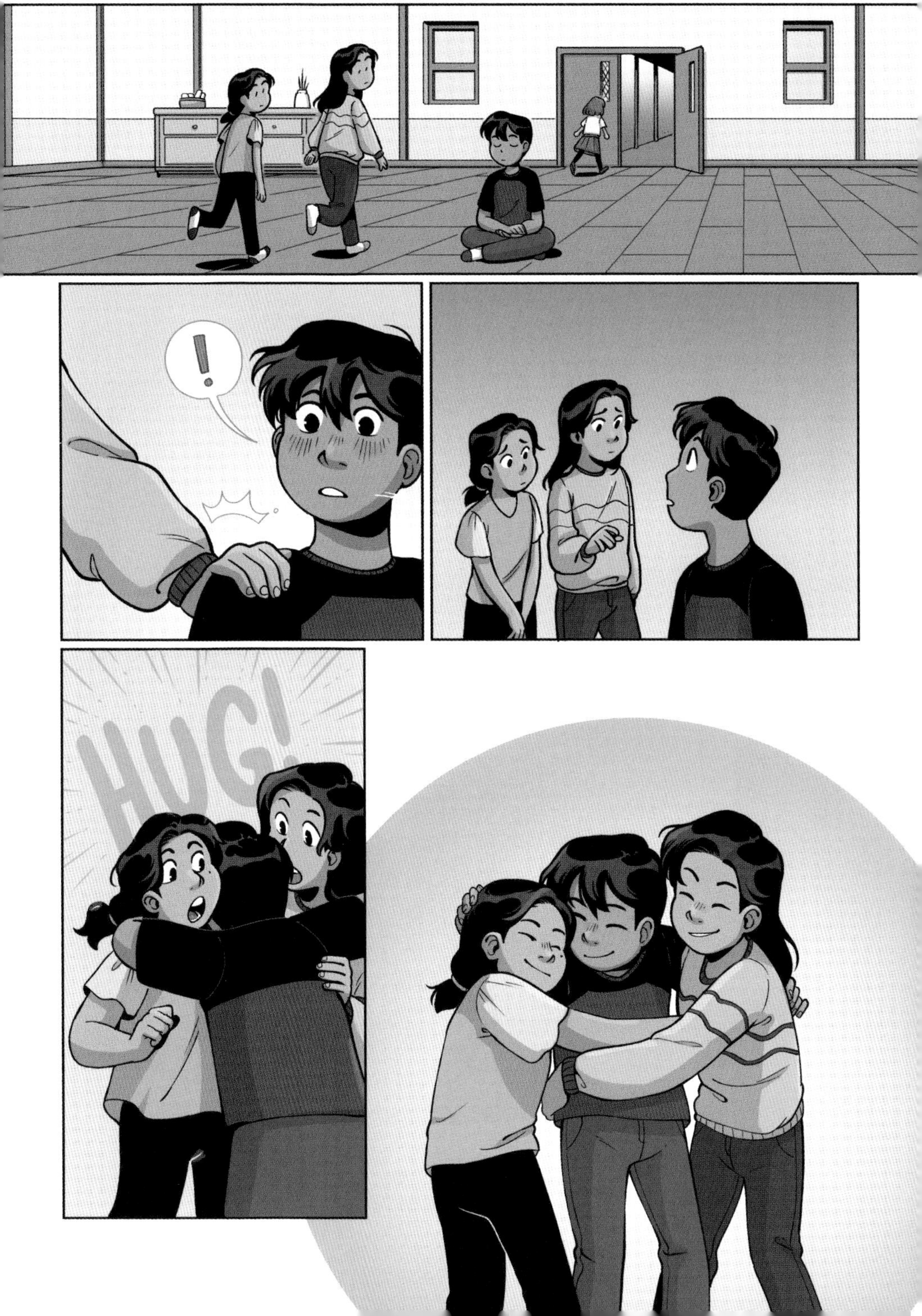
!
HUG!

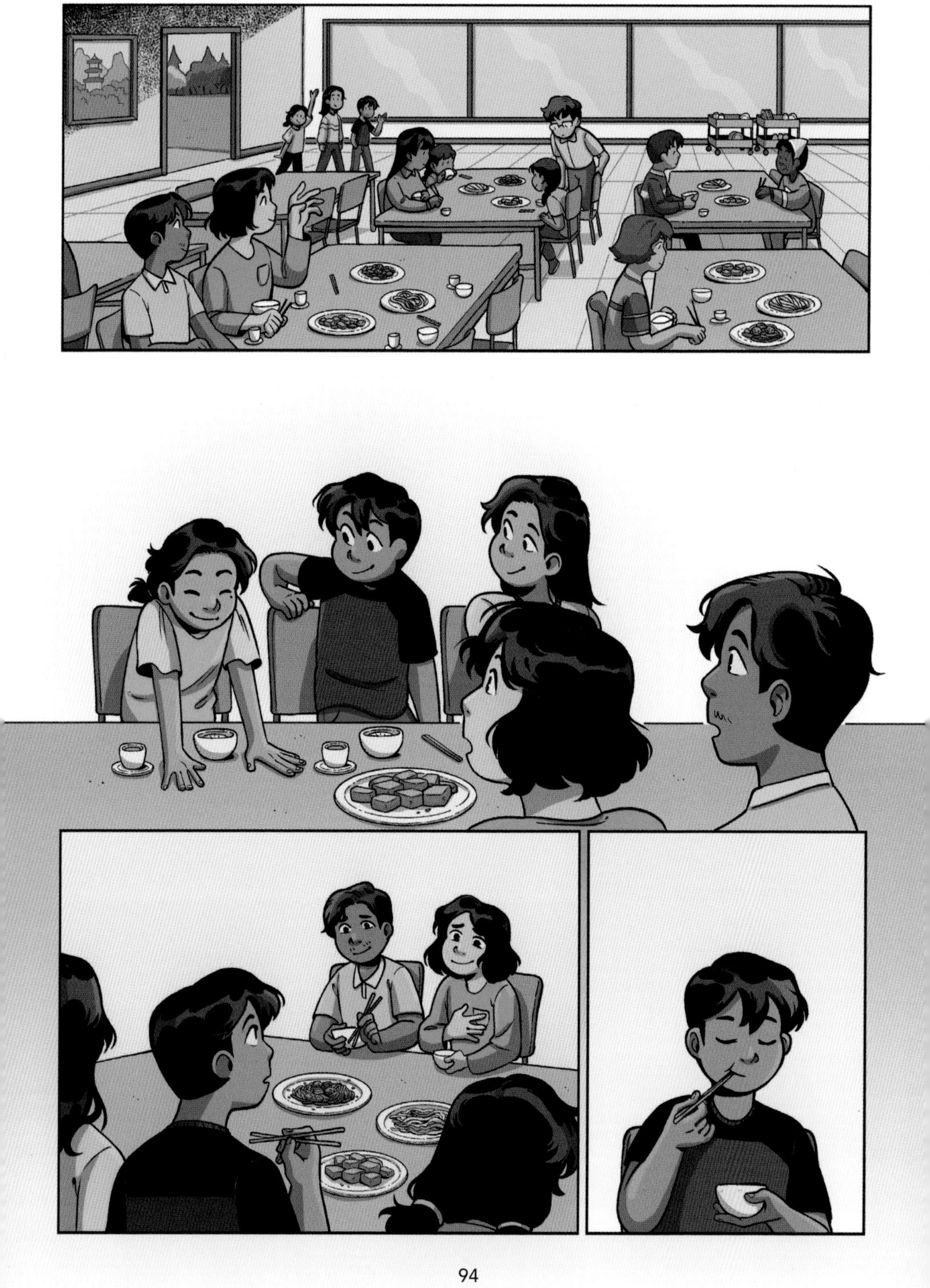

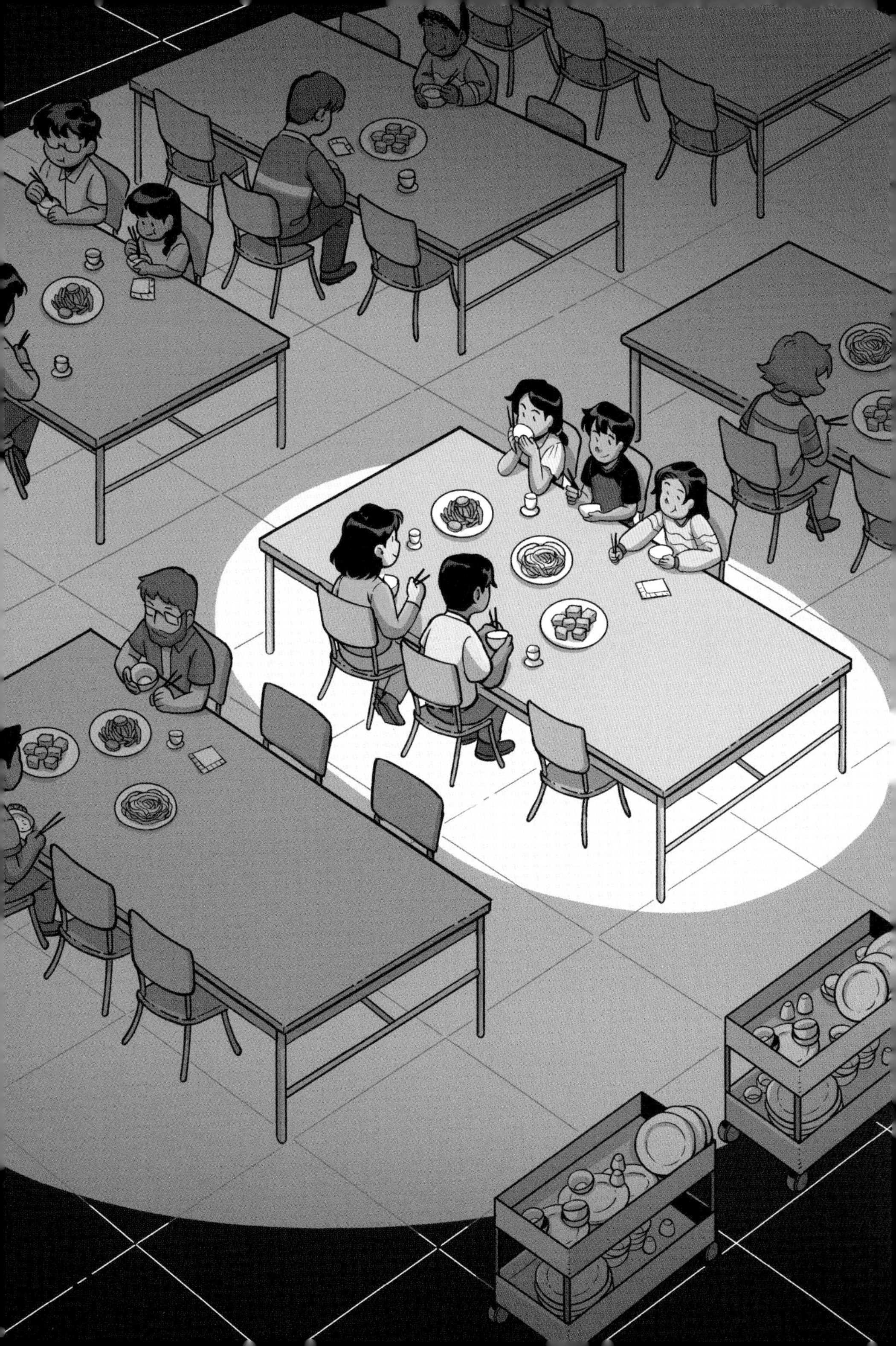

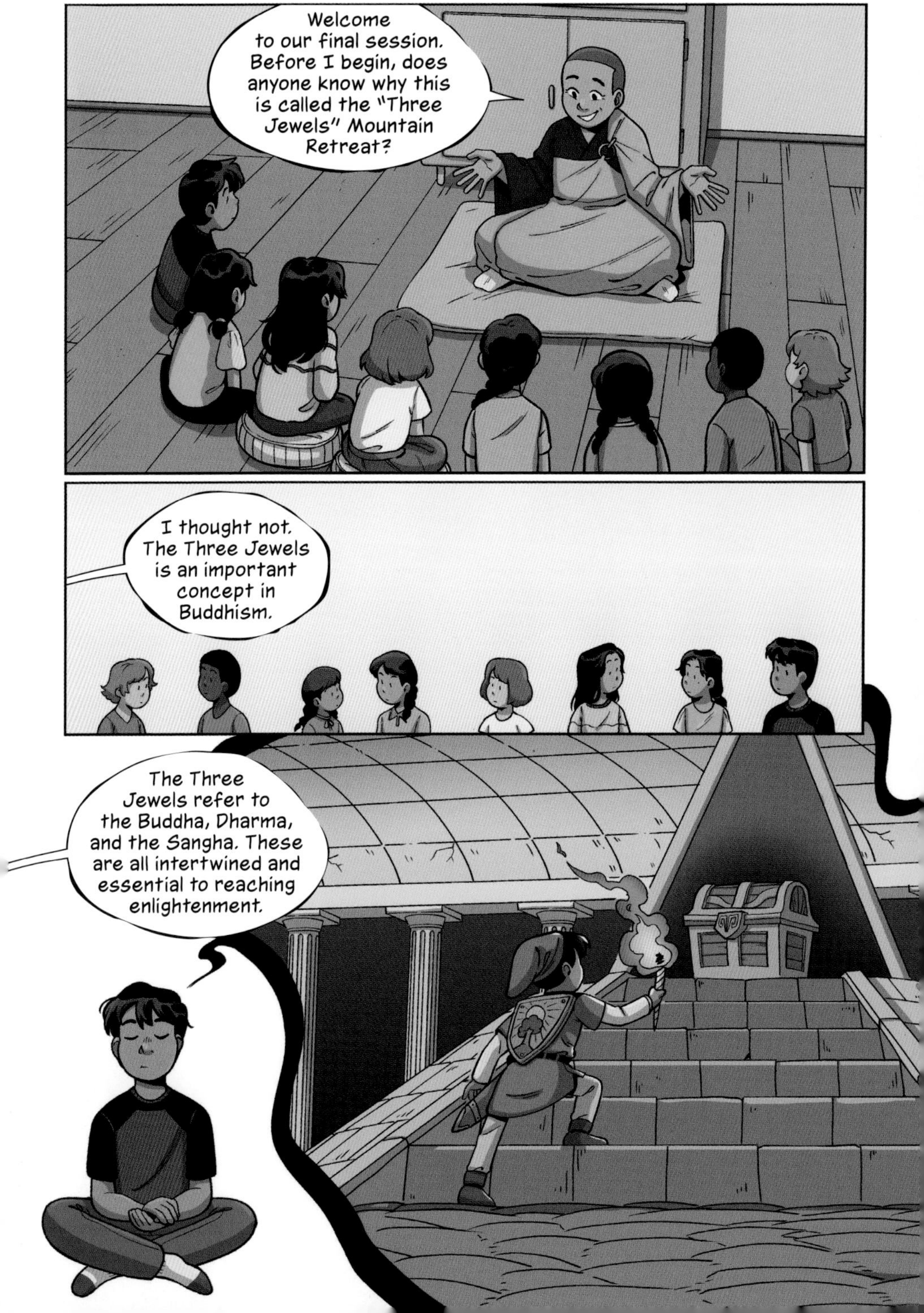
Welcome to our final session. Before I begin, does anyone know why this is called the "Three Jewels" Mountain Retreat?
I thought not. The Three Jewels is an important concept in Buddhism.
The Three Jewels refer to the Buddha, Dharma, and the Sangha. These are all intertwined and essential to reaching enlightenment.

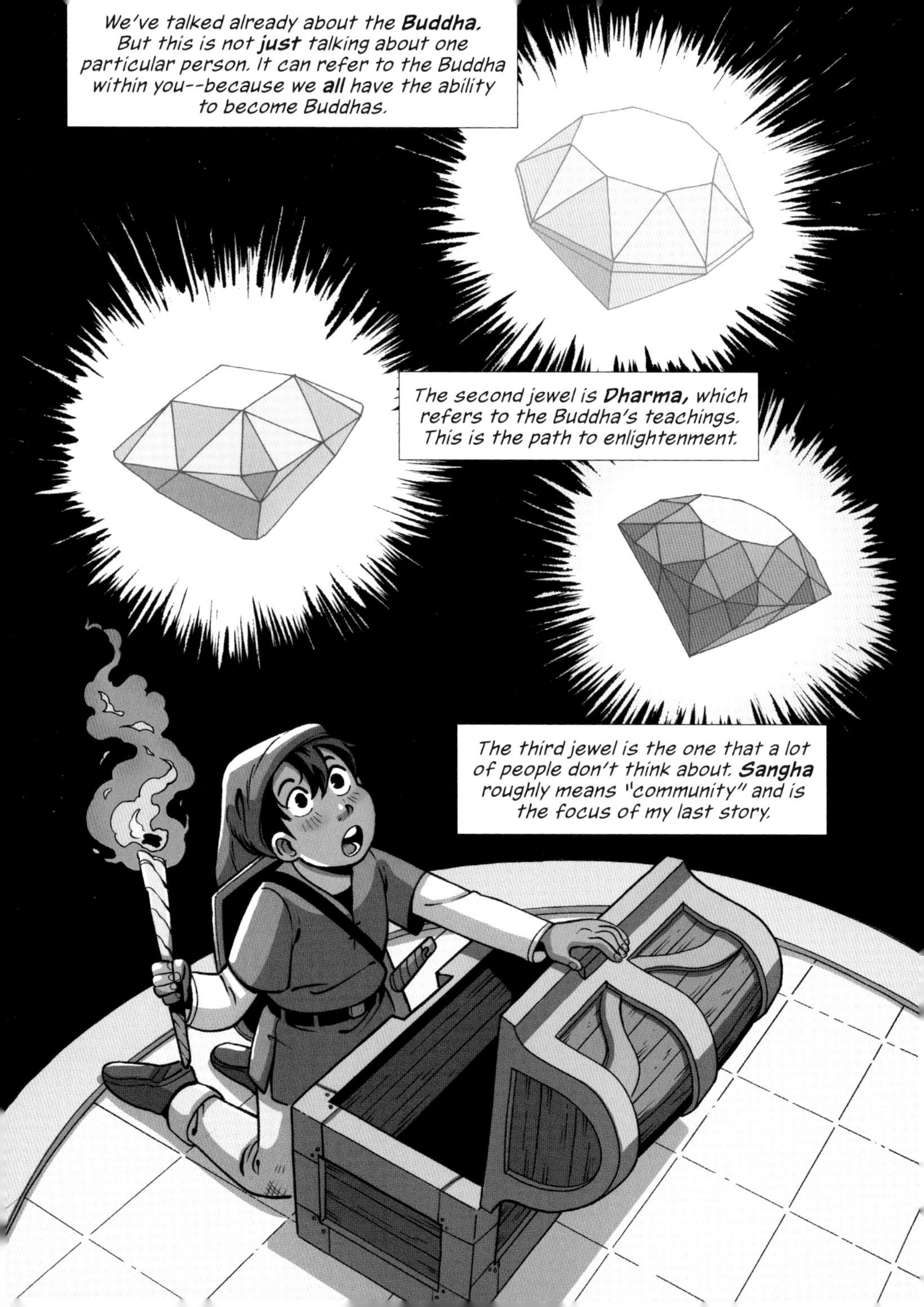
We've talked already about the **Buddha.** But this is not **just** talking about one particular person. It can refer to the Buddha within you--because we **all** have the ability to become Buddhas.
The second jewel is **Dharma,** which refers to the Buddha's teachings. This is the path to enlightenment.
The third jewel is the one that a lot of people don't think about. **Sangha** roughly means "community" and is the focus of my last story.

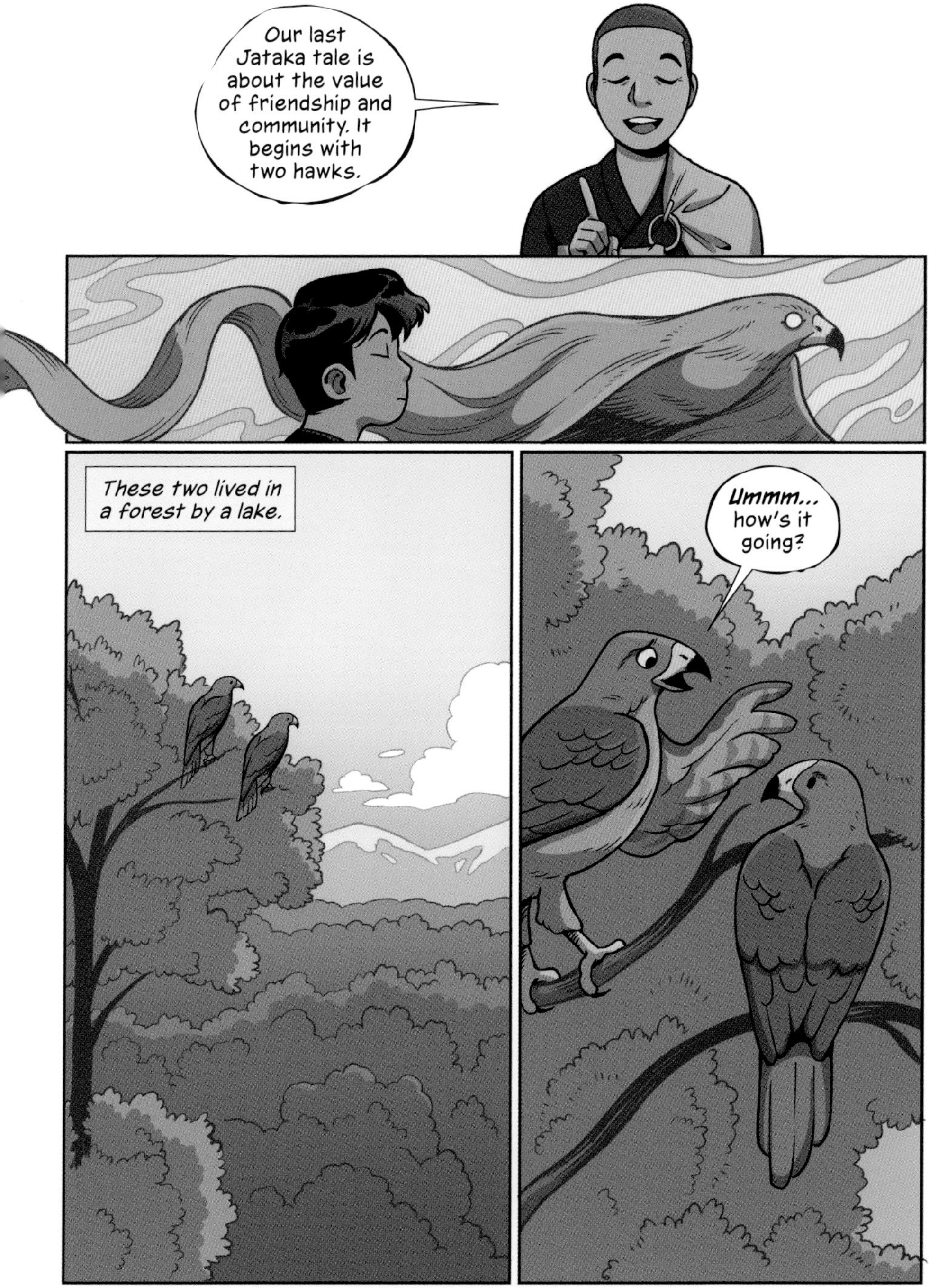
Our last Jataka tale is about the value of friendship and community. It begins with two hawks.
These two lived in a forest by a lake.
Ummm... how's it going?

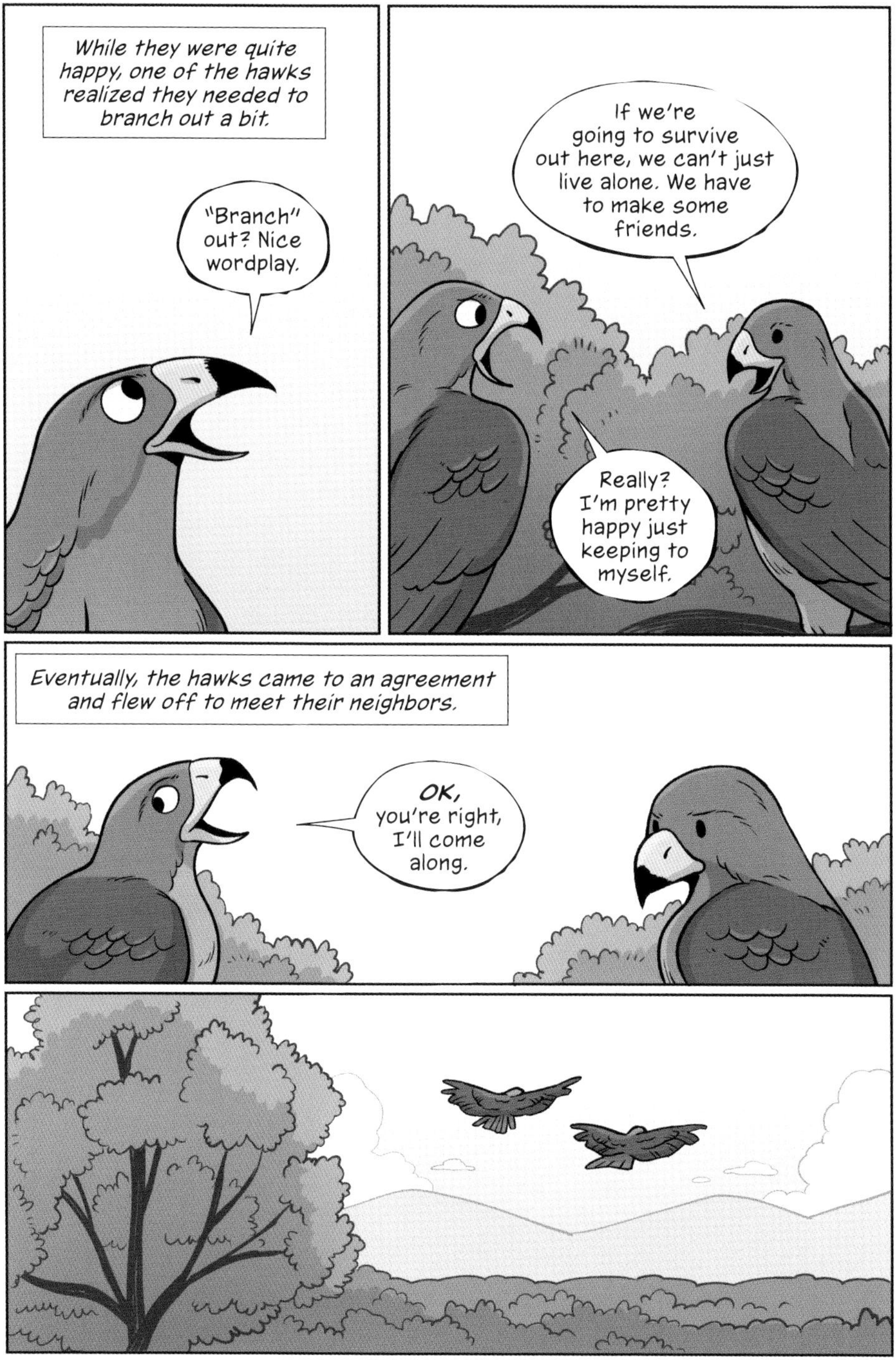
While they were quite happy, one of the hawks realized they needed to branch out a bit.
"Branch" out? Nice wordplay.
If we're going to survive out here, we can't just live alone. We have to make some friends.
Really? I'm pretty happy just keeping to myself.
Eventually, the hawks came to an agreement and flew off to meet their neighbors.
OK, you're right, I'll come along.

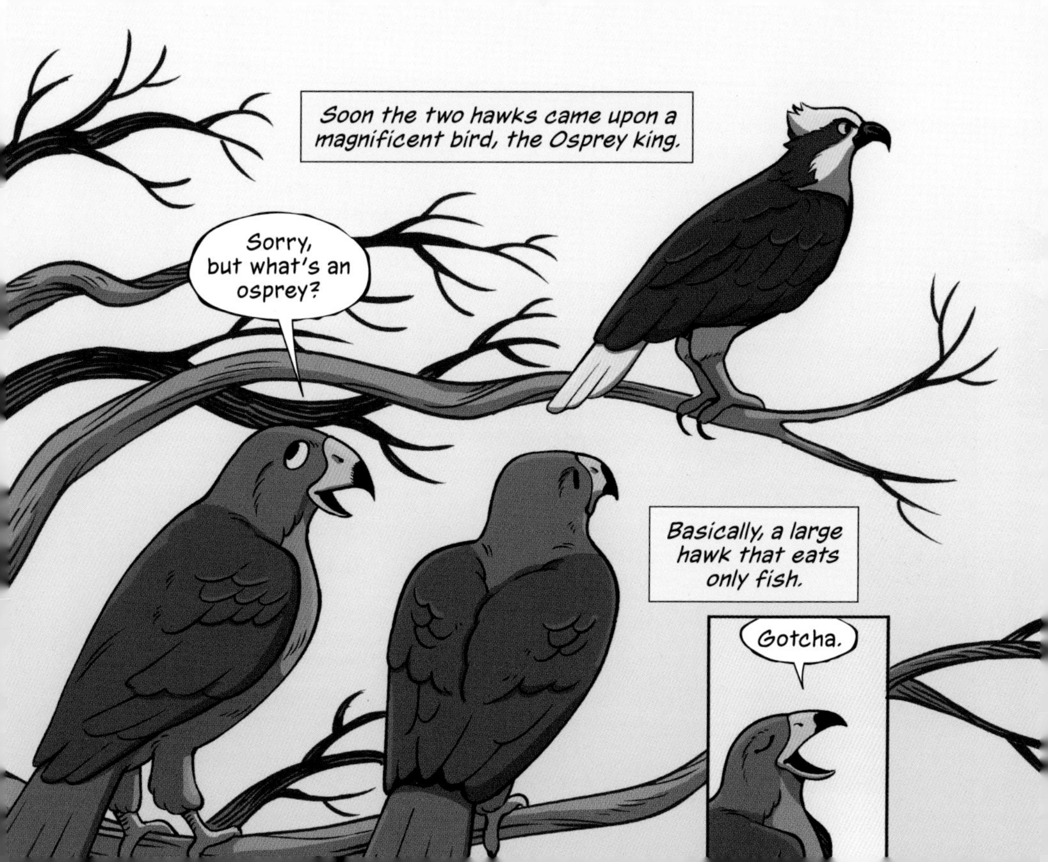

Soon the two hawks came upon a magnificent bird, the Osprey king.
Sorry, but what's an osprey?
Basically, a large hawk that eats only fish.
Gotcha.

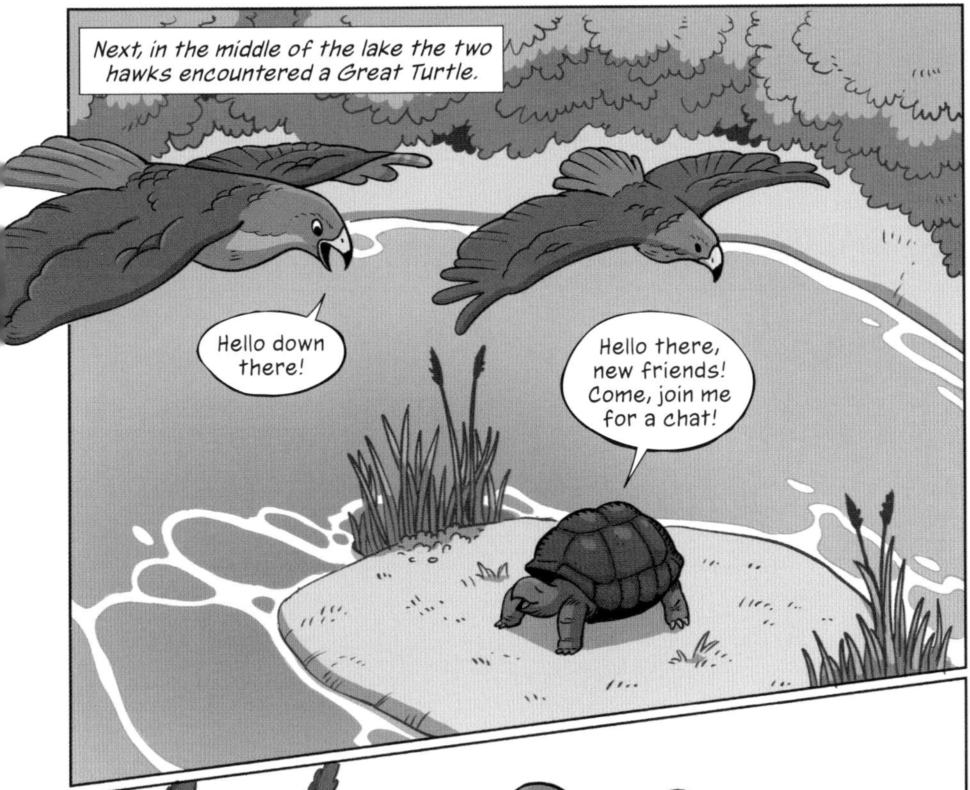
Next, in the middle of the lake the two hawks encountered a Great Turtle.
Hello down there!
Hello there, new friends! Come, join me for a chat!

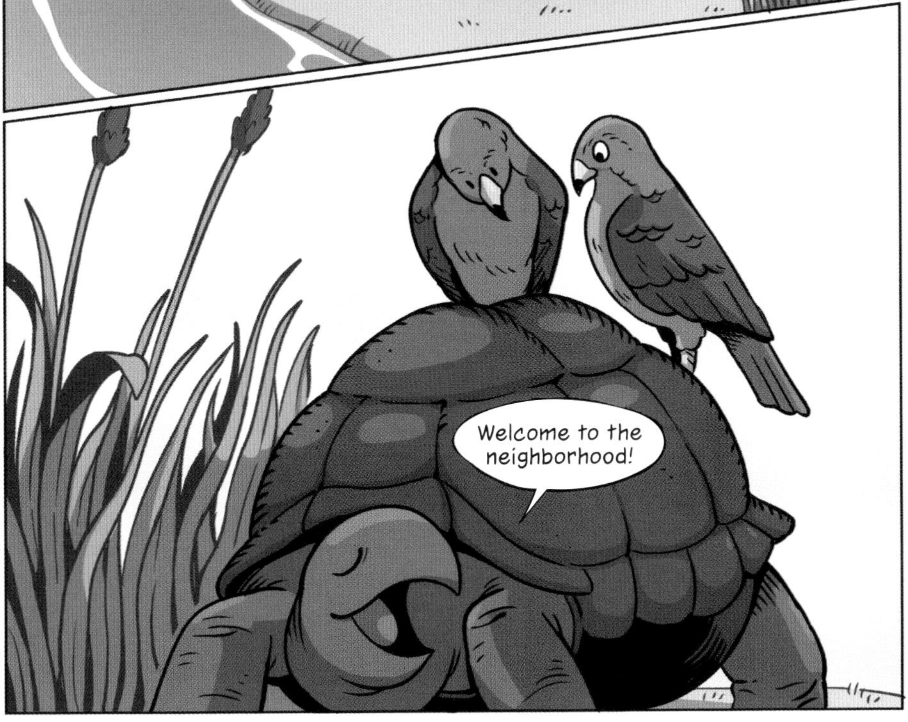
Welcome to the neighborhood!

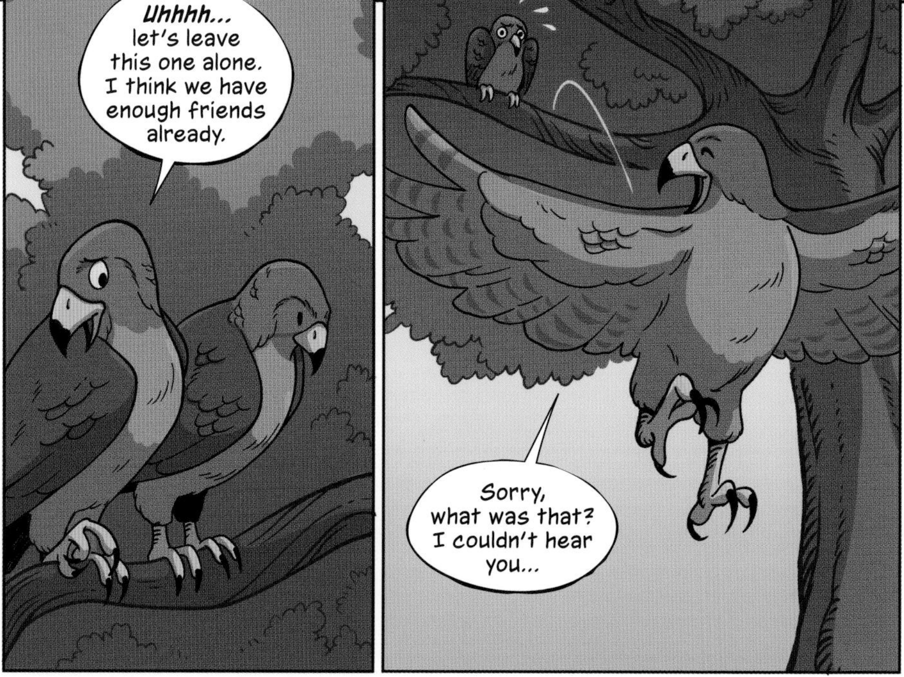
Uhhhh... let's leave this one alone. I think we have enough friends already.
Sorry, what was that? I couldn't hear you...

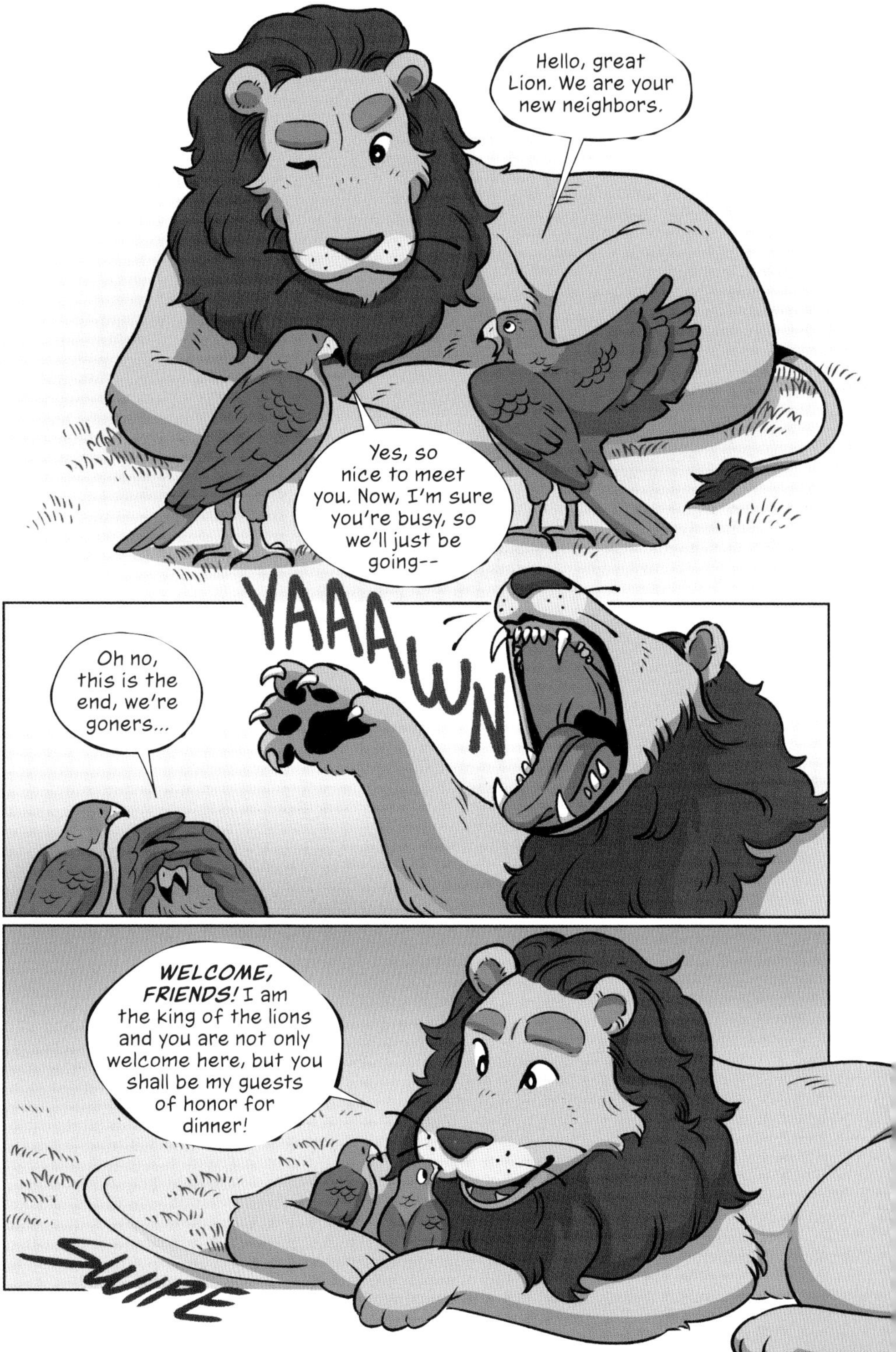
Hello, great Lion. We are your new neighbors.
Yes, so nice to meet you. Now, I'm sure you're busy, so we'll just be going--
YAAAWN
Oh no, this is the end, we're goners...
WELCOME, FRIENDS! I am the king of the lions and you are not only welcome here, but you shall be my guests of honor for dinner!
SWIPE

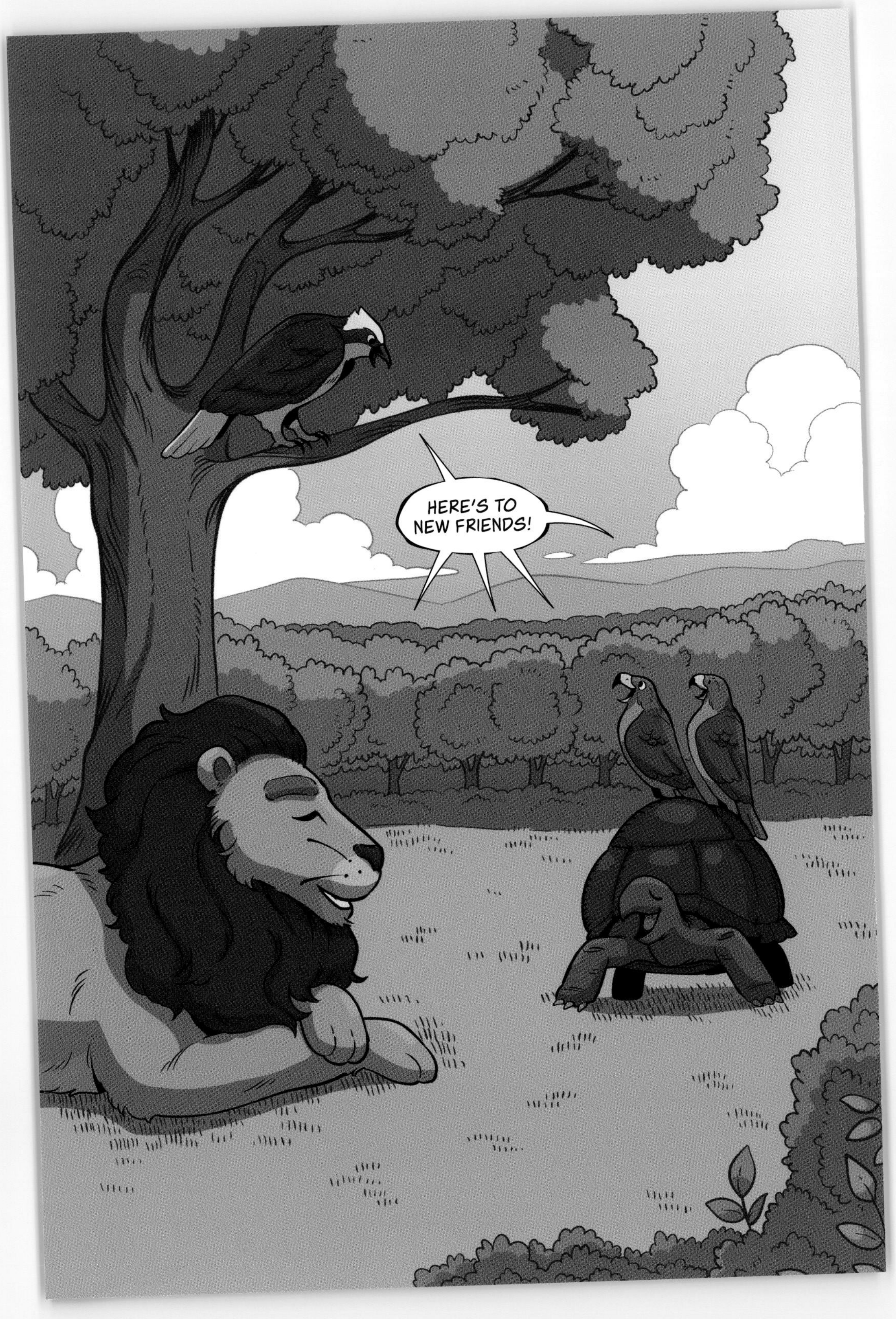
HERE'S TO NEW FRIENDS!

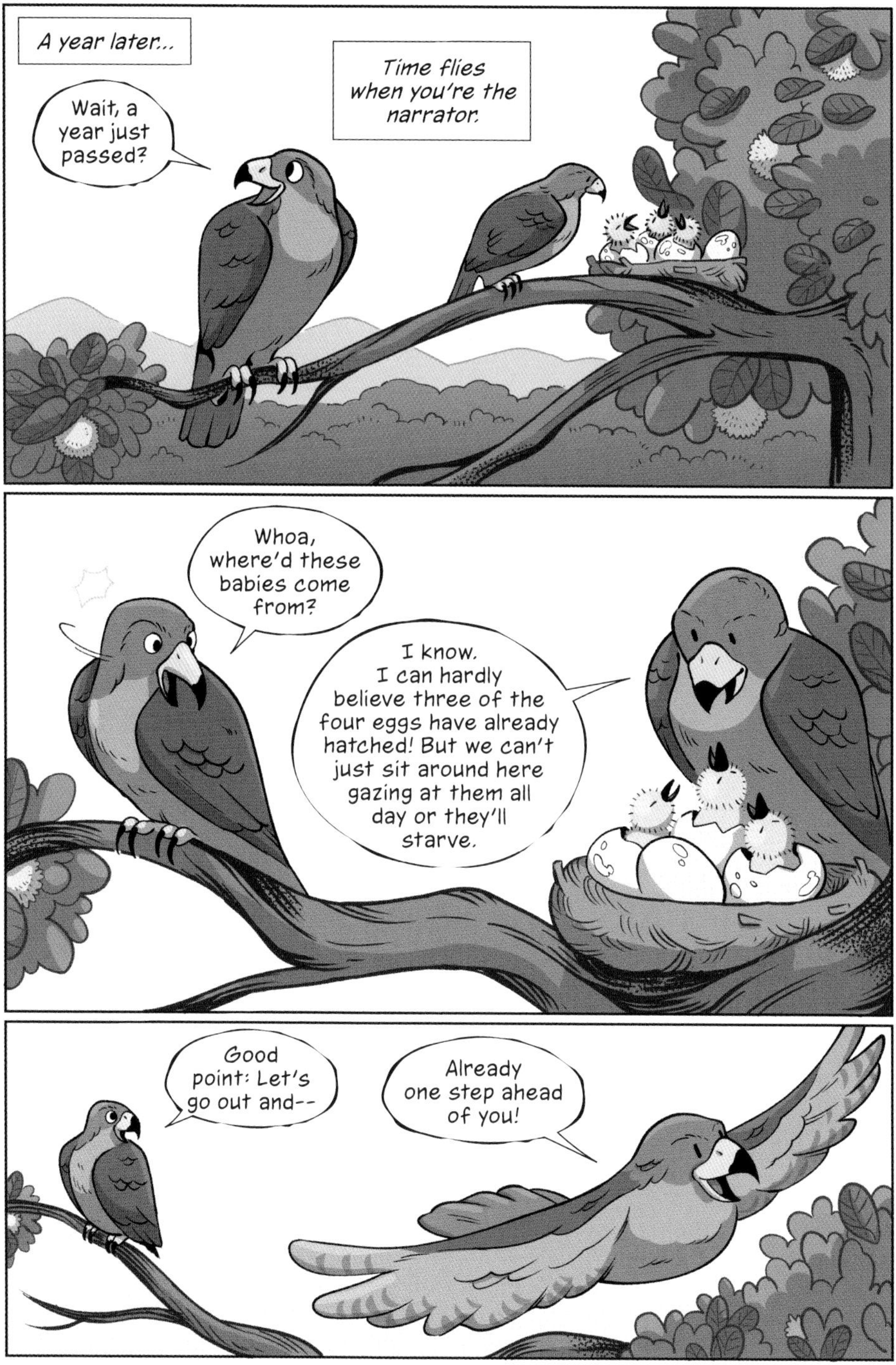
A year later...
Wait, a year just passed?
Time flies when you're the narrator.
Whoa, where'd these babies come from?
I know. I can hardly believe three of the four eggs have already hatched! But we can't just sit around here gazing at them all day or they'll starve.
Good point: Let's go out and--
Already one step ahead of you!

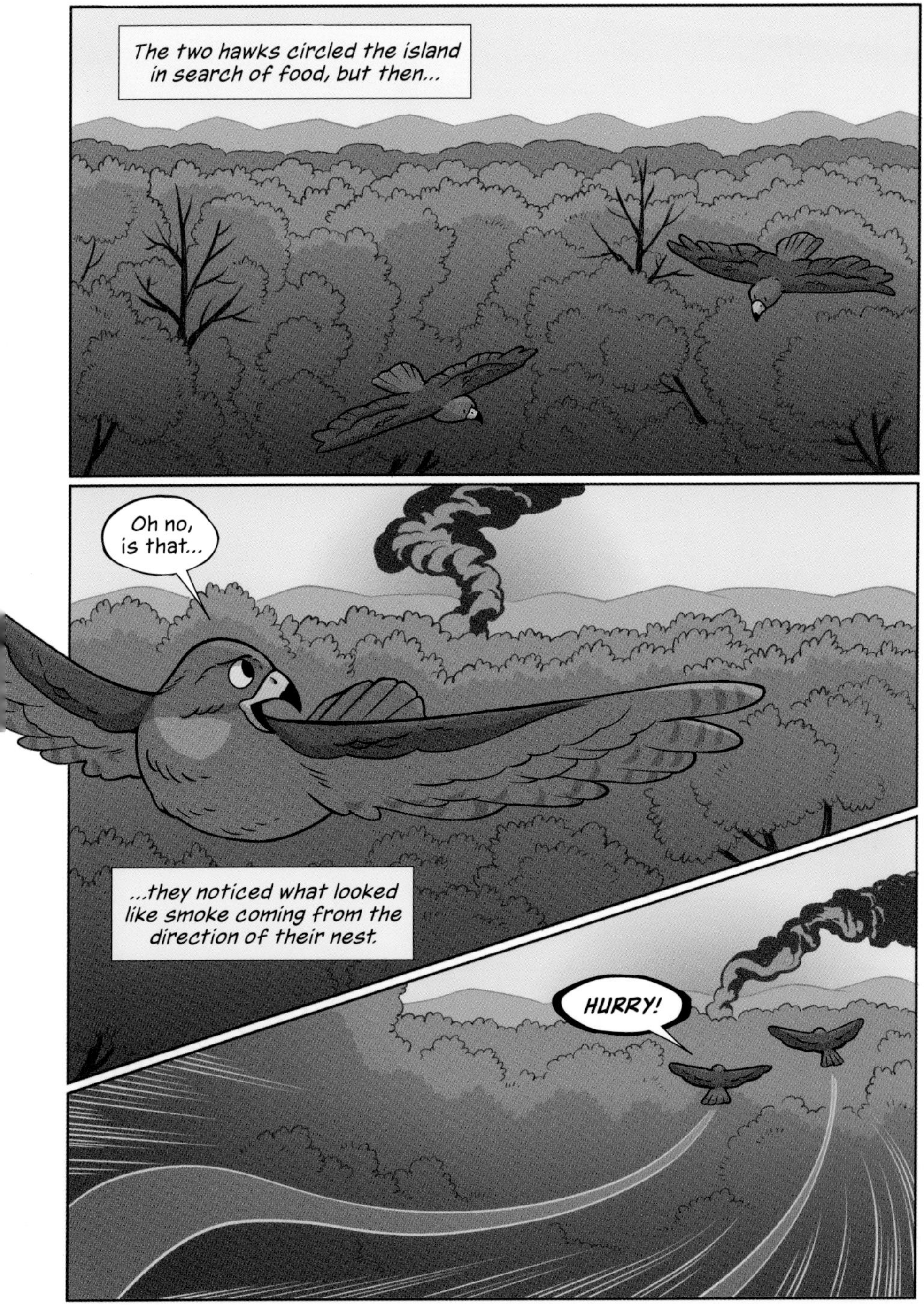
The two hawks circled the island in search of food, but then...
Oh no, is that...
...they noticed what looked like smoke coming from the direction of their nest.
HURRY!

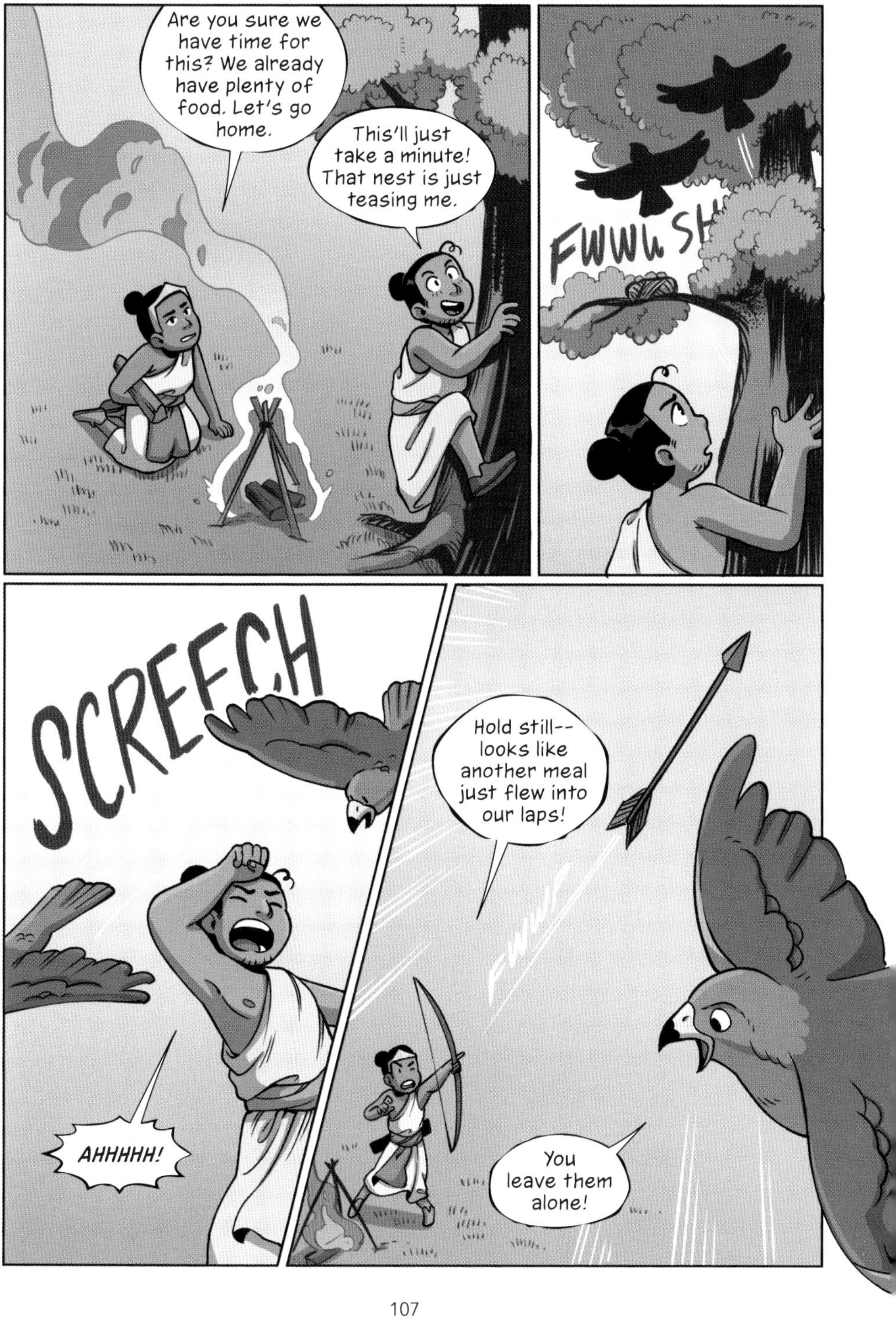
Are you sure we have time for this? We already have plenty of food. Let's go home.
This'll just take a minute! That nest is just teasing me.
FWWUSH
SCREECH
AHHHHH!
Hold still-- looks like another meal just flew into our laps!
FWWP
You leave them alone!

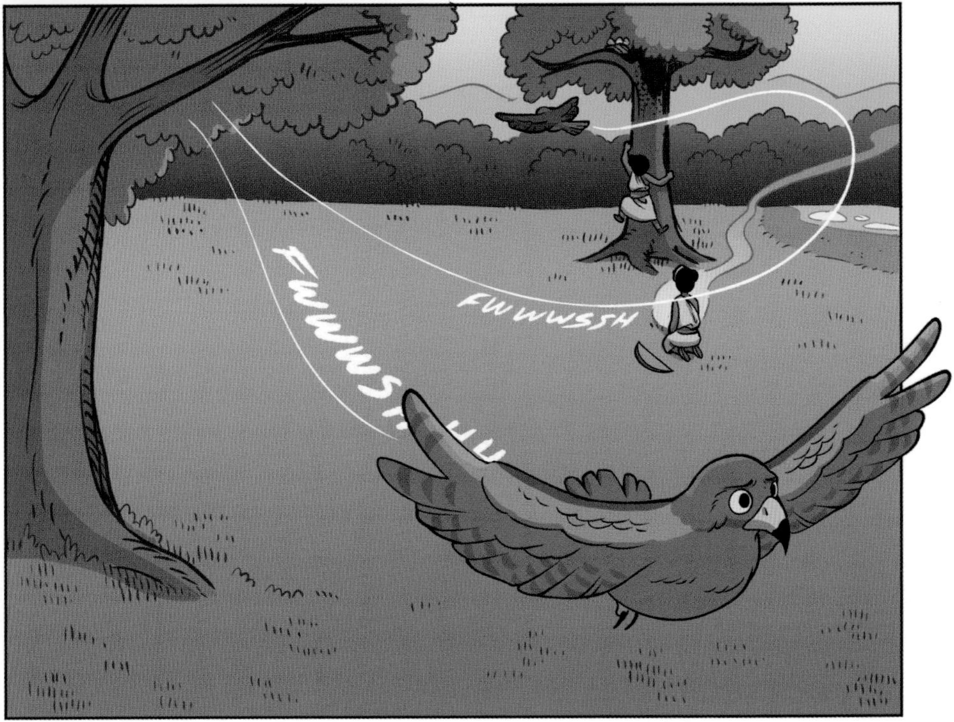
FWWWSSH

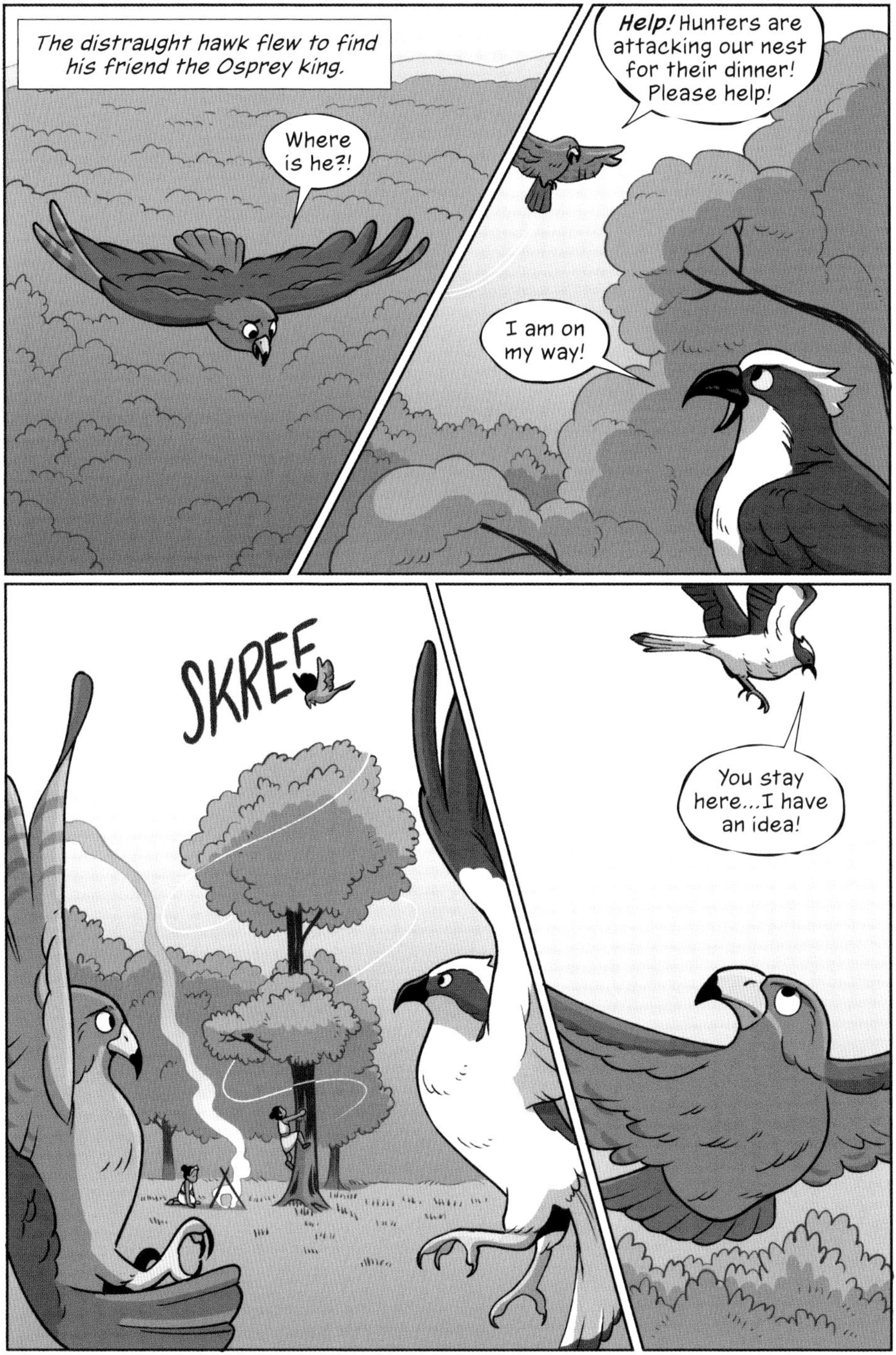
The distraught hawk flew to find his friend the Osprey king.
Where is he?!
Help! Hunters are attacking our nest for their dinner! Please help!
I am on my way!
SKREE
You stay here...I have an idea!

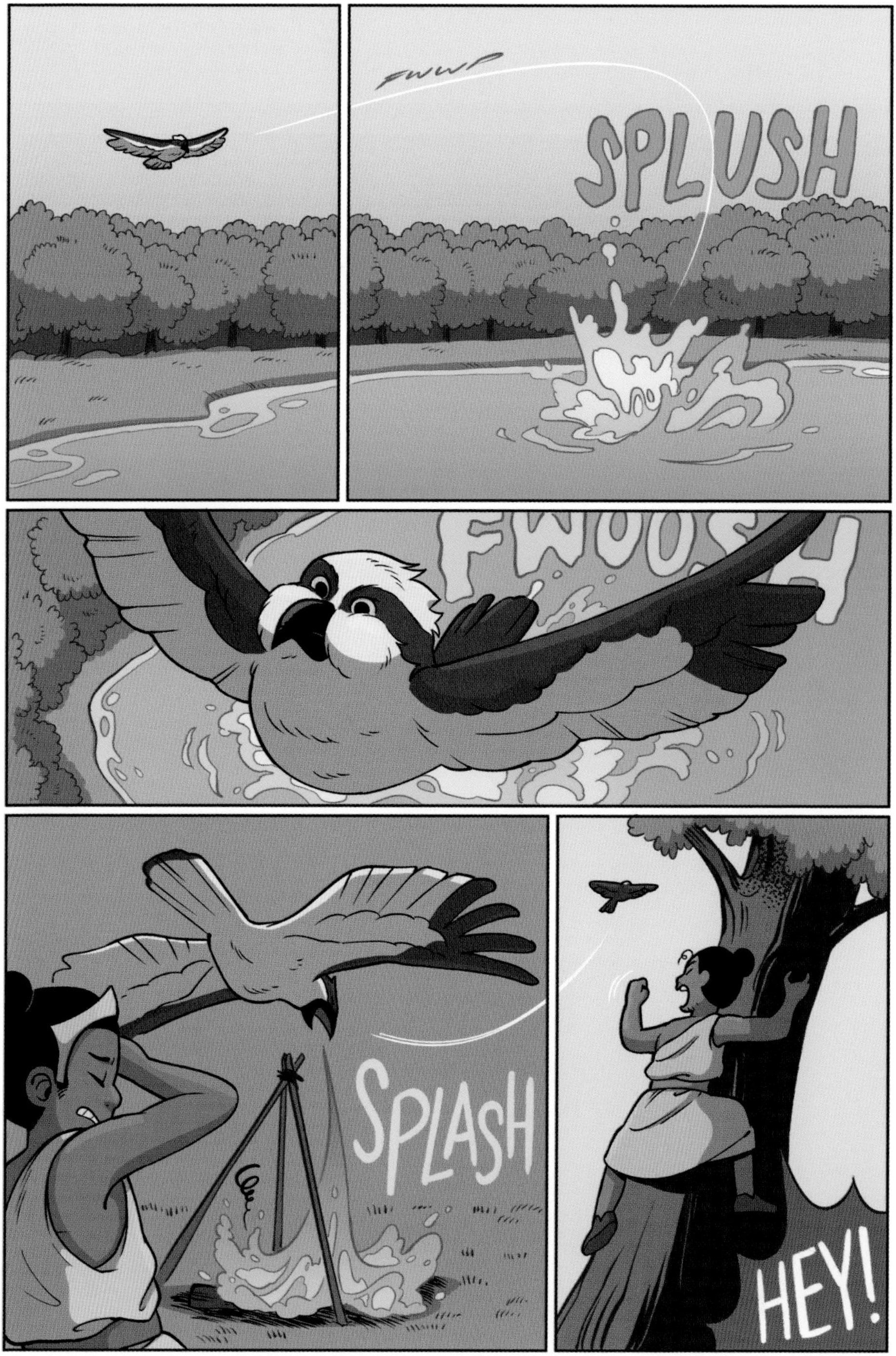
FWWP
SPLUSH
FWOOSH
SPLASH
HEY!

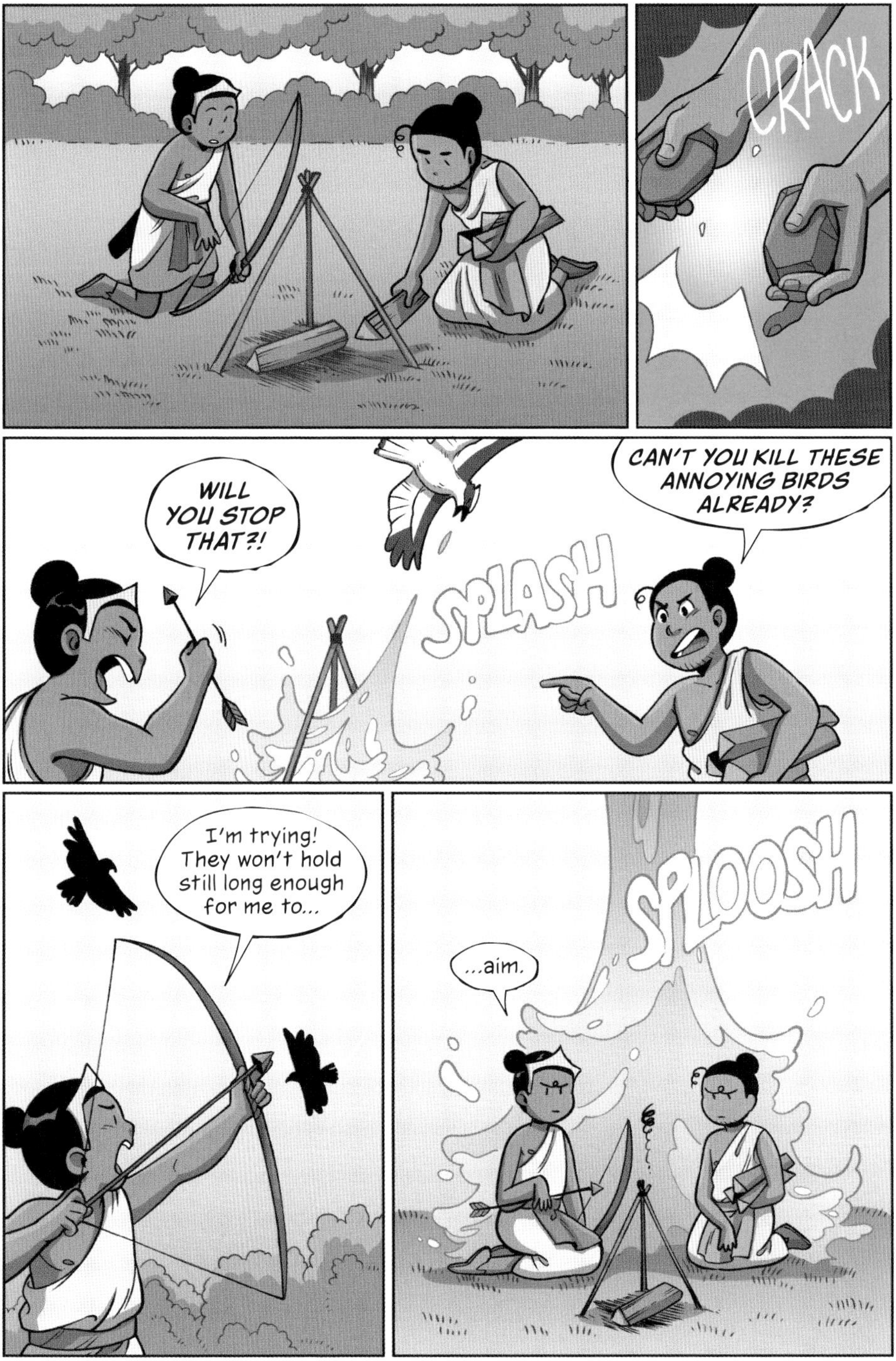
CRACK
WILL YOU STOP THAT?!
CAN'T YOU KILL THESE ANNOYING BIRDS ALREADY?
SPLASH
I'm trying! They won't hold still long enough for me to...
SPLOOSH
...aim.

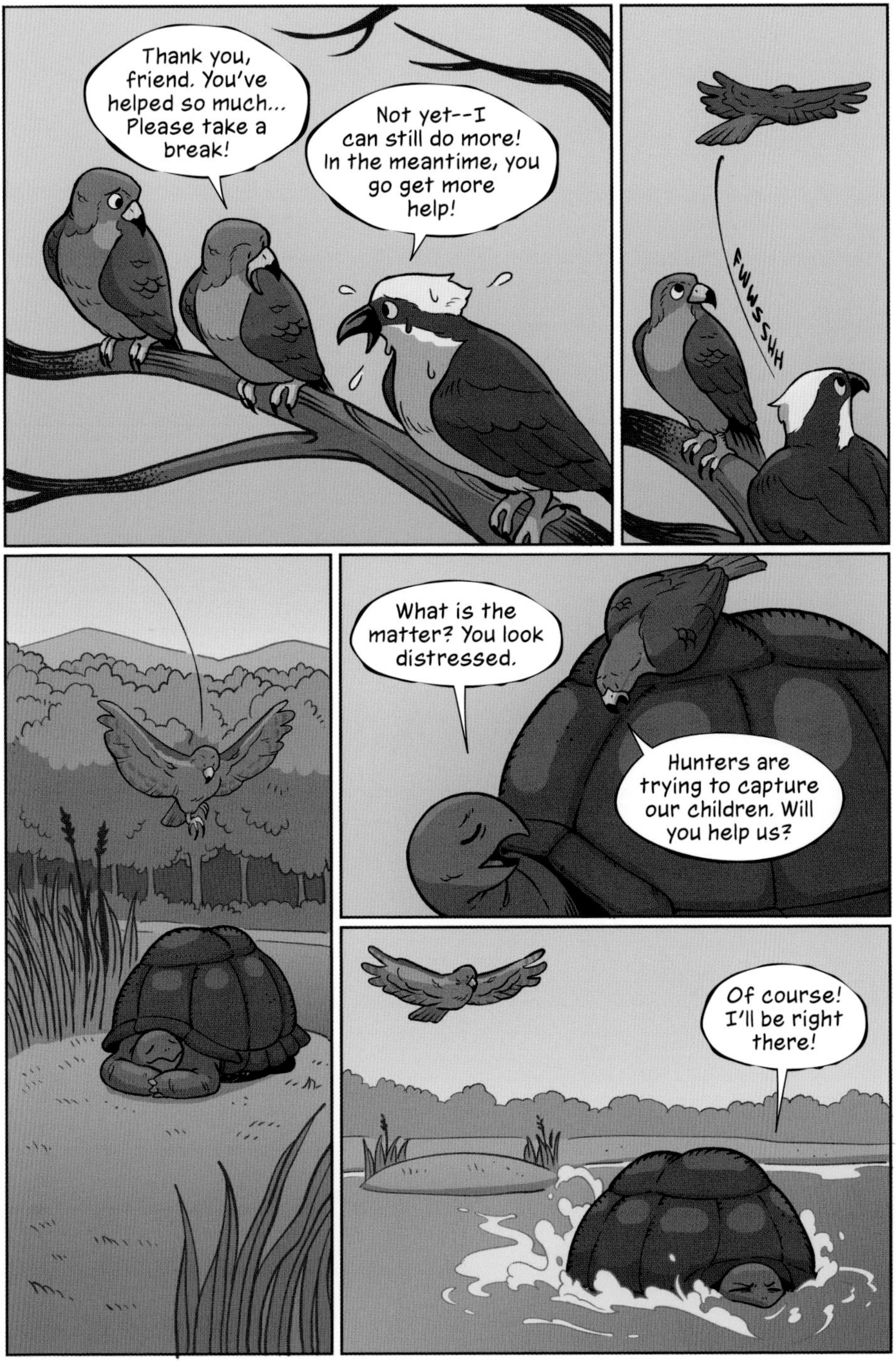
Thank you, friend. You've helped so much... Please take a break!
Not yet--I can still do more! In the meantime, you go get more help!
FWWSSHH
What is the matter? You look distressed.
Hunters are trying to capture our children. Will you help us?
Of course! I'll be right there!

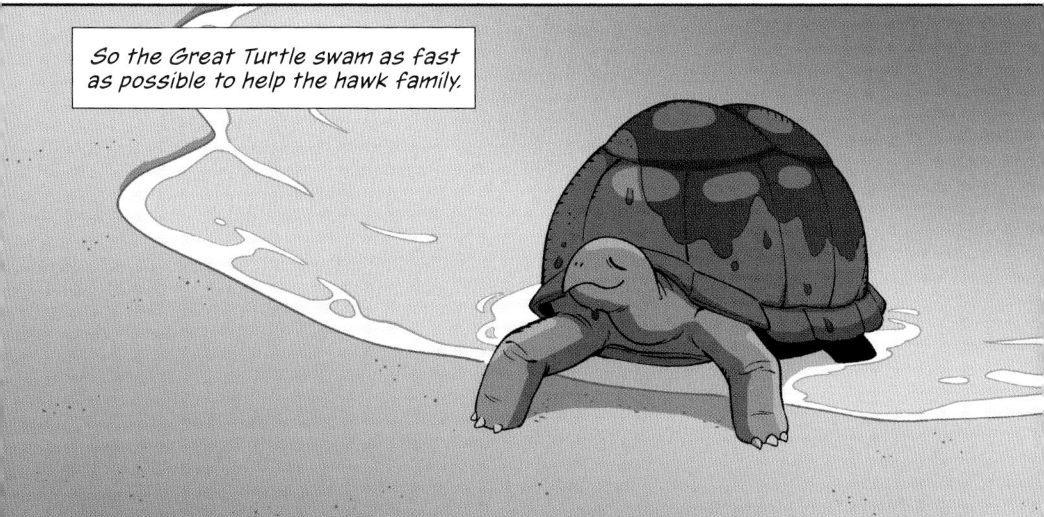
So the Great Turtle swam as fast as possible to help the hawk family.

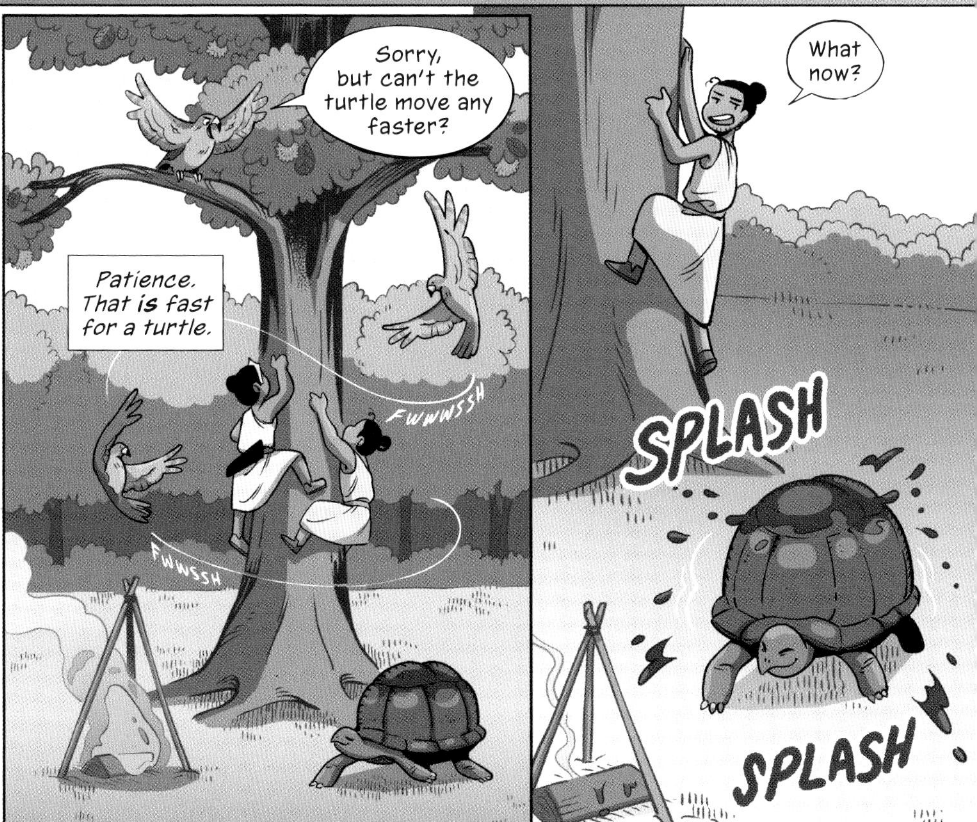
Sorry, but can't the turtle move any faster?
Patience. That **is** fast for a turtle.
FWWWSSH
FWWSSH
What now?
SPLASH
SPLASH

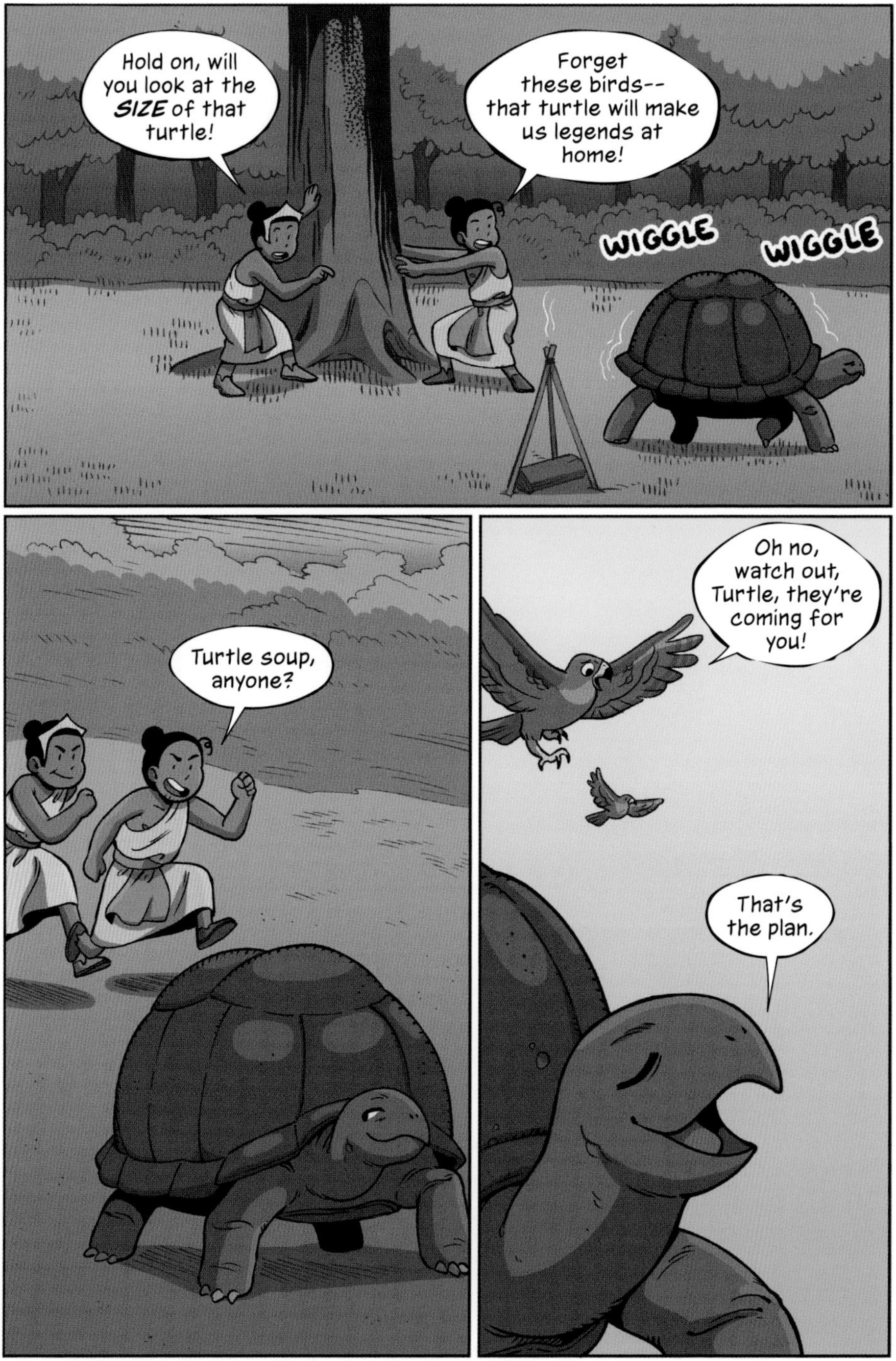
Hold on, will you look at the *SIZE* of that turtle!
Forget these birds--that turtle will make us legends at home!
WIGGLE
WIGGLE
Turtle soup, anyone?
Oh no, watch out, Turtle, they're coming for you!
That's the plan.

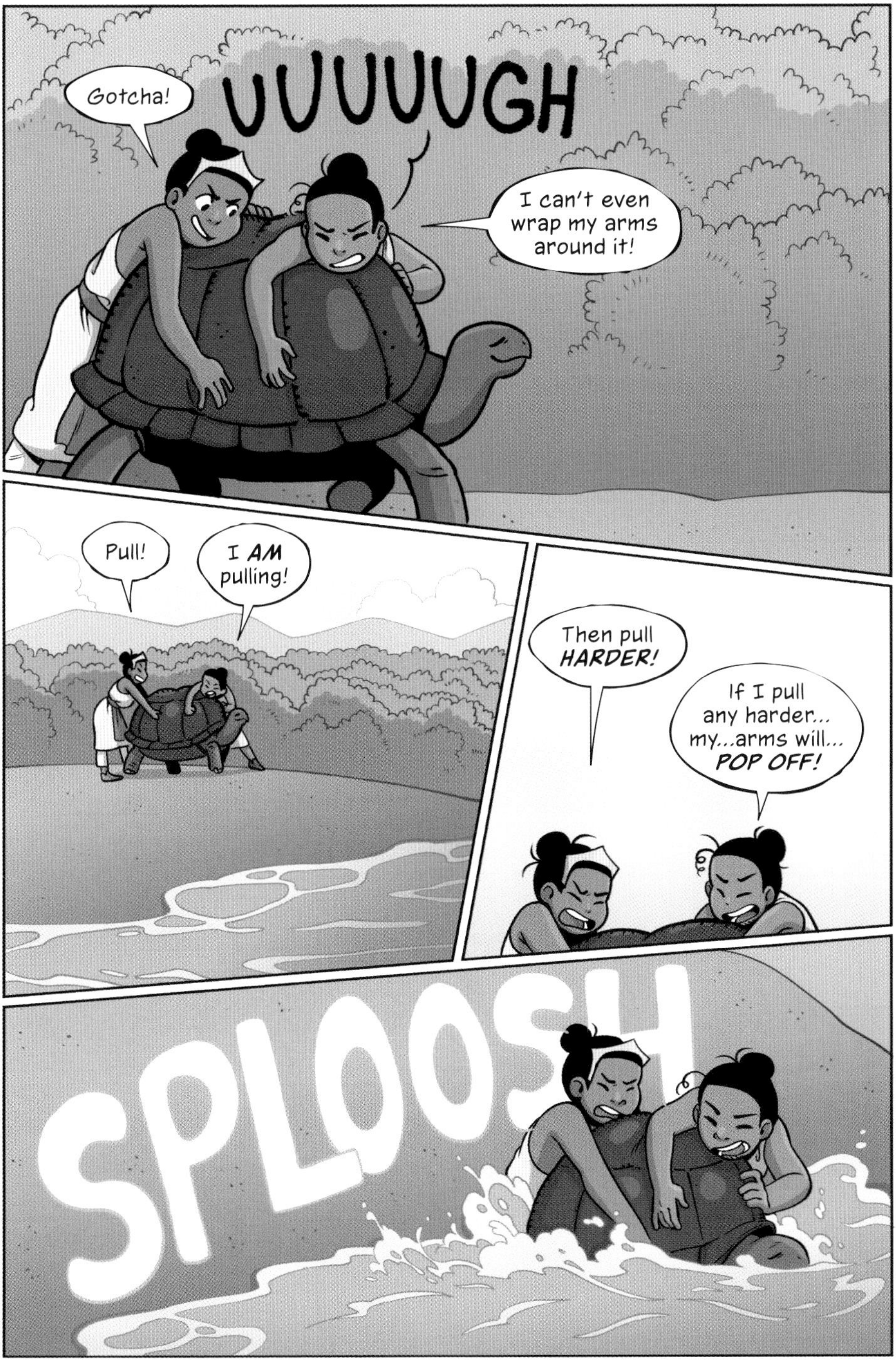
Gotcha!
UUUUUGH
I can't even wrap my arms around it!
Pull!
I **AM** pulling!
Then pull **HARDER!**
If I pull any harder... my...arms will... **POP OFF!**
SPLOOSH

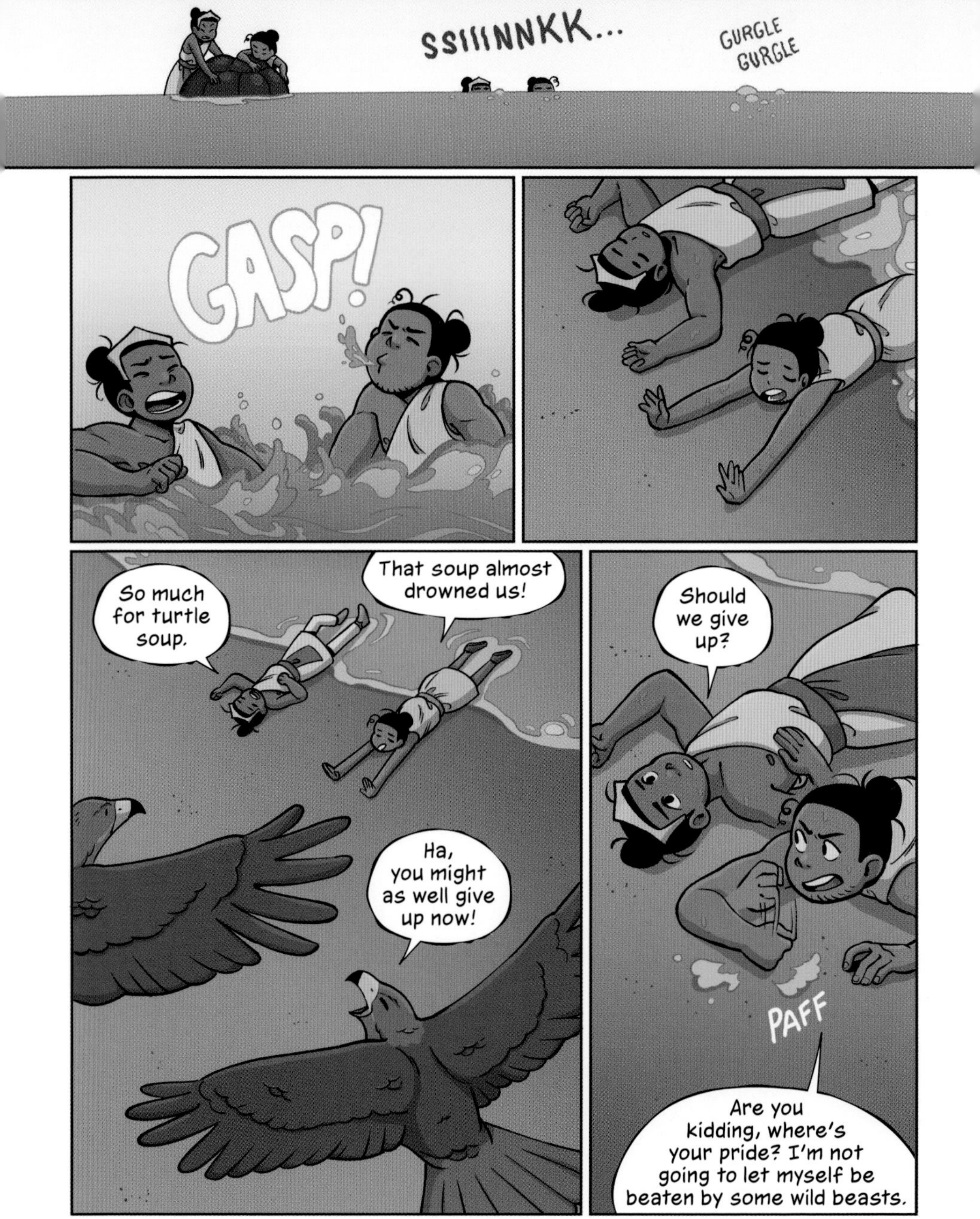
SSIIINNKK...
GURGLE GURGLE
GASP!
So much for turtle soup.
That soup almost drowned us!
Ha, you might as well give up now!
Should we give up?
PAFF
Are you kidding, where's your pride? I'm not going to let myself be beaten by some wild beasts.

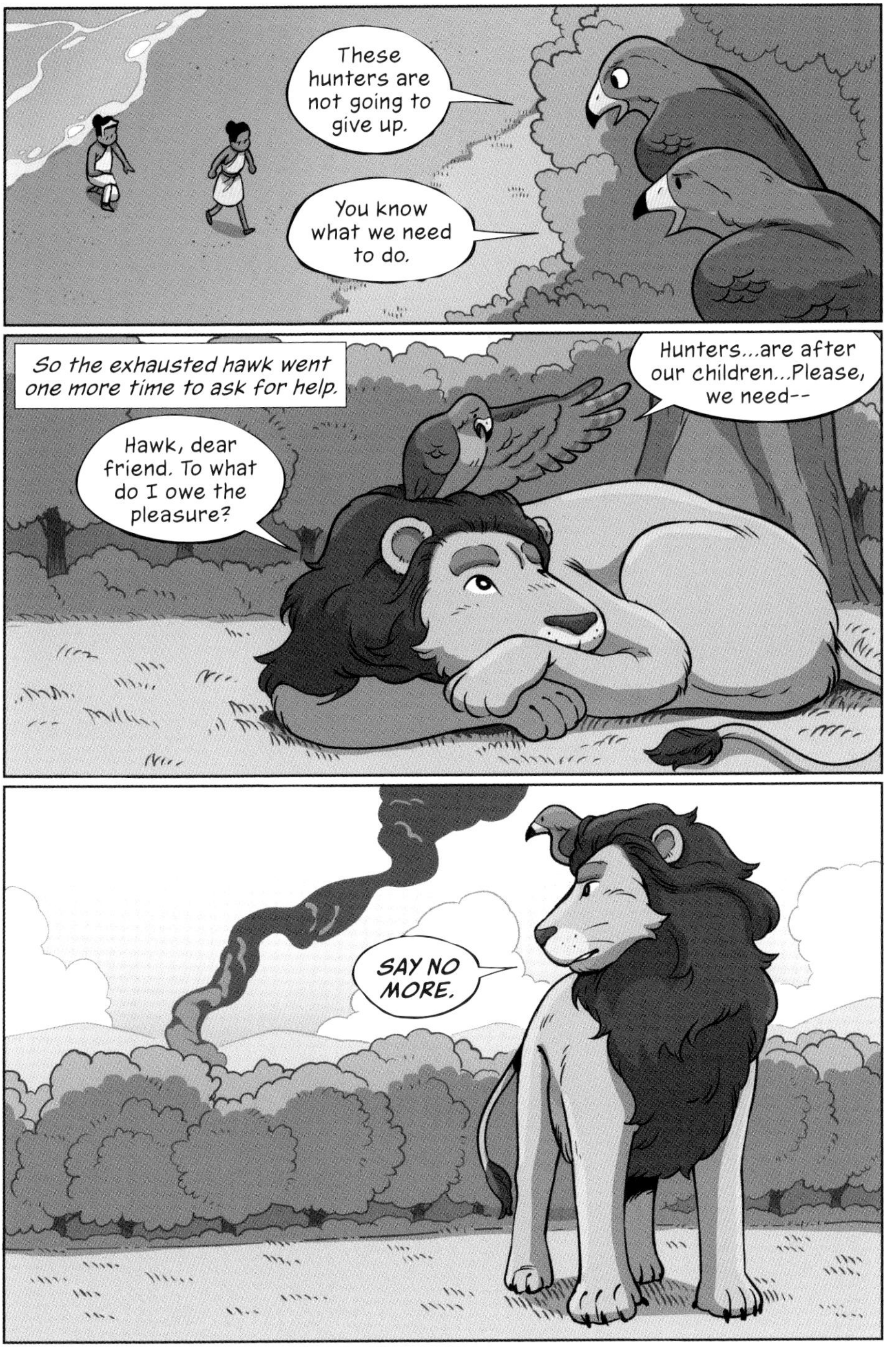
These hunters are not going to give up.
You know what we need to do.
So the exhausted hawk went one more time to ask for help.
Hunters...are after our children...Please, we need--
Hawk, dear friend. To what do I owe the pleasure?
SAY NO MORE.

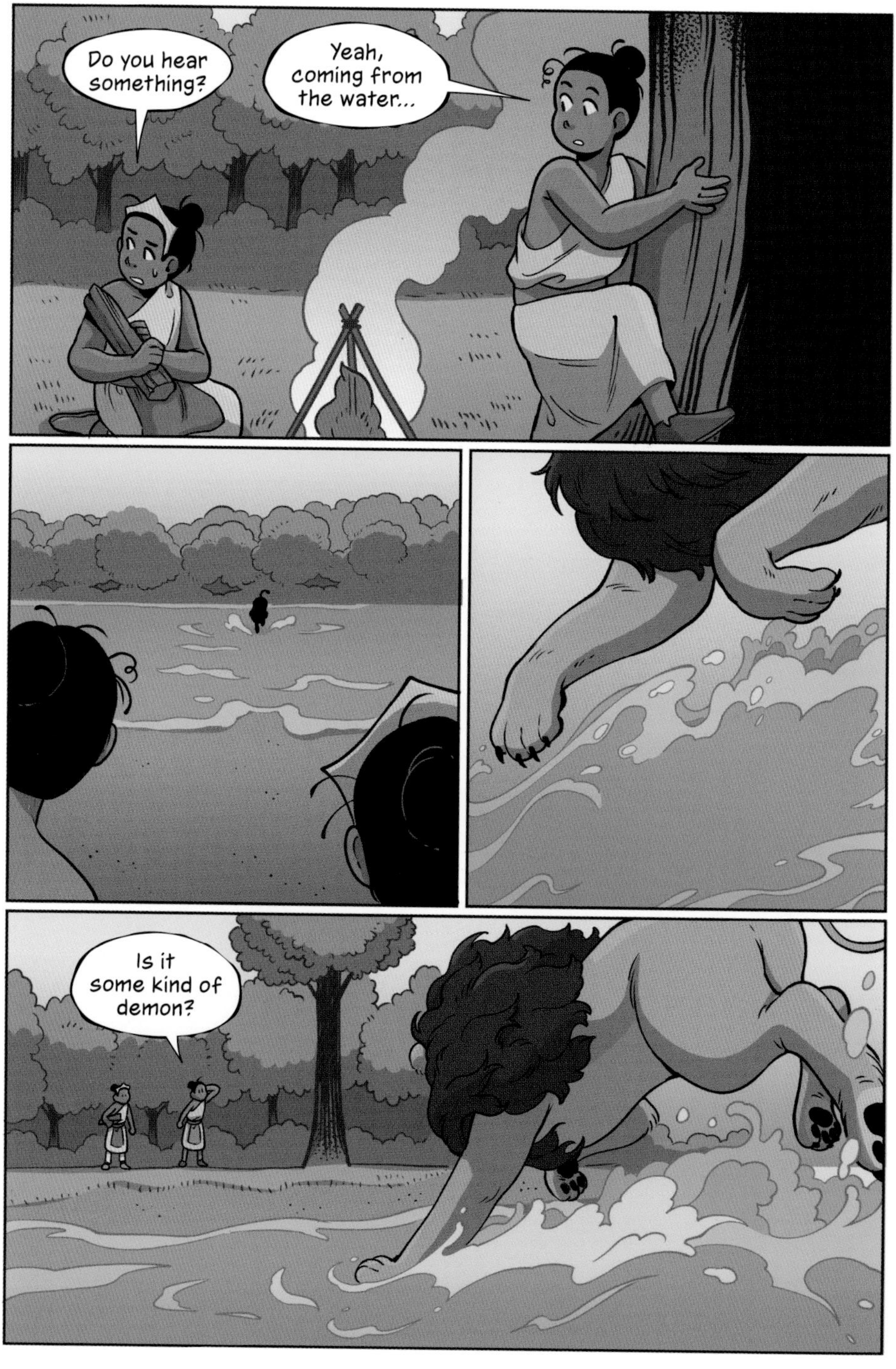
Do you hear something?
Yeah, coming from the water...
Is it some kind of demon?

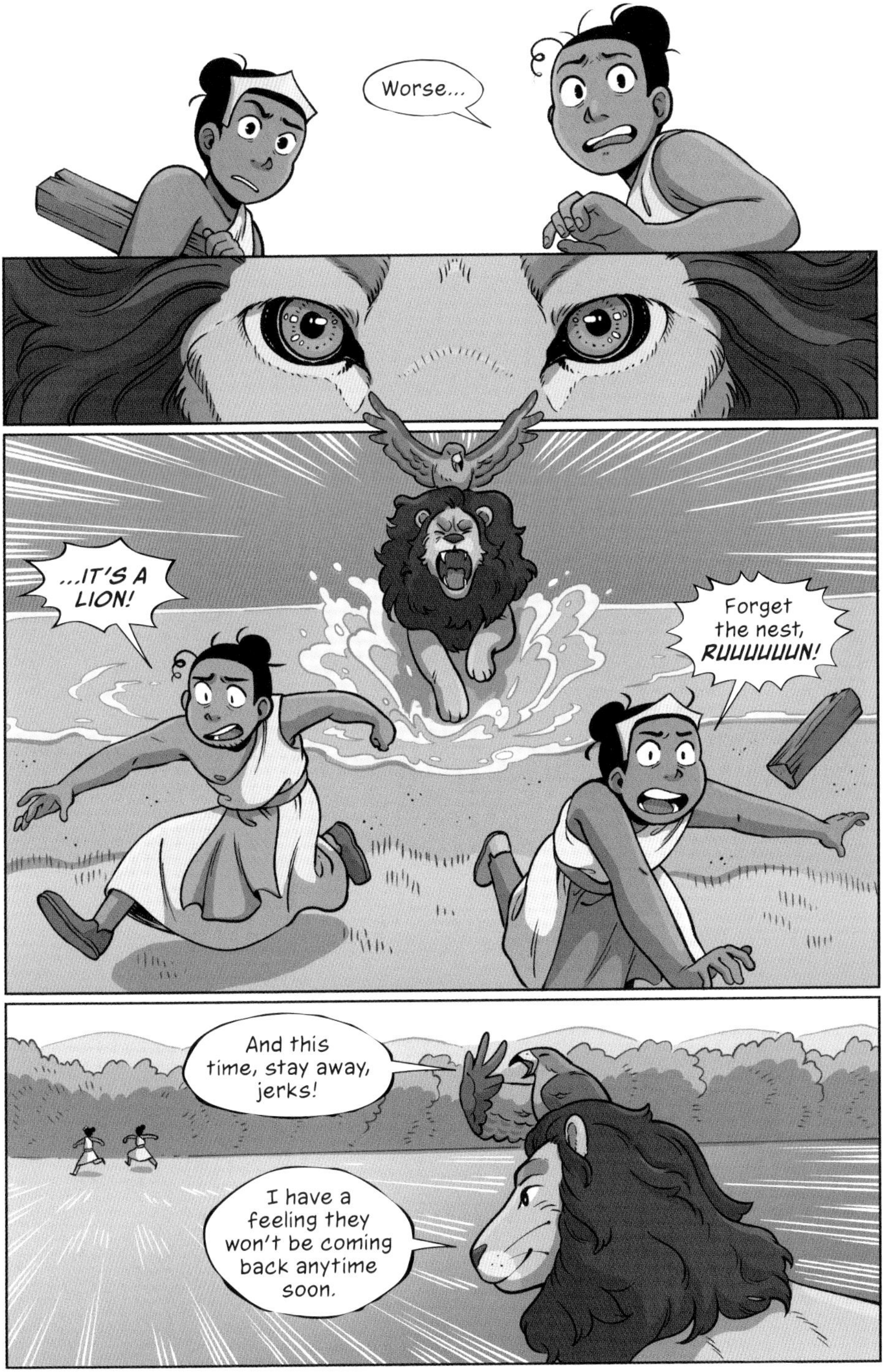
Worse...
...IT'S A LION!
Forget the nest, RUUUUUUN!
And this time, stay away, jerks!
I have a feeling they won't be coming back anytime soon.

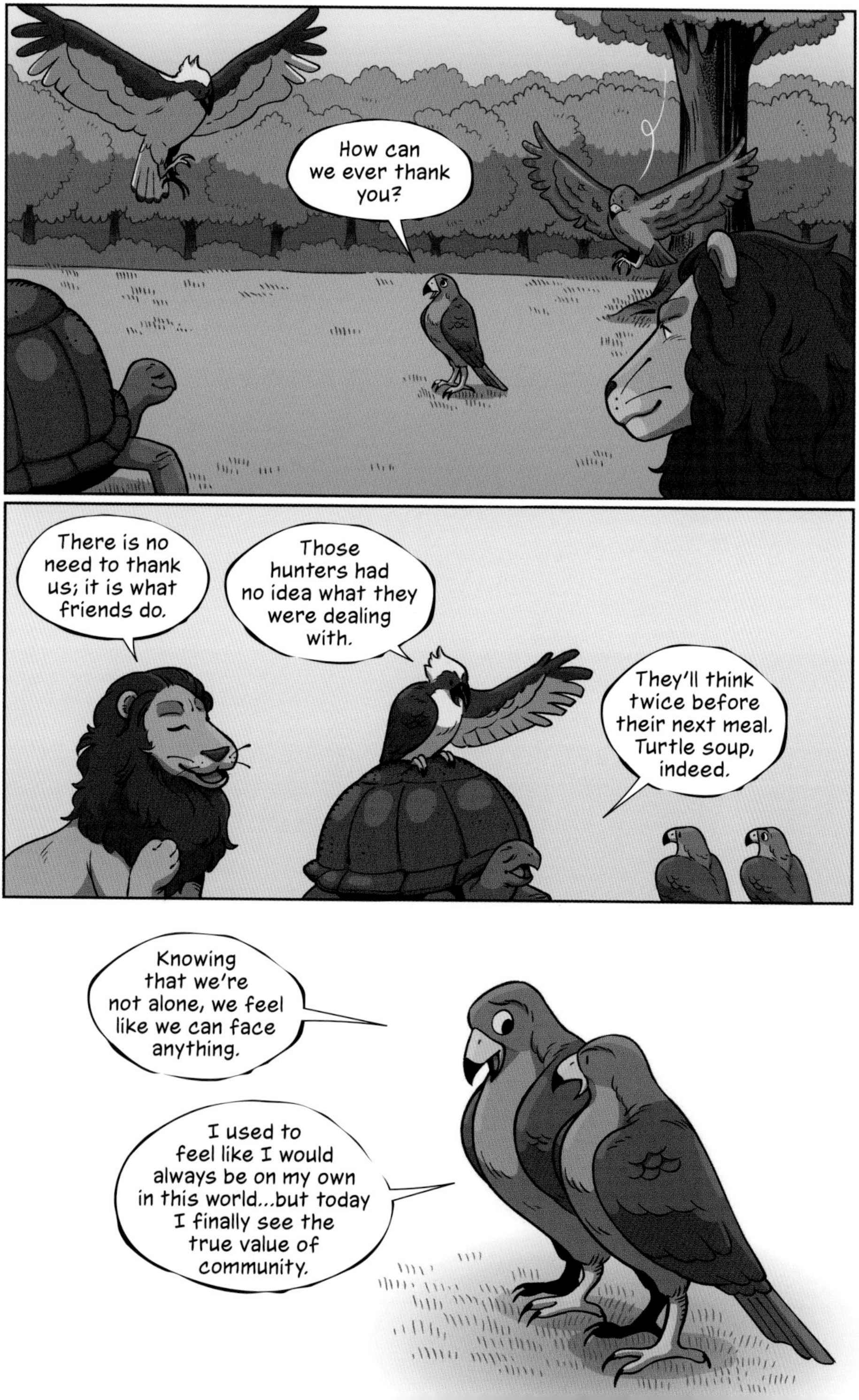
How can we ever thank you?
There is no need to thank us; it is what friends do.
Those hunters had no idea what they were dealing with.
They'll think twice before their next meal. Turtle soup, indeed.
Knowing that we're not alone, we feel like we can face anything.
I used to feel like I would always be on my own in this world...but today I finally see the true value of community.

CRAAACK CRAAACK

Listen, do you hear that?

The last egg is hatching!

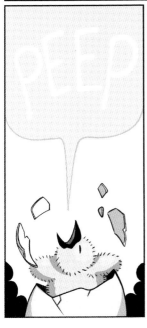

PEEP

AWWWWWWWWww

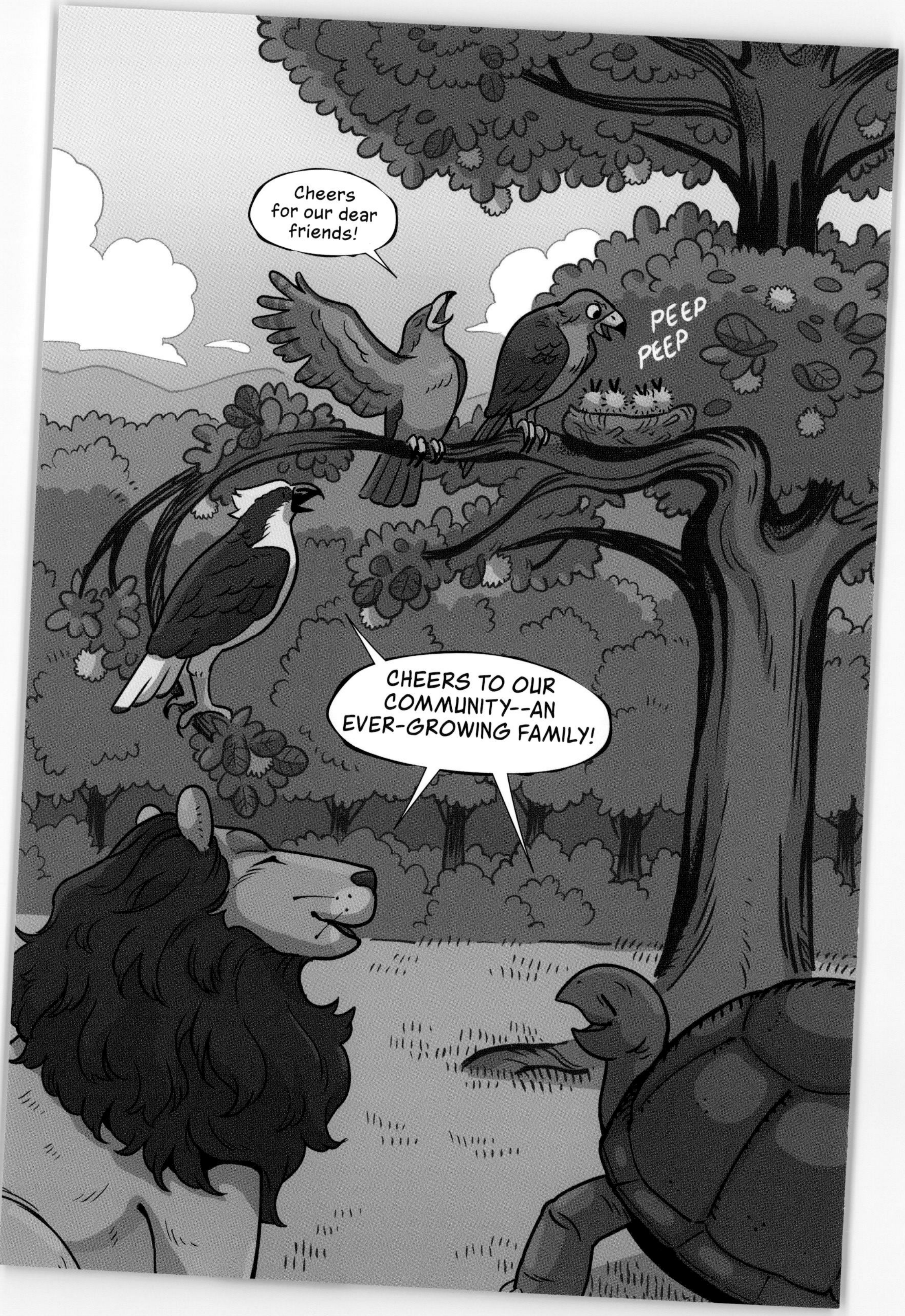
Cheers for our dear friends!
PEEP PEEP
CHEERS TO OUR COMMUNITY--AN EVER-GROWING FAMILY!

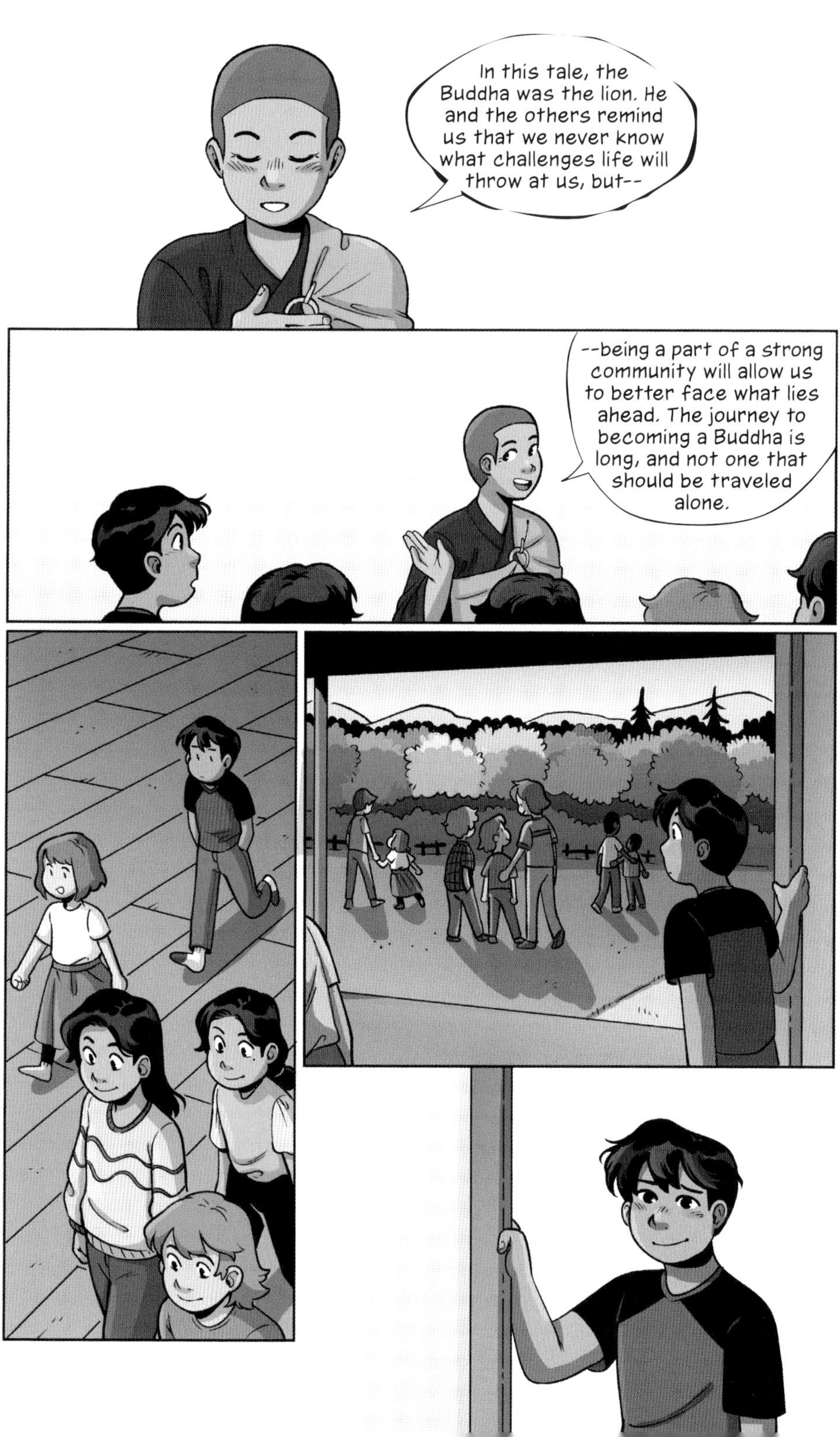
In this tale, the Buddha was the lion. He and the others remind us that we never know what challenges life will throw at us, but--
--being a part of a strong community will allow us to better face what lies ahead. The journey to becoming a Buddha is long, and not one that should be traveled alone.

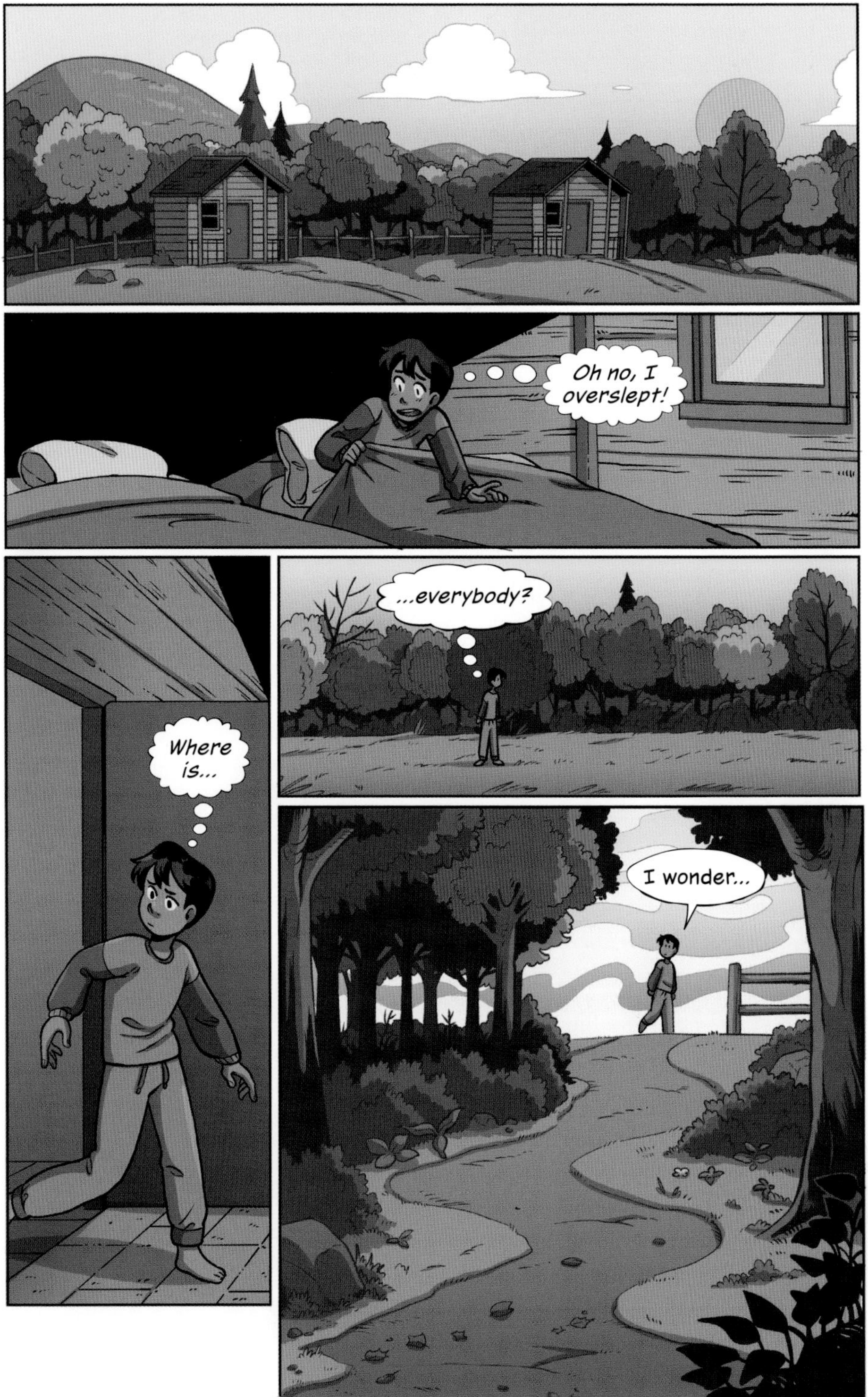
Oh no, I overslept!
Where is...
...everybody?
I wonder...

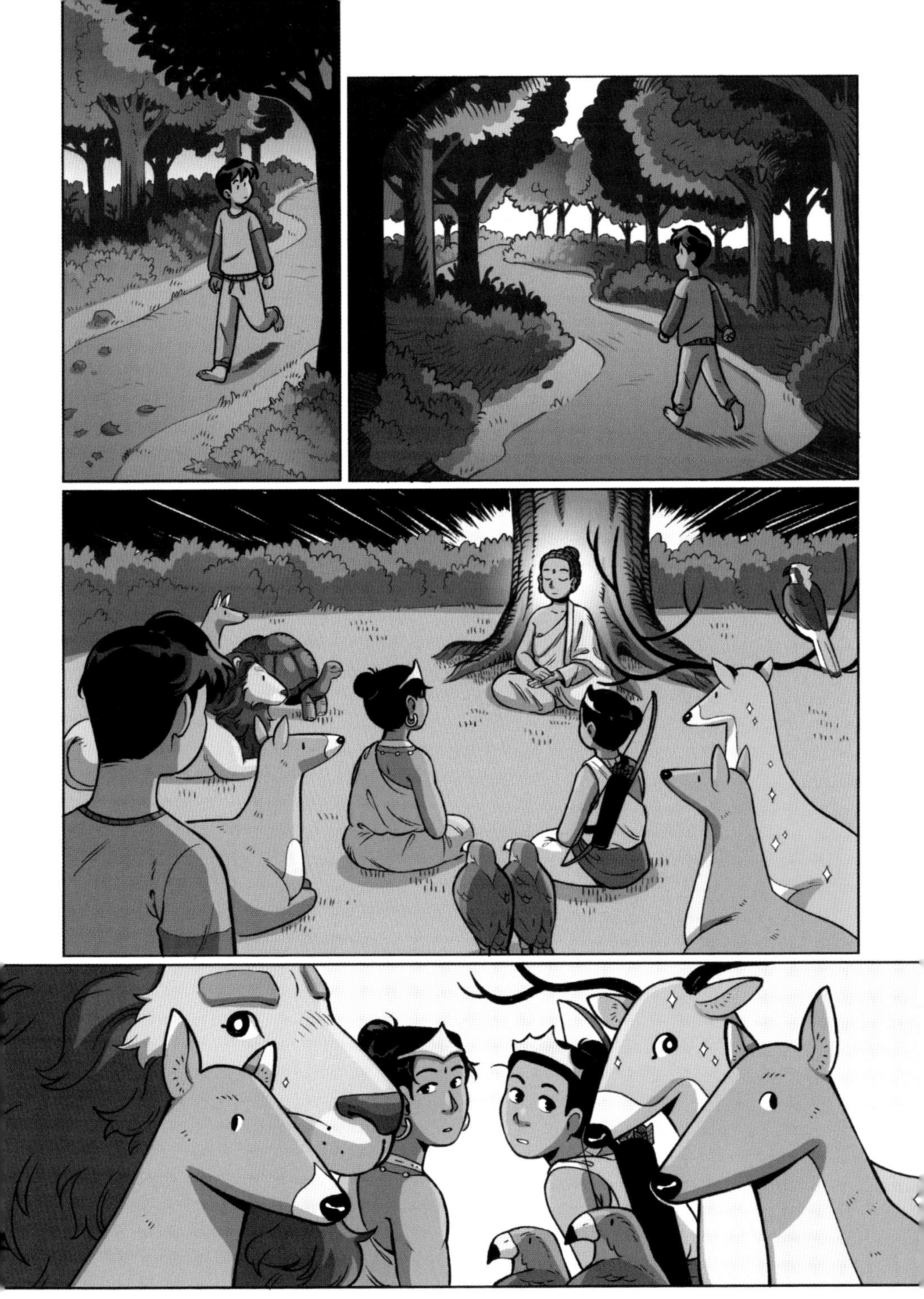

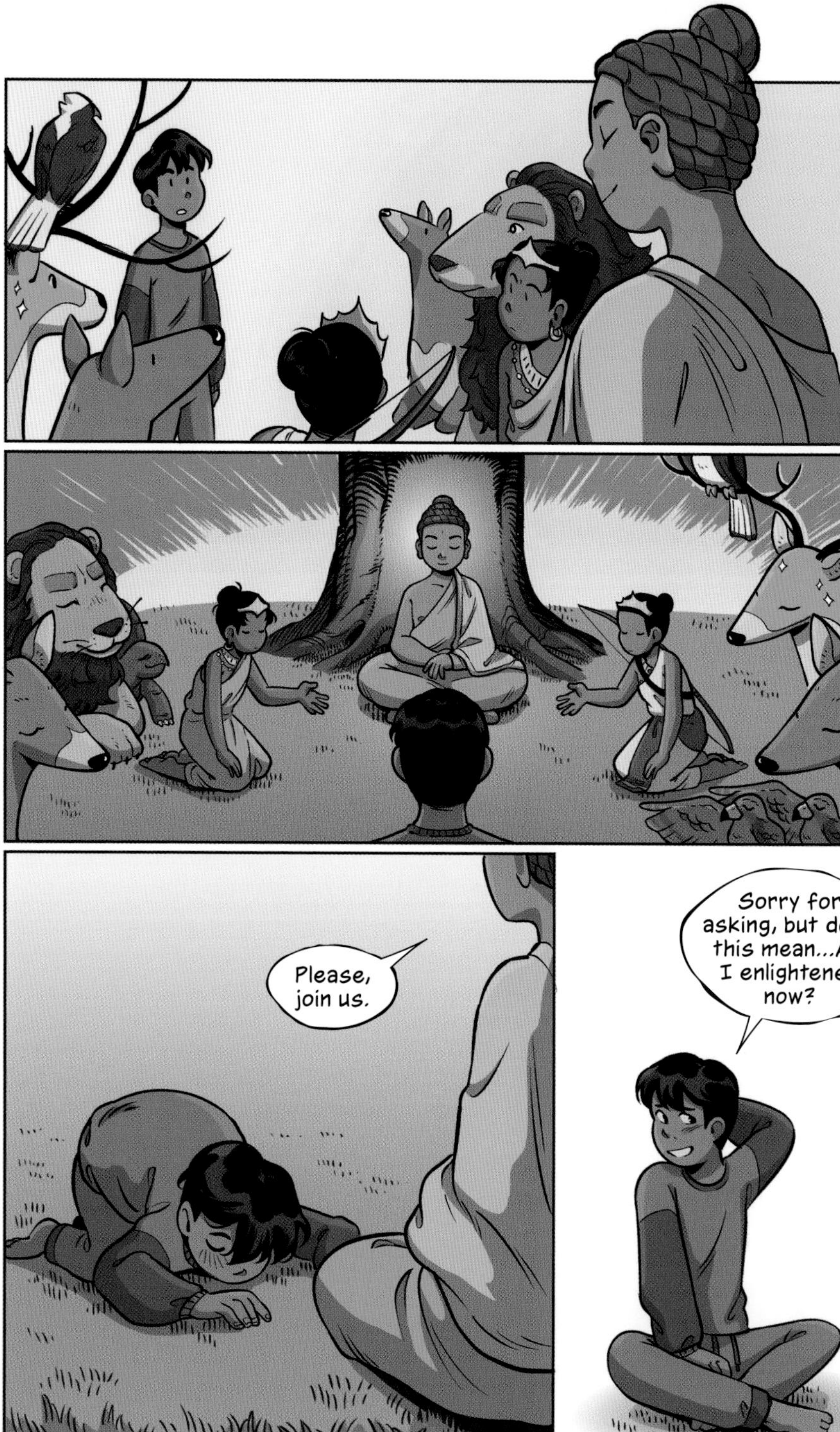
Please, join us.
Sorry for asking, but does this mean...Am I enlightened now?

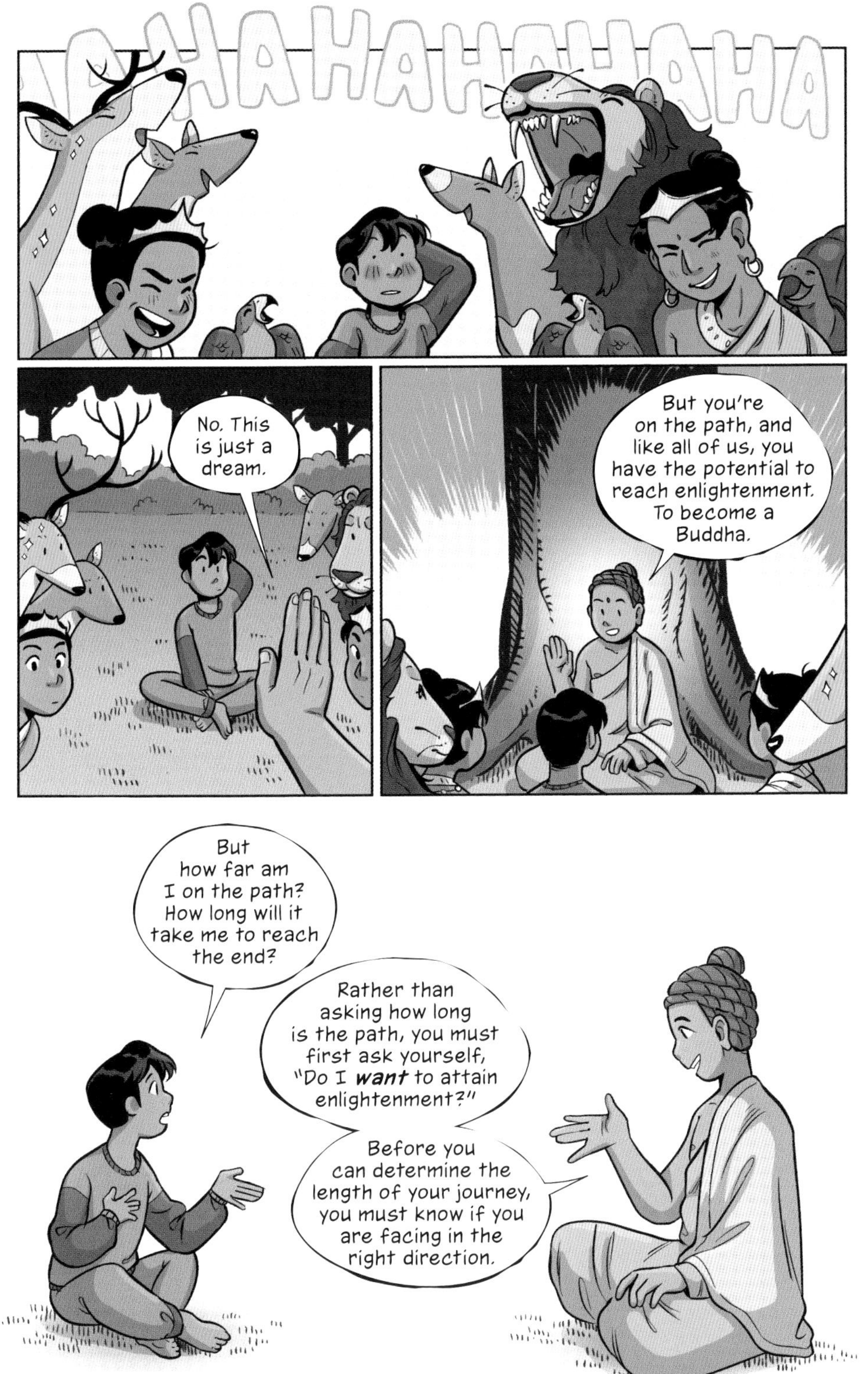
HAHAHAHAHAHA
No. This is just a dream.
But you're on the path, and like all of us, you have the potential to reach enlightenment. To become a Buddha.
But how far am I on the path? How long will it take me to reach the end?
Rather than asking how long is the path, you must first ask yourself, "Do I ***want*** to attain enlightenment?"
Before you can determine the length of your journey, you must know if you are facing in the right direction.

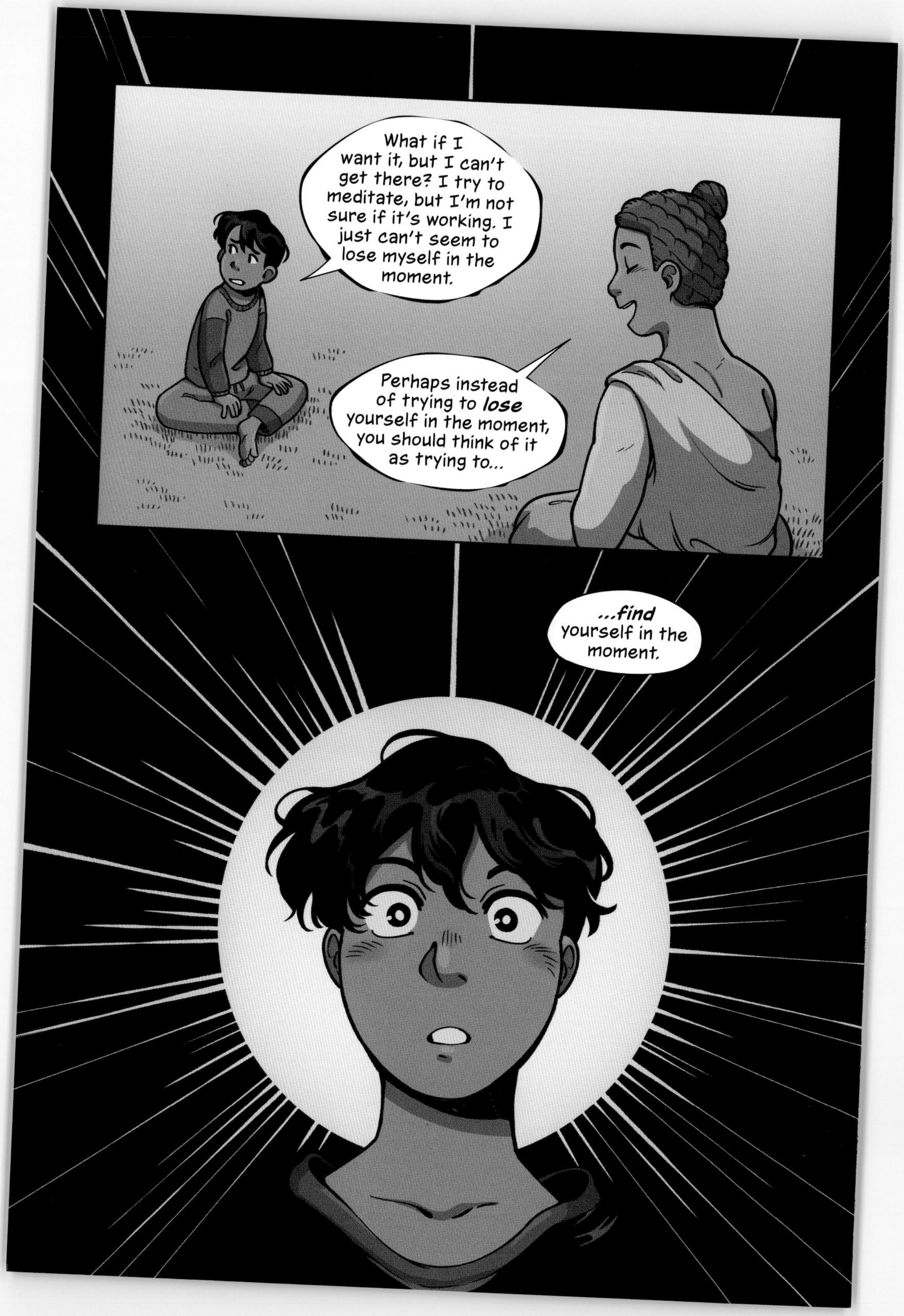

What if I want it, but I can't get there? I try to meditate, but I'm not sure if it's working. I just can't seem to lose myself in the moment.
Perhaps instead of trying to ***lose*** yourself in the moment, you should think of it as trying to...
...find yourself in the moment.

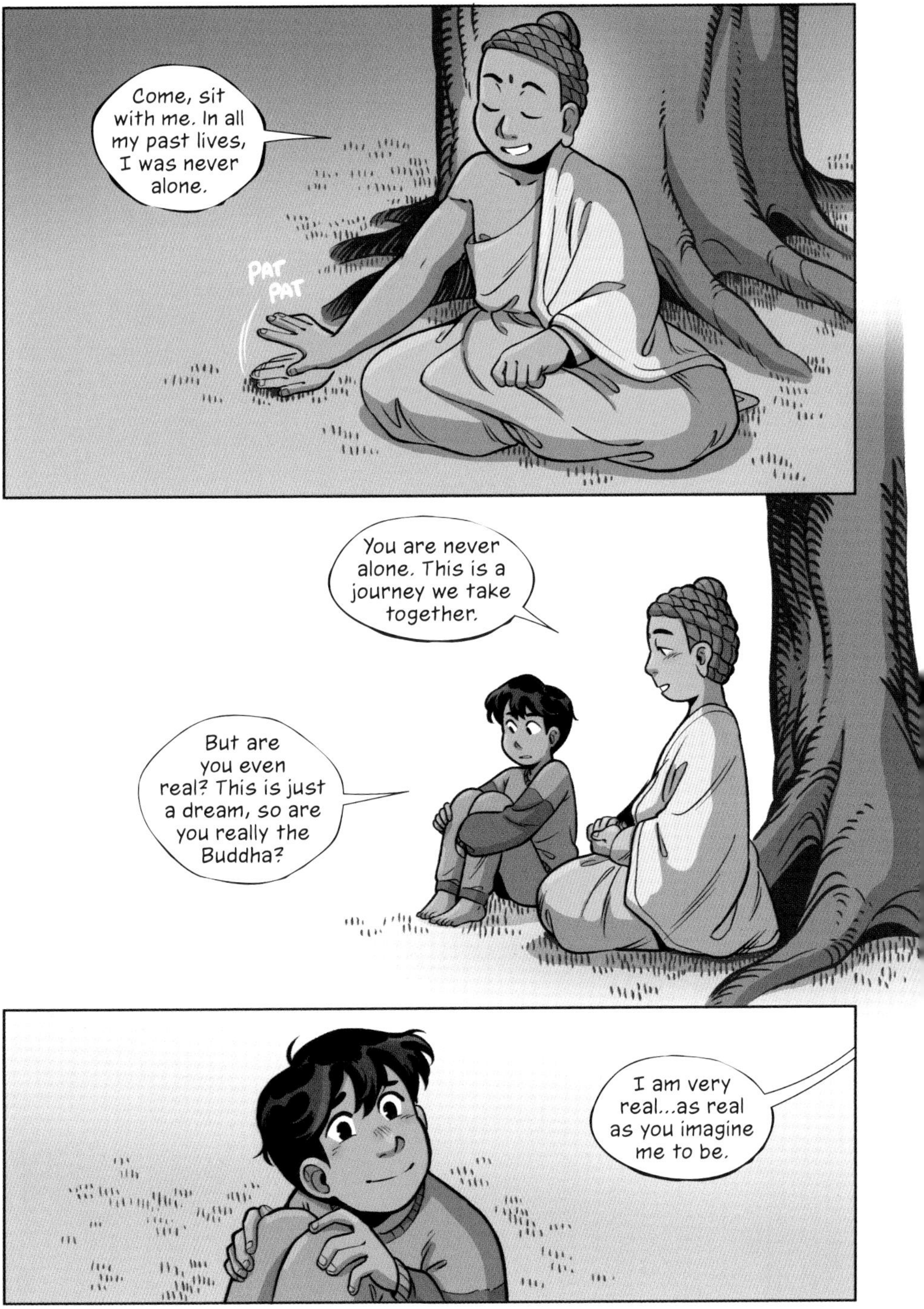
Come, sit with me. In all my past lives, I was never alone.
PAT PAT
You are never alone. This is a journey we take together.
But are you even real? This is just a dream, so are you really the Buddha?
I am very real...as real as you imagine me to be.

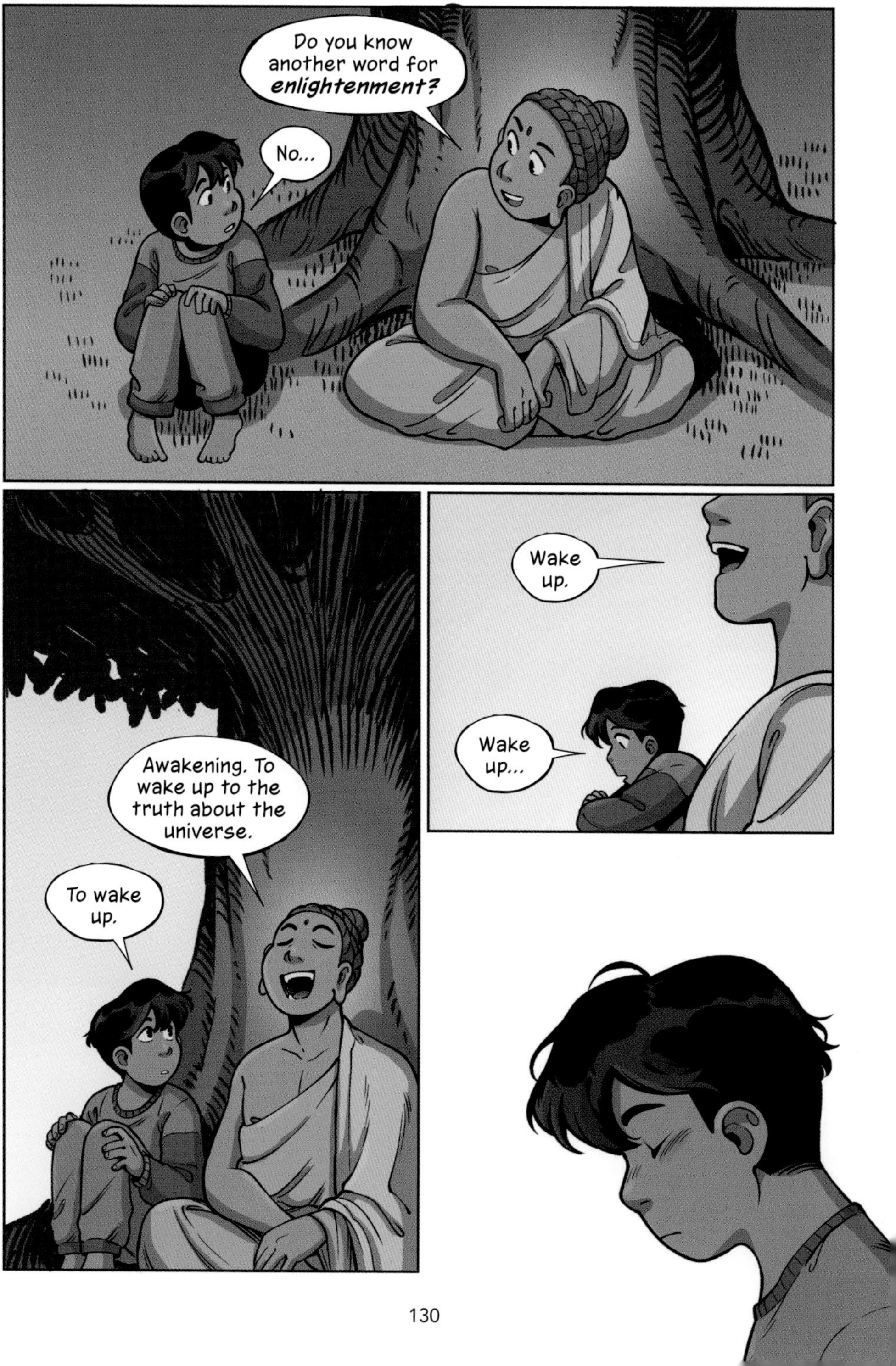

Do you know another word for *enlightenment?*
No...
Awakening. To wake up to the truth about the universe.
To wake up.
Wake up.
Wake up...

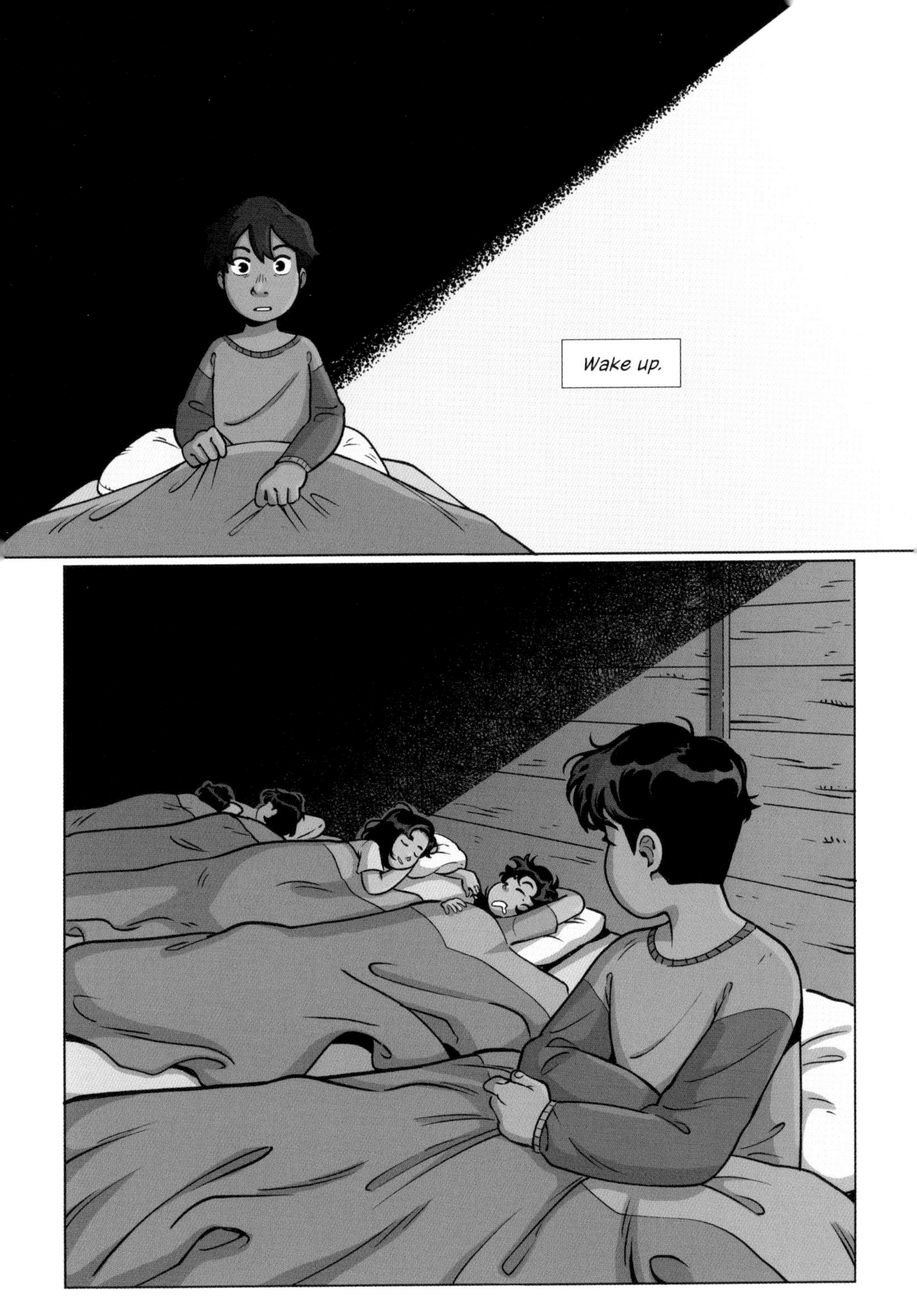
Wake up.

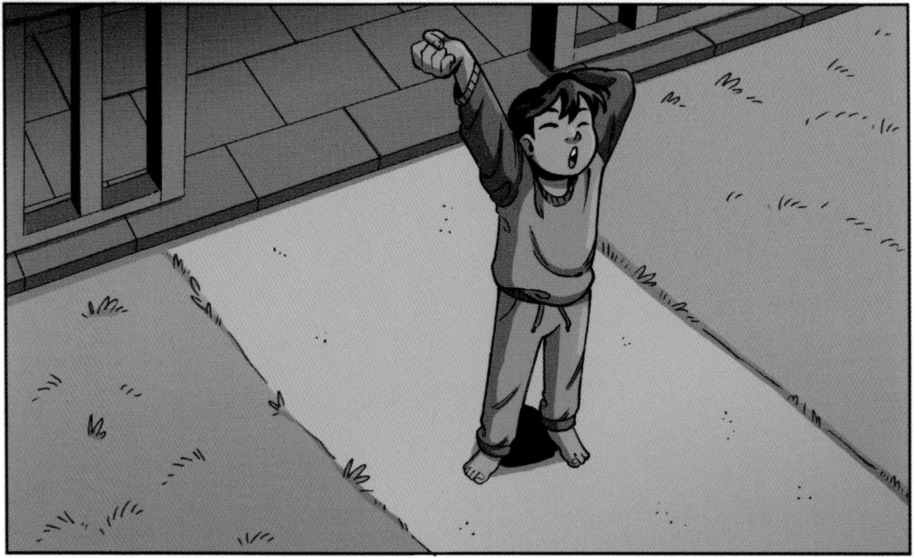

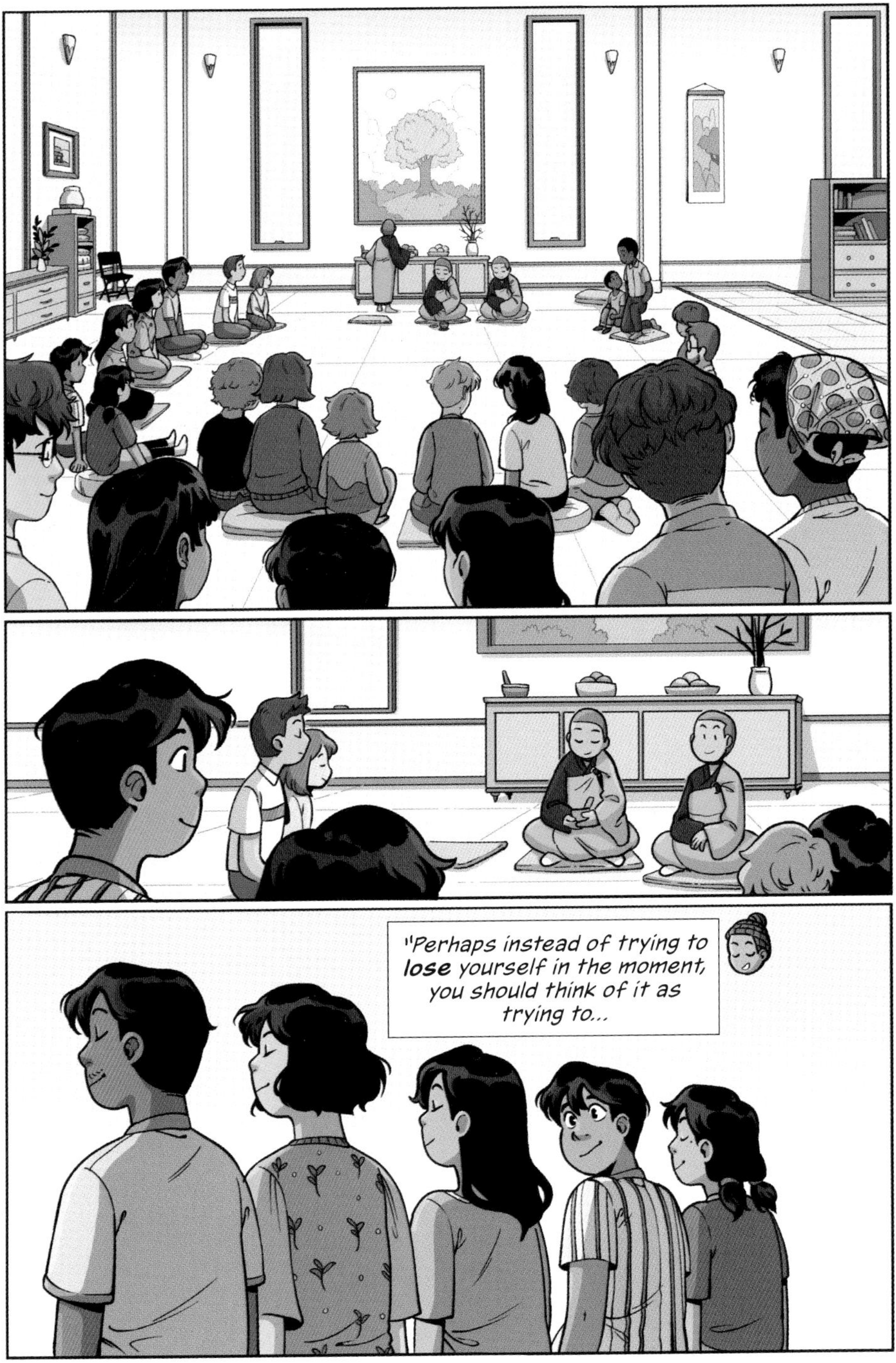
"Perhaps instead of trying to **lose** yourself in the moment, you should think of it as trying to...

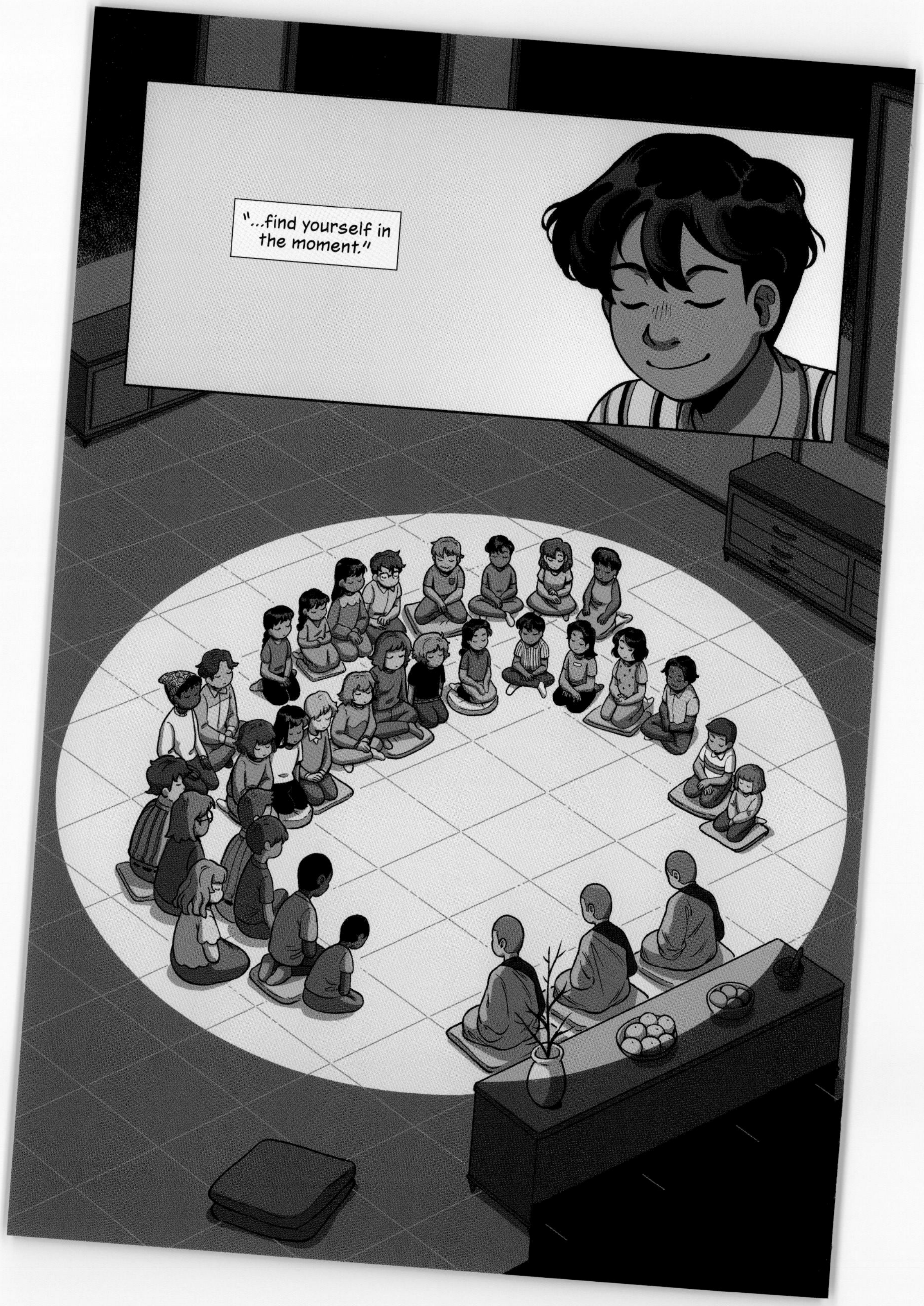
"...find yourself in the moment."

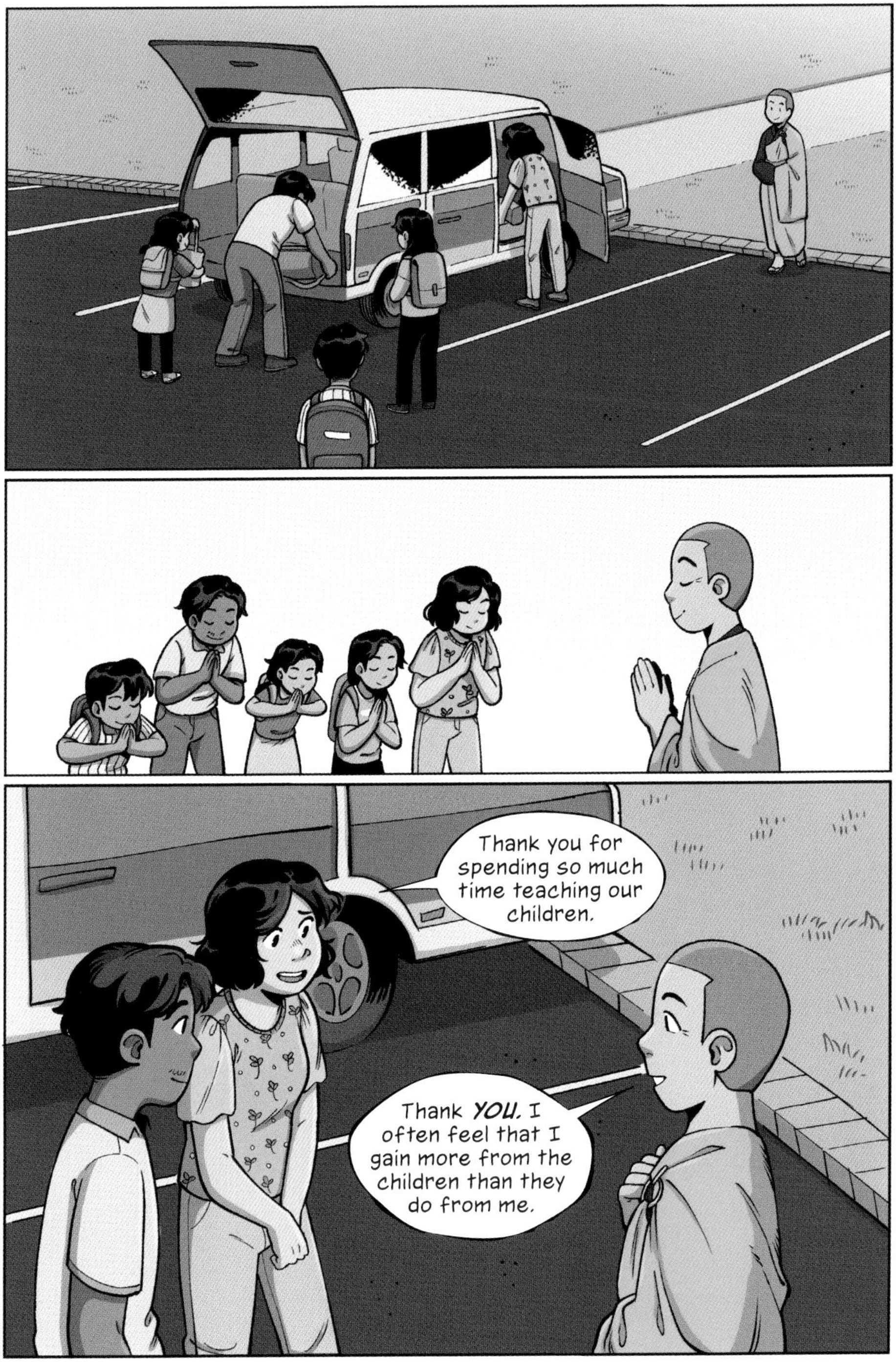
Thank you for spending so much time teaching our children.
Thank YOU. I often feel that I gain more from the children than they do from me.

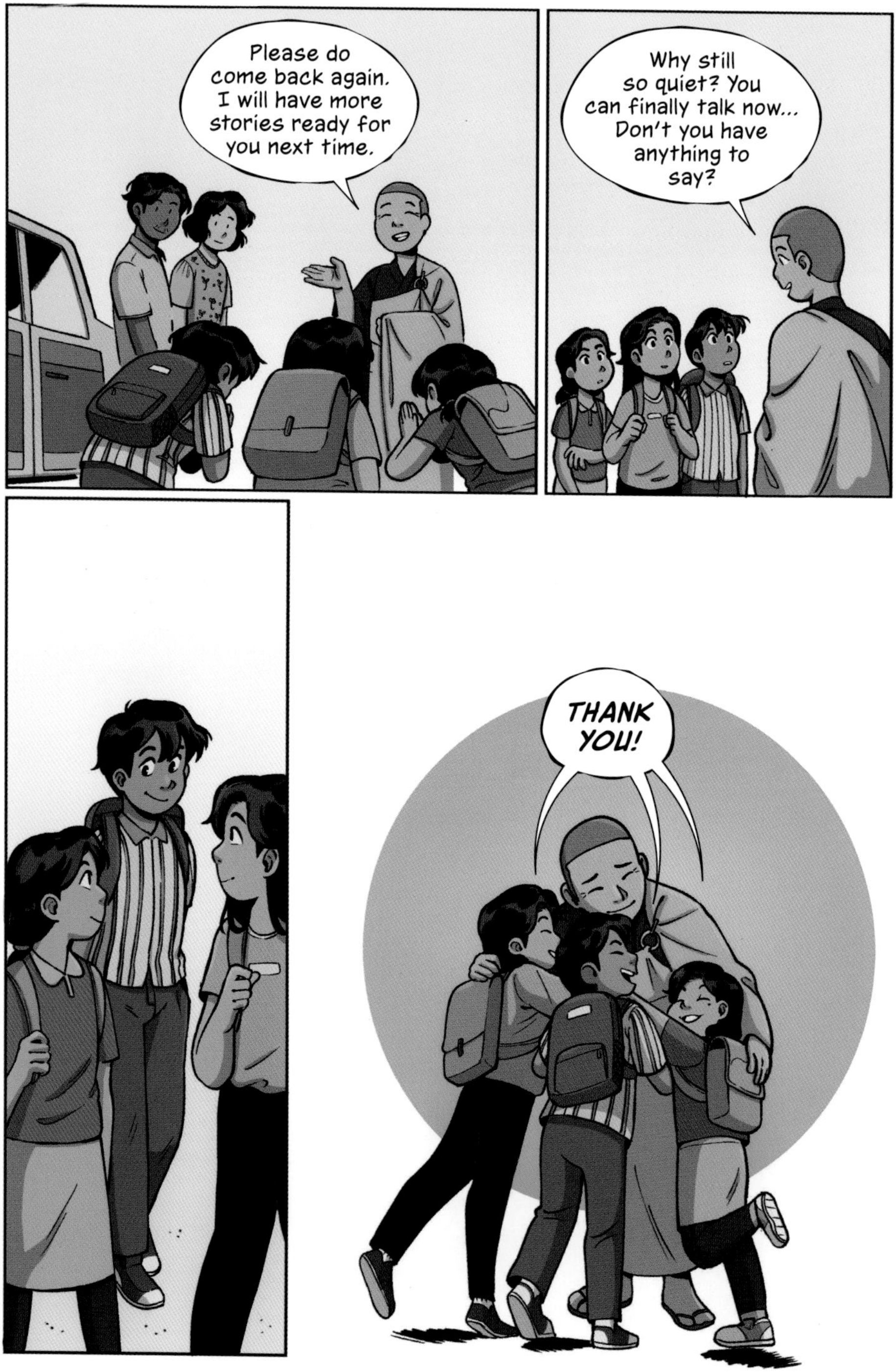
Please do come back again. I will have more stories ready for you next time.
Why still so quiet? You can finally talk now... Don't you have anything to say?
THANK YOU!

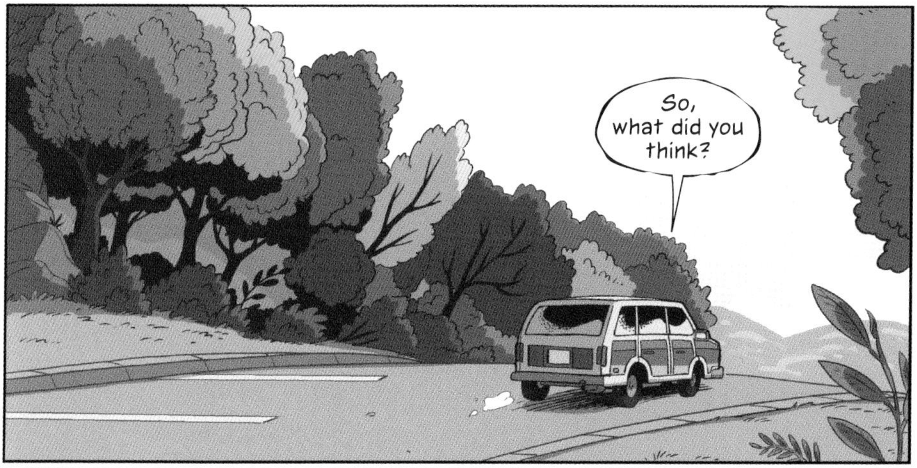
So, what did you think?

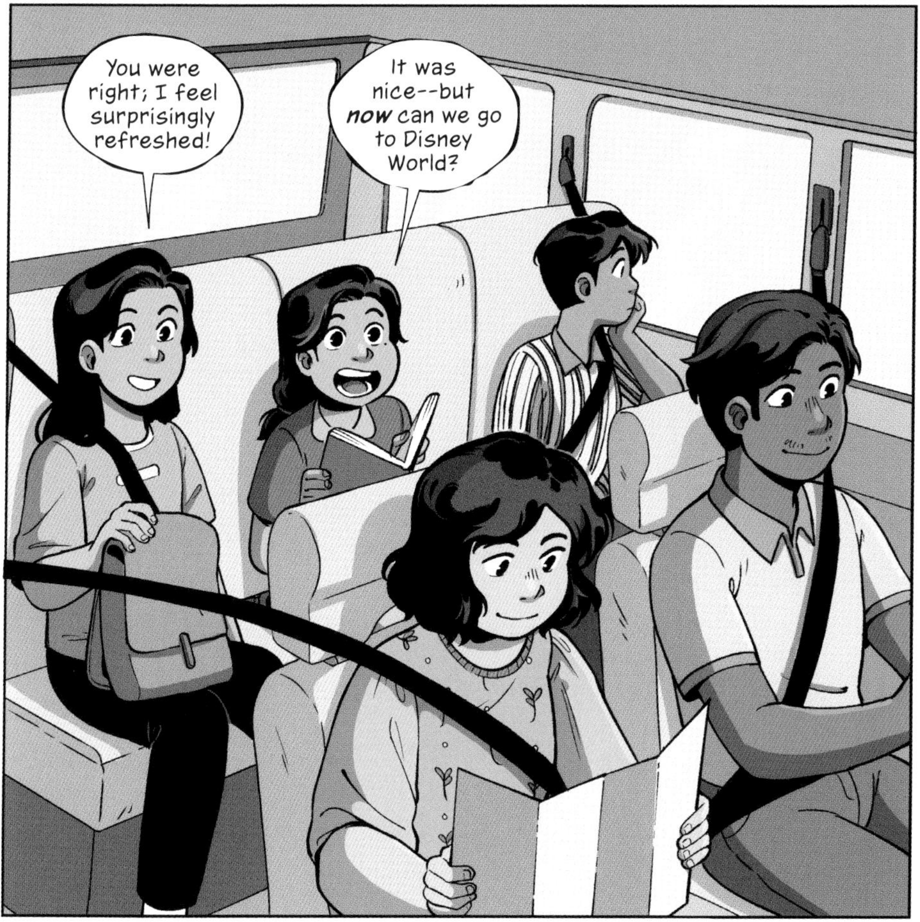
You were right; I feel surprisingly refreshed!
It was nice--but ***now*** can we go to Disney World?

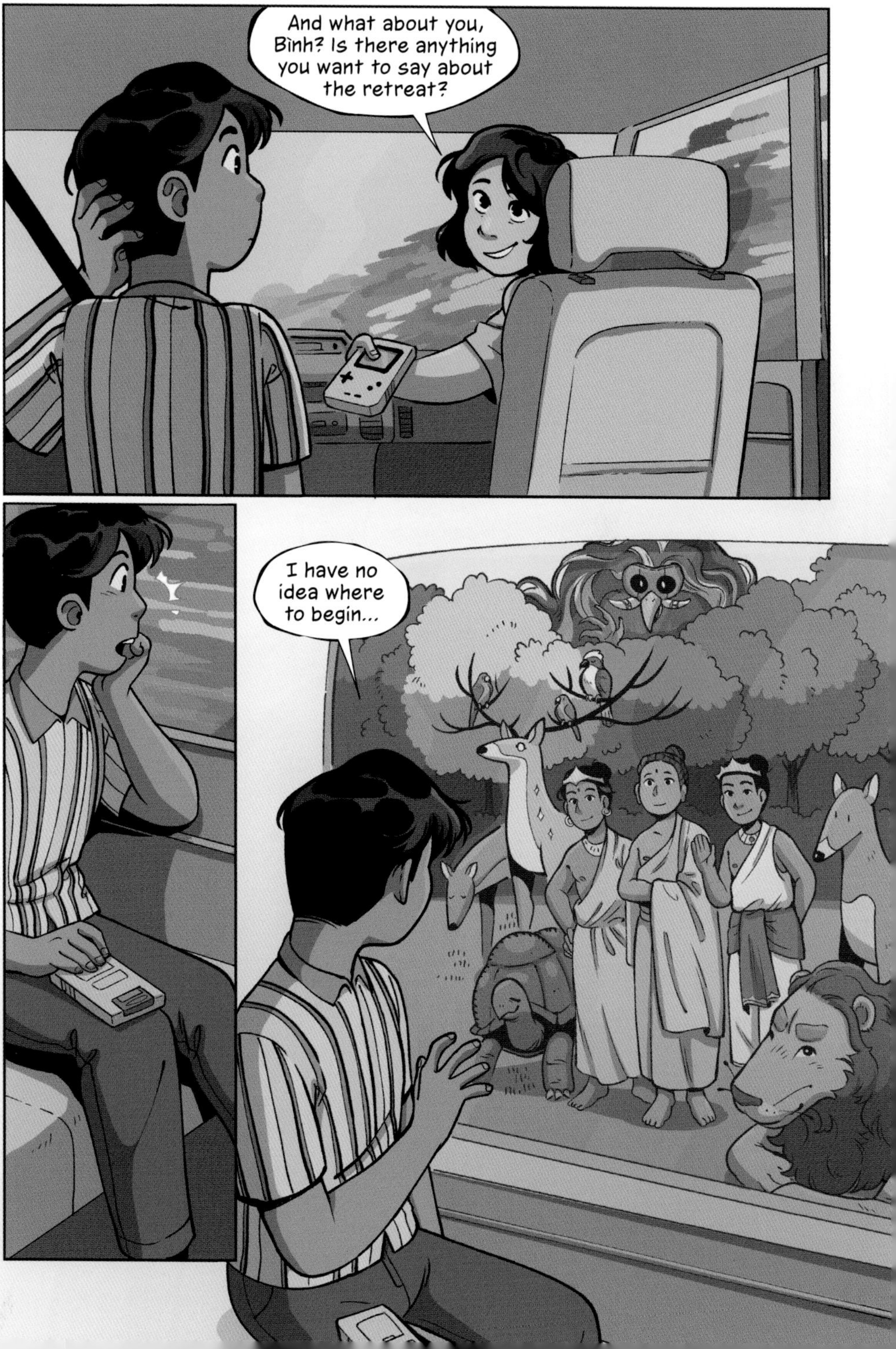
And what about you, Bình? Is there anything you want to say about the retreat?
I have no idea where to begin...

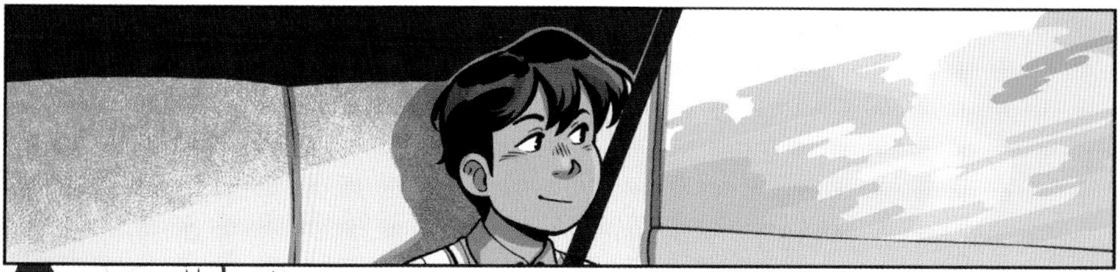

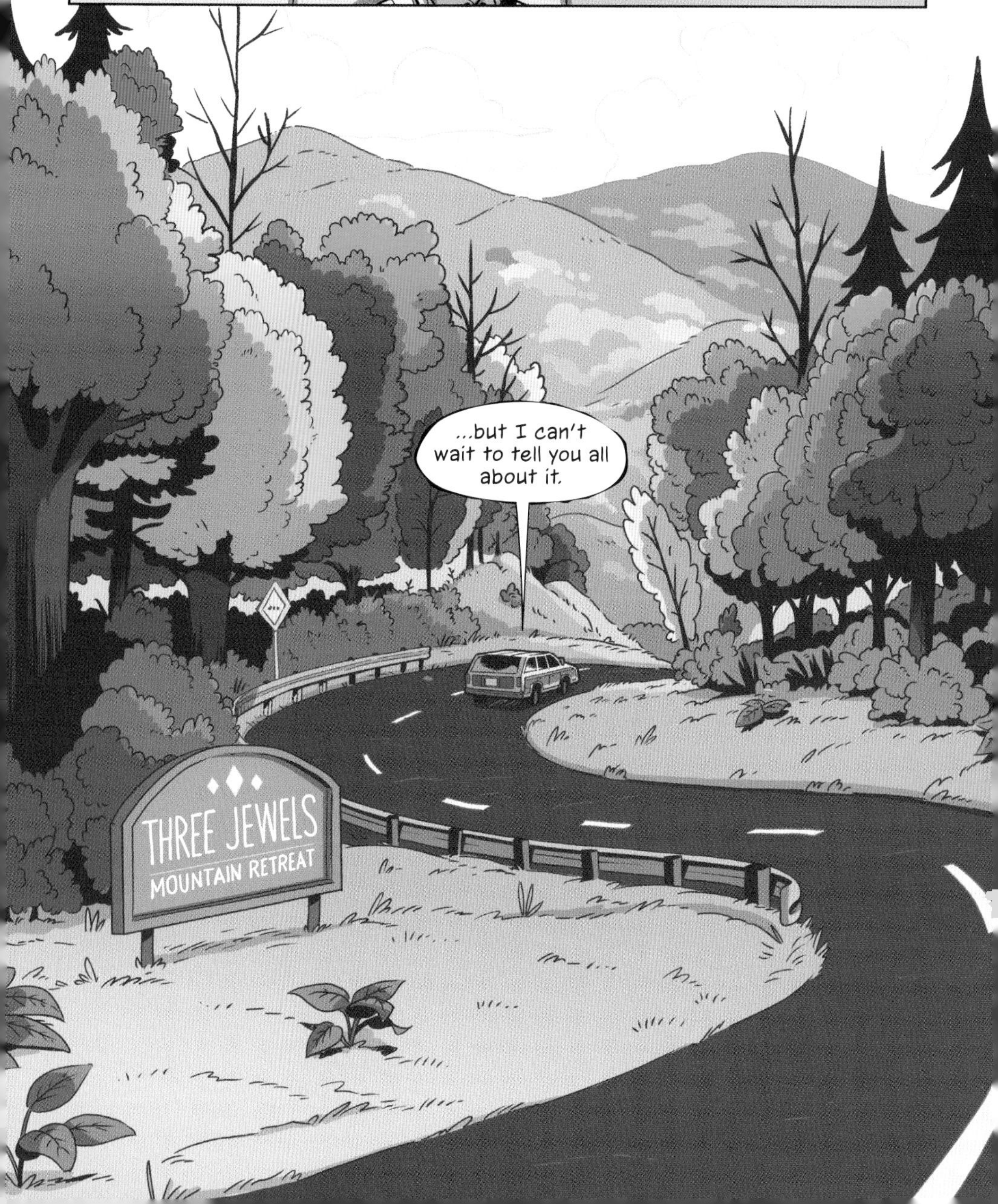
...but I can't wait to tell you all about it.
THREE JEWELS
MOUNTAIN RETREAT